I0769887

GALLIVANTER
EXPEDITION

A NEW WILD (THE GALLIVANTER SAGA BOOK TWO)

First edition. July 4, 2024.

ISBN: 979-8990210325

Written by Cassie A. H. Moore.

A New Wild
Book Two, *The Gallivanter Saga*
By Cassie A. H. Moore

PREFACE

I BIT MY LIP, URGING the automobile to go faster.

My foot pressed the pedal down as far as it could go, my leg cramping with the relentless pressure. Even though my muscles ached, I gritted my teeth and refused to slow down. The engine shuddered, but held steady.

I had to get there before he died.

Exhaling, I heard his laugh echo in my head. Almost like he was in front of me right this moment, I saw the freckles on his face wrinkle as he told me jokes. His eyes, crinkling at the corners as they looked at me.

I pushed the image of him helpless, facedown in a pool of his own blood, out of my mind.

How could they do such a barbaric thing to such a wonderful man? Who could be so evil?

He couldn't be dying.

I knew how strong he was. How his childhood had honed his strength, and how months of strenuous work had chiseled his resolve. He would beat the odds and survive this.

He had to.

The wind whistled against my helmet as my driving goggles dug into my cold cheeks. The night was inky black, and my weak headlights lit only a few feet of bumpy gravel road in front of me. More than once, I'd nearly collided with an errant tree branch that was sprawled across the path.

I swore under my breath, a steady litany of curse words. Then, I prayed.

Over and over, I repeated the refrain of swearing and praying. Anything to keep my mind off of the fact that he could be drawing his last breath at this very moment.

How could it be that only a few months ago, I had hated them so much? Now, I realized just how much they mattered to me.

Why had we been so blind to how we really felt about each other? Why couldn't we just admit that we needed each other?

We had to get there.

"Whatever it takes, Andi," I breathed, gripping the wheel so hard my fingers ached.

I had to make it there. Even though it meant this frantic race through the night, tearing across the countryside.

We had to get there. We had to beat the odds.

He had to beat the odds, too.

"Just hang on," I pleaded in my mind, my shoulders tense with worry. *"Please. Hold on. We're coming. I promise, we'll make it there. Just hang on for me."*

CHAPTER 1

BANG.

My drowsy brain registered the sound with alarm. I cracked open my eyes.

I heard noises. Straining to listen, I held my breath.

Again, I heard the sound.

Bang.

Then I heard the slow shuffle of someone moving around in the kitchen.

"Oh no," I thought. *"We're all in danger now."*

I sat up, rubbing my eyes. The sounds of Chito singing softly in Spanish from the kitchen filled my ears. He was already up, moving around in there—no doubt making us a huge breakfast from scratch.

Grinning, I listened to him sing the song his mother had taught him long ago. Though he was Hispanic, the only Spanish words he knew were those in the songs he'd learned as a child. A great big bear of a man, he only sang like this when he was happy.

Flopping back down into my warm mattress, I stared up at the ceiling. I was happy, too.

I heard a soft knock at my door a few minutes later. I threw back my down covers and tiptoed across the warped wooden floor, trying not to step on the creaky boards. I opened it.

"Hey," Cap whispered, standing outside my door in his pajamas. His blonde hair was flat on one side, like he'd just woken up and hadn't yet run his hands through it.

"Good morning," I whispered back, grinning. Even in the early morning fog, Cap was ruggedly handsome.

"Chito's up in the kitchen," Cap said, smiling back at me. "You know what this means, right?"

I wrapped my arms around myself to keep my body warm. "Another feast?"

"Yes," he replied, and we laughed softly. "How much food does he think we can possibly eat? We don't need a gourmet breakfast every single morning."

"Don't tell him that," I grinned. "He loves this. Having a real kitchen to cook in every day."

Cap smiled, and leaned in to give me a quick peck on the cheek. "I'm going to get changed. I'll see you in there. Adventure awaits."

I watched Cap go back to his room, walking down the hallway with the slightest trace of a limp. He'd been badly injured—nearly killed—in an automobile accident several months earlier. Though his Model T Ford had been repaired and Cap's numerous scars had healed, he'd had lasting nerve damage in his leg. After all these months, Cap had worked hard to stretch and build up the strength in his damaged leg, but it still affected his gait.

Crossing back into my room, I shivered as the cool breeze from the open window made goosebumps on my bare arms. I grabbed a knit blanket from the foot of my bed and wrapped it around myself, feeling the scratchy wool warm me.

I leaned out the window, my hair catching in the wind and spinning wildly around my head. Our hotel perched on the banks of the River Thames, and I watched as the water flowed by, past the large boardwalk.

Tethered boats bobbed along in the bubbling ebb, and the noises of early morning dock workers filled my ears. The colossal Tower Bridge stood proudly across the water, its spires looking like tiny castles balanced on narrow blocks.

"How strange to hear people speaking English again," I thought, listening as men on the street below tipped their flat caps at each other with a polite "g'morning, chap," newspapers clutched under their arms. We'd spent the last several months weaving across Africa, mostly speaking French, or else simply not understanding the native tongue.

I smiled. London was exciting.

It was *all* exciting. I was the luckiest girl on the planet.

After changing into my white shirt and khaki pants—the uniform my team and I had been wearing for months now—I headed into the kitchen.

"Hey sunshine," Chito greeted me, as I walked in to the smell of frying ham and toast.

"Chito," I laughed, taking in the spread he'd already started laying on the table. Slices of tomato, buttered toast, fried eggs, beans, and bacon sat on plates on the large wooden table.

"What?" he asked, looking up as he fried another piece of meat. It sizzled in the skillet.

"This is way too much food! We can't eat all this!"

"But it's a typical English breakfast."

"We're not English, though," Bernard said, without looking up from the newspaper he was reading at the table. "Thank God for that," he added, vehemently.

I peered over Chito's broad shoulder, looking at the thick, dark meat patties he was frying. "What's that?"

Chito grinned. "It's black pudding. The butcher down the street told me we had to have this, if we really wanted a flavor of England. It's a staple here."

Cap entered the kitchen and put his arm around my waist, pulling me close to him. "What's black pudding?"

"Pork blood, fat, some oatmeal," Chito listed, thinking. "Some spices, I think thyme?"

Cap and I exchanged glances, our eyebrows raised. Behind us, we heard Bernard groan.

"Come on," he grumbled. "We're not eating fried blood."

"But smell it," Chito blinked, flipping the meat patties. "It smells incredible."

"If I wanted blood for breakfast, I'd bite you," Bernard snapped. "Then maybe you'd stop feeding us so much darn food every morning. This is ridiculous."

I laughed as I helped myself to a cup of coffee, a staple we'd worked hard to get here in London, where everyone else we encountered guzzled tea. "This escalated quickly."

We dined together in the familiar companionship of people who had been living together for months. We knew each other's habits, likes and dislikes. We'd been through a lot, as a small team, and our routines reflected this.

"So I thought we could take a little drive out to the country today," Cap suggested casually, sipping his coffee. "Take in the scenery. That kind of thing."

I met his eyes. They brimmed with mischief.

"A little drive?" I narrowed mine, setting my toast down.

"Oh, good," Chito laughed. "Another race?"

"Another race," Cap nodded, his eyes still on me. "I'm not going to lose to Andi this time. Not again."

"So you're trying to prove what, exactly?" I grinned. "That you're faster than me? Or is it that you're going for a new record of longest losing streak?"

"Today's my lucky day."

"That's what you said last time."

"But I *feel* it this time."

"Sure," I tossed my head. "I'm ready for a rematch. Especially when I always win."

CHAPTER 2

THE COUNTRY MEADOWS far outside of London were green and empty, and the ideal place for racing our Fords. Only the birds and the occasional bleating sheep could spot us out here.

We'd pitted our automobiles against each other several times before, and I held the winning record. My pride was no match for Cap's fierce competitive nature, however. His adoration for me disappeared the instant he climbed behind the wheel of his car.

I pulled my helmet on and climbed into my Ford, slamming the door shut.

Reaching up, I yanked my thick driving goggles down and adjusted them on my face. They were tight, but we wore them to prevent losing our eyes if a rock ever hit the windshield of our cars and shattered thousands of tiny shards of glass into our faces. We knew from experience, unfortunately, that this could happen.

"Listen, Andi," Bernard draped himself over the driver's side as I turned the car on. The Ford rumbled loudly, and he raised his voice. "Don't be stupid out there, okay?"

"I'm never stupid. I'm always sensible."

"You might be, but he isn't," Bernard replied. "Not when he's racing you, anyway. Something comes over him. You get his competitive side going and he can't turn away. Don't let him push the cars too hard. That's all I'm asking."

"Oh, so you're not concerned about our safety? This is about the cars?"

"Of course it is," Bernard blinked. "These are expensive vehicles. They're what enable us to travel the world. Don't screw that all up with reckless driving."

"Your concern is touching, Bernard."

"Don't get any dings in the metal body, either. And definitely do not break that windshield. It'll kill you."

"Okay, Bernard."

"Remember, this car can go forty, maybe forty-five miles an hour. Don't try to push her beyond that."

I held up my gloved hand. "Stop!" I complained. "It's just racing. We've done it before. It'll be fine."

"Bah," he groaned. "There's never a need to push these cars as hard as you two do. I hate when you do this."

"See you at the finish line," I grinned cheerfully. "Thanks for the pep talk."

Bernard shot me a sour look and backed away, shoving his hands into his pockets. I looked over at the Ford next to me, and found Cap's eyes already on me. He winked.

"Maybe fourth time's a charm!" I called out, grinning.

"Ready?" Chito yelled, his deep voice clear over the reverberating engines. "On your mark, get set, and go!"

At his words, Cap and I both shot forward in our Fords. The road was wide enough for both of us to drive side-by-side, and we roared through the dirt at an even clip.

With the wind whistling in my face, I couldn't hear anything but the sounds of my own car rushing headlong into the wind. From the corner of my eye, I could see Cap keeping up with me.

I glanced over. Cap's eyes were focused on the road, his expression determined.

If only people could see me now, I smiled to myself. *Me, driving a car? A young woman actually allowed to drive an automobile by herself? They'd never believe it. And they'd certainly never believe what a good driver I am.*

Most girls in my position would let the man win.

But I wasn't like most girls. I was Andiamo Gallivanter.

The field blurred by me, a shapeless mass of green and brown. Our cars left a wake of dust behind us, drifting lazily over the head of grazing sheep. I could hear the sharp pings of rocks hitting the undercarriage of my car as we raced along.

I shifted into high gear, urging the Ford to gain speed. The action was a complicated one, but the motions were second-nature to me after months of driving for days on end. I could drive a Ford in my sleep now.

Cap's car remained glued to my side, however. I couldn't pull ahead.

Suddenly, he swerved sharply to the right, taking his car up into the soft grassy embankment. His car tilted up with the sudden motion.

"What the—" I cried, taking my foot off the pedal. I saw a flash of white frozen in place, standing in the middle of the road, as I skillfully zipped around it.

Cap's Ford thudded back onto the road. He hadn't let up, even though he'd just gone into the grass.

I glanced over. I had a clear lead now that he'd been slowed by the ditch, but his lips were pursed. He hadn't given up the fight.

Grinning, I raced all the way until the stone wall started, the finish line we'd agreed on before we started the race. I reached the stones a second before he did, and finally slowed my car.

Cap was already laughing as he pulled up beside my Ford. "Hold on," he said, pushing up his goggles. "Are you aware that we almost killed a sheep back there?"

"Is that what it was?" My forehead wrinkled in concern. "That could've ended badly, Cap. Holy smokes."

"Especially for the sheep," Cap grinned. "Good thing I have quick instincts."

"No kidding," I replied, exhaling. Then, looking slyly at him, I added, "Just not quite quick enough."

"No," Cap laughed, holding up his hands. "That wasn't a fair race. I had to slow down to avoid killing an innocent lamb."

"Sure," I smiled. "Whatever you need to tell yourself."

"Besides, isn't it more accurate if we say that *ewe* won? Get it? Ewe?"

I stared at Cap, wrinkling my nose at his pun. He laughed. "Fine. I'll wait for a rematch. Next one's mine, for sure."

We turned the cars around and drove slowly back to Chito and Bernard, who stood waiting next to our third Gallivanter Ford at the starting line. As we pulled up, Chito put his hands on his hips.

"Who won?" he hollered.

"Who do you think?" I laughed, honking my horn.

"Barely!" Cap pretended to scowl. I smiled anyway. I knew he was proud of my driving ability. Most women had never had the chance to drive an automobile, but here I was, better at racing than most men who owned cars. It was a rare accomplishment.

"Nuts," Bernard groaned. "Come on, Cap. I had a lot pinned on you winning this round."

We pulled the cars to a smooth stop, the dust settling as we popped out from the drivers' seats. "What'd you bet this time?" Cap asked, peeling off his helmet. His blonde hair caught the sun.

"He has to cook a meal for us next time we're eating on the road," Chito rubbed his hands gleefully. "I get the night off."

"Wait, what did Bernard wager?" I asked, removing my goggles.

Bernard sighed. "If Cap won, Chito agreed to ride along in silence next time we drove together. I was looking forward to a little peace and quiet."

The rest of us laughed. "Come on, Bernard," Cap said, throwing his arm around him. "We have daredevil blood in our veins, the souls of trailblazers. We're not the type of team to do well with peace and quiet, anyway."

CHAPTER 3

AS WE DROVE BACK INTO London, I thought about what Cap had told Bernard. We did indeed have daredevil blood in all our veins.

Most of my life, I'd been the oddball that never fit in anywhere. I'd always been too unladylike, too discontent, and too restless for polite society. Now, as a member of the Gallivanter Expedition, I'd finally found people who were just like me.

And what incredible people they were.

Captain Grant Gallivanter was the fearless, brave leader who had assembled our team and brought us together from the very beginning. For nearly a year, I'd been traveling around the world with him as a member of the Gallivanter Expedition. Together, three men and I were racing to be the first group of people to navigate around the world, visiting every country in an automobile.

At the end of our travels was a million dollar cash prize, sponsored by an organization called the Odysseus Society, if we could beat out the other team who was racing us. We'd both started last year, in early 1923, navigating from a preliminary base in different locations.

Only one other team, the Chinook Voyageurs, was in competition with us.

The stress of planning such an immense operation had caused every other team to drop out, even though dozens had initially applied. The Chinooks were a group of men from Canada who had grown up together. Their crew was twice the size of ours and had more funding, but we were quicker.

Captain Gallivanter was confident we'd win. Even more so now, because we'd come out on top of some serious danger already.

Cap, as we called him, was only twenty-six, but he was wise beyond his years. He'd spent years procuring our Model T Fords, planning our travel itinerary, and carefully accounting for every possible obstacle we could face. It was soul-crushing work, years of fundraising and schmoozing and meticulous planning.

Handsome, tall, and muscular, with blonde hair and blue eyes, he was every inch the disciplined leader of our team. Women threw themselves at him everywhere we went. He was charismatic and witty, but also lost himself privately in research when he was out of the spotlight. Behind the scenes, he was a bit of a perfectionist and obsessed over planning our journey.

And I was madly in love with him.

We'd fallen for each other as we traveled together for months, and had both fought our feelings, trying to remain professional. But after facing down tragedy together, we could no longer deny how we felt. We'd become engaged, secretly, before we left Africa, which was merely the first leg of our journey.

Bernard and Chito, our fellow teammates, knew that we were in love and planning to get married, but we'd all agreed to keep it a secret from the rest of the world, including our families. We didn't want it to be a distraction from the spirit of the expedition. Though we knew we'd spent a lot of time together, we realized that we hadn't known each other long enough for it to be considered decent to now be engaged.

Besides, Cap had a complicated past with a former fiancée, and he worried that she'd make our lives a living hell if we came out together now, to the world.

"You don't know Milly," he'd told me several times. "She's horrible. And we can't afford to lose the public's support, not now."

Bernard Harris, our crew mechanic, had known Cap's fiancée back when he and Cap worked together in New Orleans, a few years ago. He agreed.

"I hated her," he said bluntly. Aloof and crotchety, Bernard said little but always managed to make his opinions clear.

He'd been in the construction business before Cap plucked him for the Gallivanter crew. A lifelong bachelor, he resisted people and never opened up about his life. He was the oldest member of our team, shorter than me and wrinkled, but with exhaustive knowledge and affection for our Fords.

"Maybe she has a reason for the way she is," Chito always said, looking for the best in Milly, whenever Cap brought her up. "You liked something about her at some point, Cap. She can't be all bad."

Chito Martinez was the opposite of Bernard. A burly man with a wild beard, untamable hair, and a sizable gut, he looked intimidating but was unfailingly kind and gentle. He was a widower, and his small niece, Molly, lived with his sister in California.

His wife had died in childbirth several years ago, and the sorrow had profoundly touched Chito's soul. He treated me now like I was his own daughter. His role on our expedition was team chef, which meant he was in charge of supplies and meals. It was a perfect job for him, as he delighted in taking care of all of us.

Our early expedition itinerary a few months ago led us from France through Spain into northern Africa, and we barely escaped with our lives as we scissored through the deserts and jungles there.

Unbeknownst to us, our thrilling stories had been picked up in newspapers all over the world. By the time we crawled out of the jungle after being stranded there, exhausted, and made it back to civilization, we were global superstars.

Along with our fame had come money. More money than we ever imagined we'd get. Fans all over the world excitedly sent us more money than I could've dreamed we'd ever see. Our bank account balance spun like the spinning wheel on a slot machine. Not only did everyone in the world know us by name, but we were also incredibly wealthy now.

People loudly cried out for us to come back to Europe and share our travel stories with them—we received thousands of eager letters, telegrams, and newspaper articles urging us to tell our travel adventures. I enjoyed responding to as many as possible, dashing off a few lines and imagining the thrill when the recipient received a postcard with an exotic postmark and my signature.

"What do you think, team?" Cap had asked us a few months ago, as we rested comfortably after crawling out from a nomadic village in French Sudan. "Should we do a victory lap in Europe and take advantage of our celebrity status?"

"It couldn't hurt, could it?" Chito had replied. "We're allowed to take personal leave, according to the competition rules. Perhaps the additional funds we'd get will come in handy for funding future expeditions, too."

We'd ended up driving the cars north through Africa to do a whirlwind tour in Western Europe. Currently in between big shows here in London, we were taking a few days to rest and relax together in a shared house.

Requests flooded in from potential supporters everywhere, and we leisurely considered each one, picking out the best opportunities for sharing our stories and connecting with new people and places.

We had a special fondness for sharing our travels with school children, in the hopes that we could open up their eyes that had perhaps been clouded with prejudice and hatred by the Great War, and open a new world of possibility to the younger generation.

At dinner that evening, Cap filled us in about our upcoming commitments.

"We have a full week ahead of us, Gallivanters," Cap said as we pushed our plates away. "We've been invited to speak in Dublin, Ireland, at the request of a university travel group. They're wanting to sponsor us for the next leg of our expedition. They even asked me about providing uniforms with their logo."

"Surely we don't need their funding?" I questioned. "We have more than enough money to circle the globe, right?"

"Yes," Cap replied. "But our expedition is also about goodwill and unity. We're trying to educate people about each other. Show that just because we look different, we're still all human. Anyway, this group also hosted the Chinook Voyageurs a few weeks ago. They want to meet us, as well."

"How'd we end up traveling so close to where the Chinook team is going through?" Chito asked, wiping his hands and sitting down at the table with his own plate of food, which had been warming in the oven while he fed us and tidied the kitchen.

"They started in Finland, then crossed through Sweden and Norway. They took a ferry across to Scotland, and drove south. It's just coincidence that we're both in the United Kingdom right now, I guess. Obviously our original itinerary has changed since everything that happened in Africa."

"Will the fact that both teams are traveling so near each other cause problems for us?" I asked. "You know, will the publicity for one or the other start to fade?"

"I don't think so," Cap said, rubbing his chin. "There's plenty of room for both of us here in Europe. What could possibly go wrong?"

CHAPTER 4

THE NEXT DAY, AFTER stocking up and packing the cars, we drove northwest through the countryside from London up to Holyhead.

Fields of wildflowers swayed in the breeze as we cut across the rolling plains of England. Birds drifted above our cars, an occasional hawk swooping down on a critter in the fields.

"They used Holyhead as a port during the war," Cap said, looking out at the sea after we parked our cars at a small inn. "Imagine this place filled with soldiers, pouring off of ships and headed into battle. It's unreal to think about, isn't it?"

We walked along the shoreline in the darkness, the sound of people drunkenly singing and laughing inside a nearby bar filling the quiet night air. It was late at night now, and it felt good to stretch our legs after driving all day to get here. A lighthouse on the point shone into the darkness.

"How fast does the ferry go?" Bernard asked.

"I read that they go twenty-five knots a day," Cap replied. "Can you imagine that? We can cross from England to Ireland in a single day. It's incredible."

A group of men stood on the sidewalk in front of us, staggering over themselves. They reeked of beer. "Hoy, mate," one of them drunkenly called out as we neared them. "Join the party! Have a drink!"

The man grabbed Chito by the sleeve and tried to drag him to the center of the group. Chito peeled the man's hand off his big arm. "No thanks, sir."

"It's okay," the man slurred. "We'd rather have the pretty girlie, instead," he said, reaching for me.

I stepped back, but another man in the group grabbed me around the waist from behind.

"Get off me," I said sharply, twisting away. They laughed and swore amongst themselves.

"Don't you touch her," Cap said, his tone deadly. Chito and Bernard stepped up to either side of me, surrounding me.

"It's just a joke, mate, lighten up," one of the men said. "She's a bearcat, anyway."

I shook my head, noticing Cap's fists were balled up. He was ready to fight them.

"Let's go, they're not worth it," I uttered, pushing my way through the men. One of them whistled and they made small derogatory sounds as I marched away, my head held high.

"I hate when this happens," Chito slipped an arm around me. "Don't let it bother you."

"I don't," I said, lying as I watched Cap's face. His lips were pursed and he was walking quickly. He was still angry. This wasn't the first time I'd been grabbed in public in front of my crew. Often, it happened right after someone recognized us as the famous Gallivanters.

Being a celebrity had brought all of us our fair share of inappropriate creeps. The men had received countless letters of marriage proposals—especially Cap, who often got pictures of beautiful girls, too.

I'd gotten several strange letters, some of which threatened me for daring to be a woman who traveled across the world. *"Stop pretending to be a man,"* one had written me recently. *"You're not. You don't deserve to do what you do."*

I pushed it out of my head, trying to lighten the mood. "So what can we expect in Ireland?" I asked cheerfully. "I've always wanted to go there."

Cap answered me. "Well, we're headed into Dublin, which is a major city," he said. "They're famous for their beer and whiskey. It's an industrial city, but it's had some nasty skirmishes with England over the years. Remember the Easter Uprising, what, eight years ago or so? That's why it's good that we're going there, really. We're showing our impartiality by visiting both England and Ireland."

I noticed Cap's shoulders relax as he talked. He was in his element, teaching us about the places we visited. He studied more than anyone else I knew, and retained important facts that helped us understand local customs and cultures. He took his job seriously.

"What about food?" Chito asked.

I smiled. Chito was always eager to try the local delicacies, no matter how odd they were. Not only was he our chef, but he'd also taken on the responsibility to introduce each local culture's cuisine to us. We traveled and tasted the world, thanks to Chito.

"They do a lot of seafood," Cap replied, searching his memory to recall what he'd read. "Seafood chowder, fried fish. Oh, and something called brown bread. I seem to recall it's made with buttermilk."

"Let's make sure we get some," Chito grinned.

"The university is providing a city guide for us," Cap responded. "He's supposed to take us on a tour of the school and downtown Dublin, after we settle in, and we can ask him to take us to the best restaurants in town."

THE NEXT MORNING DAWNED clear and bright, and I breathed a prayer of thanks for good weather for the ocean crossing. Bernard and Chito were already loading the cars when I came down, and Cap was settling our bill with the innkeeper.

"We're ready to go," Chito proclaimed, as Cap returned to the front of the building where our three Fords were lined up.

"Good," Cap said, checking his pocket watch. "We need to get the cars down to the ferry and board up."

"Aye aye, Captain," Chito saluted, climbing into his Ford. Bernard and Cap and I slid into our seats, pulling on our gloves and goggles.

We drove through the small downtown streets to the port, slowing as we reached a crowd of people hurrying to board several ships of various sizes.

"We're looking for the big one, with the double smokestacks!" Cap yelled over the noise from the crowd.

"There!" Bernard pointed. The ship was large, with gleaming gold smokestacks sputtering white smoke.

We drove slowly through the crowd, beeping our horns. Many people recognized us, and shouted and waved as we went by. "The Gallivanters!" I heard voices say as I navigated the vehicle.

"Can you believe we got to see them in real life?" I heard one little boy shout to his mother.

Cap signaled for us to stop, and jumped out of his car to track down the ferry's staff. Several minutes later, he reemerged from the crowd and trotted over to my Ford.

"They're going to help get us on board, into position," he said, already walking away toward Bernard's car to tell them. "Follow me on."

Three uniformed men walked toward us a few moments later, two of them stopping the crowd and the third helping navigate us up the large metal ramp that led into a dark compartment at the bottom of the boat.

As we drove, the crowd impulsively started cheering. I grinned and waved. Catching sight of their smiling faces always made me happy. I remembered the feeling I'd had so long ago, reading about Captain Gallivanter's famous expedition around the world—I'd been in awe. I knew they felt the same about me.

"Boy, it's dark in here," Bernard said, rubbing his thin arms. "Make sure your Fords are hooked in, in case we hit rough water today."

We worked together in the dark hold of the ship, securing our automobiles with thick ropes. When we'd finished to Bernard's exacting standards, he patted each vehicle fondly and followed us upstairs. Cap remained last, standing with the deckhand, busy filling out a small mountain of paperwork.

Blinking in the bright sunlight that dazzled our eyes after being in the dark for so long, we looked for a spot against the railing on the upper deck. Whistles sounded and the last few passengers scurried on board. Soon, the ramps were pulled up and the boat started to pull away from the dock. People waved at us from the shore, calling out to their loved ones.

"I love the open sea," Cap said from behind me, squeezing next to me at the railing.

"Me too," I smiled, feeling the cold ocean breeze hit my face and flutter my hair over my shoulders. "I was so terrified to go to my boarding school when I left Boston. I was only eleven years old. But once I got on that boat, I forgot all about my fears. I just loved sailing across that big blue horizon."

"Even at that tender age, you were a little explorer," Chito teased, standing on the other side of me as we watched the shore grow distant behind us.

I watched the seagulls swoop above our heads, chirping as they wafted through the currents in the air.

"Guilty," I grinned. "It's a good thing I stumbled across that little article about you in the newspapers last year and decided to try to earn a spot on the Gallivanter crew. Imagine life without me?"

Cap grinned at me, briefly squeezing my hand. He dropped it just as quickly. We worked hard to not reveal our love for each other to the rest of the world. Chito and Bernard were the only two souls on earth who knew we were engaged. Still, we occasionally couldn't help a small show of affection.

We were human, after all, and young and in love.

Our boat cut through the waves, the wake sparkling in the sunshine. The sky was blue and the ocean smooth below us. It was a pleasant journey.

"I'm going inside to find food and a comfortable seat," Chito said, pulling away from the metal railing. "I hope they have something good. Otherwise, I'm breaking into our snacks."

"I'll go with him," Bernard said. "I'm hungry, too. And too many people are up here."

Now only the two of us remained at the railing. Cap winked at me. "Too wild and free to want to be cooped up inside, Miss Andi?"

"Yeah, something like that. I love being outside. Always have."

"Didn't you tell me once that you got in trouble in boarding school for sleeping with your windows open?"

I laughed. "My roommates hated it. They complained all the time."

"If they could see you now," he grinned. "Think of what they would say if they knew you'd slept outside in the desert for months on end, eating beans over a campfire, night after night? Washing your clothes in a bucket and going to the bathroom out in the jungle?"

"They'd rather die, I think."

"It wasn't that bad, was it?" he mused. "I rather liked the adventure of it all. Especially sleeping out there, under the stars."

"I did, too."

"What a long, strange journey this has been already," Cap leaned against the railing and watched the roiling sea under us. The boat cut through the water, the wind whistling loudly in our ears. "It staggers my mind to know that the expedition has barely started. We've only been through a handful of countries, but it seems like we've been together forever, doesn't it?"

"It's just the beginning of forever for us," I wrinkled my nose, even as I uttered it.

He laughed. "You're such a terrible romantic, Andi."

"I knew it was cheesy, even as I said it."

"Just stick to finding those little moments to remind me how you feel about me," he said quietly, leaning into my ear so the passing couple who smiled at us couldn't hear him.

"So you're going to be one of those demanding fiancés, then?" I said, poking him playfully in the ribs. He squirmed and began to laugh.

"Not so loud," he whispered back. "We can't share it in public. Not yet. But someday."

"I know," I replied, wistful. "Wouldn't it be nice to not have to hide it, though?"

"We won't have to hide it when we're back to just being with Gallivanter crew, once our travel schedule resumes. Surely we can contain ourselves when we're around strangers."

"I know," I said, then changed the subject. "What do you think Ireland will be like?"

"It's the land of enchantment. Interestingly, do you know how many famous poets and writers have come from there? A lot. They're said to have the gift of gab, those Irish."

"Think we'll find a pot of gold at the end of the rainbow while we're there?"

"No," he grinned. "But I do know it rains there, pretty much every day. Get ready for that. I wrote to our hosts at the university and asked if we should pack umbrellas for the trip. He responded, and I quote, 'nothing can keep you from getting soaked, so don't bother.'"

"Sounds like our trip will be pretty charming," I grinned.

"How can it not be?" Cap smiled, his hair blowing in the ocean breeze. "Everything's looking up for us now. Why, I bet even the sun will shine down on us while we're in Ireland."

CHAPTER 5

WE SPENT THE REST OF the day sailing across the ocean, the cold wind dusting our pink cheeks with salty spray.

Eventually, we sheltered inside the ship with Chito and Bernard, who lounged on a cozy bank of chairs next to a large glass window.

"This is the life," Chito crunched happily on an apple. "I could get used to this."

"Don't get too used to it," I teased. "We'll be back to the rugged life of travel and adventure once we make our way out of Europe."

"That's still months away," Chito mumbled through a mouthful. "I aim to enjoy the good life until then."

"Hey, is that it?" Bernard leaned forward, pointing at a craggy, large cliff barely visible in the distance. We pressed our faces against the window and peered out.

"It must be," Cap replied, staring. "It's so green."

Slowly, out of the water, Ireland rose up as a beautiful emerald landscape. Sandy beaches lay at the base of tall cliffs, layers of sediment visible in the rock. Verdant hills lay gently on top of each other like ripples in a thick, plush rug.

"It's lovely," I remarked, my nose nearly touching the glass.

Slowly, our ship pulled into the harbor and the crew lashed us into the dock. They lowered the ramps, then proceeded to let the passengers off. With our Fords stored securely below deck, we were the last to disembark the ship.

"Where are we going first?" I asked Cap as we unlashed our cars side-by-side.

"We're supposed to meet our tour guide at the American ambassador's office in downtown Dublin," Cap replied, busy with the ropes. "They arranged our hotel, meals, and have done all the planning for the event tomorrow night. We're supposed to just settle in and enjoy Dublin, according to the letters I received."

"Sounds nice," I said. "After months of you grinding away, planning every detail of our journey, isn't it nice to have a break from the work?"

Cap grinned at me. "I barely know what to do with myself."

I popped open the engine and flipped the lever on the fuel shut off valve down, allowing gasoline to once again flow into the engine. Slamming it shut, I slipped into the single door—on the passenger side of the Model T—and slid the key into the ignition. The Ford rumbled to life.

Next to me, Cap and Bernard performed the same motions on the automobiles they were driving, and we slowly pulled through the ferry floor and down the ramps to the outer dock.

"It's raining!" Cap yelled as he inched the car along the gangway.

"Great," I groaned, tugging at my driving helmet and wrapping a scarf around my face. I couldn't do much else to shield myself. The cars had open tops.

Drizzle hit me as soon as I pulled my car out from under the cover of the boat. The wind was breezy, fluttering my scarf as I drove. Carefully, I drove behind Cap as we rolled forward through the crowded streets near the harbor. Fishermen stood behind fish stands, calling to passing customers with their thick brogues. The air itself was thick and salty on my tongue. The sounds of the friendly people around me, their voices lilting in a musical tone, brought a smile to my face.

I followed behind Cap, watching as he glanced from his map to the road, guiding our convoy. After a few minutes, as we drove the wrong way down an alley and got shooed out by an angry shopkeeper, he pointed toward a bank of buildings.

"There!" he yelled over his shoulder. "That's where we're going!"

We steered our Fords toward tall and narrow buildings, in a dated Victorian fashion. As we drew closer, a handful of men in suits stepped out, waving.

"That must be the American ambassador," I thought to myself, as we eased our cars to a stop and parked behind one another in front of the offices.

"Hello, my friends!" The middle man cried, smoothing his suit as he waited for us to get out of our vehicles. He was tall and dark, with white teeth and a bushy mustache.

"Mr. Ambassador?" Cap said, climbing out of his car and offering his hand. "I'm Captain Gallivanter."

"Ah, Captain!" the ambassador grinned, slapping Cap on the back. "I'm John Ladley. Welcome to Dublin, good sir! How was your journey over?"

"Very smooth, Mr. Ambassador," Cap smiled, then motioned to our team. "Please allow me to introduce the rest of my crew. This is Miss Andi Gallivanter, Mr. Chito Martinez, and Mr. Bernard Harris. We hail from New Orleans, California, and New York, collectively."

"Greetings, greetings, my fellow countrymen!" he cried, pumping each of our hands. "It's so good to have you here."

"Thank you, sir," I replied.

"Miss Gallivanter, please allow me to comment on your refreshing beauty," he said, staring at me. I was slightly taller than him, so he lifted his eyes up to my face. "I can only imagine what sort of effect your presence has on the men you meet."

"Thank you," I smiled politely, not entirely sure if he was complimenting me or not.

"Let me introduce you to my staff here," the ambassador blustered, waving at the two staff members who flanked him. "This is George, my assistant," he said, pointing to a young man with auburn hair. He was tall, freckled, and good-looking, with an easy smile.

"Nice to meet you," he extended his hand. "George O'Malley. I run everything here."

"He's a great man, Georgie," bragged the ambassador. "Top of his class at the university. A real stellar kid. Loaded with potential."

"Thank you, sir," George replied, a hint of a smirk on his face. "It's my honor to hold such a prestigious job, with such an esteemed man."

I couldn't help but notice that Georgie had an ego to match the good looks he was obviously aware of.

"Over here, we have Samuel Smith," the ambassador said, pointing to a dark-haired man with brilliant blue eyes. "Our chief of staff. Probably the smartest man alive, our lad is."

"Nice to meet you, Mr. Smith," Cap said, shaking his hand. I hid a smile, guessing that Cap desperately wanted to pit his own knowledge against Sam but wouldn't do so out of politeness.

"Georgie here is going to show you around the city," the ambassador said, discreetly checking his pocket watch. "Lots to see. Lots of places to visit. You'll love it. He's a great tour guide, he does it for all our American celebrities."

"Wonderful," I replied, studying George. He struck me as the type who'd prefer to be out flirting with pretty girls rather than squiring American guests around town.

"Yes, I must be going," the ambassador said, as Sam whispered into his ear and led him toward the door. "But very nice to meet you, Gallivanters. Enjoy our charming city. Dublin's a special place."

"Should we get started?" George said, leaning up against Bernard's Ford. "I thought we'd stop at your hotel first, to drop off your bags."

Bernard frowned as he stared at George lolling across the hood. "Get off," he barked.

"Excuse me?"

"Get off the car," Bernard growled. "Show some respect."

"Sorry," George stepped back, holding his hands up in defense. "It's just a car."

"The Fords are like his babies," I explained. Bernard was a bit of an odd duck, but he was our odd duck. "He loves them. He's very protective of them."

"Sure, old man," George's laugh was rude, almost mocking. "I guess you don't have much else going for you if cars are what matter most in your life, huh?"

I bit my tongue. *We just have to get through a few hours with him,* I thought. *Just ignore his bad behavior. A little teasing never hurt anyone.*

Cap shot me a withering look as George opened the door of his lead car, unprompted, and sat down in the passenger seat.

"Would you like to drive with Miss Gallivanter, Mr. O'Malley?" Cap asked. "It'd be quite a special treat for you. Most men don't ever get the chance to be driven around by the famous Andi Gallivanter. She's breaking ground as the first woman to circle the globe by automobile, you know."

"Drive? With *her*?" George blurted, amused. "No."

Chito shot me a look as I tried not to roll my eyes and climbed back into my Ford.

"We'll lead," Cap yelled from the front car, and he slowly eased the vehicle out from the curb and followed George's directions to the hotel. We pulled up to the hotel, a charming brick building covered with ivy and flower boxes, and climbed out.

"I'll just wait out here until you're finished," George said, leaning against the car again and shoving his hands in his pockets, whistling irreverently.

I hurried to hand Bernard a large trunk before he noticed George, and pushed him toward the lobby door. It didn't escape my notice that George hadn't offered to help us carry anything.

We checked in, the excited hotel staff swarming us and swooping in to carry our gear. "It's our honor to serve the Gallivanter team!" the manager squeaked, before quietly sliding a newspaper across the desk to us. I stared up at a picture of my own face, beaming as I stood next to my crew, on the front page of the paper.

"The world-famous Gallivanter Expedition arrives in Ireland!" screamed the headline.

"Do you mind?" the manager asked, his voice barely above a whisper. "My children love following the stories of your travels. They have articles about you pinned up all over their rooms. Can I get your autographs?"

"Certainly," I smiled, exchanging happy glances with my teammates. Hearing about the joy we brought so many little hearts certainly never got old.

After scribbling our signatures on the newspaper and smiling our thanks, we circled up in the lobby.

"I'm excited to see the city, but do we really have to go around Dublin with this kid, Cap?" Chito grimaced. "He's a royal pain."

"It's just a few hours," Cap groaned. "Come on. Let's get it over with. At least he'll know all the best places to show us."

We trotted outside, where a bored-looking George lolled on the Ford, both elbows resting on the side. He perked up when he saw us. "Ready to go?"

"Sure."

Bernard shook his head, staring at George. "He better not scratch the paint," he muttered under his breath, just loudly enough that I could hear him.

CHAPTER 6

WE TOOLED AROUND DUBLIN for the next few hours, stopping all over the city.

George took us to Trinity College, escorting us around the campus and telling us the history of the old school. Started by Queen Elizabeth herself in the sixteenth century, the ancient campus was the oldest university in the country and one of the most prestigious institutions in all of Europe. Students and professors spilled out around us, streaming out of buildings and hurrying to classes. A number of women were walking around campus carrying books.

"Does this university have female students?" I asked, staring with curiosity. I had never seen my own gender going to college.

"Oh, yeah. A few. They voted twenty years ago to allow them in. Ridiculous, right?" George complained. "We all know women belong at home, not clogging up our schools."

He rolled his eyes and shrugged at Cap.

"Interesting take, Georgie," Cap replied, his tone even. "I know quite a few smart women. In fact, one of them is standing right next to you. Certainly higher education has plenty of room for them, don't you think?"

George just laughed and kept walking, leaving us trailing behind him. Cap glanced at me, shaking his head.

"The real treat here is the library," George called over his shoulder, leading us across the campus to a large stone building with dozens of ornate windows. He opened the door in front of us and grinned. "Prepare to be amazed."

We stepped in and stopped short. Massive wooden shelves, stacked on top of each other, soared hundreds of feet above our heads and reached to a huge arched ceiling. The carved shelves stretched down a long hallway, illuminated by the windows streaming sunlight into the dark wooden space. Dozens of marble busts dotted the room.

"Smell that," Chito breathed, sniffing the air. "I can't even describe it."

I breathed in the rich, musty smell of old books and smiled. I loved to read. I'd spent much of my childhood reading to escape the crushing loneliness I felt. It staggered my mind to gaze out on so many books and reflect on the collective wisdom of thousands of great minds, their life's work gathered here in one room.

"Dear Lord," Cap said softly, next to me. "This is heaven."

"This library boasts over two hundred thousand books," George told us. "It's the greatest library in Ireland. One of the most famous in the whole world."

Our boots echoed through the room as we walked through, craning our necks to take it all in, reverently.

"I could live here," I whispered, staring at the cracked spines and leather covers of the tomes around me.

"Me, too," Cap grinned. "Imagine how thick my notebooks would be if I spent time in here."

"Wait until you see the cathedral," George said, waiting at the door at the other end of the room. "You'll love that, too."

⎯⎯⎯◉⎯⎯⎯

AFTER PULLING UP TO the cathedral in our Fords and stepping out, several women and little kids stopped me on the sidewalk.

"It's Andi! Andi Gallivanter!" they clamored, rushing to shake my hands. "Andiamo!"

"Can you hold my little girl?" one mother cried, smiling at me. "I want her to be able to say that the famous Miss Gallivanter held her when she visited Ireland. It'll be a little extra bit o' luck for her."

The little girl reached up and pulled my hat off, grinning, and placed it on her own head. Her curls poked out underneath as she looked up at me, her tiny face beaming. She was missing several teeth.

"Oh my," I laughed, my cheeks pink. "I don't know that she needs luck—she'll do just fine on her own. She's a character, isn't she?"

"We've got to get a picture of this," Cap laughed, rushing back to the Ford. "Chito, where's the camera?"

"So *this* is why you keep Andiamo around, huh?" George said, his arms crossed. "I've always wondered why you bothered to have a woman on your crew. But if it brings in this sort of attention, I suppose I can see the reasoning."

Cap caught my eye and shook his head at me, warningly, as I started to reply, still holding the little girl. "Smile!" he called, lining us up for a shot with the cathedral in the background.

I hugged her and set her down. "Thank you," I said, kneeling on one leg so I could look her in the eyes. "Grow up to be brave and strong, little one."

"I will, Miss Gallivanter," she lisped, grinning up at me. "My mum said that even if I never get to be as tall as you, I can still be courageous just like you. You survived all on your own in that jungle!"

"You have a smart mother," I smiled. "Nice to meet you both."

I dusted my pant legs and joined the men. We walked through the giant cathedral doors into the cavernous space, the stone arching above our heads. Lamps cast a warm glow over the wooden pews and floor. Large, gothic chandeliers spanned the length, looking like crowns hovering in mid-air.

The room was full of people milling about, looking at paintings and altars, and others kneeling down to pray. It was silent inside. My boots clacked loudly against the polished floor and I tried to walk softly.

We meandered through, separating from each other, taking in the stunning space. Cap came up beside me, silently, as I stared at the intricate wooden altar.

"We could get married in a place like this someday," he whispered in my ear, his soft breath tickling my neck.

I smiled at him, my heart full. I'd had the same thought. We stood side-by-side, studying the chancel.

"Ready to see the brewery?" George appeared at Cap's side.

"Certainly," Cap said, placing his hand briefly on the small of my back as he ushered me down the stairs. He winked at me as we walked back down the aisle, as if to say, *Someday soon, Andi, we'll be walking down an aisle together."*

We hopped back into our Fords, a light drizzle again starting.

"We only average two or three days a year without rain," George commented as he climbed into Cap's car. "Irish folks don't even notice it, it's so much a part of our lives."

The roads through the city twisted around old buildings and dozens of small, dark pubs. Music spilled out into the streets as we drove by. Eventually, we reached an industrial-looking area, with railroad tracks and tall smokestacks billowing. The air smelled warm, like fresh grain.

"Here's our real pride and joy, as Dubliners," George said, pointing. "The biggest brewery in the world. And the best, too."

The massive complex was busy, alive with the hum of activity. George guided us through the building, explaining different parts of the facility.

"Here's the best part, for all our guests," he said, leading us into a warehouse. "You get to see what no one else does, when you're with me. This is where they do the coopering, making the barrels that hold the beer. I'm friends with the foreman. I bring our guests here to watch them, as a special treat."

The room was giant, with a lofty ceiling. Rows of benches and piles of tools and wood sat every few feet from each other, aisles separating workspaces. Dozens of men dressed in leather aprons held various pieces of wooden barrels in their hands, working rapidly. Some scraped wood curls off, while others shaped long boards. Still others were piling several boards together in a circular band, making the frame of a barrel.

"They do it all by hand," George explained to us, as we watched them work. "It has to be perfect, because it needs to be airtight for the liquid and able to withstand rough handling. They're artists. And they're paid well for it, too."

"Look at all their tools," Bernard said, staring. "They must have dozens of tools for each of them."

"My friend told me once that it takes thirty different tools to cut and pare the wood," George responded, as we watched the man closest to us quickly hammer a metal hoop on top of a nearly completed barrel. Within a few moments, he'd rolled it out into the courtyard outside the large open doors, where we saw another man take it and roll it toward a fire. Rapidly, he shoveled some flaming coals into the bottom and fire blazed brightly out of the top of the barrel.

Other men filled the courtyard outside, shaping metal pieces and shaving down the outside of the completed barrels.

"They're so fast," I said, staring as they worked.

George huffed. "Apparently you weren't listening earlier," he said, his tone sounding like an irritated teacher instructing a failing pupil. "They're artists, Miss Andi. This is their trade. They know what they're doing."

I frowned. "I did hear you say that earlier. I was merely commenting on their speed."

"Maybe try *not* commenting, for once," he huffed. "Know your place."

He brushed by me to stand next to Cap, who stood several feet away and hadn't overheard his rude reply.

I bit back a sharp retort. George rubbed me the wrong way, but I couldn't let him have the satisfaction of knowing that.

"Hold your tongue, Andi," I told myself, trying not to let my irritation ruin a perfectly good day.

CHAPTER 7

WE FINISHED THE DAY with a sumptuous feast at the ambassador's home.

Maids in frilly white aprons served us a large meal, then whisked our plates away for coffee and whiskey. "Thank you," I said, as the maid placed a cup of coffee in front of me and smiled.

I noticed that all of the men at the table got a small glass of whiskey along with their cup of coffee. The ambassador's wife and I alone had a single cup of coffee. Personally, I didn't care about the alcohol, but it irked me that I was frequently left out of the little rituals that the rest of my crew enjoyed. Though my crew saw me as an equal, it certainly seemed like plenty of other people didn't. I tried not to sigh as I sipped my coffee.

"Can I ask something personal, dearie?" the ambassador's wife said, leaning in to speak to me privately. We'd entertained them with stories from our trips, and she'd followed along with interest.

"Yes, ma'am?"

"What's it really like out there, for you?" she said softly, patting my arm with her gloved hand. "Do people actually respect you?"

"That's a loaded question," I thought, looking at Mrs. Ladley under furrowed brows. Just how much could I tell her? I decided to spin the truth out slowly, in bites, to see how she would respond.

"My crew does, ma'am," I responded honestly. "Most people like me. The crowds, the little kids—they're so excited to meet me. To meet the whole crew. But to tell you the truth, not everyone likes me. I've had plenty of men—and a few women—make mean comments."

"You know, I've followed your stories in the newspapers for a while," she admitted. "I've long wondered if people have softened their attitude toward you. I'm sure you remember that people had a lot of resistance to the idea of bringing a young woman along on an expedition like this, when Captain Gallivanter first announced you to the world."

"Oh," I said, thinking back and drawing a blank. Cap must've intentionally shielded me from all the negative press, when I first joined the crew. Maybe he'd worried I'd leave the team if I saw how much negativity I'd get from strangers?

"Those mean people, what do they say about you?" The ambassador's wife had an earnest expression on her face. "I want to know. I want to *think* the world's changing, but I doubt it sometimes."

"I don't think I can repeat some of their comments in polite company."

"Please, Miss Gallivanter. Be honest."

I studied her as she pursed her lips. Her face was kind and understanding. Perhaps as a foreigner, an outsider's wife living in a strange culture, she was sympathetic to my situation.

"They call me a lost kitten," I responded. "They say I'm nothing but a looker. That I'm just a pretty skirt, a nice pair of legs, and nothing else. That I don't actually have any skills."

"It's obvious that you do," she sipped her coffee. "Captain Gallivanter seems like a sensible man. He doesn't strike me as the type that would bring on a useless team member."

"He's not."

"What else do they say? Tell me."

I hesitated. "It doesn't matter."

"Andiamo," she reached across the table and patted my hand. "You can tell me. Let it out. I sense that you've kept this in for a long time. Maybe I'm just the right person, at the right time, to let you lay your burdens down for a moment. I won't judge."

The dam of my self-discipline broke at the show of her kindness. The words tumbled out before I even realized what I was saying.

"People write to me and tell me that I'm a conniving piece of work," I blurted. "I've been told I'm bossy, manipulative, a nasty woman. People send me letters saying that I'm a gold digger, intent on stealing money from Cap. They insinuate that I've slept my way onto the team, around the team."

Mrs. Ladley listened silently, her eyes full of compassion.

"That's not all," I said, the frustration from the day pouring out as I confided in her. "They tell me I'm throwing away my future. That no man will ever want to marry me, because I'm a soiled little dove after living with other men on this trip. That I'll never have a family, or a future, or anyone who will accept me. They say I'm wasting my life. And my time. That I'm throwing away the prime of my life, chasing an empty dream."

I noticed Cap glancing at me from the other end of the table, and realized my cheeks must be flushed from the anger I felt.

"It can be awful, ma'am," I said, biting my lip and lowering my voice. "Strangers can be cruel. They speculate and pass judgment on me, without even knowing me."

"It certainly sounds like it."

"People who don't know me at all assume all sorts of things about me," I admitted. "They speak down to me. So many men act like I'm an idiot, that I don't have a brain at all. They boss me around, or tell me things about the automobiles that aren't even correct. They tell the same jokes, over and over, about how I should be at home cooking dinner, and everyone always laughs. Sometimes it just gets to me. It's too much."

"Surely not everyone thinks that," Mrs. Ladley frowned. "You come across as capable, to me. Sure of yourself. Courageous. You can't let the opinions of strangers, people who have never even met you, define how you see yourself."

"I try not to," I admitted. "And it really isn't most people. But it's the one out of a hundred that gets under my skin. It's their tones that bother me the most. The way they use their words against me. They don't speak to each other like that, only to me. It doesn't matter what I do, or how carefully I speak—they just dismiss me. And I hate it. I don't know what to do about it. I can't change their minds. I know all I can do is just keep being me, but it's so hard to face the same battles day after day, in every corner of the world we visit."

"Even your own employee, George, did the same to me today," I wanted to add, but refrained. George had been wildly condescending all day, to the point where I'd kept as far away from him as possible.

Mrs. Ladley studied her coffee cup, silent.

"She's elegant and beautiful, and so poised," I thought desperately. *"She can't relate to me, sitting here in my pants and boots and jacket. We live in different worlds. What can she even say right now? She doesn't understand what I'm facing. I can't try to make her see my struggles. She has no idea."*

I sipped my coffee, regretting my outburst. Yet again, I'd put my foot in my mouth. I had a bad habit of doing that. Why couldn't I take a cue from Mrs. Ladley and keep my mouth shut about the things that bothered me? The world wasn't friendly to women who spoke their minds.

Unexpectedly, Mrs. Ladley picked up her dessert fork and stabbed it violently into the tablecloth.

"Son of a—" she muttered angrily. "I hate to see this happen to a bright young woman like you. You have too much potential to let a bunch of naysaying fools dictate your path, Andiamo."

"Ma'am?"

"Don't you make the same mistake I did and just put up with this sort of bad behavior," she hissed. "The world's different. It's time we stop letting people tell us who we should be or how we should act. Follow your own dreams, and don't give a damn about those who think they can dictate your life. You're in charge of it, not them."

"True," I blinked. Mrs. Ladley was more spirited than I'd thought.

"As the Brits say, don't give a bollocks!" she added vehemently. "Yes, that's right, I said it. I get the same kind of comments too, did you know that? I have, my whole life. And I'm sick to death of it. You're a nice girl. You don't deserve such roadblocks. I don't know why we can't just let each other do what we want. Those gobshites."

I raised my eyebrows. I certainly hadn't expected an ambassador's wife to be swearing at the dinner table in front of me.

"I'm sorry," she apologized hastily, seeing my surprised expression. "It's just that—I've dealt with a lot of the same attitude, marrying John. People insult me openly, too. Especially here. Maybe I wanted a little adventure myself, moving across the ocean, you know? What's wrong with that? You'd think they'd be more progressive in Ireland, but they're tied to the old ways."

"No, don't apologize," I smiled. "I'm glad you're honest. It's good to know I'm not alone."

"You're definitely not alone," she picked up her cup. "Keep moving forward. Remember that there are other people out there who are cheering for you, even if you don't know their faces. Don't let a bit of negativity stop you from being who you were born to be."

"Thank you. I appreciate you being candid. And asking me about this. Sometimes I just need to get it out and vent. It wears on me, dealing with it day after day."

"I could tell," Mrs. Ladley grinned. "I didn't want you to think you were alone in facing this. Keep your chin up, dearie. Don't let them kill that fire within you."

"I won't," I promised, finding comfort in her encouragement.

"Oh," she whispered, leaning forward and glancing at the men. "Do me a favor. Don't tell my husband I said 'gobshite' at the table, with important guests present."

CHAPTER 8

WE SPENT THE NEXT DAY sightseeing on our own around Dublin, walking past old buildings and dipping in and out of stores and pubs to try different foods and listen to merry music.

In order to avoid the mob of crowds that would follow us if they noticed the Gallivanter Expedition crew walking in the streets, we draped ourselves in scarves and shadowed our faces with hats.

Chito glowed with joy, ordering little cups of steaming seafood chowder and sampling breads and butters and cheeses. "I could stay here forever," he happily proclaimed, in between bites.

"You might have to, if you keep eating like this," Cap teased. "Bernard, what's the weight limit on those Fords?"

"He's not even close to it, Cap," Bernard rubbed his chin. "Those axels can handle a lot, and remember? We upgraded to the most expensive tires..."

"It's a joke, Bernard," I interrupted, laughing.

"But he asked?"

"No, no," Cap laughed, flinging his arm around Bernard. "Forget it. I was teasing."

That night, we put on our uniforms and made our way to the large auditorium where we were scheduled to speak. We stood backstage, chatting with each other and the university staff, as people filed into their seats. Soon, the house lights dimmed and we lined up behind Cap.

"Everyone ready?" he winked at all of us. Chito flashed him the thumbs up. We could do this routine in our sleep now.

We filed onto the stage, Cap first and then me, Chito, and Bernard behind him like three ducks in a row.

Four wooden chairs sat on stage, waiting for us. As the spotlights shone on us, the crowd went wild. People cheered and whistled, screaming and waving, as we took our seats. Our host, the president of the university, stood up to introduce us.

"You've seen them in the news, my friends," he said in a booming voice. "Their names are on the lips of nearly every civilized man, woman, and child in Europe, as they travel around the world in their automobiles. We're so pleased to greet you, Captain Gallivanter and crew, and welcome you here to Dublin this evening!"

The crowd thundered as a cute young redhead hurried onto the stage with a tray of beer. She smiled cheekily as she placed a beer in front of Cap, Bernard, and Chito.

"Wait, we need one more," Chito said quietly, frowning at my empty spot as she started to walk away.

"Oh, sorry," she whispered apologetically.

It wasn't the first time this had happened on stage. Because it usually happened when we were in front of a crowd or just about to start a speech, the "mistakes" were never rectified. I settled my face into a smile, willing myself to overlook the slight yet again.

Cap launched into our presentation, strolling across the stage with passion. He was a charismatic speaker, engaging the crowd in his stories. We teased him about it, but he came alive up here on the stage.

"Ladies and gentlemen, we've journeyed across the wilds of Africa and through the mountains and valleys of Europe to be here tonight!" Cap cried dramatically, taking his hat off and raking his hand through his blonde hair.

The motion caught the eye of several women in the front few rows, who bit their lips and followed his every movement with their eyes. I grinned. I'd given up being jealous a long time ago, knowing Cap kept even the most beautiful girl at arm's length.

"I only have eyes for you," he told me often. "You're the only girl who could ever possibly keep up with me, Miss Gallivanter. Besides, the adoration of strangers pays the bills."

Still, it was flattering to see that other women found him attractive.

Cap looked dashing tonight, wearing a cheetah skin draped artfully across his shoulders. "I bought it from a little flea market years ago," he laughed once, as he unpacked it from his bag to air it out before a presentation. "I thought it might come in handy. People assume I've killed a wild animal or two with my bare hands, I think. It fits my image."

"We stand before you here, my friends, as survivors. Nay, we are more than survivors—we are victors!" he raised his voice, holding up his hands.

"We have survived through the worst that Mother Nature can throw at us—sandstorms and rain, dangerous floods and treacherous driving conditions. We have crashed our cars and nearly bled to death, we've drowned and nearly died, and we've been trapped in the deepest, darkest jungles of Africa and survived by the skin of our teeth as we battled wild animals in the darkness of the forest!"

Cap dramatically illuminated the projector, and a giant picture of a snarling leopard appeared on the screen behind him. The audience murmured.

"This is the animal that the beautiful Miss Andiamo and I faced alone, together, in that jungle!" he said, whirling around to point at it. "See those fangs? Those claws? Imagine how we could have been shredded with just a swipe of those paws, ladies and gentlemen. Picture us, wounded and oozing blood, fighting to draw a last breath, as we perished tragically in the jungle."

As he re-told our very real adventure, it wasn't difficult for me to look serious and emotional, at the memory.

As dramatic as it sounded, the reality that we'd faced very real danger still tugged at my mind. Cap had started working in these moving stories along with the educational aspect of talking about new cities, people groups, and customs. He thought it hooked people in.

Cap continued through his presentation, beseeching the crowd to imagine the sites we gazed upon, as he punctuated his stories and facts with pictures and short videos we'd collected as we traveled. The crowd dragged their hungry gazes between Cap and the screen behind him, as he masterfully cycled through image after image and wove a fascinating narrative.

Occasionally, he lobbed us questions and we shared our own perspective. We had a set routine, honed to perfection from the dozens of times we'd repeated this act.

I told my story of what it had felt like to drown in the mountain stream as we traveled through Spain.

Bernard begrudgingly shared how he felt waking up after his car accident, where a rockslide had flipped his car over and pinned him inside. Somehow, his abrupt, spare manner of speaking accentuated our near tragedy. The audience had to strain to hear him, but they listened at the edge of their seats.

Chito always spoke about the unique cuisine we experienced, but also about the friendship and courage he saw in our team, and the foreigners we encountered as we faced difficult situations.

Reaching the end of the presentation, the crowd gave us a standing ovation. Cap bowed deeply, his gleaming boots reflecting the excited faces in the crowd who clapped for us.

"And now, my dear friends, we have time for a few questions," he called, looking out at the excited crowd.

From the front row, our guide George bolted to his feet.

"Captain Gallivanter!" he called, turning sideways so the audience could see him and hear his voice. Clearly, he craved the spotlight. "Sir, I have a question for you!"

"Certainly, Mr. O'Malley," Cap smiled. "Folks, Mr. O'Malley here spent the entire day with us yesterday, showing us around your lovely city. It's a charming place, full of wonderful people, for sure. We'd love to have your question?"

"Yes, Captain. My question is this—what's it like putting up with a young woman on your crew? How does that change the dynamic between the rest of you?"

"I'm not sure I know what you mean," Cap replied lightly. "I think Andiamo is the one who's putting up with *us*, not the other way around."

"Surely you don't think I'm blind, Captain," George's voice was loud enough for everyone in the room to hear him. "I spent all day yesterday with you. I can tell when things are different, when there's a woman around. I want to know how you think it affects your team?"

"I don't see what you're trying to ask," Cap's tone cooled noticeably.

"Oh, you know what I mean," George grinned back at him. "Don't we all know what I mean, gentlemen?" he said, turning to the crowd and smiling. The crowd laughed. Several men whistled and clapped.

"Tell us, Captain Gallivanter," George pressed, smirking as the other men egged him on. "I think we're all curious. What is it like, having to babysit a young lady while you travel the world on this epic adventure?"

Cap laughed, but I could tell it was for show. He wasn't amused. "I wasn't aware I was running a babysitting service," he joked, looking at me. "Look at Miss Andiamo—she's a grown woman. She hardly needs my supervision. Or anyone else's supervision, for that matter."

Chito shifted uncomfortably in his seat next to me, shooting me a pitying glance.

I'd had quite enough of this rude man. I thought back to my conversation with the ambassador's wife last night. "Don't let a bit of negativity stop you from being who you were born to be," she had told me.

I lifted my chin. There were children in this crowd, listening to me right now. This was my chance to show them what courage looked like.

I stood up from my chair and joined Cap in the center of the stage. He adjusted his position, so we both stood in the beaming spotlight together.

"Mr. O'Malley, let me cut through your implications and clear some things up," I called out, my tone smooth. "All jokes aside, I've been an invaluable member of this expedition, sir. I've repaired the cars, dealt with the natives, and done my fair share of work when it comes to all the grueling travel. I carry my own bags and I make my own repairs. I'm part of this team, and they rely on me. I'm not a burden. I hold my own here."

"Right, sweetheart," George replied gaily, grinning at the crowd. Another man whistled. "Why don't you let the men speak? When I want *your* opinion, I'll ask. I was talking to Captain Gallivanter."

The crowd erupted in laughter and I felt my cheeks go pink. I was enraged and tried not to lose my cool. Though we were no longer in the wilderness of Africa, fighting for our lives, here I was still fighting another battle.

"Can you change the oil in an automobile, Mr. O'Malley?" I asked, my voice ringing out in the boisterous room. "Can you drive for hours on end, across the Sahara, camping in the sand

and crawling under the car to check the undercarriage? Can you use your shirt to pick up dew from the moss to survive in the jungle, without water? Spend the night in the jungle, totally alone, without any supplies? Because I've done all that and more."

The crowd was electric now, chatter filling every corner. I raised my voice to be heard.

"Just because it's not what you're used to a woman doing doesn't mean that it's wrong," I added.

"This is what I'm talking about," George groaned, shaking his head. "It sounds like you should be safely at home, sweetheart. Let the boys have their adventure. You just don't know your place and you refuse to see how your presence affects the rest of your crew. You're either too naive or too arrogant to know what you should actually be doing with your life."

Cap interrupted him, his ears pink. His tone had changed subtly, but he still attempted to make light of the situation.

"Apparently, this gentlemen just wants to start a little debate here," Cap said, laughing hollowly. "Thank you for sharing your opinion, sir. That's all for tonight, folks. Thank you—"

But George interrupted Cap's words before he'd even finished speaking.

"Captain, you're the one who made this a public issue by bringing this woman onto your team in the first place. Aren't you man enough to tell us why? Or do you not have a good reason?"

Cap took the bait.

"Andi is a valuable member of our team," he responded tersely. "If you listened to her just now, you wouldn't be asking me for an explanation of why she's on this crew. She's earned her spot, just like anyone else. She adds just as much to this team as any man would."

"I was with you all day, Captain Gallivanter," George pressed. The crowd tittered as he refused to back down. "I spent all day with your crew, and with Miss Gallivanter. I can tell you, she's just like any other ordinary woman out there. Except that she's not at home, in the kitchen, where she's supposed to be."

The crowd laughed, though I watched a woman in the front row frown as her husband chuckled.

"The world has changed, Mr. O'Malley," I replied, raising my voice to be heard above the commotion of the crowd. "Women can vote now, in America and in Germany. We can own our own property, too—property that belonged to us, in the first place. Even here, in Ireland, women can attend university. We're eager to contribute to the world, and deserve to do so."

A woman clapped from the middle of the crowd, and was immediately hushed by her husband. Her small act of defiance fired me up.

"And look how women stepped in while their men were away during the Great War," I continued. "You certainly didn't seem to mind that we were keeping your businesses and factories going while you fought."

"Right, and look how men stepped back in to take over as soon as they got home," George snapped. "It's unnatural. Women belong at home. You're the weaker sex. We here in the old country know the proper roles that men and women are supposed to have. We don't fight nature."

"So by your line of reasoning, we should never see a doctor?" I tossed back. "We should never visit a hospital, or implement new technology into our lives or our factories? Forget eyeglasses and electricity, telephones and automobiles. You believe our ideas and routines should never grow or be challenged in any way. That progress is wrong."

George opened his mouth to reply, and I cut him off.

"Your opinions would have left us in the dark ages, Mr. O'Malley," I said, my voice edged in anger I couldn't hide. "We'd never have the literature or artwork or the scientific and medical advancements we use in our lives. Brilliant thoughts come from brilliant minds, regardless if they're male or female brains. It's a shame you can't see that."

I barged ahead, encouraged by a small smile the lady in the front row gave me.

"We'll never see the world, or meet anyone new, because we'll just stay in our little villages and do things the way we've always done it, right? Because that's what you're saying, sir. We're just fine doing things the way we've always done them. No need to grow or progress, to broaden our minds and our horizons. No need to see what the human spirit is capable of, whether that be man or woman contributing to a better world."

"This is what I'm talking about, see?" George yelled out over me, gesturing to the crowd. "She can't even have a rational conversation. She's too emotional to think clearly."

Chito stood up now, shoving his chair back against the wooden floor with a screech.

"Hold on, you're saying that Andi isn't rational? Do you even hear yourself?" Chito thundered. "You can't even respond to the points she's making!"

George grinned. "Oh, the big boy on stage has to speak up now for her. She can't even defend herself, huh? And you claim she's a part of your crew, just like everyone else? It doesn't seem like it. She can't even hold her own in a simple conversation."

The crowd laughed again. I bit my lip so hard I tasted blood.

I was in an impossible situation: I couldn't lose my cool, lest I be accused of being an emotional woman and lose all credibility, but I couldn't rip into him without upsetting the crowd, which was obviously sympathetic to him. I fought every instinct I had, trying not to show how upset I was.

"Is your wife here, sir?" I asked, knowing full well he wasn't wearing a wedding ring. I'd noticed that small fact yesterday, as he showed us around Dublin. *"It's hard to believe someone with such a negative opinion of the opposite gender hadn't settled down,"* I thought wryly.

"No," he frowned. "I'm not married."

"Big surprise," I replied sarcastically. The crowd screamed their laughter.

George was noticeably angry, listening to the laughs. He waited until they died down, then spoke up.

"I noticed you're not wearing a ring either, sweetheart," he spat. "What, no one wants you now that you've worked your way around the team?"

His insult drew visible rage from the men on stage next to me. I saw all their bodies stiffen with anger. He had crossed a line and shown the entire room his true colors. Shocked whispers flew through the crowd.

"Mr. O'Malley, how dare you insult her—and all of us—like that?" Cap cried, his words clipped as he struggled to control his temper. "Andiamo is a lady. And we are all gentlemen. How dare you insinuate something like that? And in such a public way? A man of honor would never speak this way to anyone."

"Yeah right, she's a lady," George sneered. "If she was *your* wife, would you be happy with her traveling the world with a bunch of unmarried men? Wouldn't you prefer her to be at home?"

"If she was my wife, I'd happily hand her the keys and hop in the passenger side," Cap shot back. "You have no idea what she's capable of. But I do. I've seen her in action, every day for a year now. Why, at one point, I was cornered in a tree by a jaguar, and if it hadn't been for Andi scaring it off, I might not even be here today. And when I got in a car accident, months ago, Andi risked her own life to pull me out of the wreckage and speed me to a hospital, stemming the wounds that could have been fatal. She's saved my life."

"Mine too," Bernard finally spoke, still sitting in his chair.

Cap glanced at me, biting his lip. "You don't think she deserves to be here? You're a fool. She doesn't have to prove herself to you. *We* know her worth."

I was still angry, though. Impulsively, I dug out the keys to my Ford from my pocket.

"Let's go outside, and I'll show you right now," I called out, holding them up to the crowd. "I can take apart the engine and put it back together. I can drive as well as any man here, probably even better. I'll show you. I'll show you what a girl can do."

The crowd hooted and rolled with laughter as I held the keys up and walked toward him, down the steps of the stage.

George made a show of backing up dramatically as I walked toward him.

"Oh, no," he said, pretending to cower in fear. "I wouldn't possibly trust any woman behind the wheel. Not even you, Leggy."

"That concludes our show tonight, folks," Cap called out, putting his hat back on his head and clapping his hands together. "A final word here for Mr. O'Malley? We'd rather have Andiamo any day over you, sir."

Cap stepped down and put his arm around me, leading me off the stage, smiling and waving with his free hand. I dutifully smiled and waved, too, as the crowd clapped and whistled.

Right before trotting me off the stage, Cap impulsively stopped and faced the crowd again, his shoulders squared. His arm remained around me.

"Let me leave you with one final thought, my friends," he called out, his voice carrying through the room. "We value the person and the skill they add to our team, not just their gender. It's made us who we are—one-of-a-kind, groundbreaking, and fearless. And the Gallivanter Expedition won't ever let anyone hold us back from doing what we love."

He smiled, his handsome face catching the spotlight. "The Gallivanter Expedition is unstoppable, and we're making history."

CHAPTER 9

AS BERNARD AND CHITO joined us backstage, the thick velvet curtains separating us from the crowd, Cap dropped his smile and paced.

"Andi, I'm sorry," he blurted as the crowd continued to clap, grabbing my hand. "I'm so sorry. He had no right to insult you like that."

"It's not your fault," I sighed. "You didn't say those things. George did."

Cap suddenly let out a barrage of words under his breath so foul that I stepped back, startled. Sometimes I forgot that he'd served in the military, as a young man. I remembered it now, listening to his language.

Chito and Bernard stared, too, as Cap paced back and forth, swearing. He paused after several moments and straightened his jacket.

"I'm sorry, everyone," he explained, his neck red. "I had to get that out or I'd explode. I'm just so tired of biting my tongue. Listening to George out there and not saying what I wanted to say to him—not punching him in the throat—it just put me clear over the edge."

"You're tired of biting *your* tongue?" I exclaimed. "I'm the one who's always made fun of. I'm constantly talked down to, or I'm enduring jokes about how I should be in the kitchen, or watching the children, or asked when I'm going to give this all up and settle down and start a family, like a respectable young woman—"

"You don't think it bothers me, too?" Cap threw up his hands. "How on earth do you think it makes me feel to hear them talking about you that way? To stand there, helplessly, not being able to shout back at them? Those damn ignorant fools! They don't even know you!"

"Don't let one opinion get to you, guys," Chito spoke up, soothingly. "People like that don't matter."

"It's not one person saying this, Chito," I groaned. "It's a lot of them. Even some of the reporters slip their opinions into their articles about me. I'm always cut down. It's always this same spin—'little Andi, playing with the big tough boys, trying to prove herself when she should be settling down with a nice, rich husband and having his babies.' Isn't it about time society finally sees women as equals to men?"

"It's not fair," I thought to myself. *"I have a thirst for adventure. I have the physical and mental strength to be on the Gallivanter team. Why am I always the target of such negativity?"*

But even though it wasn't fair, I had to get past it. I couldn't let these sorts of comments continue to get under my skin. It wasn't fair to entangle my teammates into the burdens that I alone had to carry. They were good men who saw me as an equal. I had to remember that the world contained plenty of good men, just like them.

Cap rubbed his jaw, still irritated. "I'm right there by your side, in case you haven't noticed," he said hotly. "I hear it all, too. I deal with it, too."

"Yeah, but it's not *your* character that they're attacking," I sighed. "It's me. It's always me. The butt of their jokes, the target for their stupid slurs against women, their quips that I don't have a brain. That I'm too weak. That I don't know what I'm doing. That I'm not worth listening to. That my opinion doesn't matter. It echoes through my head constantly."

Cap swore again. "You can't let them have that power over you," he groaned.

I knew Cap wasn't angry with me, but his rage was testament to how frustrated he was, too. Normally even-keeled and controlled, Cap rarely displayed his temper like this.

"I'm just tired of it," I replied, trying to reign in my frustration. "I'm tired of people acting like I'm a novelty. Not seeing me as an equal to the rest of my team."

"Not equal?" Cap uttered, running his hand through his hair. "I knew you were special before I even hired you. That first night, when you and I met in Nice, after that presentation I did there? When we talked outside the theater, overlooking the ocean? I knew then that you were fully capable. I didn't doubt it for a second."

"You're different. You're progressive. Most people see only my body—the body of a woman—and never see my brain or my spirit."

"Andi, you know why Cap didn't immediately stand up for you out there?" Chito interrupted, putting his hand on my shoulder. "Why he tried to downplay it? Why he let you take the stage and speak? It's the same reason why I didn't jump to defend you, either. Do you understand why?"

"I don't know," I pursed my lips. "Tell me."

"Because we know you're a warrior," he said gently, squeezing me. "You crash through barriers without letting them slow you down. You're out front, leading the pack. And there will always be people who criticize you because of that. You'll always have to deal with those to try to tear you down, because in life, there are only those who criticize and those who actually *do*."

I looked at him, and saw the warmth in his eyes.

"You, Andi?" Chito continued. "You're a doer. Don't let anyone stop you from doing. Ever."

For a moment, the four of us stood silent, staring at each other. The sounds of the laughing crowd exiting the auditorium contrasted with the rage I felt back here, hidden away behind the curtain.

"This is my life," I thought, catching the symbolism of the moment. *"A false, smiling face that I show to the world, the truth and hardship carefully concealed from all but a few. Up on stage, no one suspects what I actually feel. What I deal with."*

Cap sighed. "Chito's right, Andi. We can't step in to defend you because you don't need us to. You're strong enough and smart enough on your own. If either of us were to step in, we'd make you look weak. It would undermine you. We have to let you fight your own battles, especially in public. It goes against everything I want, believe me. But it's what *you* need."

I looked around the little group, suddenly feeling foolish. Here they were consoling me, after one stupid man's comments. They didn't do this for each other. If I was truly strong, I shouldn't be displaying this sort of emotion in front of them.

Straightening my back, I tossed my head. "I don't care," I replied, trying to believe my own lie. "Let's get out of here."

"Hold on," Cap said, holding up his hand. "You do care. Why are you suddenly downplaying this?"

"You men never let anything get to you. I won't, either. I need to be tougher."

Cap narrowed his eyes, studying my face. "You really think we never let anything get to us?"

"Yes."

He laughed bitterly, and took my hands in his, looking down at them. "When you almost drowned in that river in Spain, Andi? When we got back to the hotel that night, after I tucked you in? I cried."

"You did?"

"I did," he admitted. "I knew I'd nearly lost you forever. I wept for you, for the loss I'd endured in those few moments you'd been unconscious before we revived you. I suffered a lifetime of regret and blind terror, that night, over your close call. I knew if you died,

I'd never have the chance to tell you what you meant to me. How much I needed you."

"I didn't know that."

"We all have different things that get to us," Cap responded, his eyes searching mine. "We all carry scars, and sometimes those scars tear open. It hurts. But we continue pushing forward, even with our wounds."

"I feel like I'm constantly biting my tongue, trying not to blow up," I sighed.

"So do I," Cap laughed, as Chito nodded too. "I think we all can relate to that feeling of biting our tongue. Because unfortunately, our jobs thrust us into the public spotlight. We're headline news, all over the world. Of course we bite our tongues. We can't insult these people in the crowds, or turn people against us. The future of this expedition depends on us appealing to the masses. We rely on public support."

"But do we really want to live this way forever?" I asked, frustrated. "I don't. Self-discipline is exhausting."

"She has a point," Bernard grumbled. "Why are we tip-toeing around and trying to behave? We have plenty of money now. We can do what we want."

The four of us paused, looking at each other. Bernard was right. We had more money than we'd ever need. Even the million dollar prize pot at the end of the competition wasn't such a driving force now—we'd all be comfortable for the rest of our lives, living on what we had already.

"Then we do it now because it's not about getting more money, it's about our character," Cap said firmly.

"Character," Bernard groaned. "Why do you have to be such a goody-goody all the time, Cap?"

"We show the world that we're disciplined, and we're professional," Cap replied. "We preach goodwill and tolerance, and a spirit of acceptance. We have to live it out in our own lives, too. It doesn't matter what anyone throws at us. We can handle it. And it won't slow us down."

"It's like this is our new wild," Bernard drawled in his flat voice. "It's just as brutal as the jungle. Or the desert. It only appears more civilized, on the surface. But it's just as barbaric. It requires just as much courage to navigate it."

"Bernard has such a way with words," I grinned, exchanging a look with Cap. "It's a pity he's so stingy with them."

"Keep teasing and I'll clam up again," he warned.

Chito thumped him on the back and laughed. "Let's just take this as a sign that we're doing something right. We have the opportunity to re-educate society about women, and what women are capable of doing. You're the poster child for it, Andi."

"Right," Cap agreed. "Besides, throughout all of human history, the men and women who have propelled us forward faced the same criticisms. Those who stand out always draw attention, good and bad."

"You had to imagine that we'd draw *some* negative attention with all of the world's eyes on us now," Bernard said, puffing out his thin cheeks. "It was better before we were famous. When people left us alone."

"Amen to that," Chito said. "I think I know what would cheer us all up. We can use a little dinner, can't we?"

"I'm starving," Cap admitted. "Andi? Bernard?"

We nodded and slipped out of the back of the theater. Stepping into the darkness, I pulled my collar up against the cool, damp wetness outside.

The smell of thick, earthy peat moss saturated the air from fires inside homes and bars throughout the area. It was windy—always windy here in Ireland—and the road glistened with dampness as we walked down the cobblestone streets under the glow of the flickering street lights.

As we walked down the street to our cars, I reflected on the night. It certainly hadn't gone the way most of our public events did, but I wondered just how many other people had stared up at me on the stage at previous events, thinking the same things that George O'Malley had finally dared say aloud.

"How many people have watched me share my stories, thinking it was inappropriate for me to even be on stage in front of them?" I wondered.

Despite my frustration, my gratitude for the Gallivanter crew welled up. I was thankful that I had the support of these three good men who wouldn't let me fight this battle alone.

My heels clicked on the wet pavement. Internally, I resolved that I wouldn't let anyone stop me from living the adventure I wanted in life.

"I have to be myself," I thought. *"I have to keep my head up, and still see the good in people. I need to be thankful for the men out there like Cap and Chito and Bernard who see me for who I am, and don't just stop at the fact that I'm a girl."*

I thought about the picture I carried around with me, a little girl who'd sent me a photograph of herself months ago. In the photograph, she dressed up in driving goggles and boots. In her childish handwriting, she had scrawled, "I want to be just like you when I grow up."

"She'll face this, too," I mused. I saw her chubby little cheeks, glowing with optimism and pride. She didn't yet know what people would say, how they'd try to hold her back.

"Little girl, the world will try to stomp out your zest for adventure," I thought. *"You can't let it. You can't give up. And I can't give up, either. I am strong. And my shoulders can bear this load. I can't concentrate on the critics who badger me while they do nothing*

with their own lives. I have to live my life, and live it well. Not just for me, but for all the little girls watching me."

We reached the Fords. Cap tossed me the keys.

"Don't you want to drive?" I asked, puzzled. Cap usually drove one car and I drove another, as we rolled around town. It was part of our crafted image for people to see the two of us driving independently.

He opened the door and grinned at me. "I meant what I said earlier. That I'd happily hand you the keys and let you drive. So, here you go."

He waited as I slid across to the driver's seat then slipped into the passenger seat, contentedly putting his hands behind his head.

"Drive on, Miss Gallivanter," he smiled. "Drive on. And don't you ever stop."

CHAPTER 10

AMBASSADOR LADLEY HAD arranged for us to visit a school the next day, to give a short presentation about our expedition.

"It's mostly American children, and a few wealthy British and Irish kids too," he'd explained to us. "It's an expensive school. A good school. You'll love it."

Though we did many school presentations, we cringed at hearing that it was a wealthy school. In our experience, that only meant one thing: wild hellions who got their way because daddy had bought the wing of the building they sat in.

"I'd rather face the jungle again rather than deal with a bunch of spoiled brats," Bernard complained as we packed up our vehicles for the morning's visit to the school.

"Says the man who didn't get stranded in it overnight," I shot back. "Come on, Bernard. They're kids. They can't be that bad."

Bernard finished loading a bag into the back and patted the Ford's side fondly. "Yeah right. Kids are even worse than normal people."

We followed the instructions to a nearby school, a large brick building with a bright red door and cheerful flower boxes in the windows. An older man pushed out the door as we started up the sidewalk, and greeted us breathlessly.

"Oh, you're finally here! Welcome to St. John's Primary School. I'm the dean, Andrew Kelly, and you'll meet our teachers inside. We're all so excited to meet you!"

The lobby was large and decorated with colorful pictures, obviously the handiwork of their students. We could hear the quiet murmur of a class reciting a poem as we walked down the hall together.

"What a charming place, Mr. Kelly," I said, looking around. "You must have some wonderful children here."

"We have some good children," he said, nodding. "Some very good children."

Cap smiled. "We can't wait to meet the students," he said. He was great with kids. They adored him. His charisma and easy confidence captivated even the most unruly children.

"Yes, yes," Mr. Kelly replied, then lowered his voice. "But I do need to warn you about our sixth year class."

"Sixth year?" Chito asked, puzzled. "What is that, in America? How old?"

"They're all ten and eleven," Mr. Kelly replied. "You know, that age when they—well, how to describe it? They *change*."

Cap and I exchanged glances.

"You'll be fine," the dean said, noticing our looks. "Their teachers will be there. Just—don't let them throw you off course. They've been known to do that."

Now Chito stared at us, eyebrows raised. We shrugged behind the dean's back, as we made our way into a small cafeteria.

"We thought we'd set up here, and have groups of different grades cycle through," the dean said. "That way, all the children can ask questions and get the chance to meet you. Can we end with a large all-school photo when you're done presenting?"

"Sure," Cap said, looking around the space. It was meticulous, with long tables and neat chairs tucked perfectly into place.

"Let me go get the first group," the dean said, darting away. "I'll be right back. Make yourselves comfortable."

We stood awkwardly, Cap holding the box of photographs we showed around when we visited schools.

"There's still time to make a break for it," Bernard pointed out. "Can we?"

"No," Cap replied firmly. "This is our job, too. We get to inspire the next generation to see the world, and learn about different cultures. It's important."

Bernard scowled in response, crossing his arms across his chest. "I need to run to the bathroom."

"No, you don't. You're not sneaking away. Not again."

The first wave of children came in, their faces shining with excitement. A murmur went up when they saw us.

"They do wear those uniforms, just like the photographs!" one small boy said to another, as they walked by me to take their seats. They craned their necks, looking up at me.

"She's so tall!" several children whispered, giggling. Somewhere around forty children sat quietly, their hands folded on the table in front of them, as their teachers hushed the few chatty ones. They leaned forward in their seats, their enthusiasm barely contained at meeting the world-famous Gallivanter team.

Cap grinned. "Good morning, everyone, my name is Captain Gallivanter!"

"Good morning, Captain Gallivanter!" they responded in perfect unison.

"Who here can tell me where Africa is?" Cap asked, launching into the presentation we had prepared specifically for school children. He unfurled a large map as he spoke.

"See? They're not so bad," I whispered to Bernard, as we stood up front and watched Cap speak animatedly to the kids.

"He said it was the older ones who were bad. I hate this part of our job. I'd rather just wait in the cars."

"You can't hate all people, Bernard," I replied quietly. "The world's full of good folks, too. Like us."

He scowled at me.

Cap invited us each to share a bit of our story—we gave just brief outlines of our adventures to children, not wanting to scare them with the gory realities of the dangers we'd face in the wild—and finished the presentation with a stirring call to action.

"Live out your own dreams, blaze your own trails!" Cap urged them. "The world waits for what you—and *only* you—can offer it. Get on with it, my young friends. Live your adventures boldly, unapologetically, and bravely!"

They politely clapped, and stood up to follow their teachers out.

"See? Not so bad," Cap said, sipping a glass of water as we waited for the next group.

The dean reemerged after the third group of students cycled out, after the presentation. Cap smiled at him.

"Mr. Kelly, the children have been perfect angels," he said, offering his hand. "You have a wonderful group of students here."

"Thank you. But just wait. You haven't had the older ones yet."

"Surely they can't be that bad," Chito laughed. "They're just kids."

"They drove their teacher away earlier this year," Mr. Kelly responded. "She'd taught here for eight years. But she quit after only four months with this group. So just remember, don't let them get to you."

We heard the noise of students coming down the hall and entering the cafeteria.

"Do you feel a bit like we're facing down a pack of hyenas, after hearing how the dean talked about them?" Chito said, as we tilted our heads.

Mr. Kelly was scooting away, and heard his comment.

"That's probably not too far off," he called over his shoulder, as he shot through a doorway and disappeared. The four of us looked at each other in alarm.

The cafeteria door burst open, and several boys sprinted into the cafeteria yelling at the top of their lungs. Behind them, a gaggle of girls grouped together, clutching each other and whispering. A frazzled teacher pushed her way through, yelling at the boys.

"Robert! Logan!" she screamed, watching them run around the tables. "Sit down! Brendan! You sit down, too!"

The boys ignored her completely, and rounded the tables near us. We stepped back in alarm as they rushed past. It was like watching a herd of elephants nearly trample us.

If elephants screamed like wild banshees, that is.

"Hullo!" one of them yelled, pretending to tip an invisible hat at us as he ran by.

The teacher struggled for several minutes to get her class seated, as two other groups sat down and watched the chaos with wide eyes. It took all three teachers reprimanding the class to finally get them in their seats. A fourth teacher came up to the front and joined us.

"They've always been like this," she groaned, watching the other teachers try to separate troublesome children. Behind one older teacher's plump back, several of the kids quickly switched seats just after she'd moved them. "I had them last year. Couldn't wait to get rid of them. But we can't kick any of them out, their parents are the biggest donors here."

"Do they calm down eventually?" I asked, watching the girls turn to braid each other's hair. One boy waited until a braid had been started in a girl's hair, and then yanked it hard, causing her to scream and turn on him furiously.

"No," the teacher shook her head. "You heard that their homeroom teacher quit? What a shame. She was a good egg."

Cap squared his shoulders. "I like a challenge," he said, narrowing his eyes. "Besides, we have a compelling story to share. They'll listen. Let's get started."

He strode to the front of the room, his chin tilted.

"Good morning, everyone! I'm Captain Gallivanter, from the world-famous Gallivanter Expedition! I'm here with Mr. Harris, Mr. Martinez, and Miss Gallivanter," he boomed, his voice confident and clear.

A smattering of students said, "Good morning, Captain Gallivanter," but the older kids kept talking and giggling to each other like he wasn't even there.

"We're so happy to be here today, to share the exciting stories from our travels around the world," Cap continued, pushing his voice louder to drown out the talking from the kids who were ignoring him.

"I'm so sorry, Captain," the frazzled teacher murmured, joining us at the front. "Hold on."

"Class?" she yelled, clapping her hands to get their attention. A few of them looked up, but then went back to talking.

"Hey!" The teacher tried again, holding up her fingers. "One, two, three! Eyes on me!"

They disregarded her. One of the boys hopped out of his seat and started belly crawling across the table, swatting at another boy.

"That never works," the teacher admitted tiredly, as she walked over to forcibly grab the boy laying on the table and tug him back into his seat. "Stop it, Brendan. Sit down."

Cap tried again, opening up his box of oversized photographs and selecting a fierce picture of a snarling leopard. He held it up high, and made a face of fear. "Can you believe that Miss Gallivanter over here faced this, out in the jungle?"

"She looks like she could fight anything!" a little blonde boy yelled out, as his classmates covered their mouths and snickered. "She's a beast!"

I took advantage of my height and stalked over to their table. I towered above them. "You need to sit down and listen," I said in a stern tone. "You're disrupting the entire presentation. No one else can enjoy it when you're being this loud."

"Good!" shrieked one boy, standing up and grabbing for my hat. "I want to wear that!"

"Stop it," I retorted, stepping back.

"Logan!" the teacher yelled.

From the other end of the table, a curly haired girl raised her hand. "May I go to the bathroom?" she asked. "I'm bored."

"We haven't even started yet," I said desperately, looking back at my team. I wasn't sure what to do.

"Yes, but I'm still bored."

"Ladies and gentlemen," Cap boomed in his sternest tone. "I need you all to listen. Sit still and be quiet."

"Sit still and be quiet, sit still and be quiet," several of the boys whispered loudly, starting a chant. They started wriggling in their seats even more. One of them fell completely out of his chair, and lay there on the floor, laughing.

"Robert, get up!" the teacher said, pushing a lock of hair back from her forehead. "You're always falling out of your seat. It's not funny to anyone."

Robert grinned at her and stuck out his tongue, propping his feet up on the chair. I could see why their teacher had quit. Privately, I thought their replacement teacher wasn't far behind her.

Cap stepped toward the rowdy table, holding his box of photographs. "We've been all over the world, friends. Don't you want to see the pictures we brought to share with you?"

"No," several of the kids answered in perfect unison. They started laughing, poking at each other.

Brendan, the little table crawler, hopped out of his seat and stood up.

"Who am I, Captain Gallivanter?" he crowed, standing stiffly and crossing his arms across his chest. He made a face, pushing his lower lip out.

"I don't know, but please sit down so we can continue," Cap said, his tone starting to sound desperate.

This was nearly as bad as the time I'd had to reason with a nomadic tribe in a remote corner of French Sudan. And I'd initially thought that tribe was going to murder us.

Brendan ran up to the front of the room and stood next to Bernard.

"Look! I'm this guy!" he yelled, and resumed his pose. With his one foot stuck out slightly in front of the other, his arms across his chest and his lip sticking out, he did indeed look like the child-sized version of an irritated Bernard.

As I stared, Bernard's face grew red. His eyes bulged. *"Oh, no,"* I thought desperately. There was no telling what an angry Bernard might say.

"That's it!" Bernard hollered, shoving past Brendan and heading toward the door. "I'm done! You're a bunch of spoiled, ungrateful brats!"

He kicked the door open and blasted out. It swung shut with a loud bang.

"Bernard!" Chito yelled, jogging out after him. He emerged a few seconds later, forcibly dragging Bernard back into the room.

"Let go of me!" Bernard yelled, struggling. "They're monsters! I don't want to be here!"

"Get up there and be a man," Chito growled through gritted teeth. "This is our job!"

The students watched with wide eyes, completely silent for the first time.

"Dear Lord, Bernard," Cap hissed. He was mortified. We all knew Bernard was a loose cannon, at times, but we'd never expected him to lose his temper in front of children.

Chito dragged Bernard to the front of the room, next to Cap and me, and held him in place with his strong arm.

"Stand here and don't say a word," Chito commanded, his eyes angry.

"What's his deal?" Brendan asked, from behind us. He was out of his seat, mere feet away, watching us curiously.

"Shut up!" Bernard hollered, glaring at him. "Get out of my face!"

"Mr. Harris!" the older teacher sputtered, shocked. "You can't say that to a student!"

"Fine, give me detention then," Bernard shot back. "Anything to get out of here. And you, you little rat, go sit down!"

Brendan scurried to his seat and sat still. The teachers stared at us, eyes big. For a moment, it was utterly silent.

Cap cleared his throat. "Now then, let's get started. Who here knows where Africa is?"

Robert, the one who'd fallen out of his chair earlier, raised his hand. Everyone else just stared.

"Excuse me, Captain Gallivanter, sir," he said. "I don't want to hear about Africa. I want to hear *his* stories."

"What?" Cap said, staring at him. "Whose stories?"

"His, sir," Robert said, pointing at Bernard. "The funny one."

"Oh, he—he doesn't really like to share much," Cap stumbled, looking at Bernard. I could tell he was wondering if he should just have Bernard go out to the cars and wait for us. "He's our mechanic, and he—"

"I'll only speak if you don't make a single sound," Bernard interrupted gruffly. "Not a single peep. Not a burp, not a whisper. If you do, I'm out of here. For good."

The children sat frozen, spellbound, as Bernard told them about our expedition. In his terse, short words, he shared the highlights of our trip, how we'd traveled around parts of Europe and Northern Africa. He told them what it was like to drive through the desert and camp out under the stars night after night. How he repaired the cars when they faltered.

He even told them about the car accident that he and Cap had endured.

"There was so much blood," he told them, as they listened breathlessly. "I couldn't touch anything without getting it all bloody. It was everywhere. All over the cars. Dripping down my face, onto my clothes."

Cap closed his eyes and shook his head. "They don't need to know about the blood," he said to himself, softly.

I hid my smile.

Cap and Bernard were opposite personalities on stage, but Bernard had found his niche crowd: troublesome young kids.

They didn't care about a slick presentation. His blunt and matter-of-fact manner had them on the edge of their seats, hanging on every word.

When he finished, Cap tapping him on the shoulder, the children stood up to applaud. "Thank you, Mr. Harris!" they hollered, whistling irreverently. They lined up to head back to their classrooms, again shoving each other and pulling the girls' hair. Their teacher took one last desperate look at us and led them out.

"Stop it, Logan!" we heard her yell as she walked through the door. "Don't lick him, Brendan. It's annoying."

The dean peeked back in as the last of the kids filed out. "Ah, you're done. You survived."

"Barely," Chito grumbled under his breath.

"They're a handful, aren't they?" the dean said cheerfully. "We have a countdown going. When they'll be out of school here, for good."

We thanked the dean, and he walked us back out to our Fords. Cap gathered us around him before we got in, and informed us we'd be going back to the hotel.

"I thought we could all use a breather after this morning," he said, looking sideways at Bernard. "Some of us perhaps need a little reset to our day."

A few drops of rain started drifting down on us, lightly, as we stood there. The clouds were thick overhead.

"Don't ever make me do that again," Bernard complained. "I hate kids."

"Well, apparently they love you," Cap tried not to laugh. "Who'd have guessed that you'd end up being their hero?"

"I'm no hero," Bernard mumbled. "Let's go to a pub instead. I need a drink. Or maybe three."

CHAPTER 11

WE LEFT IRELAND A FEW days later, heading north to the top of the island and across the water on the ferry to Scotland.

"We're very close to the coast of Scotland," Cap said, peering up from his notes. "They say on a clear day, you can see the coast of Scotland from Ireland. At the narrowest points, they're only thirteen miles apart."

"Only thirteen miles? Let's swim it instead," Chito said, elbowing me. "Saves us the paperwork."

On the ferry ride over, Cap prepared us for our next engagement. "We've been invited to speak to a collection of wealthy private sponsors in Edinburgh. They're big deals in Scotland. Members of the government and major landowners and businessmen. A few of them are descendants of royalty, apparently."

"Royalty?" I frowned. "Do we need to bow?"

"Americans don't bow," Bernard interjected.

"No, don't bring up the royal thing," Cap waved us off. "There's quite a lot of tension between England and Scotland. England took over a few hundred years ago, and most Scots still resent them for it. It's a sore subject."

Reaching the mainland, we unloaded and traveled through the steep mountains and rolling green hills to Edinburgh. The air was fresh and cool, whistling through the mountains, and the road was empty. Other than a few tiny houses, with stone chimneys billowing smoke, we saw no signs of life out here. It was a welcome change after the crowded streets of Dublin.

"What do you say we camp out tonight, like old times?" Chito suggested, as we stopped to stretch our legs.

"I say it's cold and wet," Cap replied, tugging at his scarf. "But I have to admit, it'd be a nice change of pace from the fancy hotels."

"We'll pop the hoods up on the Fords to keep out the rain. We can just sleep in the cars," Bernard offered. "It wouldn't take long to set up."

I smiled. Despite our little team of newly-minted celebrities staying at some of the finest hotels in Europe these last few weeks, we were still a scrappy team of explorers at heart.

And that was what I loved most about us.

✦

WE SLEPT IN OUR FORDS overnight, Cap curling up in the backseat with me in the front as we shared his automobile.

We awoke to a chill in the air, wrapping up in blankets while Chito stoked the fire, heating up beans and coffee for us.

"It's been a while since we feasted like this," Bernard joked.

"It's just like the old times," Chito smiled as we warmed our hands over the fire. "Anyone feel like wandering out into the jungle and getting lost? Andi? Cap?"

"Stop it," I replied, laughing. "It was terrible. It's never happening again."

"All the more reason we should joke about it," Chito said, picking the coffee kettle up with a thick towel wrapped around his hand. He poured us each a cup and we watched the steam curl in the cold air.

"You know, we don't always travel the most logical route," Cap complained, looking out at the lonely stretch in the countryside where we sat. "It drives me insane sometimes."

"The joy's in the journey, ain't that right?" Chito grinned. "Ease up. So we cut back and forth a little bit, add a day or two or five here and there. No big deal."

"I like efficiency," Cap grumbled. "I don't want to waste our time. Or our gasoline."

"We're getting paid well, though, to speak to the group in Edinburgh, right? And we're checking another country off our list," I replied. "Those are good enough reasons for us to do a little scissoring across countries. We signed on to travel the world, anyway. We don't care. We just like to see it all."

"Fine," Cap said, leaning over his map. "We should make it to Edinburgh by nightfall, at least. The city's built on top of a dormant volcano. Their old castle is at the top of the city, at the highest peak."

We spent the rest of the day winding around steep mountains and skirting past deep, still lakes. I spotted large deer and antelope in the distance, several times, and the thick swathes of dark woods and waterfalls we passed looked magical. I soaked it all in. Scotland was a place of rugged beauty, unspoiled by human hands.

Edinburgh glimmered like a beacon as we trundled in near sunset, the glow from buildings on top of a steep hill shining down at us. The skyline was crowded, ancient and modern buildings nestled together, their gray stones reflecting the vibrant orange and pink sky.

Cap navigated us to a small hotel, tucked neatly into a small Victorian street. It was quiet here, the sound of a small barking dog the only interruption. We unpacked our Fords and headed up to our rooms, hid our faces in order to enjoy dinner in a small restaurant without being bothered by fans, and turned in early for bed.

"This is the life I always wanted," I thought to myself, as I drifted off to sleep. *"My little team, seeing the world. What more could I ever ask for?"*

THE NEXT MORNING, I took a deep breath of fresh air. My window was cracked open, and I could hear the sound of people outside, bartering. Peeking out, I saw several small stands on the sidewalk selling pastries, food, kilts, and knit goods.

I bathed, feeling the warm water and soap wash away the grit of travel. The simple luxury of a bathtub and clean clothes was something I appreciated, especially after days—sometimes weeks—of travel in remote places, without the ability to clean ourselves well.

My hair still wet, I bounded out of my room and into the lobby. As usual, Cap and Bernard had beaten me out and sat at a table together, a plate of scones sitting near them.

Chito lumbered down the hallway right behind me, craning his neck to look over my tall frame at the food.

"Oh, biscuits!" he exclaimed, nearly shoving me out of the way in his eagerness to sit down at the table.

"Scones," Cap corrected him. "Biscuits are what we call them in America."

Chito picked one up and examined it. "What's this white stuff?" he said, scooping a hefty spoonful of a thick, creamy white substance on a small plate and sniffing it.

We shrugged.

"Butter, maybe?" Bernard replied.

"It's too creamy for that," Chito said, tipping the spoon to his tongue and tasting it. "Hm. It's a bit sweet. Maybe slightly nutty."

He split his scone open and spread a bit of the white substance on it. Taking a bite, his eyes rolled up in joy.

"This is clotted cream!" he exclaimed, spraying crumbs down his shirt and on the table in front of him. "I remember now! I read about this! It's good."

He held a piece out to me, a Chito-sized bite taken out of it, and I cringed. "I'm fine. You eat that, I'll get my own."

"Try it. Wait, no," he scooped a spoonful of jam onto the top of the scone and spread it around. "That's perfect. Let's get the recipe. Don't let me forget to ask the waiter."

After breakfast, we headed to a large mansion on the outskirts of town. The rambling road took us past several old homes, most of which resembled small castles.

"This is where the rich people live, apparently," Chito said to me, from the passenger's side of my car.

"No kidding," I said, staring at the expansive lawns and manicured trees. The house we were driving by looked nearly as large as my boarding school.

In front of us, Cap pulled into a massive driveway, stopping at an ornate metal gate. A young man wearing a uniform nodded at us as we filed in behind Cap's vehicle.

"The Gallivanter Expedition, from America?" the guard called, noting the logo on the sides of the Fords.

"Yes, sir!"

"Go right on through," the guard said, pointing. "The main house is straight down that way. Don't turn right, that'll take you to the guest house. You can park in front of the main doors. They're waiting for you inside."

"Goodness gracious," I said to Chito, as we drove up the winding, tree-draped driveway. "Can you imagine having a house so big that you need to clarify that your guest house isn't the main residence?"

He stared at the mansion, his face troubled.

"I don't think I'm going to like these people," he muttered quietly, as we slowed to a halt.

CHAPTER 12

WE LINED OUR FORDS up in front of the mansion and ascended the large stone steps to two imposing doors.

Before we could knock, a butler pulled them open, bowing as he greeted us.

"Welcome, Gallivanters," he said, touching the fingertips of his white gloves together. "Please follow me to the drawing room, where you'll be meeting the guests."

"We don't belong here," Bernard whispered loudly as we walked through a huge foyer, ancient oil paintings and heavy carved tables and chairs littering the space. "This place is too fancy for us. We're wearing dirty old boots, for Pete's sake."

"Stop, Bernard," Cap tugged off his hat and ran his hand through his hair. "They're just people."

"What kind of people, though?" Bernard replied, staring up at the stuffed head of a lion mounted on the wall above us. Next to it, the glass eyes of a zebra stared out blankly at us.

I stopped short, looking guiltily at the head of a giraffe hanging on the wall. I flashed back to the moment we'd seen a herd of giraffes running in the savanna as we drove through Africa. They'd been so majestic—so free. It didn't seem right to see that beautiful creature here, cut up and tacked to a wall.

A dozen other animal heads filled the walls, snarling boars and wolves and even a large stuffed polar bear in the corner. I exchanged glances with the group. They looked uncomfortable here, too, staring at the stuffed dead animals around us.

The butler waited patiently at the end of the room, in front of a set of French doors. "In here, please, gentlemen."

He opened the doors and announced to the room, "The Gallivanter Expedition, from America."

The room was thick with cigar smoke and the sharp tang of alcohol. My eyes watered as we stepped in.

"Captain Gallivanter!" a heavyset man exclaimed around a cigar in his mouth, his mustache obscuring his upper lip. He slapped Cap on the back heartily. "Welcome to Edinburgh, my boy! I'm Lachlan McNeil. Welcome to my home."

"Thank you, sir. It's beautiful here. We can see why you love your country."

"Nothing else like it on earth, that's right," the man replied cheerfully, his thick Scottish accent garbling every word. I had to concentrate to understand him.

"Tell me about your team, Captain," Mr. McNeil added, eyeing me with interest.

Cap noticed, and stepped next to me smoothly.

"This is Miss Andiamo Gallivanter," he said, and I offered my hand. Mr. McNeil removed the cigar from his mouth and took my hand, kissing it. His mustache tickled.

"Here, we have Mr. Chito Martinez and Mr. Bernard Harris," Cap went on, deftly pushing forward so the man was forced to drop my hand as Cap herded him toward the other men.

"Together, we make up the Gallivanter crew. We currently have three brand-new Ford Model T automobiles outside, which have taken us all over Spain, northern Africa, Ireland, and England so far."

"Bah, England and Ireland, what a waste," Mr. McNeil guffawed, as the other gentlemen in the room laughed. "You're finally here, where the real men live."

He ushered us, grinning, toward the center of the room. Rapidly, he introduced us to a dozen other men, who nodded at us while holding their cigars or whisky. Most of them held both.

"Come, sit down and get comfortable," Mr. McNeil said, his arm circling my waist. I tried not to recoil as I felt his meaty hands go around my body. "Here, Miss Gallivanter, I have just the spot for you."

He led me toward a large velvet couch, his touch none too gentle, where two men in expensive suits sat nursing glasses of whisky.

"This looks cozy," he said, dropping me nearly on top of one of the men's laps. They laughed as I caught myself on his shoulders and slid into the couch cushion, my face red.

"You're playing the part," I told myself, squeezing into the small space on the couch.

The men on either side shifted so they were close to me. The one on the right of me casually put his arm up on the back of the couch, scooting so close that his side was nestled into my shoulder and hip. I could feel the heat of his body even through the thick material of my uniform.

"Acting. That's all this is. Just play the part." I told myself. *"You can do this. Just play the game. Flatter these fat cats. They're going to give you money, after all. Money to get far, far away from here."*

The man on my right leaned in close to my face, exhaling cigar smoke as he smiled at me.

"Nice to meet you, Miss Gallivanter," he said. "You're a beautiful girl. Quite an interesting one, to be traveling the world like this."

"Thank you," I said, trying to hold my breath. "I love travel. Seeing new places and meeting new people."

"I'm sure you do," he murmured, his arm creeping down so it now rested across my shoulders. "I'm sure there are a lot of new experiences you enjoy."

My skin crawled at the crude suggestion in his voice. Still, I'd encountered men like this before. I knew how to handle them.

"I'm just a simple family girl," I said, trying to dampen his obvious advances. "My mother is so proud of me, going all over the world. And my team—we're a family. It's like living with three big, burly, protective older brothers."

"And I suppose they treat you just like older brothers do?" he grinned at me. His breath smelled like whisky. "Or do they treat you a little bit differently, darling?"

"Oh no," I said, widening my eyes with innocence I certainly didn't feel. Not anymore. "They're *very* protective of me. They keep me safe. See that knife that Cap keeps in his boot?"

I pointed at Cap, across the room, who was glaring at the man next to me while Mr. McNeil was busy chatting away with him.

"I have one, too," I said, bluffing. I didn't. But he didn't need to know that.

"You have a knife on you?" The man's face was skeptical.

"I keep it even more carefully hidden than he does, but Cap there has trained me like a warrior. I have to be equipped to fend for myself, you know. It's a dangerous world. I practice stabbing every night."

"Oh?" he asked, leaning back slightly.

"Yes," I said eagerly. "And Cap showed me all the places on a man where I can inflict the most damage. It's not too difficult, really. Especially if you're as good at knife-handling as I've become."

I glanced meaningfully between his legs, and he crossed them quickly, pulling away from me.

"Fascinating," he replied, dropping his arm and standing up. "I think I need a refill on my drink. Excuse me."

I settled back into the cushions, trying to hide my smirk. He didn't return to his seat next to me, but instead pulled another man into conversation across the room.

Chito had been watching me, too. I winked at him and he winked back, a relieved smile stealing across his face.

"Now then, Captain Gallivanter," Mr. McNeil said, leading Cap over to the fireplace in the middle of the large room and turning him to face the group. "We have some things we'd like to discuss with you, as potential investors in your little expedition."

"Yes, sir," Cap replied smoothly, looking around the room as the men fell quiet, listening. "Thank you for the opportunity to share a bit about what we do. As you know, the Gallivanter team is committed to world peace, and sharing our discoveries with everyone we encounter. We carefully gather a wealth of information about each new place we visit, and—"

"Oh, skip the stump speech, laddie," Mr. McNeil interrupted. "We don't care about all of that."

"Alright. What would you like me to share, then? Would you care to see some pictures of our travels?"

"No pictures," Mr. McNeil said, grinning at the other men in the room. "Let's get down to it, shall we? What we really want to talk about is *specimens*."

"Specimens? Like plants and minerals?" Cap shook his head. "Gentlemen, I'm afraid I'm no John Audubon. I'm an explorer."

"Animals, Captain Gallivanter," another man replied, holding his whisky glass up and laughing. "We're interested in *animals*. Not flowers and rocks."

Cap frowned. "I'm not sure what you mean."

But I did. I thought back to the trophies in the main hall. The lion and zebra and giraffe heads staring at me with dead eyes.

That's what they wanted.

"Didn't you see my collection on the way in?" Mr. McNeil guffawed. "That's what we're talking about. Jack here wants a lion for his country house. Andrew wants a cheetah, a giraffe, and maybe a zebra or two."

"Two," the man named Andrew piped up, from the corner of the room. "For either side of the fireplace."

"Right," Mr. McNeil continued. "Reg wants a panther. But he'll take a lion, as well. He wants a male and female lion, actually."

"I'll take cubs, too, if you can get a few," the man called out. "Three or four would be nice."

My stomach lurched. I was disgusted at how callously they were ordering the slaughter of innocent animals. For what? To hang on their walls? They weren't even hunting for them themselves. Some trophies.

"I'm sorry, gentlemen, you must misunderstand our expedition," Cap held up his hands. "We're humanitarians, not hunters."

"For the right price, anyone's a hunter," Mr. McNeil grinned.

Cap shook his head. "Not us, sir. I'm sorry."

"Come on, Captain Gallivanter," Mr. McNeil said, draping his arm around his shoulders. "Have a drink. Let's discuss it, like friends. Money is no object to us. We'll make sure you're paid handsomely for your troubles."

Cap stood his ground. "Money's no object to us, either. We don't kill animals for anyone. Unless our own lives were threatened, I wouldn't pick up a gun to shoot anything."

"What kind of man are you, then?" one of the fellows near the whisky cart called out, his tone disgusted.

"I'm my own man," Cap replied, undaunted. He stared back at the men around him. They glared back at Cap, the mood in the room suddenly shifting.

"You accepted our invitation here," Mr. McNeil said slowly, his tone dark. "You're drinking our whisky. You're standing in my home. You at least owe us a conversation about it. It's why we brought you here."

"I don't owe anyone anything," Cap said, lifting his chin. "As I've stated from the beginning, we're explorers. We don't hunt animals. We don't work for other people. We travel, and we educate."

"We asked *you*, the Gallivanters," Mr. McNeil snapped, angry. "We could've asked the Chinook Voyageurs, but you're the ones who have a reputation for getting through dangerous situations with ease. By the way, you're not so special anymore, did you know that? The Chinooks brought on a girl, too. A real pretty thing, by the looks of her photographs."

I blinked in surprise. The Chinook Voyageurs had brought a girl onto their team? Was that because of me? Or were they trying to ride that wave to popularity, like we had? What was she like?

"Good for them," Cap replied, his voice controlled but firm. "Maybe they'll do it for you. Ask them instead."

The men glared at Cap with open hostility now.

"The murderous Scottish temper is a real thing," I thought to myself. I needed to do something to help Cap. These men, rich as they happened to be, were clearly used to getting their own way. And Cap threatened that. Most of them were heavily intoxicated, and outnumbered us. What might they do to him? To all of us?

I thought quickly, and put my hand to my head. "Captain Gallivanter?" I said in a weak voice, forcing myself to sound helpless.

"What?" Cap glanced at me, the eyes of every man in the room shifting to my face.

"It's so smoky in here, I feel sick," I said haltingly, holding my forehead and trying to rise out of my seat. "I feel like I might faint."

I intentionally wobbled on unsteady knees.

Chito beat Cap to me, reaching me first and gently holding me up. "Let me help you, Andi," he said, supporting my weight with his big arms. Cap grabbed my other side, lifting me.

"Sorry, gentlemen, but I think this meeting is over," Cap said to the room. "My associate here feels sick. These things do happen, unfortunately, when you travel the world and are exposed to different foods and germs, on top of dealing with a physically rigorous job that pushes your body to its limits. I apologize, but we'll need to get Miss Gallivanter out of here right away."

I wobbled again, to add convincing punctuation to his statement. Chito and Cap held me up.

"Please, hurry," I whispered, rolling my eyes up into my head and trying to look faint.

"Fine, go then," Mr. McNeil grumbled, as they walked me out the door. Bernard followed behind us wordlessly.

Once outside, Cap and Chito helped me into the back seat of Cap's Ford and returned to Mr. McNeil.

"I'm sorry, sir, but that's not who we are," I heard Cap say, shaking his hand. "Thank you very much for your hospitality, and for your understanding. Again, I apologize for our hasty exit, but our team's health matters greatly."

Mr. McNeil squinted at him, hard, and rolled his eyes, walking away with his whisky glass still in his hand. I waited until Mr. McNeil slammed the door of his mansion before popping up from my slump.

"I bet you didn't know you hired such a great actress," I beamed.

"Dear Lord, those men are awful," Cap groaned, leaning against the side of my car and shaking his head. Chito and Bernard leaned on either side of him.

"Nice trick there, Andi. I didn't even know you could act that helpless," Chito laughed. "Have you used that one before?"

"Nope," I smiled. "I've never really fainted before, either. But those men don't know that."

"Of course you haven't," Cap responded. "I knew you were just trying to get us out of there when you stood up, wobbling. You're quite the excellent little liar."

"I know. Aren't you proud?"

"By the way, you caught that, right?" Cap changed the subject. "The Chinook Voyageurs brought a girl onto their team? When did that happen?"

Chito shook his head. "We need to get back into town and check the newspapers. I'm sure it's in there. That's a big deal. Maybe they saw the popularity that it brought us, when we brought Andi on, and they're trying to emulate it?"

"Probably," Cap tapped the side of the Ford. "Let's get back to our hotel and look for papers there. We'll figure it out."

He slid into the driver's seat as I rested comfortably in the back.

"Thanks for driving me, Captain Gallivanter," I teased. "I'm just a helpless little lady who can't possibly do anything for herself."

"Yeah, sure," he said, adjusting the pedals, slowly pulling the car out from the front of the house. "Whatever you say, you dirty liar."

The wind lifted my hair, and I reached for my hat and goggles. Sliding them on, I tapped Cap's shoulders. He looked at me through his own goggles, his eyes a brilliant blue.

"Before I forget," I said, "We need to get me a knife. And you're going to teach me how to use it. Deal?"

He grinned back at me. "Just the words I love hearing from a lady: teach me how to stab someone."

"I'm serious, Cap."

"You've got yourself a deal there, Andiamo Gallivanter. We'll get you that knife."

CHAPTER 13

WE ARRIVED BACK AT our hotel in time for lunch. Chito went up to the front desk to ask for a restaurant recommendation from the hotel staff, while Cap and I went in search of newspapers.

We bought a few papers from the small boy on the corner, who offered us the papers with ink-stained little fingers.

"Are you—are you him?" the boy stammered, looking up at us with big eyes. "That captain, who's traveling around the world in the cars? And the woman driver, too?"

"Captain Gallivanter, at your service," Cap bowed, sweeping off his hat. "This is Andiamo Gallivanter, as well. The first woman in history to drive around the world in an automobile. You're meeting a legend, young man."

"Pleased to meet you," I smiled, offering my hand. The boy shook it with his dirty fingers, his mouth agape.

"I can't believe it," he blurted, his cheeks pink with excitement. "You're so tall in real life!"

Cap tipped him a large wad of cash.

"That's a good man, working hard for your money," he smiled. "Keep at it, son. With a can-do attitude, you'll go far."

"Thank you, sir!" the little boy shouted, unable to contain his excitement. He stuffed the cash into his shoe as we walked back to the hotel.

"Well, he got paid well today," I grinned. "That's probably more money than he's ever seen in his life. And he has quite the story to tell to his friends."

"He reminds me of myself, at that age," Cap reflected quietly, watching him scamper away with his new wealth as he folded the papers under his arm. "I never could've imagined living the life I'm experiencing now, when I was that old. Most of the time, I never knew if I'd have a next meal. I'll never be able to forget where I came from, how poor I was as a kid. And it's seeing kids like him that remind me of why what I do is important. We are inspiring people we'll never know. Giving them the chance to dream that they, too, might be something more."

He paused, and looked at me. "That's the gift we offer the world, Andi. Hope is a powerful thing."

I smiled as we walked back to the hotel, resisting the urge to slip my hand into his.

We joined up with Chito and Bernard in the lobby, unfurling the papers and searching for news of the Chinook Voyageurs.

"Here they are," Cap said, scanning his paper. "Page three. They were right, they picked up a girl."

A large photo of the newest Chinook crew member dominated the page. In the picture, a slim young woman stood proudly next to a row of gleaming Chinook Voyageur Fords, all painted with the distinctive fleur-de-lis, the logo of the Québécois team.

I leaned over his shoulder to look at the article.

"Of course," I muttered, catching sight of her beautiful face.

She wore her hair long, curled fashionably at the end. A bright, confident smile lit her face, and the tilt of her head suggested an air of pride. Though she wore a uniform that looked similar to mine, I noticed that she also wore lipstick and heels.

I hated lipstick.

"She's beautiful," I commented, because I knew none of the men would admit it in front of me.

"Yeah, she is," Bernard agreed, looking over my shoulder. Cap and Chito wisely said nothing.

I read the short paragraph about her aloud.

"Miss Dessie Hickson, a tender young beauty who has embraced this new life of adventure and travel, hails from Calgary, Canada. A modest woman, she shares with her eager fans how delighted she is to see the world. 'I embark on this journey in a spirit of goodwill,' said Miss Hickson at her press conference. 'Unlike others, I seek no fame or fortune. I don't need to see my face in the newspapers every day, like my rivals seem to crave. You won't see me embellishing my stories or thrusting myself into danger, just to catch people's eyes. I am just a good girl from a good family, hoping to see the world and make some new friends while I do it.' The Chinook Voyageurs have eagerly embraced this darling girl, a welcome addition to their team. They're looking forward to continuing their journey around the world, in an epic race against the clock. Pitted against the smaller, but more well-known Gallivanter Expedition, this competition is sure to bring out a friendly fighting spirit between these two equally matched groups."

I set the paper down with a scowl. "Yeah, I bet the Chinooks have eagerly embraced her."

"Why'd she make us look bad there?" Bernard frowned. "She makes it sound like we're money-grubbing publicity hounds."

"Yeah, and she makes me sound like I'm some sort of tramp," I complained.

"No she didn't," Chito shook his head. "She didn't say anything about you."

"Let's see here....oh, yes. Here's the line: *'You won't see me embellishing my stories or thrusting myself into danger, just to catch people's eyes. I am just a good girl from a good family.'* That implies that I'm not, right? That I'm making our adventures up, just to get noticed?"

"But we know the truth," Chito sighed. "We know this stuff really happened."

"Yeah, but the world doesn't know that," I pointed out. "She's smearing my reputation by making herself look good and making me look bad by comparison. She might as well just come right out and say that I'm a liar."

"I'm sure that's not what she meant to do," Chito protested. "She was probably just excited and swept up in the moment. You remember how hard it is to navigate fame, when it's all new."

"I'm not so sure about that," I grumbled. "In my experience, most girls know *exactly* what they're saying."

"It takes a lot of practice to handle yourself at a press conference, though," Cap mused, rereading the article. "It took me months to get good at it, when we first got started. Maybe Chito's right. Maybe this Dessie just got wrapped up in the glamor of her first press conference, and blurted out the first thing that came to her mind. We'll give her the benefit of the doubt."

"Well, I guess we'll just wait and see what else she says," I rolled my eyes. Chito and Cap were unflaggingly optimistic about others. It was a quality that was both endearing and occasionally maddening.

"She's an idiot," Bernard announced, sniffing as her picture smiled up at us. "She'll break a heel trying to drive that Ford."

I grinned. Bernard wasn't an optimist. He wasn't a fan of people at all.

"Forget about the Voyageurs," Chito said. "We do our own thing, and we do it well. In a few weeks, we'll be on another continent and they'll be long gone. Let's not waste our time worrying about them."

CHAPTER 14

THAT NIGHT'S PRESS conference ended with crowds of people lined up outside the venue, hoping to get our autographs.

Cap, Chito, and I gladly talked with people who were excited to meet us, signing pictures and newspaper clippings of ourselves. I always smiled, knowing that many of these people had been following our expedition for months in the newspapers and felt like they were a part of our journey, too.

A little girl in the crowd tonight begged to touch my boots.

"My boots?" I asked, thinking I'd misunderstood her.

"Yes, can I touch your boots, please, Miss Gallivanter?" she lisped, staring up at me with big blue eyes.

"Sure," I said, laughing and holding up my foot to her tiny hand.

"Oh Ma," she cried, giggling with delight. "I got to touch the real boots that carried Andiamo Gallivanter through all her adventures!"

Bernard always signed a few autographs, then hastily made some excuse about getting back to check on the automobiles. He typically waited in a Ford, goggles on, for us to make it back to him when we were done.

I'd lately wondered if Bernard was feigning deafness to avoid talking to fans.

"Sorry, what?" I'd heard him say several times, as people asked him questions. "I can't understand you," he repeated, pointing to his ears. "Sorry. I can't hear what you said."

The crowds were thick, and people often recognized us on the streets. Wherever we went, we had to be ready to greet fans. Our private lives were only private lately when we were safely inside the walls of our hotel rooms or boarding houses.

Cap and I could only show our affection in those rare moments as we relaxed together, hidden from the masses of people who clamored for our attention.

"I just don't want our engagement to distract people from the fact that you earned your way onto this team with that brain of yours, Andi," Cap told me as we sat lazily in the sunlit living room of our rental home, my feet resting on his lap. "You're under enough scrutiny as it is. If people find out we're together, the public might turn on us. On you, especially."

"I get it. They'll think I'm just here as a little siren. Stirring up trouble."

"That's true, too," Cap teased, shuffling a pile of maps on the table next to us. He playfully squeezed my foot as he reached for a pen. "You're nothing but trouble to me, woman. My biggest distraction."

I watched him sorting through his pile of maps, searching for a piece of paper. The stack was several inches thick. As leader of our expedition, Cap was constantly at work, making itineraries and researching locations. Though each person on our team had defined roles, the weight of responsibility was heaviest on his shoulders.

Chito plopped down next to us in an easy chair. "Nice to see you kids lounging around."

"Hey, I'm working here," Cap said, resting a map on my legs as he scribbled on the paper.

"You're always working," Chito replied.

It was true. Cap was often the last one to go to bed, and the first to rise early in the morning. None of us envied his job.

"There's a lot of work to be done," Cap responded, writing in his notebook. "It never ends."

"That's what I wanted to talk to you about, actually," Chito said slowly, looking at me with a purposeful expression. "We're back in Europe now, at least for a few months. We had a hell of a time in Africa. We made it out by the skin of our teeth. So I think we need to think about what could be different with this leg of our trip. You know, what could we improve?"

I knew exactly where Chito was going with this. He had pulled me into a quiet conversation with Bernard a few days ago, as the three of us discussed how to keep our fearless captain from burning out. We were all in on it. We each knew our lines.

"Sure," Cap replied absently, tapping the pen against his lip. "We can always improve."

Chito raised his eyebrows at me. *"Your turn,"* he mouthed silently.

"Yeah, and we could afford to add to the crew now, too," I said, picking up where Chito had left off. I was careful not to mention Paz, our crew member who'd unexpectedly deserted us a few months ago to join the Chinooks. Cap had been deeply wounded by his betrayal.

"True." Cap's eyes were still on the paper.

Bernard came in and sat down without comment on the comfiest couch in the room. He groaned as he sank into the cushions. "I'd have killed for something like this to sleep on all those months we were in the desert."

Chito and I stared at him, waiting for him to join the conversation. Clueless, he closed his eyes and leaned back in the couch.

"Bernard, what do you think?" I asked pointedly, waiting for him to catch on.

"Think about what?" he said, opening his eyes. He stared at me in confusion.

Dear Lord. We'd talked about this, at length.

"What do you think we could do to improve this leg of the trip?" I repeated.

Bernard stared back at me, eyebrows knit together. Perplexed, he turned and looked at Chito. We both shot him daggers.

"I think—" he started, and then stopped. "Wait. I forgot what I was supposed to say now. What's my line?"

"Bernard," Chito groaned as Cap paused, looking up at all three of us.

"What?" Bernard shot back. "I couldn't remember my line. What am I supposed to say?"

"Who's going to tell me what's going on?" Cap asked, eyebrows raised. "Is there a problem?"

"There's no problem, Cap," Chito replied quickly. "We're just concerned. About you."

"Me? What have I done that would make you feel concerned?"

I grabbed the map from my legs and held it up.

"This," I said. "It's not that you've done anything wrong. It's that you're *always* working, even when we're supposed to be resting. You never stop. You're wearing yourself out. Just because you managed to pull through the last few months handling all this planning and paperwork doesn't mean you can handle it for the next few months. You're the public face of our team, Cap. We need you to be healthy."

Chito nodded. "Frankly, we have more money than we could ever need. It's time we hire someone on to help you. To handle these details of preparation. It'll free you up to be our fearless leader—not a man chained to his research."

Cap rubbed his neck. "I don't know."

"Just because you can do it, doesn't mean you should do it," I replied. "We can afford to bring on someone else who can do it."

"They'd have to travel with the team, though," Cap rubbed his jaw, thinking. "Our plans change so much. They'd have to go with us, and plan things on the fly. Lodging, publicity engagements, connections with locals…it's a lot. It would take time to train them in."

"So? They travel with us," Chito offered. "They can help make hotel arrangements, and sort out supplies, and organize our press releases. It would free you up to concentrate on the actual expedition, the journey itself. We have the space in the Fords for someone else. We could use another teammate, anyway. And we'd be freed up to trade off drivers again, like we used to."

"We know our team is capable, but we're small," I said. "We could use a bit more help, Cap."

"It didn't exactly work out for us, when we brought in others before," Cap replied. "Paz? Paolo?"

We fell silent, reflecting on past team members that were no longer with our small team. We'd picked up Paz as a local guide in Spain, and kept him on because we liked him. He traveled with our crew and was a part of our little family—until he defected and joined the Chinook Voyageurs, our rivals. Paolo had been a short-term hire, a publicist we hired to help us get attention in the press. His dangerous stunts had nearly killed me in a drowning incident.

"We can't live in the past," Chito said finally, breaking the silence. "We've all grown since then. We're wiser. And closer. We know ourselves—and this team—now."

"That's true," I agreed. "Look how different the last few months have been, compared to the first. We were all still figuring out our dynamic then. Now? We're a family. And Cap, your family is worried about you. Listen to us. We need additional help. *You* need it. We want you to be healthy."

Cap looked at all our faces, and then reluctantly groaned, tossing his journal down.

"You guys are relentless," he said, laughing ruefully. "Fine. I suppose it wouldn't hurt to bring some new blood onto the team. It could help to split up some responsibilities and share some new perspective. I'll write an advertisement and post it in some local papers."

"Thank you," Chito grinned. "Do you know how long it took us to rehearse these lines?"

"Bernard flubbed his," Cap responded merrily. "I guess you didn't rehearse enough."

"What?" Bernard shot back defensively, crossing his arms on the couch. "I'm a mechanic, not an actor."

CHAPTER 15

OUR LAST MORNING IN Scotland, I slipped out of bed before dawn. Pulling a thick wool blanket around myself, I made my way outside, alone. I stared out at the green hills, damp with dew, barely discernible in the warm darkness before the sun rises.

"Don't you ever forget to enjoy the sunrise, Andi," I told myself. *"Keep your eyes on the beauty of the world around you. Even if the people you meet aren't always kind, or supportive, you keep your eyes here—on the horizon, waiting to embrace the new day's adventures. That's who you are. That's what an explorer does."*

It was increasingly easy to forget that I was an adventurer. Now that the Gallivanters were world-famous, we'd been caught up in a nearly endless cycle of making media appearances, visiting important people, and doing presentations. Everywhere we went, people clamored for our attention.

But this was all I really wanted. To breathe deeply, taking in the wonder of a new place, with my little team—my family—at my side as we experienced the excitement of travel together.

I stood outside as the sun rose, waves of thick fog gently rolling through the hills. The sky bloomed from dark blue to pale. I tucked the blanket up around my cheeks, my nose cold from the crisp air.

Behind me, the door opened. Chito ducked out, pulling on a jacket. "It's chilly," he remarked, blowing hot air into his hands.

"It's perfect."

We stood side-by-side, silent as the sun rose. Behind us, the sounds of the city coming alive started to fill our ears. People talking, in quiet tones. Horses neighing, bicycles whirring, delivery boxes thudding out of carts.

"We don't do this enough, do we?" Chito said, still staring at the sky. "We've been too busy lately. I forget how much I love these quiet moments. Taking it all in."

"Me too. I wish we could leave this publicity tour behind and just get back on the road."

Chito slipped his arm around me. "In time. We'll just make the best of it. And try to find someone to alleviate some of the pressure from Cap."

"He placed the advertisements in the newspapers, right?"

"Yesterday," Chito nodded. "Once we get back to London tonight, maybe we'll have some applications waiting for us."

I clutched my blanket around me, wondering what it would be like to have another teammate on the Gallivanter crew. The four of us were so close. Would bringing someone else in disrupt that?

"They took a chance on you," I told myself, remembering back to the day I'd talked myself into an interview with Cap. It seemed like a lifetime ago. *"You need to be open to taking a chance on someone else."*

"What do you say we make breakfast together, to celebrate our last morning here?" Chito suggested, stomping his feet to get his blood moving. "I picked up some Scottish staples. Haggis. Tatties. Tomatoes and toast."

"Haggis?" I frowned, not recognizing the word. "What's that?"

"Don't ask," he laughed. "Let's go inside."

⸺⚬⸺

WE MADE OUR WAY BACK to London, taking the ferry from the rocky landscape of Scotland to the northern shores of England, driving back south.

Cap had placed advertisements sharing our desire for additional crew in several local newspapers, and we found dozens of applications waiting for us when we checked into our hotel in London.

Chito and I volunteered to sort through the applicants, to take the burden off of Cap. "It'll be fun to pick someone out!" I smiled.

"That's what you think now," Cap hid a knowing smile. "Just wait. I've done this before. You get some real strange ones. You'll see."

He was right.

As Chito and I sorted through the names, we were staggered by the amount of odd people who volunteered to spend the next several months with us.

"This man seems like a possibility," I said, squinting as I read his letter. "He's traveled all over Europe already....he's driven a Ford before...oh, wait. No."

"What?" Chito said, looking up from his stack of applicants.

"He insists on traveling with his cat. She eats at the table with him for every meal, apparently. He says it's non-negotiable."

"Are you making this up?"

Wordlessly, I handed him the letter. He glanced over it, shaking his head. We returned to our reading. A few moments later, Chito held one up.

"What about this? They're qualified. He works for a newspaper, and she has an interest in writing, too."

"A couple?" I frowned. "Aren't we looking for one person?"

"It's not just a couple," he said, holding up the paper to show me. "It's a couple with three children. All under the age of five."

I imagined a screaming toddler stuffed next to me in the Ford as I tried to concentrate while driving up a steep, winding mountain road.

"Are they just trying to run away from their lives?"

Chito laughed. "Probably," he said, looking at the next name. "We can't take kids."

It was tough trying to find reasonably qualified candidates who didn't set off alarm bells when we read their applications. Many of the letters we got were from fans who were starstruck and simply wanted to spend time with us. Others didn't have the experience we needed, and still others had too many demands.

"Here's one," I said, reading another name to Chito. "He's willing to share his expertise with us, but in return, he requires us to accommodate his hobby."

"Huh?"

"He's a rock collector. Says we need to have room for his collection. And that we need to stop whenever he sees a good landscape, so he can find some more rocks to bring home."

Chito threw back his head and roared with laughter. "Can you just imagine the look on Cap's face when this bloke tells him we need to pull off the road so he can hunt for rocks for a few hours?"

"It's almost worth bringing him on just to see it."

"I don't know," Chito rubbed his beard. "Will we ever find someone that actually fits this team?"

"It's a tough life," I replied thoughtfully. "We balance a lot of demands and a lot of roles. We're public figures, so our private lives have to be exemplary. We're explorers, though, so we need to have grit and survival knowledge, which makes us tougher than most. We also have to speak to draw attention to what we're doing, so we're showmen."

"Don't forget the mechanical knowledge required to operate an automobile," Chito added. "On top of that, you have to be willing to adapt quickly to any number of new situations. And give up creature comforts."

"And be a good team player," I wrinkled my nose. "We spend so much time together that you have to get along well with others."

"I don't know, Andi," Chito grunted. "It felt like a miracle that Cap and Bernard and I all got along so well, before you came along and joined the team. And I have no doubt Cap saw instantly how well you'd click with us, once he met you. No wonder he snatched you up without hesitation. I know we could benefit from adding a few more people to the Gallivanter crew, but I'm worried the risk might not be worth the trouble."

We returned to the pile, heads down. After a few minutes, Chito spoke again. "I'm going to be honest, I don't have anyone good in here. Not a single one."

"Me neither," I sighed. "No one quite aligns with who we are."

Cap entered the room, a pile of maps and notebooks in his arms, and plopped down next to us. "How's the search going?"

"Not so great," I admitted. "We're having a hard time finding someone who fits the Gallivanter spirit."

"Don't you say it, Cap—" Chito warned as Cap began to laugh.

"I told you so," Cap grinned.

"Sometimes I hate how you're always right," Chito elbowed him. "Andi, do you really want to live with this for the rest of your life?"

"Look, I just knew it'd be a wasted effort," Cap laughed. "It's hard to find the right person for this sort of trek. We've been lucky, having the perfect team. And that's why we've remained small. The more people you add, the more drama you get."

"We won't be adding anyone anytime soon," Chito tossed the applications down. "Sorry, Cap. We were just trying to help you."

"Well, maybe the right person will come along someday," Cap replied. "The worst thing would be to force it and get stuck with someone we hate. It'd make our entire expedition miserable. We need to enjoy ourselves through these adventures, you know. It's hard enough as it is—the physical and mental demands of this role are very real—and to add in the wrong sort of person would make it unbearable."

"True," Chito said, collecting the applications from me and adding them to his pile. "We'll just put off the search for now. Who knows? Maybe we'll stumble into the perfect person on the road. Luck might bring the right people to us."

Cap waited until Chito left the room, and swiftly pulled me up from my chair.

"You're not trying to add more men to the team to make me jealous now, are you?" he teased, kissing me softly.

"No, we're trying to help," I wrapped my arms around him. "You work all the time, Cap. I worry about you."

"You're quite the protector. I shudder to think what would happen if I disobey. I owe you, after all. You've saved my life twice already."

"It was a life worth saving," I murmured, leaning my forehead against his and closing my eyes. His arms tightened around me.

"Oh, no," Bernard moaned, his voice coming from behind me. "Not again."

I opened my eyes, grinning guiltily, and stepped out of Cap's arms. Bernard was standing in the doorway, staring at us with a look of disgust.

"No," Bernard repeated. "Please stop. I hate walking in on you two when you're all romantic."

"Come on, Bernard," Cap smiled, grinning like a kid who was just caught sneaking candy. "I'm just a man. I can't have self-control all the time. It's a kiss between two people who love each other, that's all."

"Not in front of me, Cap," Bernard shook his head. "You don't see me out there, kissing the Fords, and I certainly love them as much as you love her."

"It's not *quite* the same," Cap could barely contain his laughter.

I plopped back down into my seat, smiling at the boys. In joining the Gallivanter Expedition, I'd found love and adventure at the same time.

"How much luckier could a person get?" I said to myself. *"My life is just about perfect."*

CHAPTER 16

"WE'RE FINALLY IN PARIS," I breathed, looking around me with wonder.

Every building seemed more exquisite than the last, a city that lived up to its own legend. It was as if romance and charm came alive here in tangible form. From the tiny sidewalk cafes, crowded with people who sipped coffee, to the people ducking through the streets, baguettes under arm, the city teemed with life.

Everywhere I looked, beauty was on display. People were well-dressed and colorfully arrayed, strolling through gardens that boasted showy flowers. The city was not made to be just seen, but marveled at: begging to be explored, enjoyed. The smells of fresh bread and sweet wine mingled with the sounds of music drifting out of the cafes.

Paris was a city to savor. Like the intricate pastries that sat in bakery windows, captivating the attention of those passing by, everything seemed delightfully intentional—a piece of art in the midst of ordinary life.

"I'm just glad to be traveling again," Chito said, looking with interest at the small cafes dotting the street. "It's hard enough to be in civilization, here in Europe, after being used to the wilderness in northern Africa, but being stuck in the same city for more than a few days feels like torture."

"We're only here for a week or two," Cap reminded us. "Just a few presentations. But we have plenty of time to explore the city. I figured we could all use a little break—we've been going hard on this publicity tour."

"I'm going to disguise myself here," Bernard muttered. "I don't want to deal with fans. Especially not French ones."

"You're going to?" Chito raised his eyebrow. "Cap and Andi attract way more attention than you or I do, bud. The whole world knows their faces."

"But I don't want anyone to recognize me," Bernard complained. "I just want to take a nice stroll here and there, without dealing with people."

"We're celebrities now," Cap reminded him. "It comes with the territory. I know you don't like the attention, but we do get a lot of money out of being well-known by the general public. And goodwill, too. We're ambassadors for America, don't forget."

"Bah, who cares," Bernard groaned. "We have plenty of money already."

"I'm going to get myself a nice beret," I chimed. "People don't usually notice us when we're out of our uniforms, and I'm going to take advantage of that. Maybe I'll buy a fancy scarf, too. I'll go in disguise with you, Bernard."

"Hold on," he said sourly, shooting me a look. "I didn't ask for you to go anywhere *with* me."

"I'd like to shop the markets," Chito proclaimed. "Paris is known for being a chef's paradise, and the markets are the heart of it all. Does anyone want to go with me?"

"I want to read the newspaper and nap," Bernard said, easing himself into a chair. "Just don't bother me, and I'll be fine."

"I want to see all the landmark sites," I confessed. "The Eiffel Tower, the Arc de Triomphe, Notre Dame—is it too much to ask to play anonymous tourist for a day?"

"Sorry, Chito," Cap replied, slipping his arm around me. "I can't pass up an opportunity to spend the day in Paris with my lovely fiancée, even if it means skipping the markets with you."

"But I'm going to pick out a charcuterie board!" Chito protested playfully.

"And I'm sure we'll enjoy that tonight, when we all meet back here."

"Fine," Chito swatted Cap's arm, pretending to kick us out the door. "Have fun, lovebirds. Don't get into too much trouble."

We laughed as we squeezed through the door together and strolled down the tiny streets toward the heart of Paris.

⸺⬦⸺

THE CITY WAS JUST AS delightful as I'd always imagined it would be, broad cobblestone streets bordered on each side by beautiful buildings with graceful arches and urns and carved reliefs.

"I can't believe we have an entire day to ourselves," I bubbled happily as we walked down the narrow streets of Paris. People zipped by on bicycles, and sat sipping drinks and eating croissants at tiny round tables on the sidewalks.

"I know," Cap smiled. "And in Paris, the most romantic city on earth."

I wanted to kiss him right there on the sidewalk, as all of Paris looked on, but we couldn't risk it. We were celebrities here, even if we hadn't been approached yet. I'd already noticed a few locals staring at us, but hoped their Parisian pride would prevent them from asking for an autograph.

"Let's head to the Eiffel Tower first," he said, gazing around. "And get a café crème and a macaroon. And see the Notre Dame later. I already plotted it out, don't worry."

"Let's see it all," I smiled at him. "If we stroll fast enough, maybe no one will recognize our faces."

We walked close to each other, our shoulders touching. A woman walking a tiny black poodle stopped us, excitedly jabbering in French as her dog circled our legs, sniffing.

I translated for Cap as the woman spoke to us, smiling.

"She says she recognizes us from the newspapers. We're the famous explorers. She says welcome to Paris, we're so pleased to have you here as guests in our beautiful city," I said, nodding my thanks to her.

I grinned at her last words as we walked away.

"What'd she say there at the end?" Cap asked.

I laughed. "She said 'enjoy Paris, this is a perfect place for lovers.'"

"Wait, hold on," Cap stopped in his tracks. "Is she—she thinks—we need to talk to her. That's our business, not hers. If she suspects we're—what if she tells—"

I pulled his arm, dragging him down the street, laughing.

"She's not going to tell anyone," I wrinkled my nose. "Not everyone runs to the newspapers with a story."

"But how did she—we aren't even holding hands!"

"She can tell by our body language, I assume, that we're in love. Come on, Captain Gallivanter. Stop worrying about other people and worry about your fiancée and what she wants to do today."

"Fine," he said, shaking his head ruefully. "We're going to have a hard time hiding our engagement, if we're not careful. We'll have to be more cautious in public."

We walked leisurely down the old stone streets together, staring at statues and monuments that seemed to be hiding around every corner. Blossoming trees framed postcard-worthy views, birds pecking at the ground around us. Couples of all ages sat on benches together, chatting.

"I love it here," I remarked, stopping to inhale the scent of fresh flowers at a small cart in the middle of the sidewalk.

We ducked in and out of small antique shops and tourist stores, looking at replicas of Parisian monuments and gaudy scarves and leather goods. In one small bakery, we breathed in the intoxicating aroma of fresh pastries and split a chocolate croissant.

"This is heaven," Cap groaned, closing his eyes. "Can we move here, after the expedition?"

"We have a lot of the world to see before talk of settling down, sir."

Stepping out of the bakery, we continued our stroll down the street, the Eiffel Tower peeking up over the old buildings around us. At the corner, Cap stopped short.

"Oh," he said, staring at the display window of the corner store. I followed his gaze.

"A jewelry store?" I said, squinting at the sign. Inside the display windows, dazzling diamond rings and necklaces glittered in the sunlight.

Cap didn't respond. I turned to look at him. His ears were pink.

"What?" I asked, amused at his sudden discomfort.

"Nothing," he replied quickly, as his neck turned red.

"Cap, what on earth?" I exclaimed. "It's just a jewelry store! Why are you acting so odd?"

"I just think, um," he cleared his throat. "Maybe I should get you something. You know."

I pressed my lips together to hide my mirth. I rarely saw Cap at a loss for words.

"What has gotten into you, Cap?"

He stared back at me, his blue eyes full of confusion.

"I don't know," he admitted. "We're engaged. And I proposed out in the middle of the jungle, without a ring or anything. I feel bad about it. You deserve a proper engagement."

"I'm not the kind of girl who cares about proper. I love how you proposed."

"But you should have a ring," he insisted, looking over my shoulder at the window display. "Shouldn't you?"

We stood in the middle of the sidewalk in front of the store. A couple walking by split up and walked around either side of us, shooting me a peeved look.

"Je suis désolé," I murmured quickly in French, apologetic.

"We can't just stand here all day," Cap replied, taking my elbow. "Let's go look, at least. Just to look."

"I guess. It won't hurt to take a peek."

"Come on," Cap said, pushing into the shop.

CHAPTER 17

A TINY BELL TINKLED as we walked inside the jewelry store.

"Monsieur and mademoiselle, welcome!"

A mustached man with oiled hair descended on us before we'd even made it all the way into the store. He wore an expensive suit, with shoes so shiny that I could see my face reflected in them as I glanced down.

"Bonjour," Cap replied. "We're just browsing."

"Ah, yes, of course," the man said smoothly, taking me by the hand and ushering me to a glass display.

Inside, dozens of rows of glimmering gemstones and diamonds shimmered in the soft overhead lights. His hand was baby soft as he held mine. I noticed with a mixture of embarrassment and irony that his fingernails appeared to be manicured, while mine still had remnants of grease from working on the cars under the nails.

"What are you looking for, my dear? A necklace? A beautiful bracelet for that slender little wrist? Some earrings, to sparkle while you toss that pretty head of yours?"

Oh my goodness, I felt like a fool in here. Give me the front seat of a Ford any day over this strange world of glitter and glitz.

"Actually, um, maybe that," I faltered, pointing at a large ruby necklace.

"Oh, yes," he said, swooping behind the counter and opening the little drawer behind it. "This one? It's incredible. Beautiful clarity, as you can see. One of the cardinal gems, of course. A treasured stone, especially in China."

"Yes," I nodded, trying to sound like I knew what he was talking about. I didn't.

"We're interested in some other pieces, too," Cap spoke up awkwardly, glancing around. His ears were still faintly pink. "Maybe a ring?"

"Certainly, monsieur," the man said, stroking his mustache. "What sort of ring are you looking for?"

"A...diamond...ring?" Cap stammered, staring at me. I wrinkled my forehead and shrugged.

"Oh my! How did I not see it until now?" The man slapped his hands down on the glass case. "Are you them?"

"What? No," Cap said quickly at the exact same moment I replied, "Yes, we are."

"That traveling team! The one going around the world, with the girl!" The man studied us, taking a step back. "Yes, you are! You're the explorer people!"

"The Gallivanter Expedition," Cap filled in. His face was crestfallen. Our cover had been blown. "Yes, that's us."

"You are so very famous, oui! How nice to meet you both!" he exclaimed, unconsciously straightening his suit jacket. "What a pleasure to have you in our store!"

"Thank you," we said automatically.

"So what exactly brings you in, then?" the salesman said, tilting his head. "You are looking for a ring?"

Cap and I stared at each other.

"Yes, a ring," I said slowly, watching his reaction. Cap's ears turned even redder.

"What type of ring, exactly? A token for your mothers? We have some very nice sapphires out here," he turned, beckoning toward another case.

"Actually, we're looking for...an engagement ring," Cap replied, his voice low.

The man swung around and looked from Cap to me, back and forth.

"An engagement ring," he repeated, nodding slowly. Suddenly, comprehension dawned on his face. "For the two of *you*?"

I looked at Cap and panicked.

"No," I blurted. "For our friend."

"Your friend?" he repeated incredulously. "You're shopping for an engagement ring for your *friend*?"

"Yes, our friend Bernard," Cap smoothly matched my lie. "He just proposed to a young lady, and he's tied up working on our Fords today. Just can't get away. He asked us to go out and look around for him, and see what sort of styles his bride-to-be might like."

"Yes, I know her taste quite well," I added. We were digging in deep to this lie now, weren't we? "She's my best friend, actually. I know just what she's looking for."

"Well, how lovely," the salesman replied, a twinkle in his eye. "So mademoiselle, what would you like to look at first? Any particular style in mind?"

"My friend likes diamonds, I guess," I replied, scrunching my nose. "Something simple. And classic?"

"Let me show you some pieces over here," the salesman said, leading us to the back of the store. Rows of pretty diamond rings sat in neat lines inside. "What size carat is your friend thinking she might enjoy?"

"Oh, just something small," I said, leaning over the case.

"But Bernard has a lot of money, don't forget," Cap leaned over my shoulder, studying the rings with me.

"Yes, of course," I nodded. "But his fiancée is pretty modest, isn't she?"

"She is, yeah," Cap responded. "But Bernard wants to spoil her, remember? He adores her."

I tried to hide my smile.

"That's true," I said, pointing to a ring in the middle. "That looks like something my friend might like."

The man pulled it out and handed it to me. "That's a half carat, set in yellow gold," he said, sliding it up on my finger.

It fit perfectly. I held it up for Cap and wiggled my fingers playfully. He laughed.

"That's nice," he smiled at me. "But I really think Bernard wants something even bigger for her. Something extravagant, to show just how deeply he cares for her."

"But Captain Gallivanter, didn't Bernard mention something about traveling for a while and maybe wanting to hold onto some of their money for that?" I tilted my head to the side. "We wouldn't want to spend *all* his money now."

"No, I don't think he did," Cap said absently, looking at the far end of the case where the biggest diamonds lay. "I'm pretty sure he told me he had a fortune to spend, since he's going to win a big competition, and that this was how he wanted to spend it. On the woman he loves."

I bit my lip, smiling, and lowered my face to the display below. So much for Cap's self-discipline. He was ready to blow our hard-earned fortune on a ring. I had to keep him in check.

"How about this one?" Cap pointed to a giant diamond, surrounded by dozens of smaller baguettes.

"Oh, sir, you have excellent taste," crooned the salesman, taking it out and offering it to me. I slid it on. The ring was an inch long on my finger.

"It's too much," I blurted, staring at it with wide eyes.

I was horrified at the thought of wearing a ring so large. Why, I'd be robbed in the street if I walked around with something like this. I certainly could never wear it on the expedition itself.

"It's one of the most expensive rings we have in here," the salesman said, turning my hand so it caught the sunlight from outside the store. "It's a rare, stunning, unique beauty. Like you."

I would've blushed if I wasn't already busy trying to keep myself from rolling my eyes in front of the salesman. It wasn't until Cap coughed that I realized what the man had said. I looked up, suddenly scarlet.

He knew.

"I mean, like your friend surely must be," the salesman corrected himself, smirking, still turning my hand so it sparkled like a dazzling rainbow as I stared at it.

"It's perfect," Cap said, standing next to me. "He's right. Stunning. Rare. Unique."

"We're still looking, Captain," I said, shooting him a look. Cap stared down at the ring, entranced. I slipped it off and handed it back to the man.

"Thank you, but I think Bernard wants something a little bit simpler," I said, glancing at the case. "Something practical. Not so flashy."

"I'm not sure Bernard thinks that, though," Cap said, pointing to another giant diamond ring. "Doesn't that look like something he might like?"

"No, definitely not," I said, looking at the ring he was pointing at. "Not his style."

"You two are just too much fun," the salesman said, twirling his mustache as he watched us with amusement. "What good friends you are, to do this for your Monsieur Bernard."

Dear Lord, we could never let Bernard know that we were making up this story about him. He'd die of embarrassment. After he murdered us both.

Cap insisted I try on a dozen other rings, each one bigger than the last. I kept veering back toward the smaller rings.

"Miss Gallivanter, don't you think Bernard would really enjoy pampering his fiancée with something stunning?" Cap cried in frustration, as I replaced a humongous five-carat ring with a one-carat diamond ring.

"I think Bernard would be happiest spending money on his travels," I said, my eyebrows raised. "His fiancée would, too. Since she knows that makes him so very happy."

"If you two don't see anything you like in here, we can always do a custom piece for you," the salesman offered, his eyes darting between us like he was a spectator at a tennis match. "Perhaps you just can't find anything that suits you?"

"Yes, our friend is apparently *quite* picky," Cap replied, glancing at me out of the corner of his eye. "Maybe we'll have to have a discussion with Bernard to make sure we're all on the same page. Because I definitely know that he wants something grand for her. Maybe he'll just have to pick it out himself."

"Oh, maybe he will," I shot back. "But he should probably think hard about the woman he's marrying. I mean, maybe she wants him to save some money for a honeymoon *around the world* or something."

Cap groaned out loud. "He has money," he said, exasperated. "What he wants most is a happy wife."

"Please, sir, give your friend my business card," the salesman said eagerly, pushing a small card into Cap's palm. "Tell your friend I'd love to work with him. I'm the best in the business. Fair prices and brilliant keepsakes. And custom jewelry, too. Anything you want to do. Remember that."

"Yes, thank you, sir," Cap said, putting his hand on my arm and guiding me out the door to the street.

"Thank you!" I called gratefully to the salesman, as he closed the door behind us and waved.

"Let's get out of here," Cap said, biting his lip to keep from laughing. "He's still watching us from the window."

"Are we the worst two liars on the planet?" I gasped out, when we finally reached an alley and dissolved into peals of laughter.

"We might be," Cap said, bent over laughing with his hands on his knees. "He had to be onto us, right? There's no way we fooled him into thinking we were shopping for our friends. Nobody does that."

"Probably not," I said, tears of laughter oozing out of the corners of my eyes. "At least we tried to have a good cover story. Let's hope he doesn't sell us out to the newspapers."

"I can see the headlines now," Cap gasped out. "'Gallivanter Secret Engagement Revealed—From Crew to 'I Do!'"

"Stop, stop," I said, holding my sides. "You're hurting me."

Impulsively, Cap grabbed me around the waist and pulled me into him for a kiss. I was breathless by the time we came up for air, partly from the laughing.

A sudden sprinkle of cold water doused us both from overhead.

"Hey!" Cap sputtered, looking up.

An old French woman wearing a robe stood on the balcony three stories above us, glaring down. She yelled at us in French, waving her watering can threateningly.

"She's telling us to clear out," I translated, grinning impishly. "This isn't a brothel, it's her backyard."

"Tell her this, then," Cap said, dipping me backwards for another kiss.

This time, we got drenched as she poured the rest of the watering can out over our heads.

"Fine, we're going!" Cap yelled, grabbing my hand as he pulled me away. "So much for the city of romance, huh?"

I smiled.

"And we find ourselves facing another unexpected adventure, even here in the quiet streets of Paris," I joked, my wet hair hanging in my face, squeezing his hand happily.

CHAPTER 18

AFTER A FEW DAYS HIDDEN away at our small cottage in Paris, we moved into a hotel.

"Sorry, everyone," Cap said, as we packed the Fords. "Part of keeping the public happy is being in the public eye, and that means being visible in a posh hotel."

"The things I do for you, Captain," Bernard grumbled, as he hauled his bag out to the Fords.

Cap navigated us to the L'Hôtel étoile du Nord, where we were planning to spend the next few days as we did public presentations. We pulled up to the gleaming white exterior, a uniformed doorman stiffly nodding and rushing to open the lobby doors for us.

"Oui, oui," Chito muttered, taking it all in. "Very nice."

We stepped inside the large marble lobby, gilt mirrors and candelabras glinting in the soft light. Cap and Chito headed to the reception desk while I sat with Bernard on a large velvet couch, our bags sprawled on the floor next to us.

"Hello, we're checking in for the Gallivanters," I heard Cap say to the clerk.

I closed my eyes and stretched my legs out in front of me, relaxing.

"How can that be?" I suddenly heard Cap say, his voice louder.

I opened my eyes and turned. Cap and Chito were standing at the counter, confused expressions on their faces.

"We made these reservations weeks ago, right?" I heard Chito say. "How can we not have rooms?"

"I'm sorry, sir." The clerk's tone was curt. "This is an exclusive property. We have the right to refuse service to anyone, at any time.

And that includes even the celebrity guests who choose to book lodging with us."

"I don't understand," Cap shook his head. "We reserved these rooms in advance. We can pay. We're a small, well-behaved crew of travelers. What's the problem?"

"I'm sorry, Captain," the clerk said, tipping his chin up. "We maintain a certain clientele here, and quite honestly, that's just not you. There's another hotel down the road. I'm sure they'll be able to accommodate you and your crew."

Chito and Cap both reeled back in surprise. I stood up.

"Let's go," I said, glaring at the clerk. "I don't feel like staying here, anyway."

We squeezed out of the lobby together, making our way back to the Fords.

"What was that?" Cap cried, once we dropped our bags in the trunks.

"What exactly did he say?" Bernard asked. "That we couldn't stay here?"

"Basically," Cap rubbed his face, his eyebrows drawn together. "He first told us that they didn't have a reservation for us. I pulled out the communication I'd had with them, dated a few weeks ago. He then confessed that they had cancelled the reservation. He wouldn't tell me why."

"What on earth?" I said, confused. "Why wouldn't they let us stay? We have money."

"*Tons* of money," Bernard corrected me. "We could buy a block of rooms there for months on end, if we wanted to."

"Maybe they don't want to deal with the crowds?" I mused. "We tend to attract a lot of attention wherever we go, now that we're so famous."

"I don't know," Cap responded. "You'd think they'd want a lot of eyes on their hotel, right? That's what every other hotel wants. They love when we stay there—it brings eyes to their business."

"Does he have an issue with the Fords being parked on the property?" Bernard offered. "Maybe they think we're blocking the view?"

"I might know why," Chito said quietly, as we stood around scratching our heads.

Wordlessly, he pointed to a man sitting at a nearby table outside a small cafe, sipping a cup of tea. He held his newspaper up as he read, and a blown-up black and white photograph of Cap's face was on the front. Underneath, bold letters declared in English, *"CAPTAIN CON MAN?"*

"What on earth?" I said, as we all stared.

"We need to get a newspaper and see what's going on," Cap flushed. "Why am I on the front page?"

"I'll go down to the corner and see if I can grab a paper there—" Chito began, but I impulsively rushed over to the stranger drinking his tea.

"He has an English newspaper," I thought to myself. *"He looks British. Who knows where he got that paper, but I need it now more than him."*

"Hello, sir," I said, forcing myself to sound cheerful. "Nice day we're having, isn't it?"

He looked up, over his paper, and blinked as he took in my height. I was tall, even compared to most men. I was used to this sort of initial reaction from strangers.

"Hullo," he responded, staring at me. His accent was indeed British.

"I couldn't help but notice your newspaper," I continued, feeling awkward. How did one approach a random stranger on the street and forcibly steal the very thing he was enjoying? I wasn't sure.

"Yes," he said, sounding confused. He looked down at his paper, and back up at me.

"I'd like to have your newspaper, please, if you're done with it."

He furrowed his brow. "I'm still reading it," he replied, perplexed.

Oh, this was hard. I forged ahead anyway.

"Right, of course," I responded hastily. "Could I just have this front page, then?"

He stared, one eyebrow raised. *Only an Englishman would hold onto a newspaper this tightly,"* I groaned internally.

"Please?" I added, hoping I had an expression of feminine distress evident on my face.

The man looked past me, noticing the crew now standing behind me. His face lit up with recognition.

"Hey, I just read about you," the man blinked, staring curiously at Cap. "You're that captain bloke."

"Yes, I am."

"Is it true?" he asked, watching Cap.

"Is what true?"

"Did you really leave your fiancée at the altar and run off around the world with another little tart?"

Cap blanched as my mouth dropped open. How had this gotten out? And how was Cap being painted in such a negative fashion? This version of the story held only the barest hint of truth. Cap had once been engaged, yes, but his fiancée had left *him*.

"Wait," the man said, looking again at me. "Are you—are you her? The one he ran off with? Whoa. You're not a little tart at all."

I blushed, feeling the heat creep up my neck like a fiery rash. What had this article said about me?

Bernard had already hit his tolerance limit for the day and simply swore. "Give us the damn paper," he said, yanking the front page out of the man's hands.

We walked away from the sputtering man, clutching at the paper together and trying to read as we hurried away.

"Captain Grant Gallivanter, parading around the world as a hero—but actually a fraud?" boasted the tagline under the blazing headline.

Cap started reading aloud.

"Familiar readers will no doubt recognize the name Captain Grant Gallivanter, leader of the world-famous Gallivanter Expedition, a small team traveling around the world in their Model T Ford automobiles. Mr. Gallivanter made history by inviting the first female driver into his team, a young beauty named Andiamo Gallivanter, in early 1923. This crew of Americans claimed to be on the up and up, but this reporter has discovered credible proof that things are not as rosy as the Gallivanters pretend."

"What the—" Cap gasped, as Chito grabbed the paper out of his hands.

"I'll read it, Cap. You shouldn't have to read these things about yourself."

Chito continued reading.

"An anonymous source recently disclosed to this reporter that Mr. Gallivanter is, in fact, a man of questionable morals. According to this source, Mr. Gallivanter jilted his fiancée at the altar, on the eve of their wedding, to run off with Andiamo, his rumored love interest. The source claims that his fiancée, Mildred Johnson, was simply devastated, and has been pining after him ever since. Apparently, she has made numerous attempts to contact Mr. Gallivanter to work things out, but Mr. Gallivanter has coldly ignored her repeated efforts and has cut her out of his life without any remorse whatsoever."

"No," Cap cried, flushed. "That's not true. Not at all. It was the opposite—she left me! And I certainly didn't know Andi back then! We met years later!"

"We're not done yet, Cap," Chito said grimly, scanning ahead.

"Furthermore, this anonymous source pointed out the obvious romance between Mr. Gallivanter and his gorgeous young crew member, Andiamo. 'It's clear to see that they're in love,' my source told me. 'Just look at the photographs and films of them together, and it's plain as day.' This reporter can't help but agree with the obvious attraction displayed, and must beg the question—who exactly is Mr. Gallivanter? A self-styled 'captain' of a team of intrepid explorers, or a con man on the run, motoring away from a betrayed woman he claimed to love? Either way, the public should think twice about believing whatever Mr. Gallivanter claims, and perhaps consider the true character of this mysterious man."

"This is insane," I exhaled. "None of that is true. How would anyone even know?"

"Where did this come from?" Chito said, folding the paper up. I noticed he glanced at the tea-drinker from across the street. I realized that the stranger's reaction—and the reaction of the hotel clerk who pulled our reservation—must be due to this article.

"Milly," Bernard groaned, shaking his head. "She always was a piece of work."

"It could only have come from Milly herself," Cap agreed, his voice husky with anger. "She's the only person who would've blabbed all this. And she *did* try to contact me last year, before the expedition even got started. You remember, Bernard? My name and photos were just starting to appear in newspapers. I ignored her attempts to talk, of course. But she's probably been waiting to sell her side of the story to the highest bidder. Putting the blame on me, instead of owning up to her mistakes."

"If you don't mind, Cap, we probably need to know the truth about Milly," Chito said gently. "We're going to have to get in front of this thing, in the press. And to do that, we need to know all the facts. From you."

"Andi already knows," Cap sighed. "So does Bernard. Bernard and I worked together, doing construction, when it all happened. When I first moved to America as a young man, from Poland, I settled in New Orleans. I met Milly at a saloon one night. She was a singer there."

He paused, meeting my eyes. He looked ashamed.

"She was manipulative from the beginning. She assumed I was rich, and I got caught up in her flattery," Cap explained. "Before I knew it, we were engaged. I tried to make it work—I *thought* it was love—but Milly was already on to someone else. Someone richer. To get rid of me, Milly reported me as a German spy to the American government. She claimed that she'd testify that she saw me writing out reports to give to the German military."

"What?" Chito said, aghast. "You? You're as American as any of us, Cap."

"I know," Cap said, rubbing his chin tiredly. "I'm an American citizen now. I have been for years. But I grew up in Poland, and I had a trace of an accent still, back then. The American men who arrested me grew up in the south, speaking Creole. They didn't know what a German accent sounded like. They assumed I had one."

I frowned. Cap's accent was so slight now, it was hard to believe it had caused him so many problems.

"Remember how it was, before the Great War?" Cap continued. "Everyone was paranoid about what was going on in Europe. Good people got thrown in prison without evidence, just because they had suspicious accents. I wasn't the only one. But by the time they got to my trial, I'd been locked up for six months. The judge dismissed my case immediately—Milly was the only witness, and she'd already skipped town with her new man. I had a good reputation with my construction crew, and bosses who backed me up. But the damage was already done."

Chito whistled. "Sounds like you dodged a bullet, my friend," he said, patting Cap on the shoulder. "Life with a woman like that would've been hell."

"I know," Cap nodded. "Since Milly, there's been no one else. I thought I was done with love for good. I'm glad that wasn't the case."

"But how'd they find out about all of this?" Chito asked. "How did someone track down Milly to dig all of this up? And why?"

"I don't know," Cap groaned. "And how do they know about Andi and me being in love? You didn't write to your mother about us, yet, did you, Andi?"

"No," I shook my head.

"Wait, I thought you were going to write to your mother and tell her we were engaged?" Cap's forehead wrinkled. "You haven't done that yet?"

"This sounds like something you two need to talk about privately," Bernard interrupted. "As far as the newspaper noticing that you and Cap love each other? Come on. The chemistry has been obvious between you two from the very beginning. You'd have to be blind not to see it."

Chito shrugged. "He's right. I know you two think you're being clever by hiding it, but it's evident just by watching the way you glance at each other and stand next to each other, even in photographs, that you're in love with each other. I'm sure reporters have taken notice, too."

"At least our engagement didn't leak out," I said, shaking my head. "Or the story of your time in prison. We'd look even worse."

"Oh, gosh," Cap groaned. "The press would skewer us with it right now. And the last thing we need is for the public to turn against us."

"So what do we do about it?" I asked. "Can we fight back? Tell the newspapers the truth?"

We fell quiet. Even if we had a press conference to share our side of the story, I knew the simple fact that this article had come out would be enough to create doubt in people's minds. As a group that relied on goodwill to open doors as we traveled, that could be problematic for us.

"I think we'll need to write our own version of the story," Cap said slowly. "Get the facts out. Tell people what really happened. I'm sure it'll all blow over eventually."

"Right," Chito said. "You haven't done anything wrong. This is libel, isn't it? Can't we go after the paper itself for making you look so bad?"

"I don't know," I said, squinting. "The reporter threw in all those disclaimers. You know, 'according to my source' and everything else he wrote? He squirmed around stating anything directly, but certainly implied a lot."

Cap groaned in frustration.

"I'm sorry, everyone," he said. "I was always concerned that my past would catch up with me somehow. I guess it finally happened."

"We all have a past we're not proud of, Cap," Chito put his arm on his shoulder and squeezed. "The only thing that matters is that you're a better man today than you were yesterday. And that's certainly the case."

We nodded in agreement, but the word "today" gave me pause. If this was what we were facing today, what fresh frustration might tomorrow bring? I shook my head, thinking about the stress our team had already gone through.

What we needed right now was peace and quiet, not more challenges. That's why we were here, in Europe, after all.

But what might tomorrow—or the coming days—bring to the Gallivanter team?

CHAPTER 19

OUR TEAM FOUND A NEW hotel the same day, an older building in a quiet area of town that was mostly residential.

We checked in to our individual rooms, the excited hotel staff nearly falling over themselves at the prospect of having celebrities stay in their hotel. They insisted on carrying our suitcases inside, dashing to tuck vases of fresh flowers and bottles of champagne in each of our rooms.

When the staff finally left, after clucking over my bedding and straightening the vase of flowers for the third time, I crossed to the window and lifted the sash, letting the humid air drift in. It was raining softly, dampening the sounds of the busy city outside.

I leaned on the window sill, trying to sort out my emotions. I felt bad for Cap, and guilty that I still hadn't written to my own mother about our engagement. I'd been putting it off for weeks now, struggling to find the right words to explain our whirlwind romance. And now I was worried that somehow, the news of my engagement to Cap would leak out and that she'd learn about it from the media, not from her own daughter.

I tried to look at the situation from her point of view and only felt worse.

She had sent me off to boarding school as a child, after my father died in the war, and I'd completely disrupted her plans by dropping out of school and running off on this expedition. Now here I was, planning to marry my boss—the very man she had trusted to take care of me, when I was hired on to be a part of this crew.

How could I possibly write all of this to my mother and not have her be disappointed in the choices I'd made? It was easier to simply push off the thought of telling her. I'd deal with it another time.

A knock sounded at my door and I smiled. I knew it was Cap before I even opened it.

"Hey," he said, stepping inside as I opened the door. "Can we talk a minute?"

"Sure," I said, pulling him against me, teasing. "You're sure all you want to do is talk?"

He raised his eyebrow at me. "This is serious, Andi."

"What?"

"I don't know how to say this, exactly, but I think we're being sabotaged by Milly. And maybe the Chinooks, too."

"Why would she do that?" I frowned. "Why now?"

He sat on the foot of my bed, shaking his head.

"I know this will sound like a leap, but I think it's the Chinook Voyageurs behind all of this, trying to discredit us," he said. "They're our only competition in this whole expedition. It *has* to be them, right? They're the only ones who would have a good reason to go after us now. I think they found a way to dig into my past, and they found out about Milly along the way. Maybe someone on their team talked to her, and is planting these stories in the press to make me look bad."

I tapped my finger against my chin. "But we've been racing against each other for months now. Why would they all of a sudden turn on us, and in such a public way? We've both been doing our own thing and respectfully staying out of each other's way. What could have possibly changed?"

Our eyes met as we both realized it at the same time.

"Dessie," we said in unison.

"It makes sense," I frowned. "The Chinooks clearly brought her on to rival me. Suddenly, we're not the only team with a girl. We're on equal footing. They need some way to stand out. They decided to make us look bad."

"And she goes after us, using her charm to spread a bunch of pretty little lies to do just that," Cap added. "She comes across as a sweet young woman, but she's manipulating the truth about us to make us look bad. To make their team look better. Get more popular."

We sat on the bed, silently thinking.

"What do we do about it?" I said, feeling anger rise. *"How dare she go after Cap,"* I thought. *"He's an incredible man. A brave and committed leader. He's poured his heart and soul into this expedition. He doesn't deserve this."*

"I don't know," Cap exhaled slowly. "You're a girl. You understand women better than I do. What do we do?"

I thought back to my lonely childhood. I'd spent my life avoiding the girls around me, even in my all-girls boarding school.

"I have no idea," I replied helplessly. Females could be manipulative and passive aggressive. How could I explain that to Cap? Men were so direct—especially him.

"What if you meet up with her and try to reason with her?" Cap mused. "You know, woman to woman? Appeal to her as an equal? It might help sooth her vanity. Make her realize you can both share the limelight, as female explorers."

"I don't know about that," I frowned. "Besides, when are we going to be in the same place at the same time?"

"We're not that far away from each other right now," Cap pointed out. "We've both been circling around Western Europe this month. We could make it work. What if you telegram her directly and ask to meet up here in Paris? She could take a train here."

"I don't know. Where are they now?"

"I'm not sure," Cap admitted. "But what girl would turn down a trip to Paris? We could offer to pay her way. Pay for her hotel stay for a few days. Bribe her a little bit. Maybe she'd like to go shopping here, take a few days off from the Chinook team?"

"Oh, Cap," I said, shaking my head. "It takes more than a shopping trip to tempt girls."

"For you, yes. I'm not so sure about that with her. She looks like a girl who'd enjoy a whirl through a Parisian boutique or two."

I glared at him.

"What?" he said defensively. "I'm talking about her, not you."

"That's not it," I sighed. "I don't want to meet with her. You want me to be honest with you, right? I don't like her. I won't ever be friends with her. Girls like us don't get along."

"You've never even met her."

"I don't have to. I know what kind of person she is already."

"Here you go being stubborn again," Cap replied, sighing. I crossed my arms and said nothing. Truth be told, I knew I'd never forgive her for what she was doing to attack the man I loved. Maybe Cap could overlook that, but I couldn't.

Cap stared back at me, meeting my glare.

"Listen, Andi," he said. "I'm going to be perfectly frank with you here. Dessie has the capability to destroy us, if she keeps going with these little articles. It doesn't take much to turn the public against you—just a scandal or two is enough. And while we have plenty of money right now, we're also relying on our fame and reputation to pave a way for us through the world. It opens a lot of doors for us. If we lose that, we risk our expedition's success."

He was right. Darn him, he was always right.

"Fine, I'll meet with her," I groaned. "I'll wire her today and ask if she wants to spend the weekend in Paris—our treat—and meet up to get acquainted. But that's all you get from me. One meeting.

If I can't win her over in that meeting, then you can't hold it against me. I'll try my best."

"Deal," Cap said, smiling ruefully at me. "I hope this works. We need to get her on our side somehow."

"What are we going to do, in the meantime?" I said slowly. "She put a pretty nasty article out there, full of half-truths about us."

"What are you thinking?" Cap said, tilting his head to the side.

"Should we fight back in the press? Stand up for ourselves?"

Cap rested his head in his hand, thinking hard.

"Maybe," he said after a few moments. "But we can't tell the world about our engagement yet. It'd be too upsetting, coming on the heels of this lie about Milly. We'd simply have to tell the truth about Milly—that *she* left me."

"So let's find a reporter and say it. We need to get our side out there."

"I don't know," he rubbed his chin. "I hate the idea of lowering ourselves to the same level that the Chinooks are at, planting stories in the press like this. It makes us look petty."

"We don't have much of a choice," I pointed out. "You just told me how important it is to keep public opinion favorably on our side. We have to correct a lie. It's the only choice we have, Cap."

"I guess." He sighed heavily, standing up. "I'll go work on a draft of it right now."

"No," I said quickly, a thought popping into my head. "I have a better idea."

"What?"

"A press conference," I grinned, warming to the idea. "You're a pro in front of the cameras. Better than anyone I've ever seen. You come alive when there's a camera focused on you, Cap. They'll eat it up."

"Oh, I don't know about this," Cap said, wrinkling his forehead. "I hate to make this a big issue. That's making it much more public than an article in the newspaper."

"You need to play to your strengths, though," I pointed out. "The Chinooks started this, with the article. You're just going to finish it, in your own way. The way you happen to excel."

Cap unexpectedly swooped in and kissed me on the forehead. "I love that brain of yours. Fine. I'll start arranging a press conference. They may command the print, but I can command the reporters."

"Don't forget, Captain Gallivanter, you can't kiss me like that on camera," I called out cheekily, as he reached for the door.

He stopped in the doorway and looked back at me.

"There are *quite* a few things I'd like to do to you that I can't do on camera," he said, grinning as he stepped out of my room.

CHAPTER 20

CAP SET UP A PRESS conference for the following afternoon. He went all out, inviting more than thirty local reporters. Apparently, all of them were coming.

"It wasn't hard to persuade them to come," he said as he put on his jacket and smoothed his hair. "They can tell that there's something in the air between us and the Chinook Voyageurs. It's like sharks sensing blood in the water."

"Are you ready to do this?" I asked. I lay across his bed, watching him as he checked his reflection in the mirror.

"What, open up to the world about my most personal, shameful mistake?" Cap said, carefully tying his tie. "Or do you mean the fact that I'll have to lie about loving you, when eventually people will notice that the two of us get married and live happily ever after?"

"Both," I replied lightly.

He turned.

"No matter what you hear today, you need to know that I'm performing," he said, taking my face between his hands. "It's a show. It's all a show, when it's in front of the public."

"I know," I held his hands with my own and sighed.

"I never felt this way about Milly," he added, looking into my eyes. "It's you, who captured my heart, in a way no one else ever has."

"I know."

"I'm sorry, Andi," he said softly. "I hate that you have to hear all of this about me again. That the whole world has to know it now. I know it's embarrassing for you, too."

"It's in the past. It's part of what made you who you are now. And I love who you are. That means loving the embarrassing parts of you, too."

He sighed. "Yeah."

"Just tell the truth," I said, squeezing his hands. "We'll get our side out, and we'll move on. No big deal."

"Thanks," he said, glancing at me. "There's one more thing."

"What?"

"I need you to leave me alone for a while," he breathed. "I need to prepare for this, mentally. And when I'm around you, well, I can't stop thinking about you."

He looked down, his ears pink.

"I need to think about Milly now," he said, avoiding my eyes. "About how she made me feel. How angry I was."

"I'll be there by your side, during it and afterwards," I smiled, kissing him. "I'm proud of you."

Closing the door behind me, I walked down to my own room. *"Poor Cap,"* I thought, imagining how I'd feel trying to explain my love life to a bunch of reporters. He had more courage than I had, to come clean about it in front of the world.

An hour later, I made my way down to the lobby. Already, several reporters were there, unpacking their cameras. Cap was chatting with them.

"Miss Gallivanter!" one of the reporters called. "Is it true what the article said about you? Are you and Captain Gallivanter romantically involved?"

"Captain Gallivanter will be addressing that today," I replied smoothly. "He'll be sure to tell everyone at the same time. We appreciate your patience as we wait for the rest of the group."

Cap gathered all the reporters in the rear of the lobby, away from the front door. A dozen curious onlookers stood behind the rows of reporters, watching as bystanders. Even with little advance notice, the Gallivanters could still draw a large crowd.

"Ladies and gentlemen, thank you for coming today," Cap said, taking off his hat solemnly and running his hand through his hair.

"Here comes the show," Chito breathed into my ear, as we stood next to Cap as a team, supporting him with our presence. "He's a master with the media."

"I appreciate you taking the time to come here for the truth," Cap's voice rang out in the room, confident. "Lately, some unfortunate rumors have persisted surrounding a long-ago relationship of mine. In the spirit of honesty and integrity—two values of vital importance to me—I wanted you to hear the real story, straight from my own lips."

He sighed and cast his gaze down at the floor.

"As a young man, newly an American citizen after a childhood of hardship, I lived in New Orleans," Cap continued. "I worked an honest job, as a construction worker on a large crew. It was difficult work—backbreaking at times. At night, I'd go out with my crew to enjoy a hot meal, and maybe a drink or two. It made the day more tolerable, to enjoy the evening with good friends and a stomach full of good food. I'm sure some of you can relate to that, yes?"

Several of the reporters nodded sympathetically. Cap was good at endearing the crowd to himself.

"At one of those dinners, I met a lovely young lady. Miss Mildred Johnson was a singer, who was sometimes featured at the restaurant where we ate. She sang a few songs, while we enjoyed our meal, and afterwards, we started chatting."

"How smooth he is," I thought, listening to him. In reality, she sang at bars. They met in a saloon. He was making her look better than she actually was, in order to maintain his reputation as a gentleman.

"You know how it goes when you're young, right, my friends?" Cap said, staring out at the crowd. "I thought I was in love. I was so young, so naive. Before I knew it, I was impulsively proposing and she just as impulsively accepted. We barely knew each other, and we were suddenly planning a future together."

It was hard to hear Cap confessing this to the world, I suddenly realized. I thought I was prepared to listen to it, but he was so convincing as he talked that I started to question if he actually still *had* warm feelings toward Milly.

"No, he doesn't love her anymore," my brain argued with me. *"She ruined his life. She threw him in prison."*

"But then again, he just said he proposed impulsively to her. Didn't he propose impulsively to you, too?" my mind argued back. *"How do you know it won't end the same way?"*

"We were caught up in the feverish passion sweeping through the country, with all of Europe at war," Cap continued. "We knew America would enter the fray any day, too. Emotions ran high. We worried that life was suddenly too short, that we had to cram as much as possible in before it was too late. People made impulsive decisions left and right. This was my impulsivity, my reckless fear taking over."

He cleared his throat. I knew he must be embarrassed to admit something like that. Cap was so self-assured and controlled.

"When you're young and inexperienced, though, you just don't know how hard it is to sustain love," Cap's voice dropped.

The room leaned forward in breathless anticipation, cameras flashing.

"Mildred and I tried to make things work, but we quickly grew apart," Cap continued. "She had a dream to work as an actress, and wanted to be famous. She hoped the whole world would come to know her name. I, on the other hand, was content to work with my two hands. Mildred wasn't a fan of my work, and wanted me to support her. We disagreed about our futures."

"Clever of you," I thought, listening. He'd managed to imply that Milly was a fame-hungry actress. Everyone knew actresses were unstable. And he'd managed to make himself look like a steady, hardworking man by contrast.

"Mildred is a nice girl," Cap added. "She wanted so much out of life, and out of the man she wanted to marry. Unfortunately, it became evident to both of us that I was not that man."

He lowered his head again, his brows knit heavily. Cameras flashed again, capturing the moment.

"Mildred decided that she wanted to break our engagement," he said softly. "She wanted more out of life, a different kind of husband. She'd realized I wasn't the person she wanted to spend her life with. More than anything, I didn't want to bind her to me with an impulsive promise she'd made during an emotional moment. We broke our engagement, and I vowed to keep this all to myself, to save her any embarrassment in the future."

"Tell them what actually happened," I thought furiously. *"Tell them that she cheated on you. That she left you for another man, while you were still engaged. Tell the world that she's a liar, and a phony, and that she went after someone with more money after she sucked up all of yours. Defend yourself, Cap. She was horrible to you."*

Cap continued calmly.

"Mildred found someone else, right away," he said. "He was a wonderful man. A man with a bright future, and lots of wealth. All the means to take care of a fledgling young actress. Mildred seemed so happy with him. I faded away into the background of her life, quietly, praying that she would enjoy a blissful marriage with this man. We lost contact—as anyone might expect, especially when one of them has moved on to another relationship—but I've wished her nothing but the best, all these years."

He paused, and appeared to struggle with emotion. The reporters and the crowd stared at him, on the edge of their seats.

"Mildred, if you're out there watching this, I truly hope you're happy," he said, biting his lip. "We've both come a long way since we last saw each other. And I wish the best of luck to you, in the life that you're living. I know I'm certainly happy with mine. And I'm so glad I've had the chance to get all of this off my chest, to share the truth—the *real* story—with the world."

He smiled, staring straight into the cameras. "I thank you, ladies and gentleman, for your continued support. The love and encouragement you've had for my team—even in finding out about our trials and struggles of the past—has been tremendous. Without your support, we'd be nothing. On behalf of the Gallivanter team, I thank you, from the bottom of my heart."

He bowed, and placed his hat back on his head. Several reporters' hands shot up instantly, vying for his attention.

"Captain Gallivanter! What say you to the article that claims that you're in love with your crew mate, Miss Andiamo?" one of them yelled.

The crowd murmured, and swiveled toward me. I kept my face perfectly still. I knew this was coming.

Cap held his hand over his heart.

"Gentlemen, can I be honest?" he asked. The room instantly hushed. "I'm just too distracted right now to answer any additional questions, my friends. The pressure of leading this expedition is already immense, and having to dredge up painful memories today to share here? It's draining."

Several of the reporters smiled sympathetically. *"Goodness gracious, can Cap ever manage a crowd,"* I thought, trying to keep my face bland.

"I can promise you, my friends, that Miss Andi is a capable, wonderful young woman who also feels that stress," Cap continued.

"I ask, out of respect to her, that you don't pester her with questions like these, either."

He looked at me with a wan smile, and I nodded back at him. To the world, we looked like two strained professionals supporting each other.

"We're well aware that people enjoy concocting stories to sell their papers, but we're real people doing real, challenging work," Cap said, with a rueful laugh. "We can't afford to waste our precious time answering silly questions. I'm not here to impugn anyone's motives, but I'm sure you can see that it would serve *some people's* interests to destroy the Gallivanter Expedition. We're in competition, after all, with others."

As expected, his pointed words got the reporters buzzing. A murmur zipped around the room.

"Now, thank you for being here," Cap said, his arms up in a gesture of gratefulness. "My team and I have a long day tomorrow and need our rest. Have a good night, everyone."

With a final smile at the crowd, which was already disbanding, Cap ushered the team to his room. We didn't say a word until he closed the door behind us.

"Well, what do you think?" Cap said, tossing his hat down onto the bed.

"I think you made Milly sound a hell of a lot nicer than she actually was," Bernard spoke up. "She was a horrible woman. You made her sound good. She wasn't. Especially not to you."

"It's all appearances, though," Chito said, studying Cap. "You intentionally made Milly sound good, so you appeared like the nice guy. So you couldn't get attacked for dumping her."

"You didn't dump her, though," I said. "She left you. For another man."

"Right," Cap said, removing his jacket and tossing it down. "I haven't forgotten that, Andi. Trust me."

I bit my lip. I hated Dessie and the Chinooks for dragging us through this. We didn't know for sure if they were responsible, but if we found out...I didn't know if I could control myself around them if we ever crossed paths.

Cap noticed my face, and stopped pulling at his tie.

"I'm sorry," he said gently. "I told you beforehand, it's all for show. I played a role today. You know that. Milly's side was full of half truths, and I addressed them the only way I could to pull us out of this mess."

I avoided his eyes.

"Andi?"

"I hate them," I blurted. "Those Chinooks. We don't dig through their personal lives like this. What gives them the right to do it to us, and make us look bad in front of the whole world?"

"It's behind us now," Cap sighed. "We move on. Our future is bright."

"I know what will help us all feel a bit better," Chito piped up. "I ordered a plateau à fromage to my room. What do you say we all go snack on that and forget about tonight?"

"They're right," I thought. *"Let it go. The truth is out there, now. We can move on."*

It was all we could do, at this point.

CHAPTER 21

I TELEGRAMMED DESSIE to invite her to Paris, as we'd planned, and I received an immediate reply.

"Thank you, I accept your kind invitation," she'd written back. *"Will arrive via train on Friday morning. Meet you at the Gare de Lyon station at nine o'clock."*

Cap planned to pick her up and take her to her hotel—the fanciest one in Paris—in an attempt to make a good first impression. He was the face of our expedition, and we wanted her to feel flattered as soon as she got off the train. We'd discussed our strategy to disarm her, at length.

"We need to make her feel important," Cap had explained. "She's used to having the attention of men, clearly, so we'll give her all of my attention right off the bat."

"And by giving her a man to interact with first, she'll also feel more in control of the situation," I replied.

"Exactly."

"Don't let her get her hooks into you," I cautioned. "She appears to be quite the expert manipulator."

He wrinkled his nose, disgusted. "I hate playing games. And clearly I'm not a fan of women who manipulate. Look at the mess that type of woman has already caused in my life."

"Just be careful, Cap. I don't trust her."

Cap left early on Friday morning, prepared to sit at the station on the off-chance that her train arrived early.

"I'm going to get her a bouquet of flowers," he told me the night before. "Don't read into it. I'm just trying to bury the hatchet, get her to let her guard down with us. Trust me, I have zero interest in her."

I rolled my eyes.

The next morning, I stepped out of my room and stopped short. The entire hallway around my door was filled with vases of roses. I grinned. I couldn't even get through them to step out of the door.

It took me a few moments to pick up all the flowers and bring them into my room. I was halfway through the process when Bernard opened his door across from my room, scowled, and slammed it shut irritably.

I heard him sputtering behind his door. "Can't even walk down the hallway, that stupid lovestruck fool..."

Chito and Bernard and I had breakfast together in the hotel, and Chito and I went out afterwards to stroll around the city, as we waited for Cap.

"You're not worried about him being alone with Dessie, are you?" Chito asked, glancing at me as we walked down the streets, our faces hidden to avoid the crowds. We passed a bakery, the smell of fresh bread tickling my nose.

"No," I replied, watching two young children giggle and run down the sidewalk, in front of their mother. "I'm more worried about what she'll do to us."

"How so?"

"What if she finds out about Cap's time in prison? What if she spins *that* story? He'll look even worse. He should've just come clean about that at the press conference, gotten ahead of the story. She's still sitting on ammunition that can damage us, as far as I'm concerned."

Chito frowned. "You don't think Dessie would dig that deep, do you? It's been years since he was in prison. And his record was cleared—he was innocent. He doesn't have to bring it up. Nothing happened."

"It doesn't matter, though, does it? As Cap keeps saying, it's all about how the press sees us. The truth can be massaged. Twisted. But if we lose their favor, we're endangering our own expedition."

The children shrieked in front of us, babbling in French. Chito and I smiled politely, ducking around them. I knew that if the children recognized us, their shrieks would become shouts of joy at meeting such famous celebrities.

"We need people to trust us," I sighed. "Think of all the interactions we have with government officials, ambassadors, and diplomats. If they suspect that we're hiding things—like the fact that one of our crew did time in jail—they might not be so willing to help us out."

"The early days of the Gallivanter Expedition were so much easier," Chito grumbled. "Before all this fame and fortune. Just a couple of guys, scrapping our way through the world together in a few nice cars."

"Before me?"

Chito glanced at me. "I didn't say that."

"It's true. You three were happy before I mucked everything up."

"Cap wasn't," Chito shook his head. "I mean, he was fine. But he changed, when you came onto the team. As soon as he met you, that night after the presentation in Nice—he was a different man when he got back home."

"Really?"

"Really."

I tucked my hair behind my ears. The wind was blowing cold. I should've worn a scarf.

"You've never told me that before," I replied. "You don't really talk about how you feel about the fact that Cap and I are together."

Chito studied me. "You want me to be honest?"

"Yes!" I blurted. "You've always been candid with me. You've become my best friend, Chito. You know that."

"I didn't think I needed to tell you how happy I am that two of the people I love most in the world are so happy together. If I'm being honest, I've always thought you two were perfect for each other."

"You never told me that, either."

He grinned. "You didn't really need my encouragement to fall in love with Cap, now, did you?"

"No," I blushed.

"I saw his soul, before he met you. I read people, you know. It's my gift. He'd been deeply wounded by Milly. I was a broken man, too. And broken people recognize each other. With you, I don't know. Cap became himself, somehow. You brought out the best in him. Sharpened him. And he did the same for you."

I nodded, smiling to myself. Chito grinned and slung his big arm around me.

"You're happy. And you're going to have moments where you're unhappy, but hold onto *this* feeling. Remember that you bring out the best in each other, and you allow each other to be who you really are. That's love, Andi. That's a special kind of love."

"You're so wise, Chito," I laughed. "Can I ask you something else?"

"Shoot," he said, his arm heavy on my shoulders. We walked through a market now, and he was staring distractedly at a stall of local honey.

"Will you be my maid of honor?"

"Sure," he said, leaning toward the honey with interest. He stopped short and looked at me, confused. "Wait, what now?"

I laughed at his face. "Will you be my maid of honor, at my wedding? I mean, someday. When we actually get married. We don't have a date or anything yet."

"Look at me," Chito laughed out loud, patting his belly. "Do I look like I'll be fitting into some silky little dress?"

"I don't care about that," I smiled. "I just know I want the other person who matters most to me standing up there, at my side, on the most important day of my life."

He laughed again, a deep laugh. "It's supposed to be a sister or a best friend up there with you, Andi."

"Yeah. A best friend," I said, pulling his beard impishly. He beamed.

"I'd love to. But you're explaining this to Cap. Don't go fighting over me, now. Maybe he wanted me as best man."

"I got to you first," I grinned.

He patted me on the head like a puppy, then playfully turned my head toward the honey. Small jars of amber honey sat neatly in a row, and the pretty French girl behind the stall smiled at us.

"Let's get back to more important things," he grinned. "How many jars should I get?"

I laughed and shrugged. "One? Two?"

"Oh, Andi," Chito groaned in mock disappointment, turning to the girl. "Bonjour, mademoiselle. I'd like five jars, please. We're going on a road trip, so go ahead and throw them in a bag for me."

CHAPTER 22

CHITO AND I MADE IT back to the hotel after lunch. Cap had just arrived back, after picking Dessie up and treating her to lunch before taking her back to her fancy lodgings several blocks away.

"Oh, you two are a sight for sore eyes," Cap moaned as he saw us walk through the lobby doors. His forehead was already creased with exasperation.

"It went that well with her, huh?" Chito replied, amused.

Cap groaned again, and put his head between his hands, sinking into a lobby chair. Chito and I exchanged glances. From behind his hands, Cap's words were muffled. "She drives me crazy. Absolutely crazy."

"Why?" I asked, trying not to openly smirk.

He lifted his head.

"She's a good-looking girl, I'm not going to lie," he sighed. "But she knows it, and she uses it like a weapon. She flirted with every single man we encountered, from the porter to the bellhop to the bum selling cigarettes on the corner outside the train station. I've never seen anything so blatant."

"Well, she sounds delightful," I sniffed.

"She's not at all like you, Andi," Cap continued, shaking his head. "You're just—I don't know. You're different. Confident in your differences. Dessie, though, she's maddening. And vain. And possibly the most high-maintenance woman I've ever met. There's no way she's pulling her weight on the Chinook team. I bet she can't even drive."

"Sounds like a real nice girl," Chito said, smirking at me. "When do we get to meet her?"

Cap rolled his eyes.

"Frankly, I'd be happy never seeing her again," he said. "But Andi, you're meeting with her at her hotel this afternoon. We'll go over in a few hours. And I need every moment of those hours to decompress from the amount of times I had to bite my tongue and smile over her vapid comments."

Cap walked me to Dessie's hotel a few hours later, wearing a trench coat and fedora pulled down over his face, to avoid being recognized. I wore a beret and coat, too. We didn't want to get held up talking to fans.

"Remember, you're trying to get her on our side," Cap reminded as we walked quickly down the winding streets to her hotel. "Be nice. Don't lose your temper. Make her like you. Pretend like you're on the same page. The only two girls in the world doing something like this, you need to be allies, you know. That kind of thing."

"I know," I replied irritably. "This is a lot of effort for one person, you know. No one's ever made such an effort for me."

Cap grimaced. "Trust me, she loves the effort we're putting into this. Into spoiling her, making a big fuss."

We reached the hotel, a beautiful old building in a central location in the middle of Paris. We'd spared no expense to put her here for two nights. Cap had greeted her with flowers, and a small box of chocolates were waiting in her room when she arrived.

"I'll be waiting outside," Cap said, watching me walk to the door.

"You're not coming in at all?"

"No, I'm afraid my presence will change her behavior, make her more competitive. It has to be the two of you women, together, talking honestly."

Sighing, I nodded. I hated this sort of thing. Too often, I put my foot in my mouth and blurted out precisely the wrong things. I didn't know how to talk to a girl like Dessie, but I'd certainly try.

I pushed open the large doors and entered the lobby. Beautifully carved antique furniture decorated the space, with large flower arrangements adding glamor around the room. It was quiet, and oozed class.

It was far nicer than our own hotel. Dessie got all the special treatment, huh?

I spotted the crowd around Dessie at the bar before I could actually see her face. Several eager young men stood around her, clearly vying for her attention. She sat on a bar stool in the middle of the crowd, laughing, her slim legs crossed and her skirt riding up on her thighs.

She saw me and squealed from across the room.

"Oh, if it isn't the famous Miss Andiamo Gallivanter!" she cried, holding her drink up. "Boys, you're in for a rare sight—*two* of the world's most famous women in one place at the same time!"

The men smiled at me and a few tried to shake my hand. Some of them were a little too friendly. I smiled in return, then ignored them.

"So nice to meet you, Dessie," I said, offering my hand to her. She sat on her stool, smiling at me, and shook hands. Her fingernails were bright red except for the half-moon at the very tips, as was the fashion, and matched her expertly applied lipstick. I tried to imagine holding up the crew while I got my nails done in each new city, and couldn't.

"The pleasure is all mine, Miss Gallivanter," she simpered as we shook hands.

"Do you think we could settle in somewhere a bit more private to talk?" I asked, glancing at the young men around us. They leaned forward, watching us like little boys staring at an ant pile they'd just set on fire.

"Sure," she cooed, sliding gracefully off of her stool and standing up. The action hitched her skirt up even higher, and every man's eyes swiveled instantly to her slender thigh.

"Boys, we're going to go chat, but don't be wandering off," Dessie purred. "I'll be looking for you when I'm done. I'm mighty lonely, here on the road. And I'm a bit of a night owl, too. I enjoy staying up *all* night sometimes."

She winked suggestively at the men and flipped her long hair over her shoulder as she sauntered away. I tried not to let my shock show. Had she just propositioned an entire group of men, all at once? Who was this woman?

"How about a drink, Miss Gallivanter?" Dessie asked, still clutching hers as we sat down in chairs in the corner of the lobby.

"Oh, that's alright," I shrugged. "I don't drink too much."

"Just one," she pleaded, her tone silky. "Come on. To toast to us girls."

"Fine," I agreed. I didn't want to set her on edge before we'd even started. *"Make her an ally,"* I reminded myself. *"We need to be friends, at the end of this. For the sake of the Gallivanters."*

Dessie smiled, held her hand up in the air, and snapped her fingers. Instantly, a bartender appeared in front of us. He must have been watching her the entire time. The thought unsettled me. Dessie was clearly used to getting attention, and used it to her advantage.

"How can I help you, Miss Hickson?" the bartender asked.

"I'd like to order something for my friend here," Dessie said sweetly. She glanced at me out of the corner of her eye. "I think something strong."

"Oh, no, I don't drink—" I started, but Dessie interrupted me.

"Let's get her a corpse revival. It's an American drink, I'm sure it's one of her favorites," she said, smiling at me. "Brandy, cognac, and sweet vermouth. It's wonderful."

"Yes, mademoiselle," the man said, bowing and hurrying away.

"You'll love it," Dessie smiled at me. "And it's on the house. All of my drinks are on the house here."

"How is it an American drink?" I asked, wrinkling my nose. "Hasn't Prohibition been going on for a few years now? You can't get alcohol there anymore."

"It's cute how innocent you are," she laughed. "You think the government outlawing it has stopped the bars? They just moved their operations to basements. They're even more profitable now. The forbidden is always enticing."

I tried to smile back, but I felt uneasy. If I drank, which was rare, it was an occasional glass of champagne or a single beer, or a small taste of something offered to me by locals as we traveled. I preferred to keep my head clear, not muddied by alcohol.

"Well, I'm sure I'll like the drink," I said, then changed the subject. *"Be conversational and friendly, get her to let her guard down,"* I told myself. *"Don't put your foot in your mouth, like you usually do."*

"How are you liking the expedition so far?" I asked.

Dessie tossed her hair and grinned at me, leaning forward.

"I love it," she confided. "The cars? The open road? All these friendly men I encounter, bending over backwards for me everywhere we go? It's the best fun I've ever had."

She was having a far different experience than me, I realized. But I recognized a woman who loved to talk about herself, so I kept prodding.

"Tell me about your crew," I said, keeping my tone casual. "How do you all get along? I don't know much about the Chinooks, to be honest."

"Oh, they adore me," she grinned, batting her eyes and taking a sip of her drink. "They do everything for me. They just love having me on the team."

"They do everything for you? Like what?"

"Oh, you know. They carry my bags around, get my meals for me, drive me around…"

"You don't drive?" I repeated before I could stop myself, blinking. Cap had been right. "Isn't that part of the reason they brought you on?"

"Andi, you're such a tease," Dessie giggled. Her laugh was delicate and yet cold, like wind chimes dancing in the bleak midwinter breeze. "You know why they brought me on. It's the same reason they brought *you* on."

"I'm not sure I know what you mean," I said lightly.

"Yes you do," she said, looking at me. "You're a fairly pretty girl, all things considered. You know you're just an eye-catcher for the boys. A face to put in front of the cameras, when they need some attention. You don't have an actual role in all of this."

"Pretty, all things considered, huh?" I thought, feeling anger bubble at her backhanded compliment. I pushed it down. I wouldn't take the bait.

"I hold my own on my team," I replied. "But that's great that you're getting along with your crew. What are they like?"

"We both know what you're doing, Andi," she pursed her lips. "You're fishing for information."

"I'm not," I protested. "I'm just trying to be friendly. I want to get to know you. There aren't many women out there, doing what we're doing. Since there are only two of us, don't you think we should get along?"

She stared at me, tilting her pretty head. The bartender returned with my drink, proffered on a silver tray. "For you, mademoiselle," he said, bowing.

"Thank you," I said, taking it.

"To us, then?" Dessie smirked, holding up her drink to toast.

"To us," I clinked my glass to hers. "The ladies brave enough to travel the world."

I took a sip and tried not to gag. The drink was very strong. No wonder they called it a 'corpse revival.' This stuff could kill a horse. Emboldened by the toxic drink in my hand, I decided to lay all my cards on the table and quit dancing around in superficial small talk.

"Dessie, I'd like to talk together woman-to-woman here," I sighed. "I think we have common ground, and I think it behooves us to get along. Be on the same page."

Dessie sat back and swirled her drink. The ice cubes clinked together softly.

"Does it?" she asked quietly.

"It does. We may be different, and maybe we don't see eye-to-eye, but we're still two women doing something that most women could never do. Or even understand. Don't you think it would be to our mutual benefit to get along? To be allies?"

She smiled, but now her smile was different. It was calculated. "I'm not sure I agree."

"Why not?"

Dessie's eyes narrowed. "It seems to me that it's to my benefit to *not* align myself with you. I'm doing pretty well on my own, even if I happen to be new to this."

"And I'm not?"

She smiled wanly. "Didn't you almost get yourself killed already? Twice?"

"Yes. So? They were honest accidents. That's the price of adventure, isn't it?"

"It sure sounds like your crew isn't very professional," she sniffed. "Our team hasn't had any close calls like you've had."

"That's because we chose to go through northern Africa first," I shot back. "Your team stuck to civilization, in Europe. We took a risk and headed to the harder route for our very first leg. Anyone would struggle through it. It's a dangerous place."

Music started, as a small trio of jazz musicians played in the center of the room. A smatter of applause interrupted us as they launched into a slow, smoky number. I took advantage of the moment and sipped my drink, trying to figure out how to outsmart Dessie.

She took advantage of the interruption, too, and went for the jugular.

"So what's the relationship between you and that handsome Captain Gallivanter, anyway? I must admit, I enjoyed getting to know him earlier."

"We're crew mates," I replied benignly. "He's our team leader."

She pursed her lips and studied me, one eyebrow raised. "Oh, is that all? You're not lovers, too?"

I tried to control myself, but my face betrayed me as I blushed involuntarily. Dessie noticed and laughed.

"I knew it," she said gleefully.

"No, that's not it at all. We're close. As teammates. I respect him."

She sipped her drink and smiled. "You're lying. Your face gives you away. You don't just respect him, you're in *love* with him."

I thought quickly. If I told her the truth, would she open up to me, too? Or would she use it against me somehow? Could I trust her? Looking at her face, I decided I couldn't. Better conceal the truth and never let her know that Cap and I were actually engaged.

She watched me, pleased at my discomfort.

"He resisted my charms today, you know," she added. "You can always tell, when a man is really in love. He didn't flirt back with me at all. He was detached, cool. Controlled. That tells me his heart is somewhere else. Now I know where."

I felt myself flush with anger. Who did she think she was, to flirt with Cap? He's a good man. *My* man. How dare she try to exploit him for her own amusement? I struggled to control myself.

"I play the same game you do, Dessie," I replied, lying. "Do you think you're the only girl that can manipulate men? I'm just stringing him along, keeping him happy with me while we're on the expedition."

"Right," she replied sarcastically. "You don't strike me as someone who possesses a single bone of subtlety, Andi."

"Think what you want," I insisted. "I'm telling you the truth. That's why I'm saying we should be friends. We're on the same page here."

Dessie looked at me, tilting her head quizzically to the side like a curious bird. "We *are* friends, Miss Gallivanter," she said. "Why would you think we're not?"

I was confused, and desperately tried to keep up with her smooth tongue. I couldn't tell where I stood with her at all. I'm sure that was her intention.

"No, I do think we're friends," I replied hastily. "I just—I want to make sure we can support each other. Publicly. You know, in the newspapers and everything? We can build each other up. Cheer each other on. Be on the same page."

Dessie smiled wide, but something about her tone still made me uneasy.

"Of course!" she exclaimed. "You mean, say nice things about each other to the reporters? Speak well of each other?"

"Yes, exactly," I exhaled, relieved she understood me.

"I'll be sure to give you all the respect you and your crew deserve, Miss Gallivanter," Dessie said, standing up and offering me her hand. "That I can promise."

I shook her hand, but took note of her words. She'd emphasized that she'd give me all the respect we *deserve*. What did that mean? What else was she planning to say?

"Thanks, Dessie. I appreciate it. And I'll be sure to support you, too. I hope you do well. I wouldn't want to diminish the accomplishments of a fellow adventurer, just to try to get ahead."

She was already walking back toward the group of men who lingered in the lobby. It appeared that most of them had stuck around, hoping she'd return. Hips swaying as she walked, Dessie abruptly stopped and turned back to me.

"Oh, Andi?" she called out. "You mentioned that you wanted us to be on the same page. Well, I do intend to be on the page. The front page, to be exact. And I'll do whatever it takes to land there, even if it means more digging into your unsavory pasts. It's not my fault the captain of your crew is hiding things. Now, if you don't mind, I have some gentlemen to entertain. I hate to keep them waiting too long."

She glided away. I noticed that every man in the vicinity watched her as she passed by them. I set my unfinished drink down and left quickly, pushing out into the cool night air outside the hotel lobby.

Cap was waiting outside for me, lounging against the wall, his fedora pulled down low over his face. In his long trench coat, instead of his usual travel uniform, no one appeared to have noticed that he was there.

"Hey, how did it go? You weren't in there very long?"

"I was in there long enough," I groaned. "And I'm not quite sure how it went. She's a hard nut to crack."

I stuffed my hands into my pockets and walked briskly down the street with him, back to our own hotel. It was cold outside, and a chilly breeze brought goosebumps to my arms.

"Do you think she's sympathetic to us now?" Cap asked, his voice low. "Did you win her over?"

"I don't know," I said, as I recounted the entire conversation to him. His mood darkened as he listened to me relay her words.

"She's playing everyone around her, isn't she?" he exhaled, rubbing his jaw. "She couldn't even give you a straight answer."

I nodded. "I think so. She is beautiful, but she uses that to her advantage. I think her crew is just delighted to have a pretty girl with them now, who gets them so much attention. Maybe they don't even see her manipulation. Or maybe they just don't want to see it."

"It concerns me especially what she said at the very end," Cap mused as we passed through a dark alley, our footsteps echoing eerily on the wet cobblestone. "She clearly loves the fame. She wants to be on the front page of the newspaper. How exactly does she plan to do that? And at what cost to us?"

"I don't know," I said, looking at my breath in the cold night air. "I'm worried, too. She specifically mentioned that you're hiding things. What else is she going to say about you?"

Cap exhaled. "I guess we'll just have to wait and see."

"We've got to get out of Europe," I groaned. "We're too close to the Chinooks. Rivals shouldn't operate this close to each other. It's bringing out the worst in all of us."

"I know. We'll keep moving. And we'll leave the Chinooks far behind us, don't worry."

"Good," I said, not bothering to keep the venom out of my voice. "Good riddance."

CHAPTER 23

WE DIDN'T WAIT LONG to find out how Dessie decided to sabotage us again. Two days after our meeting, I awoke to Bernard sliding a newspaper under my door.

"You might want to read this alone," he called through the wooden door. I heard him walk away.

I hopped out of bed and rushed to pick up the paper. The front page had a photograph of me in the center, and a tiny one of Dessie halfway through the article. The headline stared up at me.

"Andiamo Gallivanter: SAHARA SURVIVOR, OR SEDUCTIVE SIREN?"

My jaw dropped. I was the front page news? *Me*, seductive?

I quickly started reading.

"In a stunning update to the ongoing accusations of indecency about the world-famous Gallivanter Expedition crew, this reporter has just learned of new allegations against Andiamo Gallivanter, the famed young beauty of this team. According to an anonymous source close to the Gallivanters, tender Andiamo is not the good girl she desperately pretends to be. This source claims that Andiamo manipulated her way onto the team, using her feminine charms, and found her way into one of her crew member's hearts, seeking not to discover the world but to play the heartstrings of her masculine compatriots to cheat her way into her share of the winning prize. Andiamo is reportedly in an intimate romantic relationship with the dashing Captain Grant Gallivanter, leader of the small crew."

Oh, no. I felt the blood drain away from my face. I continued reading.

"Miss Gallivanter, the oldest daughter of Mrs. Megan Warren, hails from North America and dropped out of her final year of boarding school to join the expedition. One might think her refined background at prestigious European institutions would give her an understanding of how to behave like a proper young woman, but it appears that she has chosen to live as a temptress, a vixen who plays with the affections of men to benefit herself."

A temptress? A *vixen*? Words like this had never been used to describe me. Not in my wildest dreams.

I thought back to long days of driving through the desert, sunburns on my face from where my goggles didn't cover. Of the crusted clothes I wore, day after day, as we sweated and chilled and sweated again in the same uniforms. I remembered all the times where I'd crawled under the vehicles to change the oil, spattering myself with black liquid. The grime that took several washes to scrub away, the grease that was constantly under my nails.

I was a member of the crew, plain and simple. I did the same jobs the men did. I was no temptress.

Frustrated, I rattled the paper and swore under my breath as I read the last paragraph.

"According to previous reports, Captain Gallivanter unceremoniously left his own fiancée at the altar, and despite her repeated attempts to reconcile, has ignored her completely. Captain Gallivanter recently came out in the press to share his side of the story, but this reporter has to wonder why he held a press conference about all of this when he did. It is now clear, considering these new revelations about Miss Andiamo, that she may be nothing more than an old-fashioned home wrecker who had no consideration for the feelings and future of Miss Mildred Johnson, Mr. Gallivanter's ill-fated fiancée.

Miss Dessie Hickson, the beautiful and talented young woman who became a recent addition to the Gallivanter Expedition's rival team, the Chinook Voyageurs, shared her opinion on the matter. 'Some girls care more about collecting hearts than driving cars and contributing to the team,' she explained. 'Not all of us can be professionals and share a workplace with men. It's unfortunate but true that some women will just give the rest of us a bad name through their indecent behavior.'

As to the relationship between Mr. Gallivanter and Miss Andiamo, one can only speculate what the future may be. One question nags the mind of this reporter, however: was adventure all she was after, or was she looking for something more all along?"

I threw the paper down in disgust. Birds chirped outside my window, enjoying the morning sun, but I felt nothing but rage. Based on my conversation with her the other day, Dessie was obviously behind this article.

No doubt she'd orchestrated the first article, as well.

Angrily, I pictured my mother and sister reading this article once it circulated into the United States. What would they think? What about my friends, Clara and Arnau? My old classmates?

I looked like an absolute fool.

Shoving my feet into my shoes and throwing on a robe, I banged open my door and stalked down the hall to Cap's room. I knocked, but he didn't answer. I balled up my fist and hit the door again, this time harder. Still, he didn't come to the door.

"Where is he?" I growled to myself. Stomping back to my room, I quickly readied for the day. I strode into the hotel breakfast lounge, my steps clacking an angry staccato on the marble floor.

Cap and Chito sat together, untouched cups of coffee in front of both of them. Cap's head was bent, writing furiously on a notepad.

I reached the table and pulled out my chair so hard that it nearly toppled over. "Did you see it already?"

"Yes," Cap replied, looking up with a troubled expression. "I read it."

"Front page news," Chito whistled. "At least it was a flattering picture of you, Andi."

"Can you believe it?" I sputtered. "I'm no home wrecker! How dare they!"

Chito reached over and laid his big hand on my arm sympathetically. "Calm down. We know it's not true. We're on your side here. You don't need to cause a scene in the hotel."

I took a deep breath. "Now I know how you felt, Cap, when your article came out."

"It's awful," he nodded. "Slander is a vile thing. But don't worry. I'm already working on an article of our own, to counter this one."

"Are you sure we should? " I asked, shaking my head as I watched Cap return to his paper. He had nearly a page written already. "This is accelerating now. The Chinooks are playing dirty. I thought we decided not to stoop to their level?"

"It's different now," Cap said, his voice hard. "I don't care what they say about me. But when they go after the woman I love? It's war."

"What are you writing?"

"I'm telling the truth," Cap replied, tapping his pen against the table. "I'm writing out what actually happened. Clearly, it wasn't enough that I said it during a press conference. I need to get it out in print, too. And this time, I'm not holding back. I'm telling the world in no uncertain terms that Milly left me, ran off with another man, and tried to ruin my life by throwing me in jail. And that this all occurred years ago, many years before I even met you. And I'm writing about your character—your value to this team. We'll show the world that you're no home wrecker, Andi. We didn't even know each other until a year ago."

I sighed. He gently laid his hand on mine.

"We'll get through this, I promise," he said, his eyes full of meaning. "Even if I had to put up with a lifetime of this kind of garbage, I'd still choose you. I'd still fight for you."

I exhaled through my nose. Despite Cap's opinion, I wasn't sure that firing back an article of our own was the best form of defense right now. What if they twisted that one against us too? I watched as he pulled his hand away and continued scribbling, going back and crossing out phrases to add new ones in.

A few moments later, Bernard joined us and grabbed for a croissant without saying a word. He looked at me as he chewed his croissant.

"Stupid reporters," he groused, shaking his head. "Stupid Chinooks. Now you know why I don't get close to people. They just find a way to hurt you somehow."

"That's baloney," Chito replied, shaking his head. "Not all people are awful, Bernard. It's just the fact that we're rivals. We've made ourselves a target. They must genuinely feel threatened by us, or they wouldn't be going to such lengths to try to discredit us."

"We'll win," Bernard stated flatly. "We'll show those Chinooks. Their lies and half-truths can't stop us."

"Cap, what's the travel plan?" Chito asked. "Can we get back on the road anytime soon?"

"Sooner rather than later, definitely. We're getting out of Paris and going south," Cap replied. "We'll get this article out and get on the road again. I'm tired of being wrapped up in this petty drama with the Chinooks. I just want to get as far away from them as we can. It's not good for either of us to squabble like this in the eyes of the public. We'll head through southern France and keep traveling. I'll figure out the stops as soon as I've finished this article."

As he spoke, he held up the pages he'd written.

"I think this will do. It tells the rest of the story, about my stint in jail. Once this gets out, they won't have anything left to dig up about me. No skeletons left in the closet."

"I don't think you should write about your time in prison, Cap," I protested. "What if it causes people to lose trust in you? What if it affects all you've done, as the leader of our crew?"

"I need to own up to it," he frowned. "It's the last thing they could possibly try to use against me, to make us look bad. I need to get in front of it."

"But they haven't brought it up yet," I argued. "Maybe they don't even know."

"Or maybe they do, and they've been sitting on it, waiting to drop the most sensational story on the world at just the right time," Chito pointed out.

"All my life, I've tried to be a good person," Cap groaned, his voice heavy with frustration. "I worked hard to pull myself out of a terrible childhood. Out of poverty. To serve my country with pride. To work with my two hands, save my money and invest and do something that matters."

"And then—Milly," Bernard interjected.

"Exactly," Cap sighed. "Milly destroyed all of that, with her lies. And she tainted my future by turning me in to the police and telling them I was a dirty German spy, just because I have an accent. If I would've known then that a relationship with the wrong person would haunt me for this long—"

He shook his head.

"I hate her for what she's still doing to me," he continued bitterly. "And I cannot believe that the past I've tried so hard to put behind me is continuing to follow me, ruining things now that I'm happier than I've ever been. Now that I'm doing something I've always dreamed of doing."

"Your past doesn't define you," Chito said, putting his hand on Cap's shoulder sympathetically. "No one who knows you thinks less of you. It's clear that you were a victim. You were at the wrong place at the wrong time, and happened to have a European accent at the exact time that everyone in America was terrified about spies during the war. That's behind you now. *You* have to leave it behind you, and move on. Stop worrying about how people interpret your past."

Cap looked up at the ceiling, shaking his head.

"I have to get it out," he said, his jaw set. "I'll come clean about my time in prison, because it has to come from me first. If it doesn't, and the Chinooks leak that story, I'll look like a liar. I'll lose the trust of anyone who ever respected me."

"We're with you, Cap," I replied. "We'll stand beside you no matter what happens. No matter what the press says about you."

"I know," he said, lowering his gaze to his notebook. "I better finish this. I need to get it out as soon as possible."

He picked up his pen and continued writing.

Chito and Bernard and I exchanged glances over his downcast head. I could read their faces plainly, even though they didn't say a word.

"I hope this works," I echoed their sentiment in my own head.

CHAPTER 24

CAP'S ARTICLE HIT THE front page of the papers the next morning. As we expected, the dramatic story got picked up by multiple newspapers.

"FAMOUS CAPTAIN GALLIVANTER A JAILBIRD?" proclaimed one headline.

"CAPTAIN GALLIVANTER: TRAVELING AWAY FROM HIS DARK PAST?" said another.

We flipped through a stack of newspapers together at breakfast, scanning the stories. Chito and I tried to keep the mood light, knowing Cap's inward embarrassment.

"Oh, here's a good picture of you," I said, holding up one article. Cap was handsomely facing the camera and grinning, his helmet under his arm. *"INTREPID EXPLORER OR BROODING BAD BOY?"* screamed the headline above the photograph.

"They're at least following the facts correctly," I uttered, scanning the article. "You were right, it was good that you put it out. That the truth is finally out there, on your terms."

"Should I cut this one out for our scrapbook?" Chito joked, paging through another paper. "Andi, trade me. This one's in French. I can't read it."

"I'm glad you all think this is so amusing," Cap said darkly. "Let me tell you, even though I expected it, it's still not pleasant to read such nasty articles about yourself. I feel like a fool."

"We don't think it's amusing at all," Bernard piped up. "We're just trying to let you know it's not a big deal to us. We know who you are, Cap. Headlines won't change our opinion of you."

The three of us paused, staring at Bernard. He sipped his coffee, staring back.

"What?" he finally asked, nettled.

"Where did that come from?" Chito exclaimed. "You're insightful at all the wrong times, Bernard. I don't get you. You're sarcastic when we're serious, and serious when the rest of us are joking."

Bernard glared over his coffee cup. "This is exactly why I don't talk more often. You jump down my throat when I say anything."

"No, no," Chito said, holding up his hands. "It's just that...what you said was so *profound*."

"Well, I won't make that mistake again, will I?" Bernard shot back.

"You guys," Cap smiled, in spite of himself. "You're the oddest crew. Bernard, thank you. I appreciate the sentiment. And the support."

I smiled, but secretly prayed the American press hadn't picked up any of these stories. If my mother read them, she'd be disgusted. What would she think when she saw this news about Cap being in prison and judged him before I'd even told her what a good man he was? And that I was marrying him? I pushed the thought from my mind, searching to change the subject.

"So Chito and I thought we could take a boat tour on the Seine today," I said brightly. "You know, get our minds off of things. Out of the newspapers."

Bernard started to protest, and Chito cut him off. "You too, Bernard. All of us together."

"Sure," Cap said, his eyes still on the newspapers. "Whatever you think."

"Cap, come on," I said, putting my hand on his arm. "This storm will pass, too. They always do."

"I know. But being stuck in the thunderstorm still isn't any fun."

We changed into warmer clothes and headed out into the sunshine, looking for the tour boats that took us down the Seine River, through the very heart of Paris. Wearing warm coats and scarves, we blended in with the rest of the tourists who boarded the large boat near the base of the Eiffel Tower.

The rare anonymity was healing balm. For a few hours, we laughed and gazed up at the buildings, watching people on the shore as they went about their day. Every plaza we drifted by looked like a scene from a painting, filled with gorgeous old buildings and gardens and vibrant, well-dressed people.

"This is what I needed," Cap said softly, standing next to me at the railing. He wore a hat, but the wind buffeted his blonde hair and highlighted the strong cheekbones he had. "I needed to get out here and remember why we do this. That a great big global adventure waits for us, despite the frustrating interruptions along the way."

"I know," I smiled. "You have a good crew, a woman to love, and a bright future. You'll be fine."

"Don't forget, he has an exhaustive itinerary to take us around the world, too," Bernard said, from the other side of Cap. "We all know that's what he cares about most."

"We need to get back on the road and find ourselves again," Cap said thoughtfully, pushing a strand of my hair that was blowing on his face away and tucking it behind my ear for me. "This tour of Europe, going back and forth between presentations and schmoozing people, is getting old."

"I agree," I replied.

"You didn't ask for *my* opinion, I see," Chito teased. "But I'm with you on this one, Cap. This team doesn't do well in captivity."

"We'll be back at it soon enough," Cap promised, staring at the river. It flowed gently past us, alive with movement and smaller boats bobbing in our wake.

"The Gallivanters need new adventures," I said, elbowing Chito. "New experiences. New memories to make."

"But not any new troubles," Bernard's thin voice chimed in. "Let's keep that in mind, you optimistic idiots."

———◦———

WE LOUNGED BY THE GRAND fireplace in the hotel that night, as Cap consulted his maps and scribbled out new plans for us.

"We'll head south out of Paris, into Bern, Switzerland," Cap pointed to the map. "From there, we can cut back up into Germany, dip through Austria, and cut back down through Italy."

He glanced up at us, a stack of notes in his hand.

"How do you all feel about seeing some art in Italy? Some of the most incredible museums in the world are there. Why, Michelangelo's statues alone would take up a whole day..."

"Sounds great!" Chito exclaimed as Bernard groaned.

Cap ignored Bernard, scribbling notes as he muttered his thoughts. "We'll stop and take in all scenery and museums. And the Colosseum and St. Peter's Basilica in Rome, of course. Maybe the crypts? I'll need to arrange private tours. Rome needs a week, maybe more. And we'll hit Venice—oh, yes, gondola rides—the glass factories, too—and Florence, of course..."

"So you want me to get supplies for what, a few weeks?" Chito asked, taking out a notepad.

"Yes," Cap said, starting to list off things we needed. "How about we work on it for the next two or three days, and then head out? Bernard, Andi, you're on car duty."

"Sounds like a plan," Chito said, smiling over Cap's head at me. He gave me a quick thumbs up.

Cap had already rebounded back to his old self, busy plotting our journey forward. And we were finally hitting the road. After these frustrating incidents with those awful Chinook Voyageurs, things were looking up.

"Nothing can stop the Gallivanters," I thought to myself. *"We're finally back to just being a fun-loving group of friends, having an adventure around the world together."*

CHAPTER 25

WE SPENT ALL DAY PREPARING for our departure, visiting shops and market stalls, collecting food and packing supplies for the trip.

Bernard and I diligently prepared the Model T Fords, checking every part of the engines, undercarriage, and tires for signs of weakness or damage.

While the team worked, Cap sent a flurry of telegrams to arrange hotel rooms and speaking engagements. It was tedious work, and had to be done in a certain order. Our base hotel had to be established first, so all the rest of the telegrams could be sent there next. Cap had to carefully time and track each telegram, so that it didn't get sent too far ahead or get sent to a location we'd just left.

After a long day of paperwork, we tore Cap away from his desk and dragged him to dinner. The walk to the small, dimly lit restaurant was short, and we listened to a woman croon in French at a nearby bar as we walked.

"This is one of our last nights in Paris," Chito said, listening to the deep tone of the woman's husky voice. "It's a beautiful place, but I've never been so ready to leave somewhere."

"I know how you feel," I agreed. We were explorers. We weren't meant to settle down in one place for too long.

At dinner, we toasted each other with wine.

"We never drink," Cap said, laughing as Chito ordered a preposterously expensive bottle for the table.

"We're drinking tonight," Chito said firmly. "Besides, we can finally afford the good stuff. All work and no play isn't good for you, Captain. We need to take time to celebrate. So raise a toast with me, team—to leaving our personal baggage behind and heading out to new adventures, with a lightened load!"

After one bottle, Chito merrily ordered another.

"It's back to beans and rice and tinned meat after this," he guffawed, ordering a third bottle. "We deserve a little treat before we get back to roughing it!"

The four of us stumbled back to our hotel rooms that night, giggling, avoiding interactions with fans by draping ourselves in hats and scarves. I fell into bed as soon as I took off my boots.

⎯⎯⎯⎯ ◉ ⎯⎯⎯⎯

I SLEPT DREAMLESSLY, and awoke the next morning to the sound of someone swearing loudly. Cracking my eyes open, I squinted against the harsh sunlight streaming into my window.

"My head," I groaned, putting my hand up to block the light. My window was open, and I heard swearing again.

I frowned. It sounded like Cap. *He must feel as lousy as I do,* I thought, struggling to prop myself up.

I was still wearing my outfit from the night before, and my white shirt and khaki pants were wrinkled. I didn't even care.

Too much wine, I thought to myself groggily, rubbing my temples. I had a massive headache. So much for celebrating the night before. I was paying for it now.

A door slammed in the hallway and I winced. I reached for my boots, but my head spun. Instead, I shuffled out of bed and stepped into the hallway barefoot.

Chito peeked out of his door when he heard my knock. "My head," he groaned.

"Mine, too."

"We have no tolerance for alcohol," Chito moaned, squinting at me. "Don't let me drink ever again. I feel like dying."

"Why'd you order it in the first place?"

"I was trying to be nice!" he exclaimed, then closed his eyes in pain. "Cap was stressed. You were stressed. I thought we could just relax a little bit, and enjoy ourselves for once."

"Well, we did. Until now."

He looked at me through the slits in his eyes. "Did you hear someone yelling earlier? It sounded like Cap."

"Yeah. That's why I came out of my room," I said, staring down at my bare feet. "Should I go put on shoes?"

"Probably," Chito said, yawning. "Where's everyone else?"

Bernard emerged at the end of the hallway, fully dressed. "Morning," he said, taking out his key to open his door.

"Bernard, you're already up?" Chito stared at him.

"Been up for a while now," Bernard replied. "So has Cap. I just passed him."

"Where'd he go?" I asked, squinting. My head throbbed.

Bernard grimaced. "You might want to give him some time to cool off. He just read the morning papers."

"Oh no," Chito said, throwing his head back against the door frame. It thumped and he winced. "What now? What is there left to even say?"

"How bad is it?" I asked Bernard. "More articles about him?"

Bernard whistled. "It's bad. You'll see."

"Don't whistle," Chito groaned, putting his hands up to his ears to block the noise. "Andi, this one's all yours. I need to go lie down. And never get up again."

I ducked back into my room and slipped into my boots, running my fingers through my hair as I rushed down the hall. I reached the lobby, where several guests relaxed with their morning papers and breakfast. I tried to duck out without being noticed and besieged by fans. Cap was nowhere to be seen.

As I wandered through the crowd, I noticed a man reading a paper with Cap's photograph on the front.

"LAWBREAKING LEADER?" was the headline, in French. The stranger was reading with interest.

Through a window, I spotted Cap outside, his back to me, starting down a side street. I darted out the front doors after him.

"Cap!" I called, jogging down the cobblestone alley.

He whipped around. He was wearing his fedora and trench coat, and looked murderously angry. "What?"

"The papers?"

"Yes, the papers," he spat. "Go read them yourself. See what they say about me. I'm going for a walk. Don't come with me. I need to be alone."

"It can't be that bad," I protested. "There's nothing else left that they can throw at you!"

"They questioned my character, Andi," he scowled. "They're casting doubt about my leadership abilities. They're saying I'm no role model. Do you know how that makes me feel? When I've worked my whole life to be a good man, a man of integrity? Just—I—just read it. I need to think."

Without another glance, he turned around and stalked away.

Chito was downstairs, blinking painfully, as I reentered the lobby. We asked for the day's newspapers, and the receptionist handed them over.

"Sorry about your friend," the receptionist said to me, in French. "He seems like such a nice man. How terrible that the papers are talking about him like this. He's always been so kind to our staff, and to all the fans I've seen him interacting with here."

"Thank you," I replied, in French. "He is a nice man. He doesn't deserve this. But you know how newspapers are—always looking to sell the sensational."

Folding the papers under my arm, I sat down with Chito and paged through the newspapers. Every paper had an article in it about Cap, all of them negative. Every reporter seemed to be questioning his past, his motives, and his ability to lead others.

And it was no surprise to me that in every article, Dessie and Hudson Landry, the Chinook Voyageurs' captain, were quoted speaking negatively about us.

I read Hudson's remarks in several different articles with growing anger.

"'I'm sure Captain Gallivanter is a perfectly fine man, but one must wonder if an ex-convict is capable of leading an expedition for world peace? Is this the type of man we want to hold up to the world as a role model?' says Captain Hudson Landry, leader of the famed Chinook Voyageurs. Landry, a handsome, ambitious man from Quebec, Canada, brings years of reliable leadership to his team. Their crew of nine, competing against the Gallivanter team, has not been plagued by constant ugly revelations about their past like the Gallivanters have. 'We're a solid group, a respectable team,' Landry shares. 'We're professional, without a stained and unsavory past to haunt any of us. We're confident that we're the right people to bring international attention to this competition, and that we'll win it in the end. We wish the Gallivanters the best of luck. Clearly, they have a hole to dig out of, so they'll need it.'"

Chito glanced at me over the top of his paper. "Still glad he came clean about his time in prison?"

"Imagine if he hadn't? The Chinooks would've used it against him, eventually, probably telling the barest sliver of truth about it all. At least we controlled how it came out."

"If you can call this control," Chito exhaled, scanning the papers. "These articles are pretty much all the same, from what I can see. Inferring that maybe Cap shouldn't be the face of this sort of competition. They all have these same quotes from Landry and Dessie. They must've held a press conference of their own."

"Cap is in a rage," I said. "He's pacing the streets right now."

"We need to get him out of here," Chito sighed. "It's getting worse for us, and for him especially, the longer we stay in Paris. He keeps taking hit after hit, and it doesn't help him when he sees his face all over these newspapers every other day. We need to get on the road right away. Shake him out of this mood. Today."

"Today?" I blinked. "Do you think we can leave that fast? We're heading into mountain territory after this, and that requires more preparation."

"Bernard told me the cars are ready. We have plenty of fuel and supplies. I can check us out of the hotel, if you go up and tell Bernard and start packing our things."

"Fine," I tossed the paper down on the table and stood. "Let's do it."

⎯⎯⎯◉⎯⎯⎯

WE WORKED FURIOUSLY, enlisting Bernard to help us pack Cap's items from his room and load up the cars. Within the hour, the three of us were sitting in the Fords out front, waiting for Cap to return.

"What if he doesn't come back?" Bernard said, chewing on a toothpick.

Chito shot him a look. "Right. You think he's planning to abandon his fiancée, his best friends, his three vehicles, and his life's work? Do you even know the man, Bernard? He's an honorable guy. He'd never walk out on his commitments."

"I meant during the day," Bernard replied calmly. "Maybe he's clear across town, staring up at some paintings in the museums."

"He'll be back," I insisted. "Cap's anger burns hot, but burns out quickly."

Sure enough, within a few minutes, we spotted Cap trudging back down the street, his head down and both hands in his pockets. He still looked mad. Chito beeped the horn.

Cap stopped short, staring at us sitting in the Fords. "What's going on? Why are you all in the cars?"

"We're leaving," I grinned. "Get in."

"But we're not leaving yet," Cap replied, sounding confused. "I already made the hotel reservations. It's all lined up. We don't leave Paris until the day after tomorrow."

"We made a team decision, in your absence," Chito smiled. "Come on. We all need to get out of Paris."

"But my stuff is still in my room—"

"We packed it. It's already in the Fords."

"But what about the maps? The paperwork?"

"Also packed," I chirped, patting the large bag sitting next to me on the seat of my Ford.

Cap stared at us, still not moving from where he'd first stopped.

"But we don't have hotel reservations anywhere yet," he shook his head. "And we're leaving too late in the day. We should be leaving first thing in the morning."

"So we drive until we find a small town with a few open rooms," Chito shrugged. "Or we sleep in the cars. We can wing it for a few days. Come on, this is the team that scrapped our way through sandstorms and deserts and jungles. We think well on our feet. So let's get on our feet already."

Cap shook his head slowly.

"Get in," I called, beeping at him again.

"You're ridiculous," he sighed, wrinkling his nose. "You're all ridiculous."

I beeped again and Chito laughed out loud.

"Get in the car, Cap," Chito yelled. "For once in your life, do something unscripted and impulsive and enjoy it, man! You have a pretty girl ready to drive you anywhere you want, and you're just going to stand there, gawking at her?"

Cap shook his head, but now a smile slowly crept across his face.

"I give up," he said, taking off his fedora and climbing into the passenger seat of my Ford. I handed him his helmet and driving goggles.

"You have to promise me one thing, as my passenger," I said.

"What?"

"You're not allowed to talk about your past anymore. No more memories of Milly, or prison, or mistakes you've made, or regrets or anything. No more talk about the newspapers and what they've said about us. No more conversation about those damn Chinook Voyageurs. We're leaving Paris, and we're leaving all of that behind us."

"What if I disagree?"

"Then you can hitchhike your way out of Paris. I'll dump you right out of this car and leave you on the side of the road."

He laughed. "I think I've created a monster. Those Catholic nuns you had for teachers would roll over in their graves if they knew how you talked to men now."

I grinned as I started the Ford and began to inch forward. "You're assuming those old ladies are already dead. I know they're not. They'll never die. Besides, I didn't really need all their lessons about how to catch a man, now, did I?"

The sound of our laughter filled the air as we revved the engines and rolled down the streets of Paris, out to the country.

CHAPTER 26

THE FIELDS BLAZED BRILLIANTLY in the late afternoon sun, shades of greens and browns and yellows filling the horizon.

Paris was hours behind us now, and we sailed through France, alternating between navigating tiny villages and open countryside dotted with little farms.

Every so often, we passed remnants of the Great War, upturned trees and miles of trenches, the dirt now covered with a restorative layer of grass and wildflowers. The ugly black shells of burned homes and barns and random piles of broken wagons and stretchers were often the only indication that fierce fighting had stained this bucolic landscape red with misery and death only a few years before.

"I hate to say it, but you all were right," Cap said, pulling off his helmet and letting the breeze lift his hair. "I'm happier being out here on the road again."

"I knew you would be," I replied. "You've had far too much on that mind of yours lately. You need to remember why we're doing this in the first place. I think you're often too caught up in the work of planning this expedition to actually enjoy the journey itself. "

"I feel so much better being out here in nature," he reflected, staring out at the fields. Several cows stood in the plains in front of us, chewing on high grass. "I'm happiest when we're on the move, seeing the world like this. I start to feel claustrophobic when we're stuck in one place too long. I'm a wanderer, I guess."

"*We* are wanderers," I corrected him. He smiled to himself, looking out at the road in front of us.

We stopped in a small nameless town at dusk, at a simple inn with only three rooms. The innkeeper nearly keeled over with excitement at the prospect of hosting celebrities. Chito and Cap volunteered to share a room, and Bernard and I settled into our own spaces.

The furniture in my room was ancient, and my bed was covered with a handmade lace blanket. Cheap black and white photographs of Paris were hung on the walls. I could hear Chito and Cap talking from their room next door.

I thumped the wall and grinned.

"I'll hear you both snoring through this flimsy wall," I called to Chito, through the plaster. He chuckled from the other side.

Dinner was a simple affair, refreshing after the weeks of fine dining we'd enjoyed in the cities. The innkeeper's wife came over from the main house, promptly asked us for our autographs, and then made us a hearty meat stew, loaded with carrots and potatoes. She served us fresh bread with thick, salty butter. She also made us a small pot of lentils, seasoned with pepper and onion and bay leaves.

"Everything is slower out here," I observed in French, making conversation with the innkeeper's wife between bites of my meal. "It's relaxing, after being in the hectic pace of Paris."

She smiled at me, laying another slice of bread down on my plate. "Most of France is like this. It's rural and simple. We are not fancy. We choose to live like this. We prefer this way of life."

"I can see why," I replied, thinking about Arnau, my childhood beau, for the first time in a long time. He'd chosen a simple life, like this. I could see the appeal, and I enjoyed it for a time, but it wasn't where I wanted to stay.

My little sister, too, seemed content to stay in the home we'd grown up in. She had no interest in travel, no desire to even explore beyond the same city we'd lived in our entire lives. She was happy to hold onto the same friends, sleep in the same bed, and have the same experiences day after day, until she grew old.

Like Cap, I also felt claustrophobic when I was stuck in one place for long. As a child, my only mode of escape was riding horses and reading books about distant lands. Looking back, I could see clearly that I'd never been destined to live a traditional life. I thanked my lucky stars that I'd ended up traveling the world with the Gallivanters.

I tossed and turned that night, thinking about the strange journey my life had become. I realized I was essentially homeless now. I didn't belong with my mother and sister in America, nor did I belong in boarding school. I'd been traveling with the Gallivanters now for nearly a year, and we didn't have a home base anywhere. At the most, we stayed a few days at a time in every city.

Where did I belong?

How could someone like Arnau or my sister know with such certainty that they belonged where they did, but I had no idea?

Where was my home?

"Maybe home isn't so much about a location, as it is the people you choose to surround yourself with," I thought. *"And maybe family is more than who you're born to, but who you choose to let into your life and stay there."*

I drifted off to sleep, seeing glimpses of the desert and the mountains and the night sky in my dreams.

CHAPTER 27

I WOKE UP TO THE SOUND of chickens clucking in the backyard of a nearby farm. It was the familiar symphony of my childhood. I lay in bed and listened to it.

I noticed Cap and Chito's soft snoring from the room next door.

"At least I won't have any surprises, getting married to Cap," I thought with a grin. *"I've already lived with him for a year. I know all his bad habits and peculiarities."*

Outside, the sky was awash with vivid hues of pink and orange. Impulsively, I decided to take a walk in the nearby fields. I'd glimpsed a tiny grove of trees at the end of a long stone fence, and I realized how much I craved a walk through the woods upon seeing it.

"I'm feeling sentimental," I thought, pulling on my boots and tying my hair back with a ribbon. *"It's this simple country life. It reminds me of my childhood. And of boarding school in France, with the horses and the trips through the woods."*

I tiptoed out of my room, closing my door softly so I didn't wake anyone else. The fresh, cold air hit my face and I breathed deeply. My arms got goosebumps in the sudden chill. I pulled my jacket tighter, walking down the back steps into the dawn.

I meandered along the fence line toward the trees, letting my fingers brush against the cold rocks. The stone fence seemed ancient, covered in centuries of moss.

"How long can someone be happy in one place?" I thought, looking around. *"It's beautiful here, but do you tire of it eventually?"*

Would Cap and I settle down in a place like this? Or were we destined to always be traveling, constantly in search of a new destination?

The trees loomed above me as I made my way into the woods. Birds chirped in the branches above me, and I looked up at the leaves fluttering in the breeze. The forest was thick, the morning light dimmer here as the canopy crowded out the sunlight.

I froze, struck by a sudden memory of staring up into the leaves of the jungle in French Sudan.

I'd nearly died in that jungle, after being thrown from a wild stallion that dashed me through the unforgiving foliage and stranded me, alone, miles away from my team. That had been the last time I stood in a forest and looked up into the trees above me.

A cold chill went through me. I bit my lip, willing myself to stay calm. I was suddenly, and nonsensically, awash in panic.

"You're in France now," I told myself. *"You're safe. You're behind your own hotel. Your team is right inside, sleeping. You're safe. This isn't the jungle."*

I closed my eyes, and counted to ten slowly, trying to control my erratic mind. I reached ten, and kept my eyes squeezed shut, counting now to one hundred. My heart was racing.

"Calm down," I told myself. *"You're Andi Gallivanter. You can handle this. Look how far you've come. You're a survivor. You won't be trapped, not even in your own memories."*

Slowly, I opened my eyes. I stood motionless, listening to the sound of the wind rustle the leaves. I forced myself to take a step forward. I heard a rustle in the forest ahead of me.

"Keep going," I whispered to myself. *"Conquer this. You cannot live in terror of the forests. You're stronger than your fear."*

I took another step. And another.

The branches above me quivered in the wind. I walked quietly, softly, my feet barely making a sound on the dead leaves that carpeted the ground. My pulse was slowing, but my skin still crawled.

Suddenly, I stopped. My panic vanished in the face of unexpected apprehension. My entire body was on high alert, listening to the faintest sound out here in the woods.

I was not alone.

I sensed him before I even saw him. A man stood dressed in a heavy coat, facing away from me in a small clearing.

I froze and watched him with big eyes. He was violently swinging his arms. Was he killing something? Or someone?

"Ah, zut!" he exclaimed loudly, pumping his right hand in the air triumphantly. It was covered in something dark and wet.

Blood?

I squinted, trying to figure out what he was doing. He bent forward, examining something in front of him, his body blocking my view.

He made small grunting sounds now, as I crept closer, staying close to the trees. His knees were slightly bent, and he was pitched forward, off balance. If I had to, I was confident I could shove him over and run away. Out of habit, too, I had a knife in my boot. I'd practiced with Cap. I knew how to use it.

I held my breath as I slipped silently around a tree, inching closer. I still couldn't see what he was doing. With my back against a tree, I leaned forward. My jacket caught on the branch of a tree and made a slight rustling sound.

"He couldn't have heard that," I breathed.

Slowly, his head turned toward me. He met my eyes and instantly yelped.

"Mon Dieu!" he shrieked, leaping back. I looked at what was in front of him.

It was an easel, with a large canvas covered in splotches of red and orange and brown paint propped on it. In front of it, a wooden box of paints and some brushes and rags sat in the dirt.

"Who are you?" he yelled at me in French, brandishing a paintbrush in front of him like a sword.

"I'm so sorry," I responded hastily, in French. "I'm just out for a stroll in the woods. It's so early that I thought I would be alone."

"You're not!" he yelled, still crouched in position with his paintbrush pointed at me. His hands were covered in dark red paint, I noticed. Not blood, like I'd thought.

My fear turned to amusement. "Are you an artist?"

"Of course I am," he snapped, lowering his brush. "What else would I be doing out here this early? I was capturing the essence of this sunrise in this forest. It's so *alive* here. Such raw beauty."

"Oh," I replied. He still held his brush level with my face, like he was in the middle of a fencing match. "Do you really think you could defend yourself with that paintbrush?"

"Yes. Absolutely."

"How? A brush can't hurt someone."

"If I stabbed someone in the eye with it, yes, it would hurt someone very much."

"If you're going to be out here, you need a knife, like this," I said, pulling my knife out of my boot. He instantly took a step back.

"Don't kill me!" he shrieked. "I'm just an artist! I haven't even hit my prime yet!"

"I'm not threatening you," I said gently, holding the knife in my palm. "I'm showing you. If you're going to be out in the woods, alone, you need to make sure you have something to defend yourself. There are wild animals out here. People, even. You could get hurt."

"Animals don't scare me," he stared at me with big brown eyes. "But you, on the other hand? You look like you could hurt me."

"I do?"

"Yes," he shifted. He was obviously uneasy. "Are you a soldier? You're wearing a uniform."

"I'm just a girl. I'm Andiamo. I'm with the Gallivanter Expedition. The ones from the news."

"Who?" he said, squinting at me. "Gollyvander?"

"Don't you read the newspapers? We're the team traveling all over the world together. We're very famous."

He shook his head. "I'm an artist. I don't consume the drivel of the world. I live in here, in the real world—the wilderness of my own mind."

As he talked, he pointed to his forehead with the handle of his paintbrush. A blob of paint slowly oozed off the end of his brush and splattered on the ground in front of him.

"Hm," I said, watching him. I looked back at his painting. It didn't exactly resemble trees or a sunrise. It was a blotchy mess of colors and thick layers of paint.

"I'm an Impressionist," he said, following my gaze. "You know, like Degas and Monet? Renoir?"

I shook my head. He gasped, clutching his hand to his chest like I'd insulted him. "Surely you've heard of some of them. Morisot? Sisley? Pissarro? Cézanne?"

"Nothing rings a bell," I replied, studying his canvas. "It looks...colorful."

"That's the whole point, Mademoiselle Gladymatter," he said, softening as he gazed fondly on his art. "The colors meld together to create a visual feast for your eyes. You see the essence of the scene, the very soul of the woods and the sun. It is magical and inexplicable at the same time."

"It's Gallivanter, not Gladymatter,'" I said.

He shrugged. "I'm close enough."

We stood looking at each other for a moment. This was not what I expected to see out here on my morning walk.

"Well, I was just passing through, out for a stroll," I said, turning to go. "Sorry to disturb you. I have to get back, anyway. My team is leaving today."

"Where are you going?"

"We're going southeast, to Switzerland."

"Will you be passing through Besançon?" he asked, his tone suddenly interested.

"I think so," I frowned. "Why?"

"I need to get there. To Besançon."

I stared at him, blinking back confusion. In a matter of a few moments, we'd gone from me thinking he was a killer to *him* thinking I was a killer. And now he wanted me to drive him somewhere?

"We don't take passengers, I'm sorry," I replied. "We're on an expedition. It's a pretty big deal. Like I said, we're very famous."

"Famous or not, you can give me a ride," he said, tossing his paintbrush into a small box and collecting the small tubes of paint scattered on the ground. He picked up his painting and collapsed his easel in a swift motion.

"Hold on, now," I said, staring at him as he picked up his painting under one arm and grabbed the easel and box with his free hand. "I didn't agree to take you anywhere. I don't even know you."

"I'm Hubert," he said, nodding his head at me like we were shaking hands. "Pleased to meet you, Miss Gillyvant."

"It's Gallivanter, and I still haven't said yes," I protested, hurrying behind him as he strode out of the woods.

For such an odd, bulky fellow, he was moving quickly. I rushed to keep up.

"I assume you're staying at the inn?" he said, taking long strides. We cleared the woods in a few moments, and made our way back down along the stone wall.

"Well," I hesitated, not sure I wanted him to know where we were staying.

"And those three automobiles out in front of the inn belong to you?"

"Yes," I said, wrinkling my forehead. "You sure notice a lot of details for someone who claims to live only in his own brain."

"It's how all artists think," he said, weaving around a large puddle in the road. "We concentrate on the things that really matter, like the way the sunlight illuminates the delicate tendrils of an unfolding fern, or how moonlight shimmers on the still surface of the lake. We notice the trivial trappings of the world, like politicians and automobiles, but we choose not to care about them."

"Unless you want to use them, courtesy of someone else," I pointed out. He made a small sound of disgust and kept walking.

"What exactly is your plan here?" I asked, trailing behind him. Cap wasn't the type of man who was prone to pick up hitchhikers. I couldn't see Hubert getting too far with him with this line of reasoning, either.

"I'm going to endear myself to your teammates," Hubert replied, his voice cheerful. "And I will trade you this painting, as payment for your services."

I frowned. No one would want that painting. It was hideous.

We reached the back door of the inn and Hubert reached for the knob.

"Hey! You can't just let yourself in there!" I exclaimed. "This isn't your home. We're the ones paying to stay here, not you!"

"This is my neighbor's home," he sniffed. "I've lived here my whole life. They've known me since I was a petit enfant, a baby. I watch it while they are gone, visiting friends."

Of course. Small town people were all the same.

Hubert pushed through the door, letting us into the kitchen. Chito and Cap sat there in their pajamas, chatting over mugs of tea.

"What on earth?" Cap exclaimed, staring back and forth between me and Hubert in confusion. "What are you doing? Who is this man?"

"Bonjour, I'm Hubert," Hubert smiled, ignoring Cap's questions and offering his hand from under his painting.

"Bonjour," Cap replied slowly, his eyebrows knit in bewilderment.

"Bonjour, I'm Hubert," Hubert repeated, offering his hand now to Chito. Chito shook it, staring up at Hubert blankly.

"Who are you?" Cap asked again.

"I'm Hubert," he replied, smiling disarmingly at them. He turned and busied himself with setting the easel, paint box, and painting down in the corner of the room.

"Am I still dreaming?" Chito rubbed his face. "I swear there's a stranger in the kitchen with us right now."

"I went for a walk in the woods this morning," I sighed. "I wanted to see the sunrise. And I ran into Hubert. He was out there, painting a picture of the woods. We chatted, and he—well, he followed me back."

Cap and Chito stared at him. Hubert took advantage of the moment to flip the painting around to show them. "Do you like it?" he asked eagerly, watching their reaction.

"It's...colorful," Cap replied, squinting at it.

Hubert grinned. "That's what Miss Glossimander said, too."

"Gallivanter," I corrected again. "We're the *Gallivanter* Expedition."

"Have you considered changing it?" Hubert said, tilting his head at me. "This Gallivanter name, it is very hard to remember."

Cap turned to me with raised eyebrows, clearly caught between amusement and confusion. "Is Mr. Hubert here joining us for breakfast today?"

"Oh, well, not quite," I stuttered, then stopped as Hubert dropped the painting in the corner, walked over to the breadbox, and helped himself. He sliced off a large chunk of bread, opened a cabinet and took out a jar of jam, and then seated himself at the table, next to Chito. Both men looked on as Hubert slathered jam on his bread.

"Apparently he is," I finally said, shrugging my shoulders.

"Oui. And I'm driving with you today," Hubert announced, his mouth full of bread. "By the way, should I put on some more water for tea?"

I felt Cap and Chito's eye bore into me.

"What now?" Cap said. "Driving with us?"

"You're going through Besançon," Hubert answered before I could interject, taking another bite of bread. "It's not too far. She already promised that you could take me there. I have to get to Besançon."

"Why?" Chito uttered, watching him like he was a creature who had sprouted two heads right in front of us.

"I want to see the art gallery there," Hubert replied. "I'm going to be a famous artist someday. And to do that, I need to get my art into galleries. But I don't have a car. Or a horse. So I need to hitch a ride with you."

"We don't take hitchhikers," Cap informed him, as Bernard walked into the kitchen and pulled up short. "We're a professional crew. We're on a mission of goodwill and exploration around the world, abiding by a strict schedule. We—"

"Who's this?" Bernard interrupted sharply, staring at our unwanted visitor as he entered the kitchen doorway.

Hubert stood up halfway from his chair, brushing the crumbs off his shirt, and offered his hand. "Bonjour, I'm Hubert."

"I met him in the woods this morning," I explained. "He's an artist. He wants a ride to Besançon with us. He lives here, in the village. The neighbor of our innkeeper, apparently."

"I see," Bernard said, sitting down at the table with a slice of bread. *"Leave it to Bernard to accept this bizarre story without a single additional question,"* I thought, amused.

"So, Gannivallers, when do we leave?" Hubert said brightly. "Soon, I hope?"

Chito and Cap and I looked at each other, silently communicating our thoughts.

"Listen, Hubert," Cap said apologetically. "I'm sorry, but we just don't take anyone else with us. We're a professional driving team, traveling the world. We can't afford to be a transportation service for anyone."

"I'm not just anyone," he said indignantly, puffing out his chest. "I'm Hubert!"

"We don't have room, anyway," Chito added. "We travel light."

"But I'll give you this painting, as payment," Hubert said, jumping up and retrieving the painting from the corner of the kitchen. On second glance, it was even uglier than I remembered. The three of us grimaced as we viewed it again.

Unexpectedly, Bernard spoke up. "I like that."

The three of us turned, eyes wide, and looked at Bernard. He placidly chewed his bread, his eyes still on the canvas.

"You can't possibly like that," I said, my voice low.

"I do," Bernard replied, studying it. "It's strange. And colorful."

"Oui, colorful!" Hubert exclaimed happily, bringing it closer to Bernard. "See the brushstrokes? Controlled chaos. Movement. *Life*."

Bernard took another bite, staring at the painting. "Sure."

"We don't take hitchhikers," Cap said, shaking his head. "Sorry. No trip to Besançon for you, Hubert."

"Hold on," Bernard frowned, after swallowing a bite. "I can do it. I'll take him to Besançon in my car, if he gives me that painting as payment."

The air went out of the room. I stared numbly at Bernard. He hated driving with anyone. Even us, his own teammates. He was the most solitary man I'd ever known.

"What?" Cap sputtered. "You want to take *him* with you?"

Bernard shrugged. "I don't mind that painting. And you never know, sometimes the ugliest art is the most valuable. Just look at that hideous Mona Lisa painting."

We stared at him, our mouths agape. Cap found his voice first. "The Mona Lisa is an international treasure," he exhaled, shaking his head.

"Is that really what you're focusing on here?" I exclaimed. "Bernard, what's gotten into you? You don't want this strange man in your car. And believe me, he is strange."

"You think I am strange? I think *you* are all strange," Hubert huffed. "I happen to agree with my friend here. The Mona Lisa is ugly."

Turning to Bernard, he said conversationally, "Are you an art critic, sir? You have excellent taste."

"Nope," Bernard replied, taking another bite.

"Bernard," Cap tried again, but he waved him off.

"He can ride in my Ford to Besançon," Bernard repeated. "I get the painting. And I'm taking it with me, wherever we travel. It might be worth something someday."

"I must be dreaming," Chito muttered feverishly, pinching himself. "Bernard would never agree to this."

"Perfect!" Hubert said, jumping up from the table. "I just need to run home and pack a few things, and then I'll be ready to go."

He quickly grabbed his box and easel, and headed for the door. On the threshold, he stopped and paused, looking over his shoulder at us.

"I forgot to ask," he said, his hand on the door knob. "Is everyone fine with me bringing my accordion along for the trip?"

CHAPTER 28

WE DROPPED HUBERT OFF in Besançon that night, the sounds of his accordion fading as we waved goodbye and drove away. Cap insisted we put another town between us and Hubert before we stopped to find lodging.

"He's too comfortable inviting himself into our lives," Cap had explained under his breath as we stopped to refill the gasoline. "Who knows if he'll break into our hotel rooms next? Or hide in the trunk and follow us all the way to Switzerland? We can't let him know where we end up."

Much to our surprise, Bernard had tolerated the accordion—and Hubert—the entire way to Besançon. When we rolled into town and parted ways, Hubert insisted that Bernard would be the muse for his next painting.

"I shall call it *'Vieil Homme Qui En A Trop Vu,'*" Hubert said solemnly, staring at Bernard. "It will be my masterpiece. The painting that makes me famous. You will see it someday, hanging in a museum, and remember that you once were privileged to share a car ride with me."

"Good luck, Hubert," Cap called out, as we honked our horns and continued on. I was riding now with Chito, and waited until we were bumping along the country road away from Hubert before I dissolved in laughter.

"What's so funny?" Chito asked.

"The name of his next painting," I giggled. "*'Vieil Homme Qui En A Trop Vu.'* It means, 'Old Man Who Has Seen Too Much.'"

"Sounds like Bernard, alright."

We pulled over to refuel our automobiles a few kilometers later, and Cap walked back to our car.

"No more strange little vagabonds latching onto us anymore," he announced, as we watched Bernard carefully prop the painting in his passenger seat. "Let's make sure we all understand that, from here on out. We travel alone, as a group of four."

Bernard fiddled with the painting, trying now to fit it in the backseat of his Ford.

"That can't stay there," Chito said, watching Bernard adjust it so it lay flat.

"I'll move it if I have passengers," Bernard snapped. "It's my property now. Don't worry about it."

Cap shook his head, walking back to his Ford. "I don't understand. It's hideous."

"Art isn't meant to be understood!" Bernard called out, his tone defensive. "That's what Hubert told me, anyway!"

We pushed on, eager to get as far as we could before nightfall. When we finally drove into a tiny town, it was dark. We managed to persuade a small inn to rent us a few rooms, smiling at their stunned excitement at hosting the Gallivanter crew, and quickly grabbed our bags to head inside.

"We'll make it into Bern tomorrow," Cap yawned. "Let's get a good night's sleep and plan on an early morning departure. I made hotel reservations already at a nice place there. We're coming in earlier than I originally planned, but I bet they'll have rooms for us. They know we're celebrities."

"My, aren't we egotistical now?" I teased.

He smiled. "They asked if we could pose for photographs in front of their hotel so they can use the image as advertisement. I'm just being honest. I know we're not used to our fame all the time, but there are moments when it does benefit us."

"Sure. And then there are moments where we run across a guy like Hubert, who fondly says goodbye to the warm, kind-hearted 'Giddyvanter team.'"

———◦———

WE ROLLED THROUGH THE border of France the next day and continued into Switzerland. Snow-capped mountains crouched forebodingly in the distance, but the green hills that led us into Bern were gentle and mild. The sky was clear and crisp, and the city itself was charming. I spotted a stunning arched bridge over the river in the center of town, rusty red roofs of medieval buildings peeking out on either side of the winding water.

Cap directed us to park our Fords against a quiet square, and we got out to stretch our legs and explore on foot.

"It's an old city," Cap said, looking around as we walked through the town. "Unofficially considered the capital of Switzerland, as a matter of fact."

"As a matter of fact, I don't care," Bernard groaned.

"What if I tell you about the bear pits? They keep bears in the middle of town. An old tradition."

"Still don't care."

Cap looked over at me. "You'd like to know about Bern's history during the French Revolution, right?"

I scrunched my nose at him. I just wanted to enjoy the scenery.

"Well, it also had a starring role in the Thirty Years' War," Cap grumbled to himself, looking at the buildings. A group of school kids walked by us, carrying their books. "But I'll bet you guys don't care about that, either."

We ignored him. I privately thought Cap should work on a tour book, to give him an outlet for all these random facts he knew about everywhere we visited, but I wasn't going to put one more idea into his already-crowded brain.

"Is this our hotel?" Chito asked, as we approached a large building with a fluttering flag, tucked into a narrow street.

"Yes," Cap said, glancing down at his notes. "Let's go ahead and go inside and drop our bags, and then we can continue exploring the city center."

"Can't miss those bears," Bernard whispered to me.

We entered the lobby, and were greeted immediately by an eager clerk. "Welcome to Switzerland, Gallivanters!" he said cheerfully, his Swiss accent slight. He spoke flawless English.

"Thank you," Cap smiled. "We're happy to be here. And to be staying in your lovely establishment."

The hotel clerk smiled, and held up his finger. "Before you check in, Captain Gallivanter, sir, I have a telegram for you. It's marked urgent. Let me retrieve it."

"Urgent?" I repeated. "That can't be good."

The clerk hurriedly searched through a small pile of telegrams on his desk, and then rushed out from behind the counter to bring it to us.

"It came yesterday," he said. "They must've known you'd be staying here. It was sent with urgent notice. I wanted to give it to you right away, as soon as you came in the door."

"What's it about?" Bernard crowded in behind me as I tried to squint over Cap's shoulder to see the tiny text.

Cap read the small paper. His face darkened, and I saw his eyes run over the telegram again, rereading.

Fear gripped me. My mother and sister usually sent letters, but they'd telegram if something serious had happened. Had someone gotten sick? Or what about Chito's niece, Molly? Had someone died?

"What is it?" I asked. Cap shook his head.

"It's not good," he sighed irritably, turning it around so we could see.

"What does it say?" I said, trying to read the typed words under the large Western Union logo.

"Allow me to read," Cap said. "It's from the Odysseus Society. *'Gallivanters are international embarrassment. Rivalry with Chinooks must stop. Both teams required to report to Paris on February first for disciplinary action. Expeditions suspended.'"*

We stood there, stunned. For a moment, none of us said anything. Then suddenly, we all spoke at once, talking over each other.

"They can't do this, can they?" I exclaimed.

"But we haven't done anything wrong!" Chito protested. "It's been the Chinooks!"

"Suspended?" Bernard asked. "What does that mean?"

Cap read the short telegram aloud again. "It sounds like both teams are getting called in. And I assume both of our expeditions are suspended now. Those cheapskates. They could've explained it in a few more lines, don't you think? They certainly have the money."

"Can they even do that?" Chito frowned. "They can suspend us?"

Cap nodded. "It's in our contract with them. I read every word when we first assembled the crew, and went over it with a lawyer, too. The Odysseus Society reserves the right to call us back at any point, at their discretion. You know, if a crew was operating dangerously or not following the rules—they'd be bound to bring them in for rebuke. Their name is tied up in these expeditions, too. It's a private enterprise. Their money's at the end of it."

"They want us in Paris in a week?" I replied. "But we just *left* Paris!"

"We'll have to turn around and go back," Cap said. He was angry. "What an absolute waste of time."

Chito interrupted me. "Hold on, the bigger question—is this the last week we'll get to spend together?"

"I don't think so," Cap responded, rubbing his chin. "They specifically said the expeditions were *suspended*. Not cancelled."

"So what, we're just getting called in for disciplinary action?"

"I think so," Cap said. "Maybe a mediation between our crew and the Chinooks? I'd expect that they'll make both teams sit down and talk it out. End with a handshake and a promise to get along now."

"We haven't been the problem," I complained. "They've been the ones going after us publicly for weeks now. It's that Dessie, and probably Captain Landry, too, digging through our lives and planting stories in the newspapers that make us look bad."

"I know," Cap said, shaking his head. "We know that, because we know the truth. But the committee has no idea. They haven't heard our side, they've just seen the back and forth spats in the papers. And we've been on the worse end of that, for sure."

"It'll be good, then, for us to meet the committee in person and explain what's really going on," I reasoned. "We'll get a chance to share the actual truth with them. They'll hear it right from our lips. They'll see that we're innocent."

"I think you're right," Cap nodded. "Maybe it's a blessing in disguise. Let's try to look on the bright side, as frustrating as it is. We'll deal with it and move on, once and for all."

"Whatever puts an end to this madness," Bernard said shortly, cussing quietly under his breath. "I'm sick of hearing about these idiot Chinooks."

CHAPTER 29

DESPITE CAP VALIANTLY trying to explain our side of the story, sending two different telegrams back and even attempting a costly telephone call, the Odysseus Society's decision was firm.

We were to report to them in Paris, one of their headquarters, alongside the Chinook Voyageurs.

"We can't even enjoy ourselves now," Chito complained, as we sat down for lunch in Bern. "We're stuck here, miserable, worrying about the future."

"I wish they would just tell us what they want from us," Cap groaned. "The uncertainty is the hard part of this."

"Couldn't we just travel without their permission?" I mused, pushing my food around my plate. I was too anxious to have much appetite. "We have plenty of money, now, right?"

"Yes, we're financially secure, but it's not that easy to cut our ties," Cap responded. "We signed a contract with them, before we brought you on. We committed to fulfilling the expedition—or at least making a reasonable commitment to finishing it—in good faith."

"Good faith?" Chito questioned. "What's the fine print there?"

"Legally, they're able to come after us if we break off before we fulfill the terms of their contract," Cap sighed. "We signed a commitment that we'd make our best attempt to travel the world over a period of no less than thirty-six months. We're barely into it with twelve months now. I don't fancy spending the next decade tied up in a nasty legal battle with them."

"So we have to wait two more years to attempt another trip, even if they cancel our expedition now?"

"Yes. Even if it's our money. Our names are tied up with their organization, too, don't forget. They look just as bad as us if we bow out early," Cap said, rubbing his face. "However, I think that actually works in our favor here. They won't kick us all out of the competition because it'll discredit them, too. So they have to find a way to work with us."

"We all got along just fine until Dessie," I muttered irritably.

Regrettably, we packed up to head back to Paris. "At the very least, we can take a different route," Cap told us, drawing up a new map that took us north from Bern through Chaolon-sur-Saone and Auxerre.

"So we'll be seeing a little something new?" Chito asked.

"Right," Cap replied, his tone apologetic. "I do hate to retrace our exact steps. So this at least will take us through some new cities."

We left early, and made it to Chaolon-sur-Saone that evening. It was a pretty town, with leafy trees and a grand old cathedral in the middle of the old city center.

"I'm starting to feel like I've seen a million little European cities that all look just like this," I grumbled to Bernard, as we drove into town. "Quaint. Cute. Historic."

"I know. Even our hotel rooms are starting to look alike."

He was right. Sometimes I woke up and didn't even remember what city we were in, for a brief moment. Our team had begun writing our hotel room numbers down, because we so frequently forgot which rooms were ours at the rate in which we traveled and changed hotels. I carried a small notebook that held nothing but dozens and dozens of room numbers, each carefully scratched out when we arrived at a new hotel.

After our stop in Chaolon-sur-Saone, instead of plowing straight through to Paris on the main roads, Cap wound us through a series of country lanes that seemed to lead nowhere.

"This can't be right," I complained as Chito drove us through the countryside. "It's too remote. These are cowpaths, anyway. There aren't even roads out this far."

We bumped along the uneven trail, the tall grasses bending underneath our Fords and springing back up as we passed over them. Other than a few cows and the occasional weathered fence, we hadn't seen a house or farm in miles.

"Okay, we're lost," Chito finally admitted. "When's the last time we saw any sign of civilization?"

"It's been a while," I said, staring at the passing fields.

"He's our captain, though," Chito drummed the wheel. "He knows where he wants us to go."

Soon, the sun started to dip in the sky, casting long shadows over the fields. The grass turned amber and gold, a sea of moving grains that swayed gently in the breeze.

"What's the plan here? There's no city in sight," I wondered aloud to Chito. "We're losing daylight now."

"We must be connecting with a city sometime soon. Although I can't imagine we will. Look at this."

We stared blankly at the fields. I didn't know there was this much remote land anywhere, let alone here in France. Finally, Cap's car slowed in front of us, and pulled off to the side.

"He's going to get out and come tell us we're lost," I said to Chito in a low voice. "Just watch. He just didn't want to admit it three or four hours ago."

Chito laughed. "I'd bet you a dollar, but I'd lose that bet."

Cap trotted over to Chito's door and hung his arms over the side, pulling off his goggles. "What do you think?"

"About what?"

"This," Cap said, a slow grin creeping across his face. "Ready for another night camping out in the wilderness? For old time's sake?"

We stared at him blankly. Behind us, Bernard beeped his horn.

"What's going on?" he yelled. "Are we lost?"

"No," Cap yelled, grinning. "We're camping here tonight!"

Bernard didn't miss a beat. "I'll unpack the tents, then," he yelled back, turning his car off.

Chito and I sat blinking at Cap. "You tricky devil," I finally said, smiling. "You planned this, didn't you?"

"I did," he admitted. "I figured a night out here, roughing it, would be good for us again. We've gotten too soft, staying in hotels all the time. I picked a remote route, and took us way out into the most unpopulated area I could find. We need to remember that we're wilderness explorers, after all."

"I could kiss you right now, Cap, but that's Andi's job," Chito joked, turning off the automobile. "This is perfect. Just what we need."

"I hope you packed enough food," Cap laughed. "Beans for dinner, then?"

Chito grinned. "Just like the good old days, driving through the desert."

Chito and I slid out, and I helped him carry the crates of food and dining supplies out of the back of his Ford.

"I never thought I'd miss these kinds of nights, but I realize now how much I have," I said, gazing up at the sky. The moon hung low, illuminating the empty fields around us.

"Me, too."

"For so long, we've been interacting with people," I continued. "Doing presentations. Going to schools and universities. But this is who we are, right? We're not meant to stay holed up in hotels. Hosting press events. We're meant to be roughing it."

"Yes," Chito said, grinning at me. "It's a smart leader who recognizes that about us, I'll say that. Cap has an uncanny gift of understanding who the people around him are, and exactly how he can bring out the best in them. Even where he can push them and sometimes challenge them."

I looked across the road at Cap, who knelt down in the soft turf, hammering the tent pegs into the ground. I felt fresh frustration wash over me at the thought of how mercilessly the Chinook Voyageurs had attacked his character. Chito was right—Cap was a good leader. For all of us.

We set up our small camp, enjoying a simple dinner of beans and bacon. After we ate, we wrapped ourselves in blankets and sat around the fire. I leaned into Cap, who put his arm around me.

In the flickering light, even our impending meeting with the Chinook Voyageurs seemed less concerning. *"This is who we really are,"* I thought contentedly, feeling Cap's body heat behind me and watching Chito and Bernard relax and toast their feet near the fire. *"We're a little family of misfits. A merry band of explorers."*

We slept well that night in our tents, the wind whistling overhead. I rose just before dawn, tiptoeing out with my blanket wrapped around my head to start the fire. Chito joined me after I had the fire going, the warm glow matching the sun that slowly rose over the fields and bathed us in light.

"I enjoy this," he said, poking the fire. "No matter what happens with the meeting, or the Chinooks, or whatever we face next. I still wouldn't want to be anywhere else."

I smiled, adding sticks to the fire. "I feel the same way."

Cap and Bernard soon joined us, their hair still mushed from sleep. Chito brewed a kettle of coffee for us, over the open fire, and the rich aroma of the dark brew comforted me like a childhood blanket.

"Think things will change, once we get back to Paris?" Cap mused, clutching his tin cup of coffee with both hands.

"Probably," Chito said, topping my coffee off and refilling his own. "But we can't lose this. Our essence is right here. The four of us. Out on our own."

"I know," Cap said, staring at the fire. "I just wish it hadn't gotten this far with the Chinooks and the newspapers and all the nastiness. If I could just rewind time—"

"If you could rewind time, none of us would be here," I interrupted. "We've all crossed paths together, when we did, for a reason. And if we did it all over again, we wouldn't be here now. No matter what, we have this. So let's just face the music in Paris, get it over with, and move on with our lives."

Bernard silently toasted me with his cup of coffee.

"She's a philosopher, too," Chito grinned, looking at Cap. "You sure about this woman you're marrying, sir?"

"I'll keep her," Cap smiled.

We set out after breakfast and made it to Auxerre that evening, staying in a hotel there downtown. Another day of travel brought us back to Paris. Cap checked us into the same hotel as before, where they greeted us fondly.

"Ah, Captain Gallivanter!" the clerk had cried upon seeing us again. "I knew once you got a taste of Paris, you'd come back again! And so soon!"

"Something like that," Chito whispered, rolling his eyes behind the clerk's back.

We laid low in the days before our meeting with the committee. The newspapers made no mention of either one of our teams, the feud clearly stalled out as we awaited our disciplinary action.

"I wonder if the Chinooks got the exact same telegram we did," I said over dinner.

"I've wondered that, too," Cap admitted. "I mean, it seems clear to me that they started this feud. Surely the committee sees that. Maybe they'll be forcing them to make an apology to us?"

"I don't know," Chito said, spearing his roasted duck. He was the only one of us happy to be back in Paris. He loved the fancy food here. "But I can tell you one thing: I never want to talk about those Chinook Voyageurs as long as I live, after this meeting tomorrow."

CHAPTER 30

IN THE MORNING, WE bundled up and walked several blocks to the Odysseus Society's office. They'd forwarded the address to Cap, and he led us to the imposing double doors of the large building.

Pulling open the oversized golden handle, he held it open for me first.

I stepped inside the marble entryway, spotting a wooden desk down at the end of the room, a woman sitting underneath it. A large plaque sat above her head, the society's logo with smaller words, *"Discovery, Fraternity, Unity,"* underneath.

A dark-haired, attractive young woman sat there primly, wearing a fashionable dress with a pearl necklace and matching earrings. "Bonjour," she greeted us, her American accent unmistakable.

"Good morning," Cap smiled. "We're checking in for an appointment with Mr. Roberts, Mr. Franklin, and Mr. Cartwright."

"Yes, sir," she said, checking her calendar. "They'll be out in a few moments. Go ahead and make yourselves comfortable."

We sat primly in the large lounge, having arrived early, at Cap's insistence. The receptionist glanced at us curiously, every few moments. Finally, she leaned forward and whispered, "You're them, right?"

I smiled at her and nodded. "We're the Gallivanter Expedition."

"Yes!" she squealed, putting both hands up to her mouth. "I can't believe I get to see you all with my very own eyes! I've been reading about you for so long!"

"Thank you," we smiled. We'd learned to remain benignly polite at all times, knowing that the smallest interaction we had with any fan was likely to be a story that they treasured, telling and retelling for the rest of their lives.

"Oh, you're just so amazing," she gushed, her face pink with excitement. "I've read all the stories about you. You're so famous! You do know that, right?"

"We've just been doing our job as explorers, ma'am," Chito replied. "You're very kind."

"Oh, your story has been *incredible*. The drowning? And the accident, with the rocks? Oh, and the sandstorm that almost buried you? Getting trapped in the jungle?" The receptionist breathlessly listed them on her fingers.

"It's unsettling to hear someone speak so casually about the real danger we've faced," I thought, listening to her chatter. What had been simple entertainment to her—a thrill as she read some stories—had been deadly situations for us, our very lives on the line.

"Andiamo, I have to ask, because I'll just *die* if I had you in here like this and didn't ask it," she whispered loudly, catching my eye. "Is it true that you and Captain Gallivanter here are *an item?*"

"Oh, well," I sputtered, looking helplessly at Cap, who was sitting next to me. "You can't always trust what you read in the newspapers. Right?"

Cap stared at me. Suddenly, he reached his hand up behind my head and pulled me in for a kiss. Surprised, I yanked away, my face blazing, as Bernard groaned, "Cap!"

"Does that answer your question?" Cap politely asked the receptionist, hiding a mischievous grin.

Her jaw hung open in shock. "Yes, sir," she squeaked, her eyes wide as she stared at us.

I glared at Cap. We'd been so careful to keep our romance a secret from the world, and now he was making public declarations?

"What were you thinking?" I exclaimed.

He shrugged, a smile creeping across his face. "To hell with propriety. We're already in trouble, aren't we? Look where we are. Besides, I'm tired of hiding it. We've already suffered enough because of the secrets we've been keeping."

"Now is *not* the time," I said sternly. "We talked about this. It still needs to be private. I haven't even told my mother yet, for Pete's sake."

Cap still grinned, a guilty expression on his face, over my head at the other boys. They both shook their heads and sighed.

"Gosh," the receptionist said, staring at us with her head propped in her hand. "I sure wish I had a man like that."

Realizing that she'd said it out loud, she instantly covered her mouth with her hand and turned red.

Just then, the heavy wooden door of the office creaked open, and several men and Dessie paraded into the waiting area. They wore matching coats and pants of light blue wool, and all wore heavy boots. In comparison to us, they also had matching navy scarves and helmets with their logo, a blue fleur-de-lis encompassed with a stylized gale of wind, painted on the side. Their uniforms were noticeably nicer than ours.

Dessie waggled her fingers at me, the gesture feeling vaguely insulting.

"Good morning, mademoiselle," said one of the men, a tall man with broad shoulders. "We're the Chinook Voyageurs crew, here for our scheduled appointment."

He was handsome, with thick dark hair and dark stubble across his chin. When he turned to speak to the man next to him, with the trace of a French Canadian accent, I noticed his striking dark blue eyes emphasized under arched black eyebrows.

"He must be the captain of their crew, Hudson Landry," I thought, watching his obvious confidence and unquestionable air of authority. *"He's a good-looking man. Strong. Sure of himself."*

Cap stood up, straightening his own uniform. "Captain?" he said, offering his hand to the man.

"Ah, Captain Gallivanter," the man said, returning his handshake. "I'm Hudson Landry. Nice to finally meet you."

His accent was unique, the husky French and English blend characteristic of a Québécois man. He stood proudly, alertly, and I imagined that I could see the bearing of a strong woodsman, a man who'd grown up in the remote and rugged wilderness, looking at us.

"You must be the famous Miss Andiamo," he said, walking over to me. I stood and shook his hand. He grinned.

"You are very beautiful, like they say," he said, smiling warmly. "No wonder the cameras love you."

"Thank you," I blushed. Cap stepped back to my side, an unconsciously possessive action.

"See? I told you, she really *is* that tall," Dessie purred to the other men behind Hudson, who laughed.

"Hello again, Dessie," I said evenly. "How was your trip here?"

"It was good," she smiled. "We had a lot of press conferences along the way. We're doing quite well. But I'm sure you've noticed that, right?"

The Chinook crew stood clumped together, barely fitting in the space. They jostled each other, trying to squeeze into the small room, peeling off their scarves and unbuttoning their jackets in the warm room.

"Their crew is huge," I thought, staring at the men. They were nearly all the same age, in their early twenties, and almost all of them had dark hair and various states of facial hair. Lean and muscular, they had the look of young men who spent all of their time in active pursuits. I remembered that several of them had

grown up ice fishing and racing canoes across the frozen St. Lawrence River, in the middle of winter. Seeing them now, with their strong bodies, I imagined that they'd been pretty good at it.

"Allow me to introduce the rest of the Gallivanter crew," Cap spoke up. I could tell he was trying to be professional and polite, despite the obvious tension between our teams. "You already know Andi now. This is Chito, our cook, and Bernard, our mechanic."

From the middle of the crowd, we heard his familiar voice again for the first time.

"Good to see you all again," Paz piped up.

"Hello, Paz," Cap replied stiffly.

"Paz!" I exclaimed, rushing forward to hug him. I'd resolved to treat him with kindness, knowing that his decision to leave had been an act of betrayal, but a hard one for him nevertheless. We'd both been in a difficult place after our team's near-fatal accident in north Africa, and I'd considered leaving the Gallivanters, too. Though I hadn't, I could understand why he had. It would be hypocritical of me to hold it against him now.

"How are you doing? How are things going?" I smiled, conscious of Cap's soft sigh behind me.

"Good," he said, smiling back at me. He looked over my shoulder at the rest of the Gallivanters, noting their stony reception, and his smile faltered.

Paz had traveled with our crew for several months, after being picked up as a local guide through Spain. Cap had liked him and kept him on as we entered Africa. But all along, Paz had apparently had his eyes on the Chinook Voyageurs. As Cap and Bernard lay recovering in a hospital in remote Kiffa, Paz had arranged to join the Chinooks. They sent a car for him and he left us—without bothering to say goodbye.

It had been painful, though I understood in part why he'd left. Paz was the spoiled child of a rich Spanish family, and he didn't know how to live lean with us. He'd never done anything for himself. He was attracted to the Chinooks because they were bigger and better-funded than we were. Ironically, the Gallivanters were now wealthy ourselves after people all over the world had sent us money.

I'd been close with Paz, at the end, and I could overlook his decision to leave us. Cap, however, had been deeply betrayed. I doubted he would ever truly forgive him.

Cap took charge of the awkward silence and looked at Captain Hudson. "Do you mind introducing your crew, Captain?"

"Certainly," Hudson's face was smug. "It may take a minute. Obviously, we're a bit bigger than your little team."

I stared at the men's muscular arms. They certainly were, in more ways than one.

"We have Roland here—Rollie, we call him—and Willis, our lead drivers," Hudson started, and the one called Rollie waved and smiled while Willis nodded curtly.

Rollie was good-looking, with dark hair and a round, friendly face peppered with freckles. Willis was slim but appeared wily, with the look of a man who might get himself thrown out of a bar and then wait in the alley to fight you over it.

"Patrick and Marceau are our mechanics," he continued, nodding to two others.

Patrick was tall, with light brown hair and a ready smile. He had broad shoulders and an intelligent face, lifting his square chin to study us. Marceau was clean-shaven, with curly dark hair and an expressive face that gave us a genuine grin.

Hudson clapped yet another dark-haired man on the shoulder. "Claude here manages our supplies. He's the detailed one," he said. Claude nodded at us.

With his dark hair and beard, he looked like he should be chopping down trees, wearing flannel, instead of keeping logs of staple items needed for an expedition.

"Leonce is our cook," he pointed to yet another dark-haired man, who smiled shyly. "Dessie here is our little star. You already know all about her. And you know Paz, too," he said, winking at us.

We smiled wanly at each other, not knowing what to say. It was a strange feeling to be standing face to face with people we'd hated from afar. Up close, they didn't seem so terrible.

Thankfully, the receptionist interrupted us. "Gentlemen, and ladies, the committee is wrapping up a meeting and should be done any minute. Thank you for your patience in waiting."

I remained on my feet, standing next to Cap. "Dessie, would you like to take a seat?" I asked politely, indicating the two open chairs next to Bernard.

"Why, thank you, Andi," she simpered, sitting down next to Bernard. She leaned toward him. "Hello, handsome."

Bernard immediately stood up, and backed himself up against a wall without saying anything. I struggled to hide my grin. Her charms didn't work on every man, apparently.

We waited for another few minutes, packed tightly into the lobby and not knowing what to say to each other. Despite the courteous exchanges we'd just had, an air of frostiness chilled the room. Under the surface of good manners, an obvious tension between our rival crews was evident.

Suddenly, Rollie stepped forward from the Chinook group.

"I promised myself I'd do this if I ever got the chance," he said, looking at me with a wrinkled brow. "I have to. Miss Andi, could we talk privately for a moment?"

"Why?" Cap interrupted.

"That's my business, sir," Rollie replied, taking a step forward. He caught Cap's glare and met his gaze, not backing down. He was bold.

"I can handle myself," I said quietly to Cap, laying my hand on his arm. "I'll talk to him outside."

Rollie held open the door for me, and we stepped out together onto the sidewalk. A man was laying fresh flowers out on a small cart a few feet away, and the morning sun warmed my face as it hit me.

"This is mysterious," I said, breaking the ice as we faced each other. "What couldn't you say in front of the rest of your crew in there?"

Rollie laughed. "They're a bunch of hot-blooded boys. I wanted to have a private conversation with you, without them making fun of us."

"A private conversation? About what?"

He grinned back at me. "I swore to myself months ago, if I ever got the chance to meet the famous Andi Gallivanter, I'd tell her what I really thought of her."

I smiled. Despite Rollie being on a rival team, he had a definite warmth in that round face of his. If the situation was different, I could be friends with a man like this.

"I hope you're not about to curse at me?"

He laughed again. "No, not at all. My mama brought me up better than to swear in front of a lady. Or at her. Here's the truth of it. I have four sisters at home. Four little sisters. I'm the oldest."

"Sounds like you had your hands full there, then," I quipped.

"I did," he smiled, shoving his hands into his pockets. "I love my sisters. Even though they made life a living hell for me sometimes. Anyway, my sisters adore you. They've been following your stories for months now. They write to me about you all the time."

"Really?" I replied, glowing with pleasure. "I'm so glad to hear that."

He smiled. "So am I. I promised myself I'd tell you that, if I ever got the chance to meet you. I don't know if you realize what an influence you're having on little girls all over the world. You're a hero, in their eyes. They want to be like you, I think."

I blushed. "That's very kind of you to share. Thank you."

"You see why I didn't want to say it in front of my crew?" Rollie laughed. "They'd never stop teasing me about it. But I was raised with a bunch of girls. I have a bit of a soft spot, you know. I'm not just a brute."

"I understand," I replied. "It's such a strange thing to be known all over the world, isn't it? Do you struggle with it, too?"

"I do," he said, his dark eyes thoughtful. "We're simply living our lives, one day at a time, but the whole world is watching us live. They're judging us without even understanding the situations we face. And they think they know us, somehow, even though they've never met us."

"Right!" I said. Maybe Rollie could be an ally after all. "It's such a strange position to be in. To be a celebrity."

"I know," he agreed, his eyes warm. "How are—"

The door banged opened abruptly, and Cap stuck his head out. "Meeting's starting," he called, interrupting us. "Break it up."

CHAPTER 31

ROLLIE LOOKED AT ME, smiling, as he led me to the door. "It's been really great meeting you, Andi. Thanks for being willing to talk."

I returned his smile, happy to have shared a positive moment with someone I assumed would be an ill-behaved rival. Maybe the Chinook Voyageurs weren't all bad.

That being said, though, he'd still been complicit in his teammates publishing nasty lies about us. I couldn't overlook that.

Cap waited at the door, holding it open for us and staring hard at Rollie as he walked in. He waited until I got through the door, and placed his hand on the small of my back to guide me into a large conference room behind the others.

"What did he say?" he whispered as we walked.

"It's fine," I reassured him. "He's a nice guy, actually. He just wanted to compliment me."

"I bet he did," Cap said sharply.

"Stop," I replied quietly. "He has sisters. They love me. He promised to tell me that, if he ever met me."

Cap rolled his eyes, and dropped his hand from my back before anyone else saw the motion. I knew he was highly conscious of the way he treated me in front of the others, especially men. A firm believer that I was just as capable as the rest of our crew, he didn't want to give the impression that I was coddled by taking my arm or opening my car doors for me. I was an equal in his eyes. As much as I welcomed chivalry and liked his touch, I appreciated his respect even more.

We entered a large conference room, a gigantic polished oak table dominating the space that had tall beams at the peak of the soaring ceiling. Bookshelves and imposing marble busts decorated the perimeter, and rich leather chairs spanned around the table in the center.

The receptionist breezed in behind us, and set down a tray of brandy and a dozen small glasses. "For you thirsty men," she said, winking at Hudson.

I tried not to smile. Now that she knew Cap was taken, she'd apparently set her sights on Captain Landry.

Cap, Chito, Bernard and I sat down together on one side of the table, while the Chinook Voyageurs sat down across from us. Three older gentlemen in expensive suits, two of them quite portly, stayed in their chairs at the head of the table.

"Captain Gallivanter, Captain Landry," said one of the gentlemen, standing to shake their hands. "Nice to see you both again, but unfortunate, given the circumstances."

"Good to see you again, Mr. Roberts," Cap said easily. Hudson nodded politely, too. "Thank you for having us here."

"Yes, well, let's get started, shall we?" Mr. Roberts said briskly, rubbing his hands together and settling comfortably into his chair. "Most of you are new to meeting us, but we are the gentlemen who dreamed up this competition in the first place," he said, looking to his right and his left. "Mr. Cartwright and Mr. Franklin, and myself, Carl Roberts."

"We know both captains, of course," he continued, glancing at Cap and Hudson. "They've worked with our committee for a long time now—several years, in fact. We have great respect for each of them. Captain Landry and Captain Gallivanter, you're both capable, intelligent men who have exemplified the qualities of real leadership over these last few years. We know you've only made it this far because you're dedicated and passionate about our shared mission. Most men couldn't keep their teams going, facing the odds you've both faced. It's testament to who you both are, gentlemen."

Cap and Hudson nodded their thanks.

"That's what makes this so troubling, frankly," Mr. Roberts continued, looking pointedly from one team to the other. "You men, and your teams, have been accomplishing so much, and so well. We are quite concerned at the sudden explosion of animosity between you, and the public embarrassment you've brought to our friendly competition."

The suited man to Mr. Roberts' left, Mr. Franklin, spoke up.

"We've read all the newspaper articles," he said, peering at us through his spectacles. "You're hurling ridiculous accusations at each other. Tearing down each other's reputations. Making each other look bad. And by association, you're making the Odysseus Society look bad. We didn't bring you on in order to have our professional reputations, the organization we've worked so hard to build and promote, tarnished by your silly, petty squabbles. It's an absolute embarrassment. You should all be ashamed."

Mr. Cartwright pointed up at the wall, glaring at us. Another plaque with the Odysseus Society logo was there.

"Read the words, gentlemen," he said sternly. "Discovery. Fraternity. Unity. Clearly, you're glossing over that last word. And that's an important value to us here."

I stared up at the golden words and frowned. *Fraternity.* By definition, it was a men's club. I wasn't welcome.

Yet here I was.

Mr. Roberts cleared his throat. "What we want to know is why exactly is all this happening? And why now? You've been fine for months, and suddenly there's a problem? What led you to this point of such animosity?"

Our teams stared at each other across the table, agitated. I saw Hudson and several of his crew exchange tense looks. No one spoke.

"Come now," Mr. Roberts said, leaning in toward us. "Who's going to tell us what's going on here?"

"They need to hear the truth," I thought. *"That Dessie is digging through our past, manipulating the press to make us look bad. I'm the one that met with her and heard it straight from her own lips. I need to be the one to tell them."*

I cleared my throat and stood up. "Gentlemen, allow me to share—"

"Miss Gallivanter," Mr. Roberts grimaced, holding up his hand to interrupt me as Mr. Cartwright reeled back, looking disgusted. "That's *quite* enough of that."

I froze, confused. "What?"

The suited men looked at each other, then looked back at me.

"Miss Gallivanter," Mr. Franklin wheedled in his reedy voice, "Why don't you run along and let the boys have this conversation? Don't worry your pretty head about it."

"Right," Mr. Roberts replied briskly, standing up. "I'll get Miss Yvonne to get you a cup of tea in the lobby," he said, starting to head toward the door. "You too, Miss Hickson. Come along, girls."

I stood my ground. "No."

Mr. Cartwright spoke up now. "I know the newspapers all paint a pretty picture of your heroic attitude, my dear, but let the boys talk. We have business to discuss. We don't need you distracting us from the issues we need to get through here."

"No," I replied again. "I was trying to answer your question. To explain what happened between our teams. I've been the subject of half those newspaper articles. Obviously, I know what the problem is. *You* asked the question. Why can't I answer?"

"Miss Gallivanter," Mr. Roberts began, his tone smooth. "There's no reason to make a scene. This is exactly why we don't allow women in here to begin with. You're too emotional. You're never able to have a rational conversation."

"Rational conversation?" I repeated. "I haven't even shared anything yet. How could I already be irrational?"

Out of the corner of my eye, I noticed Hudson and Rollie start to smile.

"Tea, Miss Gallivanter," Mr. Roberts chided. "Come now. The boardroom is no place for a woman."

Why could they speak down to me this way, but I couldn't speak back in the same manner? Why, they were telling me I couldn't even speak. That my voice—my very presence—didn't matter at all. It was such a double standard.

I didn't move. Perhaps emboldened by my example, Dessie didn't get up either.

"You're embarrassing yourself, Miss Gallivanter," Mr. Cartwright glared at me under lowered eyebrows. "Time to stop parading yourself around here and let the teams get to work. We have things to do, and we certainly don't have time for your dramatic little displays."

Cap exhaled loudly and crossed his arms, settling into his seat. I glanced at him and saw him hiding a smile, his eyes twinkling.

Chito and Bernard were smirking, too. They knew better than to back me into a corner. And bless them, they let me stand on my own two feet without interfering. They knew I could fight my own fights.

"From what I've seen so far, the only ones here who seem incapable of having a rational discussion are you and the other gentlemen, sir," I said calmly. "I find it abhorrent that you assume that an entire half of the population isn't able to reason and speak intelligently. Then again, perhaps that just indicates the type of women you three usually associate with. And as for letting my 'team' get to work? Well, I'm a part of that team. So I'll stay right here."

Mr. Roberts sat back in shock. "Why do you allow her to talk to men this way?" he complained to Cap.

"*Allow* her?" Cap laughed humorlessly. "She's not a piece of property, sir. She has a brain. Maybe you should let her use it."

"You asked a question to my crew," I said, staring Mr. Roberts down. "Last time I checked, I'm a member of that crew. I've camped out in the desert, dug my own car out of mud, and changed the oil and the gasoline more times than I can count. I've been covered in grease, blistered my hands working in the engine, and been up to my elbows in blood and sweat over the course of the last few months. I drowned, and went hungry and thirsty, survived in the jungle by myself, and broke my wrist rescuing two of my crew mates."

I stood up out of my chair, pushing it back as stunned silence enveloped the room. I strode over to the tray of brandy and stood in front of it. The entire group stared at me, frozen.

"Maybe you haven't been paying attention to the world out there, but things are changing," I continued. "Women can vote now. We can go to universities. We can have careers. We can manage properties, keep factories going, and contribute to winning a global war. Just because you grew up in a time when women had no place in the boardroom doesn't mean we'll never have a place here. Right now, there are two women who belong right here, in *this* boardroom."

Mr. Cartwright made a small sound of disgust. It rankled me.

"Gentlemen, I haven't just been sitting around on fancy leather chairs like you, so I'm afraid the one thing I *can't* do is speak to the dangers of office life," I retorted, picking up a glass. "I've been out there in the real world, in real danger, working my ass off. So don't you dare offer me a cup of tea in the lobby."

I clanked the glass down on the table, the noise making the whole room jump. "If you're going to offer me something, make it a brandy."

Picking up the crystal decanter, I popped the stopper out. "Better yet, I'll help myself. Thanks."

I poured a large glass and gulped it down. The liquid was hot and painful as it went down my throat, and I immediately regretted my hasty gulp, but not my words.

A thrill of pride raced through my veins. *"To hell with them,"* I thought. *"The world is changing. My voice matters just as much as any man's."*

Over my cup, I glanced at Cap. He was glowing with obvious admiration.

From across the room, Hudson impulsively stood up and clapped.

"Miss Gallivanter," he laughed, shaking his head. "It's true what the papers say. You're a real force of nature. A rare woman. I tip my hat to you."

"Sit down, Miss Gallivanter, you've made your point," Mr. Roberts said sharply, then glared at Hudson. "You sit down too, Captain Landry. Clearly, she doesn't need anyone's encouragement."

I sat down, taking the brandy cup with me. It clattered against the wooden table as I settled into my seat. Apparently I had a new ally in Hudson, at the very least.

"Gentlemen, let's get back on track here," Mr. Roberts started, but Cap held up his hand to interrupt.

"What *now*?" Mr. Roberts sighed, clearly exasperated.

"I'm sorry, sir, but Miss Gallivanter here was trying to speak, and you interrupted her," Cap said, his eyes dancing but his tone serious. I realized he had waited to interrupt Mr. Roberts, just as Mr. Roberts had rudely interrupted me, just to make his point.

"I just wanted to make sure she got a chance to finish what she was saying," Cap added. "I wanted to hear what she had to share. Andi, please continue."

"Thank you," I said, leaning forward. "I want to be direct and to the point, everyone. Clearly, there's been some tension between our teams the last few weeks. In an attempt to smooth things over between our teams, Dessie and I met in Paris a few weeks back. While we talked, I was under the impression that we'd agreed to stop speaking badly about each other in the press."

I glanced over at Dessie, who sat twirling her hair innocently as I spoke.

"Dessie told me she enjoys the spotlight, and I'm not sure if her private speculations just slipped out accidentally or intentionally, but she's shared several tidbits that have certainly made my team look quite bad," I continued. "Clearly, you've all read them in the newspapers. I'm not sure who exactly has been digging into our past and finding humiliating stories, or why Dessie and Captain Landry have been so eager to share their negative opinion about us with reporters, but it's caused a stir in the newspapers."

As I talked, Dessie flipped her hair behind her back and blushed.

"Oh, goodness," she said, cutting me off. "I'm just so new to the team and all of this. I don't quite know the ropes yet, I'm so sorry. Andi, I swear I never meant to hurt your feelings—or anyone else. I was just trying to figure it all out. And you were all so interesting to me, I wanted to know more about you. I didn't even realize what I was saying."

Hudson and his crew mates exchanged furtive glances. Their expressions told me they knew exactly what game she'd been playing.

"What I'm saying is that we've had some miscommunication," I replied calmly. "Speaking for the Gallivanters, I can assure you that we'd like to stop battling each other in the newspapers and just get along again, like we used to."

In my head, I added, *before Dessie joined your crew.*

Chito spoke up. "We're all just trying to stay safe and see the world, right? That's all we're saying here. There's no need for animosity between our crews."

"Certainly not," Hudson replied, smiling amiably. "That was never our intention. We respect you. *All* of you," he said, looking meaningfully at me. I met his eyes with my own. He winked.

"Thank you, Captain Landry," Cap said. "To be clear, we're agreeing to bury the hatchet and immediately stop firing shots at each other publicly?"

"Yes, Captain Gallivanter," Hudson replied. "I apologize for everything, on behalf of the Chinook Voyageurs. Live and learn, as they say, right?"

"Great," Bernard muttered under his breath, standing up. "Are we ready to go now?"

Mr. Roberts cleared his throat.

"We're not quite done yet," he said, exchanging looks with the other two gentlemen next to him. "We've come to a conclusion about how this contest will proceed."

Suddenly, I regretted my outburst earlier. Had I made things worse for my team? Maybe I should take a card out of Dessie's playbook and stick to sitting nicely and keeping my pretty mouth shut. I bit my lip.

"As you know, your expeditions were suspended a week ago, pending this meeting," Mr. Roberts said, frowning at us. "In that time, our committee met and decided on a course of action for you, going forward."

Mr. Franklin nodded, and cut in. "We can't just cancel the prize or the expedition itself," he said, shaking his head. "We've invested a lot of time and effort into the publicity campaign. It would make us look bad, just like you, if we called it quits now."

"Right," Mr. Roberts nodded. "So the only possible action we can take now is to repair the damage that's been done in the public. And we will. More specifically, *you* will."

Cap raised his eyebrows.

"Your contracts will remain unchanged, and the suspension against both of you will be lifted," Mr. Roberts continued. "But only after you finish touring Europe for the next three months, on a positive press campaign. Together."

"Together?" Hudson exclaimed. "Why together? We've just cleared the air!"

"Did you hear anything I just explained, Captain Landry? You've been a public embarrassment to yourselves and our society. The only way forward is to publicly embrace each other, and travel as a single crew for a while, to smooth things over. Three months should be long enough to cycle out the negative media coverage and replace it with some positive stories about your joint expedition."

Cap glanced at the three of us, who grimaced.

"Is there any other way we can handle this, sir?" Cap pleaded. "We've already smoothed things out here, in the meeting. Do we really need to travel together?"

"Right," Chito said, leaning forward eagerly. "We could do a single press conference together. Make it a big deal, invite a lot of reporters to cover it."

Hudson agreed quickly, nodding. "Yes, good idea. We'd be happy to do that."

"Absolutely not!" Mr. Roberts broke in sharply, starting to sound angry. "Gentlemen, we are in charge of the committee that created this entire concept in the first place. Apparently I need to remind you, captains, that you both signed contracts several years ago and in those documents, agreed to abide by the rules and regulations of the governing board. That's us."

He glared at Cap and Hudson. "You'll serve your punishment. You'll assuage the press and polish the image of our contest by traveling together for the next three months, or your expeditions will be suspended indefinitely until we replace the necessary team members to ensure your cooperation, starting first with the captains."

Hudson sat down and whispered to his crew. Meanwhile, the four of us looked at each other. As a small team, we knew each other's faces well enough to know what we were each thinking, without using words. And right now, we didn't need to talk about the fact that we were angry—it was evident.

"We can't do anything to change their mind," I whispered to Cap. "We have to accept it."

He nodded. "You think I'm stubborn? They're way worse. If they made up their minds that this is the fix, this is what we're going to have to do. No way around it, and no way out of it."

The Chinooks continued whispering, animatedly leaning forward and talking into each other's ears.

Chito whispered to me, "It can't be that bad to travel with them, right? They don't seem that terrible."

I shrugged. I liked Rollie and Hudson so far. Paz had betrayed our team already, and there was bound to be hostility between him and Cap, going forward. I definitely didn't like Dessie. As for the rest of the crew? Who knew.

Cap spoke up, nodding at Mr. Roberts and the two men that flanked him.

"Gentlemen, we appreciate you taking the time to meet with us today and for facilitating this meeting," he said. "Though we don't necessarily agree that our teams should travel together, my team and I are willing to mend the public perception, as you see fit. We're eager to prove our commitment to this expedition. But I want to emphasize, so we're all clear, that this is only for the next three months—the European leg of our itinerary. After that, we're free to again go our own ways. Am I correct?"

"Yes. Thank you, Captain Gallivanter," Mr. Roberts sniffed. "Captain Landry?"

Hudson smiled broadly. "The French have a saying. 'Aussitôt dit, aussitôt fait.'"

"It means 'as soon as said, as soon as done,'" Rollie translated. "We'll do it."

"Thank you, gentlemen," Mr. Franklin said briskly. "Give us a few moments to draft up and type up a new clause on your contracts, and then captains, you'll both sign on behalf of your teams."

The men stood up, buttoned their suit jackets, and headed out of the room. The door banged loudly behind them, leaving the thirteen of us behind in silence.

CHAPTER 32

THE TWO TEAMS SAT MOTIONLESS, staring at each other. Despite the promises we'd just made in front of the committee members, it was evident there was no trust between us.

Rollie bravely attempted conversation, after a few moments of hostile silence. "So, how many Fords do you have?"

"Three," Bernard replied, with obvious pride. He loved those cars more than anything on earth.

"Three?" Hudson and his crew smirked, laughing with each other. Only Rollie didn't join in.

"What?" Bernard shot back.

"Oh, nothing," fair-haired Patrick said, biting his lip and nudging Marceau. They were the mechanics of their crew, I remembered.

"We never claimed to be as big a crew as you," Chito said sharply. "We're a small team. Nothing wrong with that."

Marceau grinned at Patrick. "Can you imagine? Just three cars to maintain?"

"We didn't have rich fathers bankrolling our expedition," Cap interjected. "We had to do it the old-fashioned way, working to fundraise our team."

"Right. But aren't you flush with money now?" Hudson tossed back, an irritated look on his face. "You can't afford to add another car or two to your fleet?"

"We don't need to change anything," I replied, glaring at Hudson. "We survived one of the harshest legs of the entire expedition already, even with a small crew and hardly any money.

We don't need to add people or cars. We're just fine doing it our way, thank you very much."

Hudson laughed. "Yeah. Paz told us all about how you *survived*. If that's what you call it."

Rollie held up his hand to stop us. "Listen, everyone. Clearly, we have different ways we've been doing things. But we're going to be spending the next three months traveling together, as one unit. We're going to need to learn to listen to each other and work through our differences, even if we do disagree."

I watched Rollie as he spoke. He was passionate, but measured. I recalled that he'd had the courage to step up and compliment me, his rival, despite the fact that his teammates must speak badly about us among themselves.

"He's a good man," I thought, looking at him. *"He stands up for what's right, even if others don't agree. I could be friends with a man like that. That's something I respect."*

Perhaps Rollie and I might be the bridge between teams. We could be peacemakers together.

"Rollie is right," I spoke up, looking at my team. "We need to respect each other. We both have excellent captains who have guided us through some perilous situations. Our crews are full of professionals who have all the talent in the world."

I saw Cap and Hudson exchange skeptical glances.

"It'd be a shame if we continued to waste all of that talent fighting each other," I continued. "Let's put the ugliness behind us and move on. Move forward. Together."

"We don't really have any other choice, do we?" Dessie said, flipping her hair over her shoulder. She smiled coyly at Cap. "I, for one, am looking forward to getting to know my new teammates."

Cap either didn't notice her flirting or didn't acknowledge it. "Captain Landry—"

Hudson interrupted him, hands up. "Call me Hudson," he said. "If we're going to be stuck together, we can drop the formalities, don't you think?"

"Sure," Cap responded. "Call me Cap, then."

"Your team calls you Cap?" Hudson replied, stifling a grin. "Of course. So very American. You guys shorten everything."

"We *are* Americans," Cap's jaw stiffened. "Proud Americans. And before you make fun of that, ask me how you Canadians were doing in the war in Europe without our help."

"Listen, doughboy—" Willis, the sullen-looking one, started to fire back, but Chito quickly interrupted.

"Right, so let's talk about an itinerary, gents," he said, changing the subject.

Hudson pulled a wrinkled map out of his jacket and laid it on the table in front of his team. I saw pencil lines and circled city names on it, tracing through Europe.

"We'd already mapped out our next leg," he said, pointing to the lines. "From here in Paris, we'd go across France, into Munich. In Germany, we'll cut down through Salzburg, Austria, then back through the Bavarian countryside into Switzerland. From there, we'll cut into northern Italy."

"What about all the other countries you're skipping by?" Cap frowned, thinking hard. "You could easily hit Czech, Hungary, Slovakia..."

"Yes," Hudson said, pointing at an alternate route. "But we wanted to hit our main publicity markets first, going this way all the way down through Italy, then take a ferry from Catania to the Greek islands. We'll ferry hop from the islands up to Athens, then go straight up through Greece to hit those countries we missed initially."

Cap rubbed his chin slowly. "I suppose. That could work."

"Gee," Willis scowled crossly. "It's like we know what we're doing."

"I never said you didn't," Cap replied. "But I do see a problem."

"What?"

"We don't want to go through the mountains in southern Germany and Austria if there's the possibility of snow," Cap said, frowning. "There will be that chance, at this time of year."

The Chinooks laughed. "He's from the south, right? New Orleans?" Marceau teased. "What's wrong, you're afraid of a little snow?"

"That's not it at all," Cap replied. "I've studied the terrain and the climate enough to know that a freak snowstorm could pop up, out of nowhere, and bury us in just a few minutes. Do you really want to take that gamble?"

Hudson grinned. "We grew up in the snow, Gallivanters. We know all about it. We'll show you. It'll be a good opportunity for you to learn a thing or two."

Cap rolled his eyes. "You're not the only ones you have to consider," he responded. "You boys have grown up with it, sure. And so has Andi, by the way. But we're talking about an entire team, thirteen people now, who have to make it through without injury. The risk goes up exponentially, when you add more people and more vehicles. The area is full of winding, narrow mountain roads."

Willis tossed their map over to Cap. "We don't just sit around talking about travel, Captain. We actually do it."

Cap was stung by that, I could tell. He was often deliberate in planning to the point of irritation for our team, so I anticipated this would be a recurring conflict between the Chinooks and the Gallivanters.

"One captain who's a little too casual pitted against another captain who's a little too uptight," I thought to myself.

"Fine," Cap said, glancing carelessly at the map. "Just don't get us killed."

"It's just a little drive through Europe," Rollie shrugged. "It's civilized. Our crew is large. What could go wrong?"

CHAPTER 33

CAP AND HUDSON WERE called into private conference after Mr. Roberts and Mr. Franklin returned with an updated contract. The rest of us pushed through the lobby door and out into the street.

"Where are you guys staying?" I asked Rollie.

"Le Cygne Doré," he responded. "They gave us a private banquet room to work on our planning there."

"Nice," I replied, impressed. Apparently having a large, rich crew had benefits. We typically worked out of Cap's hotel room, or sat in the lobby and tried to deal with the distractions of eager fans and overly helpful hotel staff. Though we could afford to stay in nicer places now, we preferred our time-tested routine.

The door opened, and Hudson and Cap stepped out together, into the bright sun.

"It's official," Cap announced. "Three months. The clock starts on Monday."

"Cap and I were just discussing our departure details," Hudson nodded. "We'll meet at our hotel on Sunday afternoon to go through things, and then hit the road first thing Monday morning."

He grinned and added, "Don't worry, Gallivanters. You're in good hands. The Chinook Voyageurs definitely know what they are doing. Maybe this will be a nice little break for you. A vacation."

A group of children were giggling together as they walked toward us on the sidewalk, still in their neat school uniforms. "Bonjour, Mademoiselle Andiamo!" one of them shouted, as they came closer.

"Good afternoon, young ladies," I responded in French, smiling. "Would you like my autograph?"

"Yes, please!" they grinned, jostling each other excitedly, surrounding me. As they swarmed, chattering, the Chinook team was forced to take a step back.

"See you Sunday," I smirked as the Chinooks gave me a withering look and walked away, grumbling amongst themselves.

"That'll show them," I thought in satisfaction. *"They may have a bigger crew, but they still can't compete with our popularity."*

Chito and Bernard and Cap waited until I was done talking with the girls, who shot them adoring expressions as they smiled, then continued walking back to our hotel. Cap lingered behind the other two, and waited until they were several feet in front of us before putting his arm around my waist.

"Nice stunt with that glass of brandy. I don't know that I've ever been more proud."

"Thanks," I laughed. "I had to do something dramatic to get through to those idiots. I'm getting sick of dealing with small-minded men like that everywhere we go."

"You're something else, Miss Andi," Cap said, pulling me in tight to his side. His lips grazed my ear as he whispered, "I could use a girl like you in my life. Want to get hitched?"

"Stop," I blushed. "You already know my answer."

He grinned, removing his hand from my hip before anyone noticed.

"I know," he said, his ears pink. "I just had to remind myself that you said yes. How did I ever get so lucky?"

⚬

WE BEGRUDGINGLY MET up with the Chinook Voyageurs at Le Cygne Doré the next day, where they indeed had a beautiful private room set up with multiple tables for laying out their maps and itineraries. Cap studied the space, chagrined. In comparison, our team meetings were primitive. We often sat on the floor in hotel rooms with maps and lists surrounding us.

Watching Hudson and Cap try to join forces became a spectator sport, the equivalent of watching two rams lock heads. Within minutes, it was obvious that both were strong-willed and used to being in charge, and their self-control was being tested as they interacted with each other with absurd politeness.

"We have food supplies for our crew," Cap tapped his notes. "I take it we won't be cooking for your team?"

"That'd be correct, Captain Gallivanter," Hudson replied. "We have our own cook, Leonce. He's brilliant."

"Very well, Captain Landry," Cap continued. "How do you propose we deal with gasoline?"

"We each carry our own reserve," Hudson answered. "We'll use what we have, and you use what you have. No sharing."

"Hotel arrangements?" Cap asked. "Will we both be staying at the same establishments, or staying in different locations each night? Who will make those arrangements?"

"We'll make our own arrangements, for our team," Hudson said. "You can make plans for yours. I'd prefer that we don't stay in the same place, personally."

I tried to meet Cap's eye. He avoided me.

"This is ridiculous," I grumbled to Chito, under my breath. "It'll waste so much time."

Rollie, who was sitting by me, looked up at my words and leaned toward us. "What?"

"Cap and Hudson think we should stay at separate hotels while we travel," I explained, staring as the two of them glared at each other while discussing the first planned stop. "I get that we're all feeling a little tense, but that's a complete waste of time. Both teams making separate plans for lodging, instead of just getting multiple rooms together?"

"You're right," Chito mused. "We'll have to arrange meet up times each morning, and decide which hotel we'll be driving over to, in order to connect to travel for the day. It'll easily be an hour a day lost on that."

Rollie stood up. "Hudson?"

"Yeah?"

"Andi and Chito and I would like to talk about your decision," he said.

Chito and I glanced at each other. It didn't escape our notice that Rollie had lumped himself in with us. *"He's earnest,"* I thought again. *"He does what's right. He's trying to be a peacemaker."*

Both Cap and Hudson shot us a look.

"What?" Hudson said sharply.

"We've been discussing it, and we think it'd be wiser to make our hotel plans together, whenever possible," Rollie explained. "It'll save us a lot of time and effort. Think of how long it takes you to set up our hotels as we're traveling, Hudson. If we could split that time in half, it'd benefit all of us. One person could be designated to make all the arrangements, or you could take turns. I mean, if we're getting a bunch of rooms already, what's three or four more?"

I nodded along with Rollie. If he was going to be brave enough to stand up for us like this, I'd step up, too. We needed some common sense to smooth things over between these alpha personalities.

"We're traveling together for the next three months, whether we want to or not," I said. "It's up to us to make the best of it. And there are certainly a lot of ways we can put our habits to the side and compromise with each other, for the short term."

Cap glanced pointedly at Rollie, then at me with a disappointed look. I ignored it. So what if I was making friends with the enemy? Rollie wasn't so bad.

"I'm willing to compromise," Hudson's forehead wrinkled, looking at Cap. "Despite what you may think, Captain Gallivanter, I do respect the hell out of you. I read all about your trip through Africa. You're resourceful and brave, I know that much."

"Thank you," Cap softened. "And I do trust that you lead your team well, Captain Landry. They seem like decent men and women."

Hudson stuck out his hand. "Three months together is a long time to keep addressing each other as 'Captain Gallivanter' and 'Captain Landry', don't you think?" he grinned. "How about just Hudson and Cap, from now on?"

Cap grinned back. "Our first compromise, then," he said, shaking his hand.

Rollie and I exchanged triumphant smiles.

We spent the rest of the day planning out the details, discovering that both teams were well-stocked and well-matched. It was clear that we were all travel experts, at this point in our exploration careers.

"I feel like this should take longer to plan, combining teams," Hudson announced as all thirteen of us gathered that evening in the banquet room. "But actually, we're all prepared to leave. This was easier than I thought. We'll hit the road tomorrow morning."

"We'll load at dawn, and depart at daybreak," Cap took over. "The route will take us through France and into Germany. Our first major stop will be Munich, where we have a joint press conference scheduled."

"Enemy territory," Willis growled. "Can I tell those Krauts what I really think of them?"

"Hey now," Chito cautioned. "We're all about world peace. The war's over. Let's leave it in the past."

"Dinner's on your own—in groups or in teams," Hudson cut in. "Eat, and then get to bed early. We have a long day ahead of us tomorrow."

We stood up, gathering our papers. "I was thinking about a restaurant down the street," Hudson said, turning toward his own group. "Anyone have any other thoughts?"

Rollie stacked his notebooks up and turned to Chito and me. "Do you guys have dinner plans yet?"

I glanced at Cap, who was putting his papers and maps away in his bag. He hadn't heard us. "We haven't talked about it yet, why?"

"I thought maybe we could get something together?"

Chito jerked his head toward Bernard and Cap. "I think we'll probably take tonight on our own, as a crew," he said. "Thanks, though. Enjoy your meal."

"Sure thing," Rollie smiled. "See you in the morning."

We watched him join his group on the other side of the room. He slapped Willis on the back as he stepped into the huddle.

"He's pretty friendly," Chito observed quietly. "With you, especially."

I rolled my eyes. "You're too protective. He's just being nice."

Cap stepped over to us, holding his bag. "Let's throw this into the Fords and go across town to eat," he said. "We can find something close to our hotel."

We dined in a cozy, candlelit restaurant that night. The staff nearly fell over themselves, excitedly serving the faces they'd seen in the news. The waiter brought us dessert, chocolate mousse, compliments of the chef. Across the top of each, the chef had written *Bonne Chance!* in chocolate icing.

"For the famous Gallivanters," the waiter said, laying the goblets in front of each of us. "We are all cheering for you, mes amies."

"Thank you, that's kind of you," I responded in French.

"Do you think the Chinooks get this kind of special treatment?" Cap frowned, looking at his dessert.

"Who cares?" Chito said, digging in. "It's free food. I'll take that perk any day, without question."

I crawled into bed that night and laid awake for a long time. My window was open, and I listened to the sound of the night outside my window, trying to slow my mind.

"What will the next few weeks be like, traveling with the Chinook Voyageurs?" I thought. *"Can we put our differences aside and get along? How will our joint press conferences go? Will my team behave itself? Will Cap blow up at Paz, at some point?"*

CHAPTER 34

I WOKE UP EARLY, IN the darkness, as I heard the sound of the doors next to me opening and closing.

"Cap or Bernard must be already packing the Fords," I sighed tiredly. I rolled out of bed and prepared for the day. As soon as I shoved my boots on, I ducked out of my room with my bag and joined the others outside.

"Let's get moving," Cap greeted me, checking his pocket watch. His tone betrayed his mood. "I'd like to be out there waiting when the Chinooks finally get out of bed."

"Great," I groaned to myself as I loaded the back of my Ford. *"Competitive Cap is already in high gear."*

It was still dark when we made it over to the Le Cygne Doré. The entire Chinook crew was already outside, waiting for us, their six vehicles completely loaded.

"About time you sleepyheads showed up!" Willis called out, as we pulled in next to them.

Oh dear. Was this how the next few weeks would be?

"Good morning, Gallivanters!" Rollie said, standing outside his car and waving. I parked my car on the opposite side of the street, behind Cap, and got out. Rollie and Paz met me in the middle of the street, holding their goggles in their hands.

"How'd you sleep?" Rollie asked cheerfully.

"Fine, and you?"

"Forget sleep," Paz muttered, pulling me aside. "How's Cap? I haven't had the chance to ask you yet. How much does he still hate me?"

I looked over at Cap, who was glaring openly at Paz and Rollie. "Maybe right now isn't the best time to discuss this," I muttered.

Paz stole a quick glance, and shifted so his face was hidden from Cap. "It's been a few months," he said quietly to me. "I thought maybe his temper would've settled down a little bit. He usually burns hot and then calms down."

"Yeah, well, you're the one who left. It's up to you to apologize to him and make amends. And besides, I don't think it helped that your team went after us publicly like you did. It was a lousy move, Paz. I thought we were friends."

"We are," he protested. "You know how it works with a big team. I didn't have much say in the matter. Hudson and Dessie were the ones that mostly dealt with the press."

Rollie listened silently, his brown eyes darting back and forth between us. I decided to change the subject. "What's the mood like with your crew?"

They looked at each other.

"What do you mean?" Rollie hesitated. "Like how we feel about you guys?"

"Yeah. Are the next few months going to be miserable? Or is there any chance we might find some common ground?"

Paz shook his head. "Mixed feelings across the board, honestly. Patrick and Rollie and I like you. Willis and Hudson are hard to read. I think Hudson respects Cap, at the very least, but I'm not sure I'd say they'll ever be friends. The others haven't really said much."

"How do you think the next few weeks are going to be?"

Rollie shrugged. "I'm looking forward to it, honestly. We can make the best of it, right? It's not what any of us expected, but it's kind of nice having some new faces around."

I laughed. "Isn't Dessie a new enough face for you? She hasn't been with you that long."

"She's not really my type," he shrugged again, his cheeks turning pink.

Cap interrupted us, walking over toward our trio. "Let's go," he said brusquely. "We have a schedule to keep."

"Happy travels, guys. Be safe, Andi!" Rollie called over his shoulder, as he crossed the street with Paz to get in his car.

"Thanks," I said, pulling on my gloves and sliding into the driver's seat. Chito leaned over the door, holding his goggles.

"You want me, or should I ride with Cap this first leg?"

"I always like riding together," I replied, watching Cap as he strode back to his Ford. "But maybe ask Cap. He looks irritated. Maybe he needs a little friendly conversation as he drives?"

Chito nodded. "You're probably right." He took off, jogging up to Cap's car. "Hey! Can I hop in with you?"

I feared Hudson and Cap might collide with each other, as both shot out from the front of our convoys and whipped down the road. Hudson edged out first, taking the lead. Cap followed right on his heels behind him. Willis and Claude pulled out next, but Rollie and Paz were behind them and waved me forward. I smiled, and smoothly pulled into the line of automobiles.

Our nine cars rumbled through the city, and people stood out on their balconies and sidewalks to wave at us as we drove through.

I couldn't help but smile at their excitement. Despite being forced to travel with our rivals, it was still a rare sight for these people to see both world-famous crews in the same place, at the same time.

"How thrilling to know I'm a part of so many strangers' fond memories," I thought to myself, watching their shining faces. *"Why, they'll save scraps of newspapers and tell their grandchildren someday that they saw the Gallivanters and Chinook Voyageurs drive through their own city with their very own eyes!"*

The sprawl of buildings gradually tapered off as we drove out of Paris and into the countryside. For as far as I could see, I saw fields and farms and grazing livestock. Occasionally, a row of fences or a burned barn, an unhealed remnant of the Great War, popped up as we made our way through France. After a few hours, we stopped to stretch our legs and take a break.

"How's it going?" I asked Cap, as he walked back to my car with Chito.

"Fine, how are you?" he said. "Do you need to switch out and sit for a while? Chito can drive."

Chito raised his hand. "I'm right here. I can hear you."

"That's fine with me," I smiled. "I wouldn't mind walking a bit. Get the blood flowing."

I sauntered out into the nearby field, stretching. Driving the Fords required constant attention to pedals and levers and brakes, requiring the use of both hands and feet as we drove, and it was nice to relax after concentrating for so long. Tiny white flowers carpeted the soft ground, and I walked on them, staring down. They looked delicate next to my scuffed leather boots.

"Hey," I heard a male voice say behind me. I looked up and saw Patrick. He was standing a few feet away on a small rise, hands in his pockets, looking out at the sloping fields below.

"Hey," I responded. "Sorry, I didn't mean to intrude. I just wanted to stretch my legs."

"Me too," he said, smiling. "There's plenty of room for both of us."

We stood awkwardly for a moment, gazing out at the fields. I decided to break the tension. "You're a mechanic?"

Patrick rubbed his neck, his dark blonde hair catching in the long rays of afternoon sun. He was tall, like me.

"Dropped out of university to join the crew," he said, staring out at the fields. "My dad's an engineer. Real high-powered guy.

I was in school for it, too. But I've always been good with my hands, taking radios and cameras and cars apart. I couldn't pass this opportunity up."

I nodded. "I dropped out of school, too."

He looked at me. "You were in university?"

"No, boarding school."

"I forgot, you're the baby of the group," Patrick laughed good-naturedly. "I don't know how you've gotten so far for such a young woman. It's impressive. Most young people don't know what they want to do with their lives yet, and here you are, seeing the world. You must be very determined."

"Thanks. I am." I replied, and we both fell quiet again.

"Patrick!" I heard a male voice yell. "Let's go!"

I turned and Patrick walked back with me. Impulsively, I stopped him. "I don't hate you," I said, wrinkling my nose. "I mean, I don't hate your team. I know you probably assume we do. But I don't. You seem like good guys."

"I feel the same way," he said, smiling. "I've been telling my boys to make the best of it. That they have to have more open minds."

"It's going to take some time, though, for the ice to thaw between some of the people on our crews," I added. "Cap and Paz, for sure. Cap and Hudson, too."

"And that Bernard of yours?" Patrick asked. "How long will it take for him to accept us?"

"The ice won't ever thaw for him," I laughed. "He's always going to be like that."

CHAPTER 35

CHITO DROVE AND I TOOK a break, letting my hand hang out the window and feel the wind between my fingers.

As much as possible, I tried to find moments to connect with nature. Now that we were back in Europe, hopping between hotels, I missed the wilderness. I'd spent most of my childhood outdoors, working on our farm when I was a child and then roaming the woods all the years I was stuck at boarding school. Sometimes I closed my eyes and let the rushing wind take me back to the pleasant afternoons I used to spend galloping my horse around the fields near my school.

Dessie complained about our hotel as we pulled up to the small establishment that night.

"Can't we at least stay in a nice place?" she whined, as Leonce carried her bag into the lobby for her.

"Doll, you have to know this is the only joint in town," Hudson said. "It's this or sleeping in the cars. And I know how you feel about that."

She pouted, then glanced at Paz. "I hope someone can buy me a nice drink and make up for it."

Encouraged, he inched closer and grabbed her bag from Leonce. "Don't worry, we'll make sure you enjoy your night," he promised happily.

I tried not to roll my eyes as I watched the two of them flirt together. Of all the women on earth, I had to be stuck with this one for three months? She was unbearable. And I knew Paz had a reputation as a ladies' man, but this girl? He could do better.

Cap came up alongside me. "Let's drop our stuff in our rooms and meet back down here for dinner before Rollie hunts us down."

"Why are you singling him out?" I frowned.

"He tried to invite us to dinner last night," Cap responded. "I don't want to eat with him. We've served our time with them already today, driving behind them all day long."

"You did," I responded. "I was behind you. Rollie and Paz were behind *me*."

He grimaced. "Of course they were."

"What's that supposed to mean?"

"I don't like Rollie," he said shortly. "He's far too interested in you. He has been, since the first day you two met."

I tilted my head to the side and looked at him through narrow eyes. "I don't like this side of you."

"What, honesty?"

"No, jealousy," I replied. "You've been irritable since we met with the Chinooks in Paris. I get that they have a bigger crew, and started with more money, and have been nasty to us in the newspapers. But we have to make the best of it now. We're stuck together for the next three months. Do you want to be miserable that whole time? Better yet, do you want to make the entire Gallivanter team miserable along with you?"

"You're supposed to be on my side about this."

I exhaled, frustrated. "I am on your side. But you're not thinking logically. And you're usually so logical, Cap. We have no choice but to make the best of it."

"This is so stupid," he muttered, shaking his head. "It's supposed to be us. We're supposed to be happy. We're engaged, and we barely survived Africa, and we have all the money we could ever want now—why can't we just be happy?"

"I *am* happy," I replied. "Despite all of this. Forget the Chinooks and the papers and the press and all that. It's you and me, in the end. You know that. It's still an adventure."

"Hey now," Chito pouted, appearing at my shoulder. "What about me and Bernard?"

I laughed. "Fine. It's the four of us."

"You already know what I'm going to say about this, right?" Chito asked.

"What?"

"Let's eat," he said, grinning. "We'll all feel better after a good meal."

CHAPTER 36

CAP MADE AN EFFORT to be more cheerful at dinner, and I thanked him with a stolen kiss as we walked back to our hotel in the darkness, behind Chito and Bernard.

"I'm trying," he said, his arm around my shoulders. He dropped it as soon as we neared the glowing lights of restaurants, where patrons excitedly pointed and waved at us through the windows as they noticed us walk by.

"I know," I smiled. "Just give them a chance. Remember, it's only three months. It's temporary."

We entered the hotel lobby to find Hudson, Rollie, Willis, and Patrick sitting together, sipping drinks. Paz and Dessie sat off to the side, leaning in toward each other. She was twirling her hair and smiling at him through fluttering lashes.

"Join the party!" Hudson cried, raising his glass to us.

"No thanks," Cap answered before we could say anything. Bernard was already halfway down the hall, having not bothered to stop to talk.

"Come on," Willis urged, scooting over so there was an open space between him and Rollie on the couch and patting the cushion. "Here, Andi, sit down. We were just talking about you, actually."

"You were? I hope it was all good things," I teased, crossing the room to sit down between them.

"Oh, trust me, they were," Willis laughed.

Hudson leaned forward. "Seriously, tell us about yourself. I feel like you're just like us, but you know...a girl."

"Well, sort of," I said. "I grew up in New York, but my father's Canadian. Well, *was* Canadian."

"We've read that about you," Willis nodded. "That's why we like you. Well, the Canadian part of you, I mean. Not the Yankee side."

I grinned. Cap sat down in a nearby chair, looking chagrined, while Chito dragged an armchair over, setting his feet up on a coffee table comfortably.

"What kind of kid were you, growing up?" Rollie asked, sipping his drink.

"I'm not sure how to answer that," I mused. "I spent a lot of time out in nature. I read a lot of adventure books. I was never inside, playing dolls with the girls or doing embroidery. I grew up around horses, and rode all the time."

Hudson nodded approvingly. "A horse girl is my kind of girl."

"And what about school?" Rollie continued, settling back into the couch, next to me. "You went to school in France, right?"

I entertained them with vivid descriptions of my Catholic boarding school, of how I got kicked out for punching a fellow student when she bullied my friend Clara, and how I clashed with the other girls. The more I shared, the more the Chinook boys laughed, peppering me with questions.

"I couldn't wait to join this expedition," I admitted. "I wasn't cut out for finishing school. I'm better at changing a tire than I ever was at making needlepoint pillows."

"I sure like you," Hudson declared, slapping his knee. "Tell us more. How does it feel, being a girl and seeing the world like this?"

Cap cleared his throat, calling across the room. "Why are you so interested in Andi, gentlemen?"

Hudson sipped his wine and smiled at him impishly. "Maybe we're thinking of taking her onto our team, Cap," he said, winking at Rollie.

Cap started to respond, but I beat him to it.

"You couldn't possibly handle me," I grinned and shook my head.

"Why not?"

"Not many men can keep up with me. Not even you Quebeckers."

They laughed again, slapping each other on the back. "I knew we'd get along with her, if we just had the chance to spend some time together," Hudson exclaimed.

"Je m'en fiche," I quipped mischievously, and they rolled with laughter again.

"What'd you say?" Chito asked, confused. "Not fair. You know Cap and I don't speak French."

"It was improper. Don't worry about it," I admitted, grinning, as Hudson wiped tears from his eyes.

"This isn't so bad," I thought, listening to the Chinooks joke around and elbow each other. Despite their bravado, they were genuinely nice, capable men who enjoyed being around each other. Their sense of fun was infectious. And they liked having me around, too. It was flattering to be found entertaining.

"I'm going to bed," Cap said, standing up. "Andi? Chito?"

"I'll go to bed in a bit," I promised.

Chito looked up at Cap and shrugged. "I'll stay down here for a while, too," he said, putting his arms up behind his head.

"Fine," Cap said shortly. "Goodnight, everyone."

"What, is he your babysitter?" Willis grinned, patting me on the back. "He controls your bedtime?"

"No," I said, shooting a glance at Chito. We couldn't let the Chinooks know that Cap and I were engaged. It was too soon to share with the world. And I wasn't about to trust the Chinooks with anything. At the end of the day, they were still our rivals.

"Some guys need to learn how to lighten up," Hudson sipped his wine. "Cap is one of those guys. He seems like a good man, but he's wound too tight."

"He's a perfectly good leader," I said, feeling the heat creep up my neck. I had to tread lightly here, or else the Chinooks might suspect my real feelings about Cap.

"Sure he is," Rollie said, smiling from where he sat next to me. "We like him, don't worry. We like all of you guys."

Hudson and Willis crowed with laughter at Rollie's comment, elbowing each other.

"Stop it," Rollie commanded sharply. They continued laughing.

"Maybe I should go to my room after all," I thought. I didn't relish the idea of upsetting Cap by sitting down here with our competition, while they all got slowly drunk. I feigned a yawn, and stood up.

"I think I'm headed to bed, after all," I announced.

Rollie was on his feet before I even finished my sentence. "I'll walk you to your room," he offered.

"No, that's fine," I insisted. "It's just down the hallway."

"Please, it's the least I can do for a lady," he said, offering me his arm. I took it awkwardly, not sure how to refuse it in front of the whole group.

"Thanks," I said. Chito stood up abruptly.

"I can take her," he said, stepping next to me.

Rollie's smile faltered as he took in Chito's burly frame. With his wild, curly hair, long beard, and broad chest and arms, Chito was an intimidating man. Only his closest friends knew that his gruff looks cloaked the heart of a soft, compassionate man.

"Sure," Rollie said, dropping his arm. "Goodnight, guys. Sleep well. We'll see you in the morning."

"Goodnight," I said, as Chito nodded.

Together, Chito and I walked down the hallway in silence. My irritation grew with every step. Chito and I had been teammates for a year now, and he'd never before felt the need to walk me to my hotel room. Why now?

We reached my room, and I whirled around angrily.

"What is this all about?" I snapped. "You've never walked me to my hotel room before. Do you suddenly think I'm helpless, that I can't take care of myself?"

"No," Chito said, staring hard at me. "I think you're not thinking clearly, though."

"What's that supposed to mean?"

"I think you're not seeing that men find you attractive," he said quietly. "And now that we're traveling with a new crew, and we don't know these men, you need to be more careful."

"Careful?" I repeated. "I'm not doing anything dangerous."

"Don't play with men's hearts, Andi. That's not you."

I flushed with anger. "I'm not playing with anyone's hearts! I'm being friendly. There's a difference."

"Yes. Do you know what it is?"

"Chito, stop it," I said. "I'm not Dessie. I don't play games."

Chito studied my face, and his stern expression softened. "You're not," he admitted. "But you're a beautiful, strong woman and you'll always catch the attention of men. Sometimes they won't like you—you know that, you've put up with those men who've dismissed you and told you that you don't matter. But there are bound to be some men who *are* attracted to you. And you simply being you, being comfortable with who you are, will drive them wild. You need to recognize that, and make sure you don't end up in a dangerous situation."

"I'm not stupid," I said, still irritated. "And I didn't ask for your advice on this. And I'm just being friendly with the Chinooks, I'm not doing anything wrong."

"I'm a man, Andi. I can read other men."

"Yeah, well, I'm not a *man*," I said, my voice rising. "I'm getting pretty sick of always dealing with that. You don't know what it's like for me to try to get by in this world. I have to put up with being ignored, and made fun of, and talked down to by so many of the people I encounter. Do you know what that's like, Chito? Do you know what it's like to be given a dirty look every time you sit down with your crew at a restaurant, simply because you're the only woman with a bunch of men?"

"No."

"I'm so sick of everything I have to deal with, that you never even think about!" I blurted, giving in to anger.

In frustration, I closed my eyes. Keeping them closed to avoid eye contact with Chito, I let my words spill out.

"You boys can change clothes in the car, no problem," I cried. "No, for me, it takes several minutes to find a secluded place, change out of a bunch of layers, lace things up...I hate it! You never have to worry about a restroom, when we're on the road all day. I do! You've never had someone look at you with disgust, because they don't think you deserve to be driving a car, even though you know more about it than they do."

I shook my head, biting my lip. "People call me all sorts of names, behind my back. I've heard the whispers. Sometimes they even say it to my face, like that vile George in Ireland. How do you think that makes me feel? Just because I'm doing the same exact thing as a man, I should be called names like that?"

"I'm sorry," Chito said softly. I opened my eyes to see him staring at me, an expression of sympathy on his face.

"Yeah, I'm sorry too," I spat. "I'm sorry this is the world I live in. That I don't matter as much as a man."

"I don't think that. I've never thought that."

"Everyone else does," I pressed my hands against my temples, trying to restrain myself. "As a woman, I'm looked down on if I want to go on an adventure. Or go to college. Or be a doctor. Or fight for my country. Do you know how ridiculous that is? If someone has an interest and a passion, let them do it! It's not fair!"

"Andi," Chito said softly. I shook my head.

"No," I responded, my voice raised. "There are a million more things I could say about this. How it's wrong. And pointless. But it doesn't matter how intelligent my points are, does it? They're coming from a woman. So they'll never even be considered, let alone valued. My voice doesn't matter, Chito."

"Andi," he said again. "That's not at all what I was trying to say."

"You stand here, lecturing me about flirting with the Chinook boys, but you miss the bigger issue," I argued. "The issue is that you're telling me I can't be myself. I can't be friends with any of these men. I can't be me, because they *might* find me attractive. That I can't trust anyone. Why, you and Cap and Bernard can sit there and talk with anyone you want, but I can't? Because they *might* fall for me? How preposterous for me to change my entire personality for a possibility, Chito. None of you men have to do it. So why me? If I have to change my behavior but none of you do, then how am I truly an equal on this team?"

I shook my head, angry. "We're stuck together for the next few months, whether we like it or not. And now you're telling me that I can't even be me, in front of my new teammates. What, should I not even be in the room with them at all? That's what those men at the Odysseus Society believe. How is that fair?"

Chito looked back at me silently, his dark eyes studying mine.

I bit my lip. "How on earth can I ever navigate the world, Chito? I can't. It's impossible. The rules aren't the same for men and women. And *that*—that's not fair at all."

Chito sighed. "You're right, Andi. The world isn't always fair to women."

"We deserve better, Chito. Think of your little Molly at home. This is the world she's growing up in. You always say she's just like me, right? Well, this is probably how the world will treat her, too."

"I'm aware. You think I've never thought of the similarities between you two? Of course I've seen it. And you're right. She'll face an uphill battle, too."

"I'm strong, Chito," I replied angrily. "I grew up alone. Independent. I've always followed my own path. But that strength—the strength that everyone commends in Cap, because he's a man—is the same trait that others condemn in me."

I took a deep breath and sighed. "And if I feel this pressure? Imagine what all the other women are feeling. If it hurts me this much—and I'm strong enough to bear it—what are other women dealing with inside? How many women are beat down and discouraged? How many have just given up completely?"

Abruptly, the fight went out of me as I noticed the sadness in Chito's eyes. He always got this look when he remembered his niece at home, living with his sister in California. I felt remorse. Chito had always been my dearest friend and confidant. I shouldn't take my frustrations out on him.

"I'm sorry," I started, but he waved me off.

"No, you deserve better. Don't apologize. I know this is your reality, and that you rarely complain about it, even though it must bother you."

Slowly, he rolled up his sleeve and held up his arm. The thick, dark hair of his arms peeked out from under his sleeve, his tan skin illuminated by the sconce above our heads.

"You know I understand, more than the others," he said softly. "I deal with my own fair share of people judging me. Talking down to me. Giving me looks. Whispering derogatory words. Treating me with contempt. For no reason other than the color of my hair and skin—my heritage—the language I spoke when I was born. Trust me, I know."

I shook my head again, staring at him miserably. "I don't know what to say. I don't know how to fix it. It's all such a mess."

"I don't know either," Chito admitted. "But I recognize that it's a problem. And I'm not happy with it. I'm at your side as we try to figure it out together. And we're doing what we can, in our own way, to level the playing field. You're the first woman in history to drive the Ford on this expedition around the world, after all. I'm a Hispanic man, on this same team. We're both making a statement, just by being here. So maybe that's enough, for now."

I pulled my key out, my shoulders tense. "Thanks for walking me to my room. Thanks for listening."

"I'm on your side," Chito said, pulling me into a big bear hug. "I'd pick you over any man, any day."

I nodded gratefully and let myself into my room. Finally alone, I sat down on my bed and punched my pillow furiously, giving in to all the rage I still kept hidden—even from dear Chito.

CHAPTER 37

THE NEXT MORNING WAS tense, with Cap and Chito and Rollie all appearing to be avoiding me. I ate with Paz alone at a small table, instead of with my own team.

"So how's Dessie, really?" I asked, in between bites of egg. "I noticed you two spending a lot of time together."

"She's incredible," Paz groaned. "She's beautiful. And smart and funny. Like you, in some ways. But wittier. And way more attractive."

"Oh, thanks," I said wryly.

"You know what I mean," Paz wrinkled his nose. "You're not my type. You're too tall. And you're like a sister to me. If my sister was a giant."

"Stop making me feel like a freak."

"You said it, not me," he said, sipping his coffee.

"So you think she's pretty. And funny."

"I mean, yeah. But there's more to her, too. I don't know. She has depth. She just hides it well. I want to get to know her story. The whole story, you know?"

I rolled my eyes. "Will you ever stop chasing after girls that are bound to break your heart, Paz?"

He grinned. "Will I ever stop chasing after girls? No. Never. It's my favorite hobby."

"She's probably just toying with you, you know. Don't let her mess with you too much."

Paz groaned again. "I know. But I don't even care. I just can't stop thinking about her."

"Maybe you should try thinking about Cap," I said, cutting into a slice of ham. "Have you guys said more than a few words to each other since we joined up?"

"What can I even say?" he said, setting his cup down on the table. "I blew it. I left the Gallivanters and joined the enemy. He hates me, and he has every right to hate me. How do I possibly make it right?"

"Why'd you leave us like that, Paz?" I frowned. "You were one of us. You knew that. You had to know how much it hurt all of us. And after what we'd just been through, nearly losing Cap and Bernard in that car accident? You never bothered to explain it to us. Or say goodbye. You just left."

"You think I wanted to hurt you?" he said darkly. "You have no idea how conflicted I was, Andi. It killed me to leave. But you also don't know my family at all. What a disappointment I've been to them."

"Why?"

He bit his lip. "You know my family's wealthy. But you don't know how rich they are. Or what that actually means. How much they expect out of me. My father was furious I didn't make it onto the Chinook Voyageurs when I applied."

"You applied to their team?" I exclaimed. "Before you joined ours?"

"Yes," he admitted. "They're bigger. And they were much better funded, back when we started. By all accounts, they were the better team—guaranteed to win the competition."

I felt angry. "They're not the better team."

Paz laughed bitterly. "Well, they didn't want me. Not until they saw my face in the newspaper, anyway. I guess Hudson figured I had something to offer, after reading all our stories about how we cleverly escaped serious danger. He's read a lot about us, you know.

Don't let his cavalier attitude fool you. He's just as disciplined as Cap, but he plays up that devil-may-care attitude more, that's all."

"So you left to make your father proud?"

Paz grimaced. "I thought he'd be proud. But I thought wrong."

I tried to imagine what Paz's life must be like. He was vain and self-centered, and couldn't do a whole lot for himself. He'd mentioned before that he'd grown up with servants. And I'd certainly seen him freeze in the face of danger, helpless.

But he wasn't a bad guy, either. He'd been a good friend. A patient listener. An encourager and a sounding board when I was distressed. I'd come to think of him as family, those six months we'd been together.

"Make an effort with Cap," I told him. "You're stuck with him for three months. You can't each pretend that the two of you don't exist. You need to apologize and clear the air."

"Do you know how absolutely terrible it was for me to find out we'd be traveling together?" Paz groaned. "I mean, if I would've known I'd end up being forced to work with the crew I abandoned..."

"Then why'd you let them publish so many nasty things about us?"

"I didn't! I have no problem with you. I mean, Cap rubs me the wrong way sometimes. And Bernard, well, no one really likes him, right? But I never wanted to destroy your lives. And besides, I know you guys. I never would've implied such terrible things—that Cap's a criminal, or that you're promiscuous and in love with him. They're not true."

I tried not to blush. He'd been around for the blossoming of our romance, but he'd left before Cap and I got engaged. He had no idea I *was* in love with Cap.

"We can't go back and change things now," I insisted. "We have to focus on the future. And it's going to take effort, Paz. You'll have to earn back Cap's respect."

"Boy, that'll be fun."

"Just like *I* have to earn Hudson's respect," I reminded him. "And Patrick's, and Rollie's, and everyone else on your crew. It goes both ways. Effort on both sides."

Paz started to grin.

"What?" I said crossly.

"Oh, nothing," he said lightly. "Just that I don't think you need to worry much about Rollie respecting you. I think he already has his mind made up about you."

"Stop right there," I said, brandishing a crust of bread like a weapon. "I don't want to hear another word about him."

"Fine," Paz grinned. "Let's go back to talking about me, then. My favorite subject."

I chucked the crust at his face as he dodged it. "I didn't miss you at all," I teased.

"I feel the same way," he laughed.

CHAPTER 38

WE CONTINUED THROUGH France, exploring small cities along the way, finally stopping at a little town near Metz.

Hudson had a friend there, who'd relocated with his French wife after the war. "I promised him we'd stop if we were ever in the area," he told us. "I know it's a bit selfish to hold up all thirteen of us now, but I'd love to see him, if we can."

To my relief, Cap relented.

"It matters to make time for friends," he said. "What if we do a joint presentation there? It could serve as a good warm up, so we're a bit more rehearsed once we get to the bigger cities, where we'll have massive crowds."

"Yes!" Dessie shrieked, clapping her hands. "A presentation sounds perfect! I love being on stage, don't you?"

"Of course," Paz agreed warmly, while the rest of us rolled our eyes.

"Great idea," Patrick said. "Should we start working up our talking points? Between the two teams, we have quite a lot of material."

"I'd love to help sort things out," Rollie offered. "Maybe Chito and Andi could help me? Anyone else want to work on it? Marceau? Leonce?"

Cap rubbed his face. "I don't think we need that many people working on it," he said. "How about just one person from each crew?"

"Andi?" Rollie asked. "Want to work on it together?"

Cap interrupted me before I could answer. "Let's let Chito work on it. Andi has some other duties."

"No, I think I'm done with those," I replied stubbornly. "I can help, I have time."

Secretly, I was tired of Cap trying to control my interactions with the Chinooks. Why couldn't he just loosen up? They weren't that bad.

"Fine, Chito and Andi," Cap said shortly. "Pick someone else from your team, too, Rollie. Four of you can do it."

We decided to stay a few days in Metz, and Hudson and Cap worked together to put out the press releases and make arrangements for our impromptu presentation. Soon, our faces peppered all the pubs and light poles in town.

"ONCE IN A LIFETIME OPPORTUNITY TO SEE THE WORLD-FAMOUS GALLIVANTERS AND CHINOOK VOYAGEURS IN PERSON! HEAR FROM THE HEROES THEMSELVES!" the posters screamed, our black and white faces smiling up from the flyer.

We used Metz as a base to explore other small villages and towns in the surrounding area. The more time our teams spent together, the more common ground we found.

I frequently paired off with Patrick, Rollie, Marceau, Chito and Cap, and often Paz and Dessie, as we explored cities and cathedrals, encountered people at little markets, and got a flavor of small town life. Even Cap seemed to slowly warm up to the Chinooks, though he remained maddeningly aloof when they were around.

Hudson's friend was a warm, thoughtful man who made us feel like royalty in the small town. Fresh loaves of bread and bottles of wine and cheese and chocolates were dropped off at our hotel every day. School children gathered in front of our hotel after classes were done for the day, and excitedly begged us for stories if they glimpsed us.

One older couple even asked if they could travel with us. "We don't have much time left," the wrinkly man told us, bent over his cane. "But you kids have sure inspired us. What stories you'll have when you're our age."

We'd laughed about it afterwards until tears rolled down our faces. "Imagine them trying to drive," Chito had roared.

Even Bernard saw the humor.

"There's no way they could climb into the driver's seats, let alone use all those foot pedals and knobs," he said.

"It's sweet though, isn't it?" I replied. "Here we thought we were just changing the minds of young people. Turns out we're changing the minds of the old folks, too."

Rollie and Patrick helped Chito and me sort through the best of our photographs and videos. Patrick had been right, saying we had a lot of material. It took a few afternoons of debate and careful consideration to put together a cohesive presentation—one that did justice to the adventures that both teams had experienced—but we stepped back finally and were satisfied with what we compiled.

Cap and Hudson, on the other hand, butted heads again as soon as we presented our final product to them.

"Why's your team speaking first?" Hudson complained, looking at the notes.

"We're the more famous crew," Cap replied. "It's only natural that the bigger headliner speaks first."

"Maybe you should speak last."

"Maybe we should speak first *and* last."

"Listen, guys," Patrick interrupted. "We're both getting the chance to speak equally. We split everything right down the middle. Cap's team starts, but Hudson's team closes. Don't make this harder than it has to be."

"We're famous, too," Hudson muttered irritably, dropping our notes on the table.

"No one said you weren't," Chito replied.

Hudson and Cap both stalked away from the table, and the four of us stood looking blankly at each other.

"It'll get better eventually, right?" I asked. "They can't keep this up for three months."

"Hudson will come around," Patrick sighed. "He's stubborn, but we can wear him down. He listens to us."

⸺◈⸺

THE NIGHT OF THE PRESENTATION was festive in the hotel. Willis and Leonce ordered a round of champagne for the group, and Dessie tossed her hat into the air as we toasted each other. Chito and I were intentionally upbeat, trying hard to warm Cap and Bernard up to the Chinooks.

Rollie and I had bumped into each other in the lobby earlier, before we changed for the presentation. "Are you ready for tonight?" I'd asked.

He'd grinned back. "Of course. Are you?"

"I am," I smiled. "It's a historic night. Two teams, appearing on the stage together for the very first time."

"And to think that we helped orchestrate it. Bravo, Miss Andi. Just look at the good you've done here."

Now, as I watched Rollie across the group, refilling Hudson's champagne glass, I saw him wink at me and raise his own glass. "Bravo," he mouthed.

"Bravo," I mouthed back, smiling.

We departed for the theater in the middle of the town square, where residents had decorated with ribbons and banners for the big night.

"*Bienvenue, voyageurs du monde!*" they'd painted on one of the banners. "Welcome, world travelers!" I translated for my teammates.

We lined our Fords up in a neat row out front, making a spectacle of our entrance by honking our horns enthusiastically and waving to the crowd gathered out front. Cap pulled in first, followed by Hudson, then me. Rollie pulled in behind me, then Chito, Willis, Bernard, and the last two Chinook Voyageurs' cars.

We sat in our cars for a few moments after parking, waving and allowing the small group of reporters and cameramen present to film us.

As we walked inside together, the crowd cheered. My heart swelled with gratitude. Despite the negativity that dogged me, mostly from disgruntle men, it was the good people like these that made it all worth it.

"Ready?" Cap said, as they started to open the doors at the back of the room.

Thirteen chairs sat crammed together on the small stage, leaving us shoulder-to-shoulder with each other when we sat down. Hudson and Cap were sectioned off on the far right, as they both had to stand up frequently to speak. I was sandwiched between Willis and Rollie, with Patrick and Chito just down the row.

"I'm not complaining about my seat," Willis joked, leaning into me. "I rather like sitting up here, nice and snug next to a pretty girl like you."

I blushed. Rollie leaned over across me and glared at Willis. "Knock it off. People are watching. We're supposed to be professionals."

Willis just laughed and took a sip of water.

"Sorry," Rollie said, frowning at Willis. "This must happen to you a lot."

"Sometimes."

"Sorry. He's just being stupid. That's Willis' thing."

"Don't worry about it," I replied. "I can take care of myself."

"I know you can," he murmured. Cap and Hudson crossed in front of us, Cap shooting me a look. They stood in the middle of the stage, waiting for the spotlight to hit them.

As soon as it centered on them, illuminating the stage, both Cap and Hudson changed. They beamed, and Hudson threw his arm around Cap like they were old friends.

"Welcome, ladies and gentlemen!" Cap boomed, a wide smile lighting up his face. "We're overjoyed to be here tonight, sharing the thrilling stories of our adventures around the world with you! I'm here with my good friend, Captain Hudson Landry, ready to take you on a whirlwind adventure this evening."

"Whoa," Rollie breathed quietly, just loud enough for me to hear him. I wasn't sure if he was shocked by seeing Cap's on-stage charisma for the first time, or by the fact that Cap and Hudson were acting like best friends when we all knew how they loathed each other.

Hudson and Cap launched themselves into an impressive presentation, looking for all the world like two pals who were having the time of their lives as we traveled together. I glanced at Chito a few times, who simply stared at me with big eyes.

Cap could act better than any of us realized.

The pictures and clips that we'd sorted appeared on screen, and Cap and Hudson lobbed each of us questions to answer for the crowd. They joked back and forth, their wit and stories electric.

Despite the tales that the Chinook team shared, the audience was clearly more fascinated by the stories that Cap, Chito and I shared about ourselves and the danger we'd faced. While the Chinook Voyageurs had taken their crew through tame, sedate Europe, we'd nearly lost our lives in the wilds of rural Africa.

Out of the corner of my eye, I could see Rollie and Willis staring at me with shock as I shared how I'd drowned in a flooded stream in Spain, blacking out and being revived by Cap forcing air into my lungs. I told how I'd been flung off the wild stallion in the jungle in French Sudan, and had been forced to fight for my life, stranded alone out there.

I heard Rollie inhale as I told how I'd been temporarily paralyzed from my fall off the horse and watched as a venomous snake crept toward me, only managing to scare it off at the last moment.

Nearly an hour and a half later, Hudson wrapped up the presentation, inviting the audience to meet us and take photographs if they wanted to stay. We stood up and bowed, together, as the audience clapped wildly, giving us a standing ovation that lasted several minutes.

As the crowd hooted and cheered, Rollie leaned over to me and spoke into my ear. "I've read those stories about you, but I've never heard them come from you yourself," he whispered. "Andi, you're incredible. Honestly. Just incredible."

"I just did what I had to do to survive," I grinned, speaking into his ear.

"That doesn't change the fact that you're remarkable, though," Rollie replied, his eyebrows raised.

Cap glanced at us as he turned to head off the stage, a slight frown marring his otherwise satisfied expression.

He nodded at me, indicating I should follow him. I smiled at Rollie, and waved Chito and Bernard along with me.

We walked down the steps and lined up in front of the stage to greet our excited fans.

CHAPTER 39

WOMEN BOMBARDED ME with questions the moment I stepped off the bottom step, surging toward me in a cloud of perfume and colorful dresses.

"What was it like to survive, all on your own out there in the jungle, with no one else around?" one young woman cried, a sleeping baby in her arms.

"It was scary," I said, wracking my brain for words to describe it. "I wasn't sure I'd make it out. I had nothing, no food or water or supplies. I had only the clothes on my back, and I had to figure out how to use those to get water. It took all my will not to give up."

"I can't imagine," the woman breathed, smoothing her baby's hair. "I could never be that brave."

"Strength comes in all forms," I smiled at her. "You have to be strong, for your little one. That takes brains, and courage and will, too."

Another woman tapped me on the arm, her brown eyes curious. "What's it like, being the only girl on a crew of men?"

"It has its own challenges," I laughed. "We always have separate hotel rooms, but when we're camping or sleeping in our cars, I have to be just like them. I pack the cars, I change the oil and the gasoline and get dirty, and haul things around like they do."

"Do they give you any privacy, or do they tease you?" she asked curiously. "I couldn't imagine sleeping next to a bunch of strange guys."

"The Gallivanter crew is a bunch of gentlemen," I replied. "They're some of the most wonderful people I've ever known.

They've showed me nothing but respect from the day I joined their team."

"I always thought that Captain Gallivanter was a good man," she said absently, blushing.

I grinned. I wouldn't mention this to him. He got enough of an ego boost being on stage and having scores of beautiful young women throw themselves at him after every public event. Even now, he had a crowd of them around him, clamoring for his attention.

Dozens of people of all ages stuck around to talk to me and have me sign autographs for them. A young couple stood at the back of the crowd, waiting patiently for everyone else to clear out. She was heavily pregnant.

"Hello, folks," I said, discreetly checking the clock on the wall behind them. I'd been here for an hour already, after the conference ended. On the other side of the stage, Cap still had a line of people waiting to talk to him.

"Miss Gallivanter?" the man said shyly, smiling at me, his pregnant wife leaning on his arm.

"Yes?"

"It's good to see you," he said, a grin slowly lighting up his face. "It's been a while."

I stared at him and cocked my head. Suddenly, I placed him.

"You!" I cried, running into his arms and laughing. "Sergeant Durant!"

"I wasn't sure you'd recognize me!" he said, clutching me in an enthusiastic hug.

"Oh, you were my hero," I said, laughing as we pulled apart. "Look at you! Are you still in the army?"

"I got out a while ago, after we got home to France," he replied. "Andi, I want to introduce you to someone. My wife, Marie."

The pretty, dark-haired woman stepped forward. Her face was radiant. "I'm so happy to meet you, Miss Andi," she said, pulling me into a hug. I laughed as Marie's big belly smushed against me.

"Congratulations are in order, I see?" I smiled at her. Durant put his arm around her and grinned.

"We want a big family," he said proudly. "Remember, I told you I had a sweetheart? We married right away, when I returned from the service."

"I remember," I said, thinking back to the strange circumstances that had brought us together more than a year ago, as we sailed from France to Spain together.

The rest of the Gallivanter crew had headed to Spain before me, to prepare the vehicles and supplies, while I waited on getting my visas in order. I'd boarded the ship on my own and walked straight into the company of an entire ship's worth of rowdy French soldiers, who plagued me with cat calls and improper comments until I fended off Marius, a nasty man who'd crept into my room late one night to take advantage of me.

"I've told Marie all about you," Durant's eyes twinkled. "How you talked your way on board a ship full of soldiers, all by yourself, and got stuck in our room with a bunch of smelly men."

"He has," Marie interrupted. She was beautiful and vivacious, too. I liked her spirit. "He said the ship's captain made a pass at you?"

"Yes, he did," I said ruefully. "Did he also tell you what a brave man he was, to notice what was going on and step up to help me? He saved me from that vile Captain Charles."

Durant glowed. "It was nothing," he replied modestly.

"No, it wasn't," I said, laying my hand on his arm. "It was courageous. You stuck your neck out to help me. And I appreciate it. You're a good man."

"I know he is," Marie said, swatting him playfully. "Is it really true that you slept with your boots on and smashed a man's teeth out when he tried to attack you in the middle of the night?"

I rubbed my face in embarrassment. "I did. I knocked out two teeth, apparently."

Durant started laughing hard. "Oh, Miss Andi, I think it was more like three or four teeth. It wasn't funny then, but it's amusing now, isn't it? You've come so far since then!"

"I have," I grinned. "You have too! You're married now? And having a baby?"

"We are," he smiled. "We bought a farm, too. Not a big one, but a nice house and some barns. My brother-in-law works on the farm with me. And I enjoy it. Working with my hands, on my own property. I built the baby's crib a few weeks ago. No more military life for me. It's all domestic bliss now."

"I'm so happy for you," I said warmly. In the midst of a chaotic ocean voyage where I felt overwhelmed by the male attention I was getting, Sergeant Durant had been the calm, cool presence that protected me and delivered me safely to the Gallivanter team. I owed him a lot. I had still been finding my feet then, trying to figure out how to navigate the world as an independent young woman.

"I've followed all your stories in the papers," he said. Marie stopped him, her eyes mirthful.

"You've followed them? He's lying!" she teased. "I'm the one who's followed you religiously. I can't believe Edgar is lying to your face right now."

"What?" Durant pretended to be angry, but a smile played at his lips. "I buy you the newspapers, you're just the one that devours the stories first before I have a chance—"

"I read them out loud!"

"Yes, and you cut the stories out and paste them in your scrapbook, too," Durant told me, his eyes gleaming. "She won't tell you herself but Marie's your biggest fan. She can't believe I actually knew you, way back before you were famous."

"Stop making me look bad!" she hissed as I laughed. I liked Marie. I was glad Durant was so happy.

"Well, the feeling is mutual," I said to Marie. "I adore your husband. And I'm glad you two are happy. Sorry, you three!"

"Are you going to settle down with someone someday, Miss Andi, or will you always be an adventurer?" Marie asked.

I smiled and leaned in, my voice low. "Maybe a little bit of both?"

Durant's eyebrows knit together. "What does that mean?"

I looked around to make sure no one else could overhear. Cap was still talking to fans, several paces away from me. He seemed tired, I thought, as I glanced at him.

"I'm only telling you two because it's you, Sergeant—I'm sorry, Edgar," I smiled quietly. "No one else knows this, except for my team. But I'm engaged to Captain Gallivanter. We're keeping it a secret, for now."

"YES!" Marie clapped her hands and let out an ear-splitting shriek.

Cap and the few lingering guests stared at us. Durant looked mortified.

"Honey!" he hissed, clapping his hand over her mouth and laughing. "It's a secret! Don't cause a scene!"

She pulled his hand off her mouth and clutched my arms with both hands.

"Oh, oh, I'm just so happy for you," she whispered excitedly. "Oh, Edgar, tell her—I've been telling him for months! Captain Gallivanter and Andi are meant for each other! Tell her, I've said it for months now!"

"She has," Durant grinned. "She says she has a sense about these things."

"I do!" Marie insisted, still holding my arms. "Oh, I'm so happy. I won't tell anyone, I swear. But I just know you're perfect together. Oh, the way he looks at you on stage—Andi, he loves you. It's so plain to see!"

"Thanks," I said, smothering a grin as Cap looked over at me again, and started to walk toward me. "We're happy, too."

"Thank you for coming out, again, have a wonderful night," I heard Cap call out as he crossed the room over to the three of us.

"Hey," I beamed as he walked up. "I want you to meet someone special."

Cap looked at me, eyebrows raised, as I introduced Durant. "Cap, this is Edgard Durant and his wife, Marie."

He politely stuck out his hand. "How do you do?"

"Remember the sergeant on the ship from France? The one who pulled me away from that lecherous captain and helped me with Marius, the man who tried to attack me in my cabin?"

Cap stared at Durant. "Is this him?"

"Yep!" I grinned.

Unexpectedly, Cap enveloped Durant in a hug. "Oh, thank God for you!" he cried, then stepped back, embarrassed at his uncharacteristic show of affection.

Marie cupped her hands around her face and sighed romantically. "This is just *perfect*."

"It's a pleasure to meet you, sir," Durant said. "I'm thankful I was able to be there for her when she needed it. Your fiancée is a wonderful woman, Captain."

Cap glanced again at me, confused. "What—?" he started, and I hushed him by grabbing his hand impulsively.

Marie sighed again, her eyes shining.

"You have a lifetime of happiness to look forward to," Marie said, squeezing me in another hug. "So do we. Congratulations to us all."

CHAPTER 40

WE LEFT METZ AND CONTINUED on with our expedition the next morning, driving through the pastoral French countryside.

Here, the roads were lonely and secluded. Open fields of hills were bordered by dark stands of leafy green trees. Horses lifted their heads from grazing in shimmering fields, ragged weeds up to their big chests, watching us as we drove by them.

Occasionally, we caught sight of the ocean in the distance, a blue haze on the horizon. Rocky cliffs jutted out from the coast, and fence posts rambled through the greens and browns of the landscape.

As we meandered along small country roads, we sometimes spotted the abandoned wreckage of a small stone house, the black destruction cutting a stark contrast to the peaceful nature we saw all around us. We glimpsed the telltale signs of heavy tanks that had rolled through the fields, gashing the ground and slicing off trees at their bases as they fired heavy artillery during the war that had destroyed this land only a few years before.

The land was trying to heal, with weeds and plants springing up in the middle of the blackened and charred destruction. But it would never be the same.

Every so often, we'd see a small cluster of crosses in the middle of nowhere, marking the graves of the dead.

As we drove, Bernard and I sat in silence. We rounded a corner and started to trundle uphill, when I spotted a large grouping of crosses at the top of a gentle rise.

"Bernard, look," I pointed. "There must be a hundred graves there. Maybe more."

Unexpectedly, sorrow rose up in my soul.

"Those are men," I told myself. *"Men like my father. Living, breathing, wonderful men who kissed their kids goodbye, hugged their wives and girlfriends tight. They laughed together. They teased each other. And now, they lay together, their bodies rotting."*

Tears came to my eyes, and I blinked hard. When my father had died, I was only nine. It had turned my world upside down.

If he hadn't died in battle, and had instead returned from the Great War to us, my entire life would've been different. I never would've gone to boarding school in France. My childhood would've been happier. I wouldn't have been so miserable and lonely all the time, feeling the pressure of filling his empty shoes.

Then again, I wouldn't have ever gone on this expedition around the world. I never would've met Chito and Bernard, or any of the Chinook Voyageurs. I never would've gotten engaged to Cap.

"I miss you," I thought, trying to remember my father's face. I hadn't thought about him in a long time—and in large part, that was because I felt guilty. My memory of his strong jaw, the tone of his laughter, and his face had faded. In place of the razor sharp memories that once plagued me every night, I recalled only a dim blur of a tall, dark man who had loved me, his little girl.

We drove slowly up the hill. Next to me, Bernard stared at the crosses. "My brother's here," he said quietly.

"What?"

"He's here." Bernard repeated, his voice low.

"Right here? This battleground?"

Bernard shook his head slowly. "I don't know, exactly. He's buried somewhere in France. They weren't sure where his platoon ended up, but they speculated it was somewhere in northern France."

"I'm sorry," I whispered. "That's awful."

"It broke my mother's heart. And my father's, too," Bernard replied. "They died, one after another, shortly after he did. Spanish flu got them both."

"And you were alone?"

"Alone. Always alone, from that moment on."

"Let's stop," I said impulsively, laying my hand on his arm. "Come on. Let's pay our respects."

For once, Bernard didn't pull away or argue. "Fine," he said, easing the car over to the side.

We crunched to a halt on some loose gravel and opened our doors. A cool breeze blew my hair into my face as I walked on the spongy ground, my boots leaving faint footprints as we walked together, silently, toward the graveyard.

"Hey, why are we stopping?" I heard Willis yell from behind us, and someone shushed him. I didn't care to explain myself. I concentrated on putting one foot in front of the other, my hair swirling around my head, as I listened to the hollow sound of the wind sweeping across the field.

Bernard and I separated as we reached the wooden crosses, walking slowly through them, our heads bowed. Several crosses had names and ranks carved in, but most were blank.

"Two or three words summed up the life of a man who had loved, grieved, hoped, and wished," I thought. A few graves had dog tags draped across them, tinkling gently in the wind.

I'd imagined my father's death in horrific detail for a long time. I'd been haunted by images of him drooling blood or holding his chest as he bled out painfully. Here, in this barren field, my imagination raged again.

As I walked, my heart sank further into despair. *"Why did you leave us?"* I cried out to no one, as I internally screamed. *"You had so much life left to live. You never got to see me grow up. You never had the chance to be proud of me, to know who I became. Why? It's not fair!"*

I stopped in the midst of the graveyard of small crosses, the wind howling around me. I was surrounded by death, everywhere I stepped. For a long few minutes, I stood there, my head bowed.

Behind me, I heard soft footsteps. I knew it was Cap. Blindly, I reached for him as he joined me, standing next to me.

"I'm sorry, Andi," Cap said gently. He put his arm around my shoulders.

"I don't know what's wrong with me," I choked out, as tears started down my cold cheeks. "He died so long ago. How can it bother me like this, when it happened so long ago? This doesn't even mark his grave. He's buried in France somewhere—I don't know where."

"Grief has no timeline," Cap said simply, holding me tighter. I could feel his muscles flexing under his jacket. He had known loss, too. His father died when he was small, and his older brother had been killed in a freak accident when he was a teenager. He'd valiantly tried to provide for his sick mother, all on his own, but she'd passed away when he was sixteen.

"Why did he have to die?" I asked angrily, wiping the tears from my face. "He was young. He was a good man, a loving father. He adored my mother. Why? Why was he taken? Why not someone else?"

"I don't know," Cap shook his head, his voice quiet. "I'm sorry. It's not fair."

"Nothing's fair! Why him? It destroyed my family. It nearly killed my mother. I spent years—*years*—crying about him. And his life was snuffed out for what? A stupid war that didn't even matter, in the end? Why?"

I looked at Cap with tear-stained cheeks, and he looked back at me, his face sympathetic.

"He didn't even get to meet you!" I cried out, my voice cracking. "I'm marrying you, and he didn't get to meet the man I'm going to spend my life with! Why? He was supposed to be here. He *should* be here."

For a long moment, Cap just held me and said nothing. I leaned into him, feeling the comfort of his strong body against mine. *"This is what love is,"* I thought, in the midst of my sorrow. *"He'll be here to hold me up, when I can't hold myself up. He'll let me borrow his strength when I need it."*

Suddenly, Cap dropped his arm and knelt down in the wet turf. He stared at the wooden cross in front of him, and leaned across his knee toward it.

"Mr. Warren," he said quietly. "We haven't had the pleasure to meet until now, but I wanted to tell you how much I adore your daughter."

"Cap, stop," I protested, trying to pull him up. "That's not even his grave."

"No," he said, looking up at me. "Let me finish. He'll hear it, somehow."

I gave up, and took a step back. Cap looked back at the grave. He stared for a moment, then began speaking again.

"Mr. Warren, you're a man I admire. A man who's raised such a fine girl is a good man, in my book. And sir, I need to thank you. You raised the woman of my dreams. Andi is genuine, she's brilliant, and she's fearless. She lives and loves passionately. Her spirit is true and brave, and I've never met a person who inspires me quite so much."

Tears sprang to my eyes again as I watched Cap talk to my father like he was right in front of us.

"Sir, I love your daughter. I need her in my life. She lights up every day for me. When I say I love her, I don't say it lightly. She is the best, purest thing that's ever happened to me. She is a gift, an absolute treasure. For all that you raised her to be, I thank you. And for all that she is, and will become, I'm grateful."

My emotions threatened to overtake me as Cap continued talking to my father.

"With every beat of my heart, I promise to love and care for Andi. With my dying breath, I'll thank God that I had the chance to be with her. Without a doubt, she is the best thing that's ever happened to me. Sir, I humbly ask you for your permission to marry your daughter."

I knelt down in the ground next to Cap, my knees soaking through the thick fabric of my pants. I reached for his hand, and folded mine around his cold fingers. "I love you," I smiled, through my tears.

"I love you," he smiled back, holding me. We knelt in the wet together, our pants slowly soaking with cold.

Cap finally broke the silence. "You're not supposed to be the one kneeling. I am. You know, when I propose. I mean, I already did. You know what I'm saying."

"Since when have we ever done things properly?"

He laughed, putting his arms around me and laying his head on top of mine. "We don't. We probably never will. That's why we're perfect for each other."

We walked back slowly to the car, Cap's arm around my shoulders. When we reached my Ford, Cap opened the door for me and then sauntered over to speak with Hudson.

Rollie had been watching me, and came over to me as I dusted mud off my pants. "I'm so sorry, Andi," he said. His face was somber, understanding.

"My father," I replied. We all had people we'd lost in the war, and more after the soldiers returned home and brought the deadly Spanish flu pandemic with them. Few explanations were necessary.

He nodded. "My cousin. And my best friend, from school."

"I'm sorry, too," I said, looking at the field of crosses again. So many brave young men had died. Sometimes I wasn't even sure why. The political skirmishes had settled down, but still, empty chairs sat at so many dining tables all over the world.

"I hope you know he'd be proud of you," Rollie said, adjusting his goggles and starting to walk away. "Your father. I'm proud, too. We all are."

CHAPTER 41

THE SCENERY AROUND us changed as we drove into southern Germany, rocky mountains and tall, dense pine forests replacing the wide fields and flat land.

Snow dusted the top of the mountains all around us, and fast-moving, gurgling alpine streams appeared out of nowhere, as we hugged the sides of mountains. Tall pines blocked the sky, their boughs thick with snow that hadn't yet melted in the cold mountain air.

We moved slowly, spending a few nights in small hotels along the route. Now that we were weeks into the expedition together, sharing close quarters, our inhibitions had mostly broken down. The tension between our teams had dissolved, and we mingled freely with each other as we stopped, dined, and boarded at hotels in every new city we hit. As we crammed into hotel lobbies and rooms together, we shared stories and laughter, teasing each other.

Patrick was witty and intelligent, and Rollie was a skilled conversationalist, drawing everyone around him into discussion. Marceau regaled us with stories about the Chinook boys' childhoods, while Willis and Paz added their own colorful tales to the mix.

Hudson kept us all on our toes with his irreverent humor, and even Claude and Leonce, with their quiet manner, were easy to talk to and full of good-natured humor. I avoided Dessie at all costs, which worked out as she spent more and more time alone with Paz.

Despite trying to remind myself that the Chinooks would still be our rivals when we stopped traveling together in a few weeks, I found myself looking forward to their company.

"Don't get so close to them," I warned myself, wrinkling my nose as I remembered we were going to beat them and win that million dollar prize at the end of our global competition. Still, I found myself laughing with Rollie and Patrick more often than I could've imagined. They both had a genuine warmth, an easy friendship about them that drew me in.

As we traveled through the mountains together, my heart was in my throat. I looked down outside my passenger door, gulping at the valley hundreds of feet below. Only a narrow cliff ledge separated us from the drop.

Our Model Ts weren't capable of traveling roads with a steep grade, as the position of the gas tank didn't allow fuel to flow to the transmission if the car tilted backward at too sharp of an angle. If the fuel stopped flowing, the cars would shudder to a stop, and we'd quickly have to pull the brake lever, easing the car to a stop, and then coast back to a place where we could safely turn around and instead reverse up the steepest part of the hill.

Out on the steep mountain roads, with nine cars to repeat this process, we continued to lose valuable time. The anxiety of trying to reverse up steep mountain passes, the cliffs next to our automobiles dropping down hundreds of feet, wore on our emotions.

We snapped at each other here, in the mountains, the constant tension making us terse.

"How do people possibly travel these roads?" I asked Chito, through gritted teeth, as he drove us in reverse.

"I'm not sure they do," he said, wiping beads of sweat off his forehead with the back of his gloved hand as he stared behind him, backing slowly up the road. "We're the only autos on the road, haven't you noticed?"

It took so long to travel through the narrow mountain passes that we ended up losing daylight before getting to civilization.

With the sky darkening rapidly, we had no choice but to pull the cars over in a flat grove of trees and set up camp for the night. We arranged all nine Fords in a large circle, the headlights all pointing in at the open space in the middle so we could get fires going to warm ourselves.

"We need to slow down and be careful here," Cap told us quietly, as we listened to Hudson and Willis exchange amusing horror stories about the perils of winter driving in Quebec as we unpacked the cars.

Marceau guffawed. "What, you Americans can't handle a little snow and some hills?"

"You call these hills?" I replied, staring up at the sheer granite that dwarfed us where we camped that night. The mountains were so tall that they had completely blotted out the sunset, and we saw only the barest glimpse of sky darken overhead as we sat in the cold shadows.

"What, these? I've seen bigger," Marceau grinned at me.

"Right," I said skeptically. "In Quebec, let me guess. A place known for mountains. Oh, wait."

"Well, you caught me there," he said, smirking. "But it's not that bad. We're professional drivers, right? We're doing just fine."

Snow flurries started drifting down on us as we set up camp, making two fires so everyone could huddle around to stay warm. I wrapped my scarf securely around my ears and chin. It was already cold, and the temperature was bound to drop overnight. We'd have to sleep in the cars because the ground was too frigid to lay on. For now, we sat as close to the fires as possible. I feared I might accidentally ignite my pant legs, I was so near the flames.

"Remember the good old days, when we camped out in the sand in the Sahara?" Chito joked, hugging himself.

"Oh, yeah, let's go back there," Bernard said miserably. "That was great."

"Do you guys have any extra hot water bottles?" Cap asked Claude, raising his voice as he shouted across the clearing. "We only have four."

"No," Claude said, pulling out a small book from his jacket pocket and consulting it. "We have extra gloves, blankets, and socks, though."

I alternated between turning different sides of my face toward the fire, trying to warm each side.

"We definitely need to wear extra socks and gloves tonight," I told my team. "Our extremities are the most likely places to get frostbite."

"True," Cap said, holding his hands in front of him as the fire crackled away, sending sparks showering. "We probably need to sleep together, too, in pairs. Two bodies together will be warmer than one, alone."

"No," Bernard whined. "I'm not sleeping with anyone."

"It's about survival," Chito said, rubbing his pink cheeks with his gloved hands. "It's not like we planned this. And it's just for tonight. We'll be back near lodging tomorrow, hopefully."

"If you're going to force me, I call dibs on Andi," Bernard said sourly.

"What?" I exclaimed. "You can't do that. I'm not the last piece of cake that someone gets to claim."

"I'm not sharing a tiny seat with that giant oaf," Bernard scowled, looking at Chito. "And I'm not about to cram in with Mr. Long Legs Gallivanter over there, either."

"I'm as tall as Cap," I laughed, seeing the amused expression in Chito and Cap's eyes. "I have long legs, too."

"You're skinnier, though. More room for me."

"I'd think you want someone bigger," Chito winked, patting his belly. "More fat to keep you warm. Like a polar bear."

Marceau slapped Bernard on the back. "I bet Dessie would keep you company tonight," he said, and Willis laughed as they overheard.

"Hey Dessie!" Willis shouted, and she looked up from across the fire, where she was bundled up and wedged between Hudson and Paz.

"Yeah?" she called back.

Bernard shoved Marceau over, and struggled to his feet. "*No,*" he said, rushing to the closest Ford and wrenching open the door. He climbed inside and disappeared from view as we laughed.

"He's an odd one," Marceau said, laughing as he righted himself, dusting the snow off. It was starting to accumulate on the ground, I noticed.

"We probably need to get the tarps out of the back and drape it over the seats above us, after we pop up the canvas roof. This snow looks like it might be pretty heavy," I told Cap, looking up at the sky. Sure enough, the snowflakes fell faster and bigger now. Out here in the mountains, the snow swirled in strange patterns. We could potentially have to deal with snow drifts faster than we were used to—even those of us from northern states.

"Good idea," he nodded. Together, we unpacked the tarps and popped the canvas roof into place for each Ford. Cap held one up for Hudson to see from his fire.

"Thanks," Hudson yelled, as his crew joined us in unwrapping several heavy tarps from their trunks. "Good call. Keep the snow off and keep us dry."

After a simple dinner of rice and beans and sliced sausage, it was too cold to sit around the fires without our backs getting chilled. We rotated ourselves, but it was freezing.

"The temperature's plummeted," Chito said, his scarf now wrapped up around his face so that we could only see his eyes. We each had a thick blanket draped over our heads and bodies. Snow was several inches thick around us, and we fought a losing battle as we dusted off our jackets and boots.

"I think it's probably time for us to pack into our vehicles," Cap said. "Remember to wear extra gloves and extra socks, everyone. Keep your boots on. Keep your head warm. If you start to feel pins and needles, get up and jog around a bit. That's the first stage of frostbite."

"Poke a hole or two in your tarp, too," I added. "You'll need breathing holes overnight."

"What a way for our story to end, eh?" Hudson laughed, his dark eyes shining. "The world-famous Chinook Voyageurs and the Gallivanter Expedition, frozen to death in one single night."

Willis laughed. "That'd be sure to land us on the front page of every newspaper out there. We wanted to be famous, right?"

CHAPTER 42

CAP AND I CLIMBED INTO one of the automobiles together, clumsy in the many layers we wore to protect us from the cold.

I crawled in first, and lay flat on my side along the bench seat, my back up against the cushion. Cap awkwardly crawled in behind me, closing the door and pulling the tarp over our heads, showering us with snow and muffling the outside noise.

"How romantic," he groaned, as we squeezed together, his body half off the bench. "Do you have any more room to move?"

"No. You're already smashing me."

"Why don't they make these cars bigger?" he grumbled, his body pressed tightly against mine. "This is ridiculous. Why are we both so tall, anyway?"

"Sheer dumb luck," I laughed. Our boots clanked together as we shifted and tried to get comfortable. Nothing worked. We gave up, and tucked in with our hands crossed against our chests like mummies. Our faces were so close that our cold noses bumped against each other when we shifted.

"Don't you dare ever tell my mother that we slept together out here," I said, staring into Cap's eyes in the darkness.

Cap laughed. "I won't tell your mother about a lot of things. Mostly about all the times I've put you in danger on this expedition."

"Hey, I chose to be here," I reminded him. "Sure, it has its moments of glamor and fame, but it's these days of roughing it without proper meals and clothing that really keep me invested."

The sound of the wind rattling the tarp above us soon lulled me to sleep. I slept fitfully, the stiffness of not being able to move an inch disturbing me. At one point, I started to feel claustrophobic and cold. I stirred, and groaned. The tarp above us was bowed in—heavy with snow, I'd guess.

My nose ached, and I worried that it had gotten too cold. I slowly reached my hand up and pulled my two pairs of gloves off with my teeth, trying not to disturb Cap. He shifted as I felt my freezing nose with my hand, prodding it. Fortunately, it still had feeling, which likely meant that it was just chilled and not permanently damaged.

Cap's eyes cracked open slowly.

"Are we dead?" he whispered, looking up at the tarp that hovered inches above his head.

"Maybe," I said, reaching up with my hand to touch the canvas roof and tarp above our heads. It was heavy. "I think we got a good amount of snow last night."

He frowned. "That'll slow us down even more."

"You did try to tell them that you wanted to avoid snow in the mountains."

Cap sighed. "I'll be sure to tell Hudson I told him so when we get covered by an avalanche."

I had been thinking about avalanches, too. Despite a childhood in northern New York and France, I didn't know mountains well.

"Do you really think we need to worry about an avalanche? Are the conditions right?"

Cap shrugged. Nestled against my body, the movement pulled at my jacket. "I'm not sure. I think the angle of the mountains isn't quite conducive to it. I believe the rule of thumb is a thirty degree angle or so can be dangerous. But up here? With these wild wind patterns and these deep canyons? It could be a problem."

"If the sun comes out, too, and melts the top layer of snow, that could be bad," I replied.

"Great, twice the deadly peril," Cap said, smiling at me. "Still want to forge ahead, Miss Gallivanter?"

"Always," I replied, wrinkling my nose. "What's a little snow? Just the icing on a grand adventure."

In the warmth of our human cocoon, I felt happy. At peace. How had I ever found a man like Cap to share my life with? The thought that I was marrying him still took me by surprise sometimes. We'd faced so many battles together, and yet we still had the spirit to laugh and tease each other. It was all I could have hoped for out of life—someone who shared my adventurous spirit and was willing to happily partner with me through the ups and downs.

Cap groaned. "I don't want to climb out of here," he confessed. "It's going to be freezing out there."

"I know."

"We should check on the others, though," he said. "Get the fires going so everyone can warm up."

Together, we reached up with one hand and carefully pushed the tarp up, the movement sending the accumulated snow whooshing down to the ground. Starting at one end, we slowly peeled the tarp back, blinking in the sudden brightness.

"Incredible," I breathed, sitting up and staring at the woods around us.

We'd gotten several inches of snow overnight, and it had transformed the world into a place of beauty. The craggy pine trees and boulders were coated with snow, like a painter had dabbed white into their branches and tops. The ground and all the Fords were covered in heaps of powdery snow, which glimmered like it had a crust of tiny diamonds. The air was still, and when I took a breath it felt icy and dry.

"The world is ruggedly beautiful in all its forms," I thought.

Across the clearing, Hudson, Rollie, Claude and Leonce were already up, their cars brushed clean of snow. Leonce had both fires started, the heat melting the snow around them in large rings. A kettle sat steaming on the fire, and another large pot sat low in the flames. As I watched, Leonce dug deep into the snow with his gloved hand, finding the snow closer to the earth, and pulled out a handful. He dropped it into the pot.

"Is he making water?" Cap asked, following my gaze.

"Yes," I said, the motions of digging to find the freshest snow familiar to me from my childhood days at the farm. My father, a Canadian citizen, had grown up learning cold weather survival skills. And like any self-respecting Canadian man, he'd passed them onto me. The Chinook boys were undoubtedly in their element right now.

"That's good," I added, pulling my scarf around my ears and nose tightly. "When it's this cold, your body needs more water than normal. We need to keep drinking. And consuming more food, too."

"Make sure you pass that tidbit on to Chito," Cap said, rubbing his hands to warm them. "He'll be happy to hear that we need to eat more."

I climbed out of the Ford first, crawling over Cap. I stepped into the snow, which came up to my knees. "Let's help build up the fires," I said, stomping my feet to get the blood flowing.

"Good morning, Gallivanters," Rollie greeted us, his cheeks pink from the chill. He was squatting by the fire, poking pine branches in. Next to him, Claude worked on a kettle of coffee.

"Good morning," Cap replied. "Need help?"

"I could use some help splitting these bigger branches and stumps behind me," Rollie said, pointing to a haphazard pile that had obviously just been collected. "We need to get to the interior wood so it'll light, since the outside was covered in snow overnight."

"Got it," Cap said, picking up a nearby hatchet and heading toward the mound.

"What, the famous Andi Gallivanter isn't going to go swing an axe and chop down a tree?" Rollie teased as I joined him at the fire.

"Hey, I split enough logs repairing our farm's fence to last a lifetime," I laughed, pulling off my double gloves to show him my hands. "See these calluses? Those thick ones? I've had those since I was ten. All the other girls thought they were disgusting. Unladylike."

Rollie examined my hands with interest. "Gee, Andi. I think we would've been friends, growing up."

"That would've been nice. I didn't have many."

"Really?"

"If you count books, though, I had a ton."

Rollie laughed. "Too bad we didn't know each other as kids. Our lives could've been different."

"I could've been a part of the Chinook childhood gang, huh?" I teased. "I can't imagine what it was like with all of you growing up together. You must have been holy terrors."

"We were," he said, standing up to help Cap as he carried over a bundle of freshly chopped chunks of wood. I grabbed several pieces and knelt with him as he used a large piece to brush away the snow that had accumulated on the rocks of the second fire pit.

"All of us, except for Dessie and Patrick, grew up in the same town," Rollie talked as we worked. "We went to school together, went ice fishing, and played pond hockey nearly every day. Our families all know each other, too. In the springtime, we used to go hunting for maple syrup in the woods around us. Sometimes we'd camp out, overnight, in search of a good haul."

"You hunted for maple syrup? What tough boys," I laughed, lining up the wood to make a sturdy fire. "You don't share that story with the public, do you?"

"No," he replied, grinning at he squatted to arrange the kindling. "We prefer that people think of us as warriors."

He walked over to the other fire and held a dry branch in it, waiting for it to ignite. When it caught, he carefully carried it over and placed it in the base of our unlit fire. The small flame slowly caught the other branches and needles, and started curling up.

"Hudson likes to portray us as a group of tough guys, descendants of lumber jacks and fur traders," Rollie continued, watching the fire. "He loves telling those stories about us racing our ice canoes in the St. Lawrence River in February. I mean, we did—don't get me wrong. But we're not just brawny outdoorsmen. Hudson and Patrick were at university together, and left school to assemble this team."

"That throws off the image, for sure," I said.

"How strange it is that everyone has a backstory, and each person is so interesting when you actually take the time to get to know them," I mused. People were just as fascinating as the scenery around us.

Tarps were starting to peel back as the rest of the crew woke up. Dessie and Paz had apparently shared a car together overnight, and she hurriedly smoothed her long hair, which she had braided, as she sat up, yawning.

"Are they a thing now?" I asked Rollie in a low tone, looking toward them.

Rollie glanced over, and shook his head. "I don't know," he said quietly. "If you ask me, Dessie is willing to be a 'thing' with just about anyone here."

"How do you guys not see it?"

He rolled his eyes. "My boys see it, trust me. It's just that some of them don't care that much. She's pretty, and she gets us attention in the papers. That's all we really hoped for, out of her. Not every girl is Andi Gallivanter, saving lives and building fires."

Cap dropped another pile of wood at our feet. He'd removed his outer jacket, to keep from sweating, and he tossed it at me. "Need an extra layer?"

"Thanks," I said, draping it over my head. It was still warm with his body heat.

"You're good together," Rollie commented, studying Cap as he walked away.

"We're just friends," I responded, trying not to blush.

Rollie laughed. "Okay."

"What?"

Bernard stumbled over to us, rubbing his hands together. "I'm freezing," he said, frowning. "My hands won't stop tingling."

Rollie and I swiftly met eyes with a knowing look. We both recognized the warning signs of frostbite. Depending on the severity of the cold, you tended to feel aching, tingling, or a dull sort of throb.

"Can you show me your hands, Bernard?" I asked casually, standing up to help him pull off his gloves.

"Yeah, why?" he said, shivering as the cold air touched his bare skin.

I peeled off Bernard's outer glove, then carefully tugged at the interior one. "Does that hurt at all?" I asked, pulling.

"No. I can't feel anything."

Underneath the glove, his skin was dull, grayish white on the tips of several of his fingers and the entire left side of his hand.

"What is that?" Bernard cried out in shock. I swiftly wrapped my hands around his, feeling the cold flesh. He pulled against me, but I held fast.

"Don't, Bernard," I said. "You have frostbite. We need to warm it up."

"Let me get to the fire then!" Bernard yelled, wrestling with me. I planted my legs firmly and refused to move.

"No," I shook my head. "That's too hot. It needs to be warmed slowly."

"Leonce! Claude!" Rollie yelled, standing up and cupping his hands around his mouth. "We need hot water over here! And rags!"

"Stop it," Bernard struggled against me. His fingers were freezing, like holding ice cubes in my hands.

"Listen to me, Bernard, please," I said gently, trying to calm him down. I was sure his panic was worsened by the fact that he was our crew's mechanic, and needed functional hands more than anyone else. "Calm down and listen. You're going to be fine, but we need to warm them up slowly. With warm wet rags."

Cap carried a load of firewood over to us and dropped it in a messy heap. "What's going on?" he exclaimed, staring at me holding Bernard's hands.

"Frostbite," Rollie responded as Claude set a small bowl of steaming water and a rag in front of him. He pulled off his gloves and tucked them into his pocket, dipping his bare hands into the hot water to dunk the rag and squeeze it out.

Cap watched as I removed my own hands and Rollie carefully wrapped the wet rag around Bernard's fingers. He winced when he saw the white flesh.

Hudson and Leonce joined us, and stood watching. Bernard looked self-conscious, standing awkwardly in the middle of the clearing with his hands wrapped in a towel.

"Did any of your crew experience this?" Cap asked Hudson, glancing at the others.

"We carry fur-lined gloves with us," he shrugged. "We're Canadian. It's habit."

Cap grunted. "I told you we shouldn't have planned a trek through the mountains this time of year," he grumbled. "It was foolish."

"Hey, *you* agreed to it," Hudson replied, his face darkening. "Don't blame me now!"

"He's our mechanic," Cap protested. "He needs his hands. What are we going to do if he can't use them?"

"Well, we have two mechanics on our crew," Hudson shrugged, pointing to Patrick and Marceau, who were standing over by the farthest fire. "We can share."

"Right," Cap sniffed. "So for the next few months, we have access to them. And then what? We have a mechanic who doesn't have fingers as we travel around the rest of the world? Real helpful, I'm sure."

"Stop," Chito said, joining the group standing around the fire, watching Bernard. "He's going to be fine. You're just upsetting Bernard right now."

"Can I see?" Willis said, peeking under the rags. He studied Bernard's hands, slowly bending the tips of his fingers. "Frostbite, but not too severe. The skin will die, but you should be fine. I think you'll regain feeling right away."

Bernard was still now, his eyes darting nervously between all of us. He hated being the center of attention. "How do you know?"

Willis pulled off his right glove and waggled his fingers.

"Had frostbite on them all," he said, holding them up in front of us. "Was tracking a moose through the woods. I saw him out the cabin window, and threw on my coat and hat and rushed out without gloves. The hand that held the gun got it worst."

"Oh yeah," Rollie and Claude laughed, as Hudson slapped Leonce and guffawed. "I forgot about that. You wore a bandage for weeks, that's right. Remember what Sarah said?"

They laughed uproariously at the inside joke.

"Shut up," Willis shot back, smiling at the memory. "Anyway, the skin turned completely white, just like yours. But it slowly started to grow back new layers. In a few weeks, I was fine. I regained feeling and everything."

"A few weeks?" Bernard repeated.

"Yeah, but I could move them after a few days," Willis responded.

Bernard rolled his eyes and looked at Cap. "I quit."

"You can't quit," Cap shook his head. "We have to keep going. We're out in the middle of nowhere."

"Fine," Bernard sniffed. "Then I quit...when we get to the nearest hotel."

CHAPTER 43

AFTER EATING BREAKFAST and drinking some piping hot coffee—"You Yanks call it cowboy coffee, right?" Leonce had grinned—we cleared off the cars and repacked the trunks so we could get back to driving.

"We should be able to make it to Nuremberg, I think," Cap said, tracing the map. "From there, Munich isn't far. Maybe another day or two of driving."

We piled into our Fords after warming the engines with our kerosene lamps, which mercifully started up right away even in the cold.

"It's going to be freezing as we drive," I said, pulling my hat down low and wrapping my scarf up over my nose and ears. I tucked the bottom of my scarf under my goggles, to keep it in place against the wind.

Chito did the same, standing outside my car. "Did you ever think we'd miss the desert?"

I flashed back to the snake that had slithered slowly toward me as I lay injured in the jungle in French Sudan several months earlier and shuddered. Sometimes I woke up in a cold sweat, reliving the moment. I didn't miss the desert that much. I'd nearly died in it.

I pulled out slowly behind Cap's car, where Bernard sat nursing his hand. Reluctantly, Bernard had given up driving his own Ford for the time being and Chito was driving in his place. We no longer had a relief driver, which meant the responsibility of driving would now fall on only three of us. We wouldn't get a break at all.

It was going to be a difficult journey, without a fourth driver to rotate in and give us some time to rest. It already required a lot of endurance and strength to constantly use both hands and feet to keep the cars moving, not even factoring in the constant rattling of the steering wheel and the uncomfortable bumping of the car trundling down the road. My body was always sore after driving for hours on end.

Hudson led the caravan of nine cars as we drove up and down the tiny winding roads through the alpine scenery.

Within a few hours, we'd made it out of the treacherous, snow-covered mountains and into gentler woods. As we drove, we crossed in front of small villages. Wooden houses sat perched merrily in the snow, their distinctive wooden beams crisscrossing over colorful paint.

We slowed as we neared Nuremberg. The roads around it were clogged with horses and carriages and automobiles like ours. I gazed around, curious.

Looking at the ordinary people on the streets, it was hard to believe that we'd been at war with them just five years ago.

"These are the people who killed your father," I thought, looking at the faces I passed. *"These are the people who killed so many men, destroyed so many families. And for what? We don't even really remember now, do we?"*

Pulling slowly through the busy streets, I studied the city. The buildings were mostly brick and stone, and statues and cathedrals soared all around us. Many of the buildings were tall and narrow, and looked centuries old. It was beautiful and quaint.

We reached a wide center square and pulled over, lining our automobiles up next to each other. Cap helped Bernard out of the Ford, and walked over to my door to open it for me.

"Nuremberg's a rich city," Cap said, staring around. "It's an art center, too. Did you ever hear of the famous painter, Albrecht Dürer? He's from here."

Chito and I smiled at each other. Cap was a wealth of random facts, and he couldn't help sharing them with us, whether we had interest in them or not.

"It's also a bit of a political hotbed," he continued. "Germany is going through some power struggles right now, after losing the war. They just arrested one of their young opposing political leaders, some guy named Hitler."

"I remember reading about that in the papers," I responded. "He was charged with treason, right?"

"Yes. You can't go against the government publicly, like he did. But he's in jail now, so who knows who'll be grabbing power here next," Cap replied. "Besides, we all know the Versailles Treaty limits Germany to no more than a hundred thousand soldiers, after all the problems they caused in the Great War. They have no chance to cause issues anymore."

"Dear Lord, Cap," Bernard groaned. "Stop. No one cares about German politics."

"Fine, I'll talk about food instead," Cap replied, his forehead wrinkling. "I read that we're supposed to try a particular kind of food here. They're famous for these tiny little sausages. Supposedly, they invented them during the Black Plague. They're small, so they could be shoved through the doors of quarantined houses."

"Now you're speaking my language, Cap," Chito grinned. "Where do we get some?"

We walked until we found our hotel, a tall old building in the center of a thriving town square. A cart was set up nearby with large pretzels, which Chito and Leonce and Marceau examined with interest as we pushed open the lobby doors.

I'd always had a knack for languages, and spoke a fair amount of German. I walked up to the lobby desk and greeted the fair haired, stocky man standing there.

"Hallo. Wir wurden gerne einchecken, bitte?" I said politely in German. "Checking in for the Gallivanters and Chinook Voyageurs, please. We will need thirteen rooms."

Next to me, Hudson laughed.

"She speaks German, too? She really does it all," he said, winking at me. "Can we have her when you're done?"

"Yeah, we'll trade," Rollie joked. "You guys can have Dessie, we'll take Andi."

"No," Cap replied shortly.

"What, Dessie doesn't speak German?" I teased, looking over my shoulder. The four of us watched as Dessie smiled and flirted openly with two good-looking German men in the lobby. One of them was already holding her suitcase for her.

"She's still useful," Hudson replied, leaning back and running his gaze over her slim body. "She certainly catches everyone's eyes, wherever we go."

I rolled my eyes as the clerk handed me the room keys.

After settling into our rooms, we bathed and dressed again for dinner, drifting back into our teams. The Chinooks wanted to eat at a local beer hall, and Chito was already leading us on a hunt to find the famous local sausages Cap had told us about.

I tried not to pout as I saw the Chinooks walk away together, laughing in the cold air. They were so lively. I didn't realize how much I enjoyed their company until I saw them leave without us.

The hotel staff pointed us helpfully toward a small, crumbling dwelling outside the ancient castle walls in the heart of the town. "It's right across the street from Dürer's home," they told us, drawing us a crude map on a scrap of paper. "Look for the old well, and the best sausages in town will be right next to it."

We spotted the building, a skinny building propped against a steep rise with the castle fort walls directly behind it.

"This place looks medieval, doesn't it?" I said, pushing open the tiny door.

The warm scent of fried sausage and beer filled my nostrils and the host greeted us.

"Welcome, my friends," he said in German. "You have a good eye, Fräulein. This building is indeed that old. We've been serving bratwurst here since the fourteenth century. We're the best in town."

"Oh boy," Chito rubbed his hands together gleefully.

We were served heaping platters of tiny sweet sausages the size of my pinky fingers, with large round mounds of potato salad on the side. In the dim wood paneled room with its checkered tablecloths, electric lights blazing overhead as a fire in the corner of the room warmed us, we drank our beer and laughed together.

"This is the life I always dreamed of," Chito confessed, after eating a third helping of sausages. "Traveling the world with friends and trying new foods in every city? It's too good to be true."

The waiter smiled indulgently as he asked to hear about the desserts, and ordered a trifle that the kitchen recommended.

"I'd order the Lebkuchen Dessert im Glas mit Sahne, Orangen, und Granatapfel," the waiter explained to me, as I translated for Chito. "It sounds like a gingerbread dessert with cream, oranges, and pomegranate."

"Sounds good. Let's get four? Three?" Chito said, looking at us. We shook our heads, smiling. "Two, then," he said, leaning back and sipping his beer contentedly.

"I haven't had much chance to ask you all, but are you ready to part ways and leave the Chinooks behind?" Cap asked, settling in with his arm draped around the back of my chair. "We've nearly served our sentence with them. Finally."

The three of us exchanged glances.

"They're not so bad," Chito shrugged.

Bernard nodded in agreement. "I haven't been nearly as miserable as I figured I'd be," he said, swigging his beer.

"Honestly? I've enjoyed our time together," I replied, reaching for my drink. "They're fun. Some of them are pretty nice guys."

"Like Rollie, for instance?" Cap asked lightly.

"Yes," I said slowly, glancing at him. Was he jealous? "Patrick, too. And Marceau."

"Hm," Cap pursed his lips, taking a long gulp of beer.

"What?" I said, trying to keep my tone casual, to match him.

"Nothing," Cap said, leaning back. "Anyway, let's talk about our next leg, after we get done with dealing with them. We'll be down near Italy next month, when we finish up. I say we go straight south from—"

"Hold on," I interrupted, frowning. "Why don't you like Rollie? Or Patrick? They're good men. And Hudson runs his crew just like you do, Cap. Surely you see it."

He laughed sarcastically, removing his arm from the back of my seat. "Leave it to you to be friends with the enemy."

"Enemy?" Chito said, shaking his head. "No, they're not bad guys. She's right. Maybe we had issue with them before, but I've come around. They're good people."

"They're our competition," Cap responded, his tone darkening. "We're both going after the same prize. Did you forget about that?"

"No one's saying that," I frowned. Cap was being uncharacteristically sour about this. He was usually calm and rational, not petty.

"Sure you are," he said, taking another swig of beer. "You want to be friends with them. Spend time getting to know them. Sharing jokes and learning about each other's lives. Why? In a few weeks, we'll separate and hopefully never see their faces again. Ever."

Chito and I looked at each other across the table and raised our eyebrows. He shook his head slightly, indicating I should back off. I bit my tongue from throwing back a sharp retort at Cap. I couldn't believe he was so resistant to being friendly with the Chinook Voyageurs. Why not make the best of it?

The waiter came back, wiping his hands off on his dark apron. "What else can I get you, my friends?" he said, a smile on his face.

"Nothing. I'm done," Cap retorted, standing up and throwing his napkin on the table. He bolted out the door.

"I'm sorry," I said, standing up. I was taller than the waiter, who took a step back, confused by our hasty movements. "He's not feeling well," I lied, speaking in German. "His stomach can't handle...potatoes."

"Oh, that's too bad," the waiter grimaced. "We have so many potatoes here, too. With every meal."

"He'll pay the bill," I pointed to Chito, who was taking the last bite of the lebkuchen trifle. "I'm going to check on my friend. With his bad stomach."

"Yes, of course," the waiter replied sympathetically, as I pushed out the door.

Cap was standing several paces away, his back to me. The night was dark and starless, clouds overhead. Tiny flakes of snow floated down like grains of salt as I pulled my coat on, throwing my scarf around my throat against the cold.

"What's going on with you?" I exclaimed, reaching out to grab his arm. Cap yanked away, and my fingers grazed his sleeve.

"Stop it," he said, turning around to face me. He was angry.

"What? Why are you acting like this?"

He glared at me. "You know why," he spat. The snowflakes dusted his shoulders, falling faster now. Couples strode through the plaza around us, chatting happily in German. I was thankful no one recognized us as celebrities.

"Is this about the other team?" I asked, keeping my voice low. "You don't like us hanging out with them? With Rollie and Patrick?"

"Rollie again, huh? You sure enjoy talking about him, don't you?"

"We're friends. I don't know why you're so upset about it."

"You're being ridiculous," Cap replied. "You have to see it."

"See what?"

"Rollie's falling for you, Andi."

"What? No. We're friends, nothing more!"

He turned to look as Chito and Bernard opened the door, pulling on their coats. Chito saw me and waved. They headed toward us.

"You're being unreasonable," I said quietly, as they neared us. "I don't have feelings for him. For any of them. I love *you*."

"Yeah, well, maybe that's only because you met me first," he replied, shoving his hands into his pockets and walking away.

"Let's get back," he said over his shoulder, as Chito and Bernard caught up to where I was standing. "I'm tired. I'm going straight to bed when we get back. It's been a long day."

CHAPTER 44

I LAY IN BED THE NEXT morning, feeling the cold wind push through the small crack in my partially opened hotel room window. I pulled my blanket up to my chin, my mind racing as I thought hard.

Cap loved me. And I loved him. I couldn't wait to spend the rest of my life with him.

But Rollie was a good man, too. Did he really have feelings for me? Was I leading him on?

"No," I told myself honestly. *"From the very beginning, I've been friendly with him, nothing more. I haven't told him outright that Cap and I are engaged, but he has to see that we're closer than anyone else, right?"*

I thought about Rollie's face as he told me about how much his sisters adored me. Smiling at me as we told jokes around the fire. The way he looked at me, amused, with a grin on his face. It was so easy to talk to him.

"Life is so confusing," I thought in utter frustration. *"Why can't it be easy? Why is love and friendship so hard?"*

I waited for Cap to come knock on my door and give me a secret morning kiss, like he usually did, but he didn't come.

At breakfast, he ignored me, sitting with Hudson and plotting the route for the day on a large map. "We'll make it to Munich today, for sure," I heard Hudson say, tracing the drive down.

I tried to catch him after breakfast, as we loaded the cars, but he brushed me off.

"I'm busy," he said, pushing past me as I waited at his Ford. I stood there, leaning against the shiny black door as he loaded up the back and tied the items down. Dusting his hands off on his pants, he pulled on his driving gloves and goggles and started to open the door.

"Hey, come on," I said quietly, trying not to make a scene. "What's going on? Why are you so mad at me?"

"We're leaving," he said, avoiding my eyes and reaching for the handle.

"Cap," I said, reaching for his arm. He stepped back quickly.

"We're leaving," he repeated. "Get in your car."

"Since when do you order me around?"

"I'm the captain here," he replied. His blue eyes, normally full of happiness when he met mine, were cold. "I'm in charge of my team."

"Fine," I shot back. *I'll show him not to boss me around like this,* I thought angrily.

My boots clipped through the dusting of snow on the ground as they carried me across the road to Rollie's Ford.

"Rollie!" I said brightly. "Want to hop in with me? I could use a friendly face today in my car. I'll drive the first leg."

He was already sitting in the driver's seat with Marceau as his passenger, but his face lit up. "Sure!" he said eagerly, wrenching open the door and pushing Marceau out. He immediately followed me to my car, keeping up with my long strides.

"Where are you going?" Marceau called out after him, but Rollie waved him off.

"I'm riding with Andi!" he called out, getting into my passenger seat as I climbed behind the wheel.

I started the engine and waited for Cap to pull out in front of me. He was lead car today, and Hudson followed behind him. I studiously avoided his gaze as he stared at Rollie and me through his goggles, his wheels crunching in the crusted layer of snow on the street.

"What are you doing?" I asked myself, groaning inwardly.

Was I trying to make Cap even more jealous, or was I trying to prove a point to him? I didn't even know. It wasn't the first time my impulsive nature complicated my life.

I consoled myself with the thought that I'd at least enjoy the company of Rollie as we drove.

As we drove out of Nuremberg and headed south, we rolled through thick swathes of forest, tall pines towering on either side of the road. Birds chirped, and Rollie pointed out a deer to me as we passed it, standing in a meadow, flicking its tiny tail.

"I love the feeling of the wind in my hair," I said, leaning my head back. "Even though it's freezing wind today."

"I love it, too," Rollie agreed. "It's freedom. A release from worry."

"Right," I said, smiling at him. "The same reason I always loved riding horses."

"I love to ride, too," he laughed. "My sisters and I used to fight all the time over who could ride together. We had two horses, but there were five of us kids. We'd tackle each other to the ground, running across the field, racing to see who could saddle up first."

I grinned. "Your family sounds a bit like a zoo."

"It was," he replied. "You'd love them. You'd fit right in."

"I'd like to meet them someday," I said. "Especially your little sisters. They sound like a lot of fun."

"Well, let's hope you do meet them," Rollie said lightly. Was he saying he wanted me to meet his family for a particular reason? I couldn't tell. I rapidly searched for something else to talk about.

"Tell me about your life outside of this team," I said. "You play hockey, right? I've always wanted to learn. Tell me about it."

Rollie launched into a detailed and animated discussion about every Canadian boy's favorite subject. I'd heard enough about their little national hockey league in the last few weeks to know that their blood ran hot at the mention of the sport.

I tried to keep up as Rollie babbled about the intricacies of line changes and rivalries and some guy named Howie.

"You're not a Boston fan, right?" Rollie interrupted suddenly, looking at me.

"What?"

"The new team. The Boston Bruins. It's the only American team," Rollie said, now frowning at me. "You're not a fan, right? Oh, tell me you're not."

I had no idea what he was talking about. "No, I've never heard of them."

"Oh, thank God," he groaned dramatically. "I could never respect you again if you told me you were."

The more Rollie talked, the more I felt at ease. *"We're just friends,"* I repeated to myself. *"He's not interested in me as anything more than a friend. It's just that I've never really had many friends, so I'm not used to how this goes."*

Rollie continued to chat, his tone animated, as I snuck furtive glances at him out of the corner of my eye and drove.

"Cap doesn't know what he's talking about," I told myself again, willing myself to believe it.

CHAPTER 45

AS WE PULLED OVER TO eat lunch a few hours later, I noticed Cap watching Rollie and me closely as we got out of the car, laughing with each other. He wore a scowl.

"Hey," I said, ignoring Cap and heading over to Paz and Leonce, who were dragging out supplies from the back of one of the Chinook Fords. If Cap couldn't play nice with the Chinooks, at least I would. "Need some help?"

"Thanks," Paz smiled. "How was your drive?"

"Fine. Why?"

"You enjoyed driving with Rollie?" Paz said, watching me out of the corner of his eyes. "I'm sure he did, too. He's a big fan of yours."

"Oh, yeah?" I said lightly, turning to stack the box on a rock. "What does he say about me, behind my back? I hope he's not complaining about my driving."

"Oh, he's not complaining about you," Paz smirked. I pursed my lips.

"He's just friendly," I told myself firmly. *"Rollie is just a friend. He sees me as a friend. He says nice things because he enjoys hanging around me. We get along together."*

"So what's going on with you and Dessie, anyway?" I said, changing the subject. "You spend a whole lot of time with her. A lot of time alone."

Paz sighed dramatically, and put his leg up on the rock ledge we were setting up with plates. "I don't understand women," he said, running his hand through his dark hair in frustration. "I'm a young, attractive, wealthy man. How does she not see it?"

"Maybe she does, and she's just messing with you," I shrugged. "She's a flirt."

"I know," Paz groaned. "She's gorgeous, though."

I rolled my eyes. Paz was always chasing after beautiful women. He was never happier than after a press conference, as girls surrounded him and excitedly asked about his travels. He continued moaning about Dessie as we set up the lunch spread, carrying his plate over to the rocks near her and glancing her way every few moments, listening as she chatted with Willis and Hudson.

We ate lunch perched on rocks in a small clearing off the side of the road, listening to the birds chirp. It was cold, but the sun warmed our faces now that we weren't driving into the wind. Cap and I sat on opposites sides of the clearing, ignoring each other. Chito and Rollie sat next to me, trading jokes with Claude and Marceau.

I finished eating the sliced sausages and bread Chito had packed for our lunches and stood up, brushing the crumbs off my lap.

"You done already?" Chito asked, looking up from his second sandwich.

"Yeah, I'm not that hungry today," I said, thinking absently about Cap. How long could we ignore each other?

Willis and Patrick walked over, chewing on a hunk of sausage. "Rollie, you driving this next leg?" Willis asked, between bites.

"Oh, I haven't really figured it out yet," Rollie replied, glancing at me. "I've been driving with Andi all day."

"Right. As passenger. So are you her passenger again, or are you driving her car now or what?"

Rollie looked at me, shrugging. "I don't know. We haven't talked about it."

I looked down at him. *"Why is this so complicated?"* I said to myself. *"It's the same car, for Pete's sake. Both teams drive Fords. And you have no relief driver anymore, you might as well use the other team while you still can. Stop reading into this."*

"I don't care," I said, pulling my scarf around my neck. "I could use a break from driving. I haven't had one now, since Bernard got frostbite and can't rotate in with us."

"Great, I'll drive then," Rollie chirped, biting into his bread. Chito looked at me, one eyebrow raised.

I shrugged, already feeling a twinge of guilt. I hoped Cap wouldn't be livid over the thought of a Chinook teammate driving one of the Gallivanter Expedition Fords.

"Let me help you put this back," Chito said to me, laying his sandwich on a napkin and grabbing the box I had started to pick up.

"What?" I hissed furiously, as we each carried a corner.

"Why am I constantly interfering with you and Cap?" Chito shot back. "I get that you kids are younger, but you need to learn how to control your tempers better. You fight like children sometimes."

"I haven't done anything wrong!" I blurted as we reached the back of the Ford. He grunted, and slid the box into place, then turned and put his hands on his hips and glared at me.

"Andi, you know exactly what you're doing," he said. "You're driving him crazy on purpose. It's bad enough that you let Rollie drive as your passenger today but since when do we have the Chinook team driving *our* cars? Cap's going to lose it when he sees Rollie drive out behind the wheel of a Gallivanter car."

"So?"

"So? He's your fiancé. Do you really want to push this?"

"Rollie's a good guy. A good friend. You know that. You like him, too."

Chito groaned and grabbed at his beard with one hand, twisting it in frustration. "You know *nothing* about men, Andi. You missed the signs of Cap falling for you, too."

"I don't need a lecture," I glared. "I'm friends with you. And Bernard. And Paz. None of you are in love with me. So I'd appreciate if you just keep your nose out of my business. It's my life."

"It's my life, too," Chito said, glaring. "I'm the one that has to put up with your tantrums and fights and still have to keep on good terms with both of you. Maybe you can try thinking about your other teammates, for a change, not just yourself. Rollie likes you, and if you deny it, you're either clueless or just leading him on, which isn't fair to Cap. Plain and simple."

My cheeks blazed with hot shame. Chito had always been a trusted confidant for me, a friendly ear when I struggled.

"Andi," Chito continued, his tone gentler now as he saw my face. "You know I care about you. I'm trying to help you. You're young, I know, but you need to try to understand the men around you better. Sure, a lot of them just want to be your friends. But some of them are bound to want more. You need to learn how to spot the difference."

"Sorry," I said thickly. My throat suddenly felt tight. "It's too late now, though. He's driving and that's that."

I stomped back to my Ford. The rest of the team was nearly finished packing up and were getting into the cars. I leaned against my Ford, waiting and seething.

Rollie was talking to Hudson, leaning across his car a few spots down. He waved at me, and kept talking.

What was I doing? Proving a point and upsetting my whole team in the process? Was it worth it?

"Chito's right," I said, watching Rollie's face as he talked to Hudson. *"He's always looked out for me, like I'm his own daughter.*

He's always told me the truth. And he's saying the same thing as Cap. So maybe Rollie is attracted to me and I just haven't seen it."

But why was it that Dessie could flirt all the time, every moment of the day, and the moment someone else showed interest in me, I had to stop talking to him? That wasn't fair. It was a double standard.

I shoved these thoughts out of my mind as Rollie got into the car. I slid into the passenger seat next to him.

"It sure feels weird to drive a car with your team's logo on the door," he quipped, settling into his seat as the car rumbled.

I desperately wished I could have Rollie switch cars, but it was too late. There was no way I could get myself out of the mess now. *"You have to be more careful, going forward, to not spend as much time with Rollie,"* I chided myself.

Chito and Cap were probably right, as much as I didn't want to admit it. Rollie probably had interest in me. And I couldn't lead him on, knowing he had feelings for me. It wasn't right, and it wasn't who I was.

We pulled out slowly into the caravan, and I leaned my head in my hand as we drove, feeling the ends of my hair fluttering in the wind. Rollie chatted occasionally, sharing little stories that came to his mind as we passed different sites on the road. I tried hard not to engage him in any deep conversation, but watched the scenery quietly.

Snow-capped mountains sat on the distant horizon as we drove, and tall evergreens sat thickly, crowded, on both sides of the road. It was beautiful here, with its raw alpine nature, and remote.

When we made it into the outskirts of Munich, I was ready for some time to myself. We pulled in front of the hotel, and crowds formed quickly as we lined up our automobiles. They were waiting for us, eager and excited as we pulled in. We had a large press conference planned that night, one that we'd plugged in the newspapers for several weeks. Clearly, we'd have a massive crowd this evening.

I smiled as I shook hands with dozens of excited men and women, and nodded my thanks as the hotel porters rushed out to carry my suitcase in. The lobby was full of more guests, who applauded when they saw us enter.

"I'm going up to my room," I said to Bernard, who was inching toward the stairs, too.

"You don't have to tell me twice," he said gruffly, smiling half-heartedly at a man who tipped his hat to him.

Once inside, I flung my bag down and headed straight for the bathroom. I needed to soak in the bath for a while and clear my head.

CHAPTER 46

BOTH TEAMS MET IN THE lobby that evening, dressed and ready for our big press conference.

Dessie had carefully curled her hair and wore bright red lipstick. She hung back at the edge of our group, chatting with a handsome man who was staring openly at her. Paz stood near her, watching with obvious irritation.

"We're all here, then," Cap said as Leonce joined the group, the last one to arrive. "Let's get over there and put on a show."

Tonight's event was larger than normal, and officials had offered us a concert venue for our use. Police officers lined the perimeter of the crowd, as we pulled the cars up. Cameras flashed and people clapped as we opened our doors and stood smiling at the sea of faces.

"It feels like we're movie stars," Chito grinned, as we stepped out to a cheering crowd.

"Yeah, let's hope that never happens," Bernard groaned. "I miss the days when we were anonymous."

Once inside, we took our seats on the stage. People filed in, and newspaper journalists and photographers stood in the back, scribbling and snapping pictures as we presented. When it was our turn to share, we stepped up to the center stage and spoke under the dazzling, blinding spotlight.

We used the same presentation we'd done in France, but added in several compelling short films, which the Gallivanters had shot on our state-of-the-art portable Kinamo camera. People watched our clips of nomadic African tribes dancing, a large sandstorm bearing down on us, and people bartering in the streets of Morocco with fascination.

Hudson and Cap charmed the crowd with their electric performance. Their charisma was unparalleled tonight.

After we finished sharing, Cap invited the crowd to ask questions.

"Here it comes," Chito whispered to Patrick and Marceau, who sat next to me.

We all exchanged amused glances. No matter where we were, the questions typically ended up being the same. People asked us the farthest we'd ever driven at one time, what animals we encountered on the road, or what had surprised us most about the expedition.

Sure enough, the very first question was one that someone asked at every presentation.

"What's been the most surprising thing about the expedition so far?" a young man asked nervously, wringing the hat brim in his hands.

Cap smothered a grin, looking at Hudson, and lobbed it to him. "My dear friend Captain Landry would love to share about that."

Several more hands went up, impressing me with the variety of questions. This crowd was smart, I realized. Cap and Hudson took turns calling on us equally to answer. Cap skipped over me, I noticed, but Hudson invited me to answer a few questions.

"I think we have time for one final question," Cap said, pointing to a young man near the front who'd had his hand raised for several minutes.

"Thank you, Captain Gallivanter," the man said, standing. "My question is about how you're all getting along. Your teams had a public spat a few months ago. Now you're driving around Europe together. Can you speak to the relationship you've developed? Do you respect each other now?"

I could tell that Cap's body language changed. He stiffened slightly, but smiled wide as he responded, "I have nothing but respect for Captain Landry and his entire crew. They're a team of professionals, and they conduct themselves with integrity and discipline at all times. We're getting along just swell."

The man sat down, nodding.

"If I may," I heard Rollie pipe up, standing from his seat. "I can speak to that, Captain Gallivanter."

"Of course," Cap turned and smiled woodenly at Rollie. "Be my guest, Roland."

"*Oh no, oh no,*" I thought desperately, as I watched Rollie walk to the center of the shiny wooden stage, next to Cap.

What was he going to say? Please tell me he wouldn't bring me into this, somehow. Cap was likely to punch him right then and there, in front of everyone, if he did.

Rollie cleared his throat as the spotlight swiveled to him, illuminating his dark hair with a halo of light. His face was handsome and relaxed as he lifted it and stared out at the crowd.

"Ladies and gentlemen, I've truly enjoyed traveling with the Gallivanter crew," he spoke, his voice confident. "They're brave, and funny, and friendly. In fact, I spent the entire day driving with Miss Andi, in her automobile."

He turned his head to look at me and smiled before turning back to the crowd.

"Andi is an excellent driver, and a witty and admirable woman. She's brave and beautiful, smart and kind and resourceful, too. It's been the greatest few weeks of my life, getting to know such remarkable people," he said. "The Gallivanters are class acts. I, for one, am glad we've had this chance to get to know each other. It's an honor to be making history with them, as friends—not enemies. I truly hope they remain in our lives forever."

My heart sank. Oh, dear Lord, Rollie *was* falling in love with me. There was no denying it now. He'd just about confessed it to an entire room of strangers. He'd even called me beautiful.

Cap and Chito had been right.

The crowd thundered their applause, and shouted their approval in German. Apparently the world loved seeing us together, getting along.

"Thank you so much, ladies and gentlemen," Cap shouted, bowing low and smiling warmly. "Your support means everything to us. We simply wouldn't be here without the generous love and cheer of all of you. Thank you, from the bottom of our hearts. Enjoy your evening, and don't forget to keep your eyes open, your loved ones close, and always be ready for adventure!"

I hid a smile, despite my unease. Cap always ended each public event with that line. And each time, it always drew a standing ovation.

We smiled and waved as we stepped off the stage, into the quiet and dark backstage area. We crowded together in the dim gloom, little conversations happening all around me.

"I'm starving," Chito said to Leonce, who nodded.

"I saw a good restaurant not too far from here, I think...there's a beer hall next to it, too," Leonce responded.

Cap pushed through the huddle and grabbed my elbow. "Andi, let's talk for a minute," he said under his breath, smiling at Claude and Bernard, who stood next to me.

"Should we save you a seat?" Bernard called, as Cap walked out briskly, holding my elbow.

"Don't bother. We'll eat at the hotel," Cap answered for me. "You drive my car back, Chito. We'll walk."

He was angry.

"Listen, Cap," I began, but he waved me off, grinning as he walked me out the door through the crowded hallway.

"Not here," he said, smiling politely at strangers. "Slap a smile on that face, Andi, and walk with purpose. I'm not about to stop and talk with fans right now."

I grinned, automatically, and kept up with his fast strides. We reached the side door, and pushed out into the alley. He pulled his coat on, and shoved his hat down onto his head, pulling it low across his forehead. Wordlessly, he handed me my scarf and jacket and I bundled up as he put on his gloves.

"Cap," I started again.

"No," he said sternly. "Not yet."

"Why?" I replied, looking around. "We're alone."

"You just stepped off the stage, and the crowd is still emptying off into the streets all around here," Cap growled. "They'll recognize you right away. And me. We'll keep walking. You better keep up."

CHAPTER 47

CAP TOOK OFF DOWN THE street without me. I hurried to catch up with him.

The night was moonless and chilly. We walked briskly through the streets, our hands in our pockets, without speaking to each other for several blocks. I glanced at Cap's face as we walked, but he wasn't betraying anything. Was he disappointed? Frustrated with me? Would he listen, if I tried to reason with him?

Finally, he reached an empty street of closed businesses, and exhaled loudly. He stopped. For a moment, he bowed his head and closed his eyes, like he was summoning the strength to face me.

"I know," I said, before he could open his mouth. "Chito talked to me, too. About Rollie."

"Great," he exploded. "So please explain what the hell you've been doing, then?"

"I didn't realize it," I said, feeling foolish. It seemed obvious now, especially after Rollie's declaration on the stage. I'd had time to think about Rollie's looks and conversations and analyze them, as I soaked in the bathtub earlier.

"Right," he yelled. "You're full of it. You played along with him, flirted right back!"

I flushed. "I swear, in my mind, Rollie and I were just friends. I didn't think he liked me. I wasn't flirting, I was just being friendly. It wasn't like I ever talked about anything intimate with him."

"Sure."

"What?" I said, defensively.

Unexpectedly, Cap slammed his fist into the side of a brick wall. His gloved hand popped violently in the silence.

"You let him drive your car," Cap said, his voice rising to a shout. "*Your* car. *My* car. With *my* name on the side!"

I took a step back, surprised at Cap's sudden outburst. "So? It's just a car!"

"It's *my* expedition. The Gallivanters are my creation. My life's dream. And you let him sit behind the wheel of my Ford—the car I worked for years to get—and think it's no big deal?"

"Calm down."

"Calm down?" he repeated angrily. "It's bad enough that I'm stuck dealing with Paz again, the man who broke my trust and abandoned us. And dealing with the team who publicly dragged my name through the mud, damaging my reputation—forcing me to admit embarrassing things to all those reporters? Getting hauled back to Paris and reprimanded by our sponsors—men whose trust I worked hard to earn? And now I have to watch another man flirt with you right in front of me? How much do you think I can take, Andi?"

I crossed my arms and bit my lip, unsure of what to say.

He misinterpreted my actions and glared at me. "You're on my team. Rollie's a Chinook. Have you forgotten that? Or are you planning to pull the same trick Paz did and join them?"

"What?" I exclaimed, now feeling angry. "How could you even say something like that? You're being irrational."

"Think how it looks for the cameras!" he yelled at me, pacing. "Think what it looks like, when you're letting one of them sit in our cars, and someone gets a photograph of that? You can't! They're our competition, Andi! In a few weeks, we're separating and going our own ways again. We can't get friendly with them! We're in this to *beat* them!"

"It sounds like you just don't want me to have anyone," I shot back. "You'd rather control me, keep me all to yourself on our little crew. Where you have no competition."

Cap swore violently.

"So you acknowledge it, then?" he glared at me. "You think of him that way. As my competition."

"That's not what I meant," I backtracked quickly, trying to correct my blunder. "Not competition. You're possessive. You don't want to share me."

"Of course I don't want to share you!" he shouted. "You're my fiancée! Why should I share you with anyone else?"

Now I was mad, too. How dare Cap think he could control me? He'd always praised me for being a strong, independent, intelligent woman. How hypocritical of him to now walk back on that when I was thinking for myself, when it came to whom I chose to make my friends.

"So what you're really saying is that you don't trust me?" I yelled back. "Even if Rollie does have a thing for me, fine. So what? I'm in charge of my own actions. You don't trust me, that I could ever be friends with another man. You think I belong to you exclusively."

Cap groaned. "You don't understand men at all, Andi."

"I wish men would stop telling me that, and just explain what's on their damn minds already," I exclaimed. "I can't understand it. I should be able to have friends. Look at Dessie. She flirts with every man on earth, even Bernard. No one ever calls her on it!"

"So you want to be like Dessie now?" Cap hollered. "You want every man around you to think of you that way, to see you only as—as a fling, a floozy?"

I threw my head back. "Maybe that'd be nice! Look at the attention she gets. She doesn't actually work, she just looks pretty and helpless. She's allowed to flirt and manipulate and gets whatever she wants. I wonder what that's like."

"You're not Dessie," Cap snapped. "That's not who you are!"

"Don't tell me who I am!" I shouted back. "You don't even know!"

"I don't know?" he cried. "So few women are like you, Andi! You're funny and beautiful and real and courageous—"

The words were kind, but his voice was furious.

"Yeah, yeah," I interrupted, holding up my gloved hand. "I get it. I just heard that same thing from Rollie, from the stage."

Cap reeled back, hurt. *"Good,"* I thought angrily. *"Put him in his place."*

"You didn't think he was in love with you until Chito told you, huh?" Cap laughed bitterly. "No man gets on stage and publicly says those things about a woman he's just friends with, Andi. Don't be so naive. No man would sit in a car all day with a woman unless he's interested. And trust me, he is. He's *very* interested in you."

"I just didn't see it," I protested, hot anger bubbling in my veins. "I thought he was a friend. And even so, who cares? Can't I have my own friends? Can't I choose who I spend time with?"

"How can you not see how men are, Andi? You can't possibly expect a team of men to live around you for months on end without some of them falling for you."

"That's ridiculous," I shouted. "Not everyone is like you, you know. Some men just want to be my friend, nothing more. Look at Chito. And Bernard. Paz!"

"You have fun with Rollie, don't you?" Cap's voice was raised, ignoring my point. "I see you laugh together. Spending all your time talking. Sharing jokes around the fire. I'm just a drag, huh? The leader, always with my nose in a book or a map, trying to figure out what we're doing? I'm no fun. Not like him."

"That's not it."

"Right," he spat, then paused. His shoulders fell. Slowly, he said, "Maybe you wish I was more like him."

"Stop," I said crossly.

"How do I know, Andi?" he sighed. "You once thought you were in love with Arnau, and then you fell in love with me on one of these adventures. Who's to say that I can trust that you won't fall for Rollie now? Or someone else?"

I stared at him, angrily. *"But I love you!"* I screamed internally as I glared. *"I love you, you thick-headed fool!"*

Instead of telling him, I stood fuming, my mouth shut. I didn't know how to prove to him that my love to Arnau, my childhood best friend, had been the innocent love of a wistful, lonely girl. I was more than that now.

"You really don't think you can trust me?" I finally said, after we squared off for several tense moments.

"I—I don't know anymore."

"You don't know?" I exclaimed. "You, who told me you needed me on this team? Told me that I belonged here, right next to you, as a partner? Real love *does* trust, Cap. It doesn't control. It allows for someone to follow her own interests, to have friends, to not just spend all her time with one person—"

Cap interrupted me, holding up a hand. "Were you just wrapped up in the whirlwind adventure of it all, when you said yes to me out there in the jungle?"

I thought back to the moment of passion we'd shared, as he proposed so many months before. We'd struggled against untamed nature itself out there in the wilderness, together. We'd declared our love out there in the darkness of the jungle. It was a memory I treasured. Did he think I faked that?

"How can you say that?" I cried.

"You'd just fought tooth and nail for survival, alone," Cap pressed. He sounded tired. "You weren't sure you'd survive the night. Maybe you just jumped at me impulsively, the first man you saw on the other side of near catastrophe."

"Cap!"

"Maybe I'm not actually the man you want to spend your life with. Maybe you prefer someone else. Like Rollie. Or someone you haven't even met yet."

Furious tears came to my eyes. I didn't know what to say. I didn't think he'd hear me right now, anyway. We stood there, facing each other, staring. After several moments, he broke the silence.

"You can't say anything now?" he said, the anger back in his voice. "Andi Gallivanter's never afraid to speak her mind. At least, that's what I've thought, all this time. Maybe I didn't know you that well after all. Not as well as I thought."

Was it Cap that no longer had feelings for me? Was he trying to get out somehow, and using this situation with Rollie to cut *me* loose? My mind felt thick.

"Seriously?" Cap scowled, throwing his hat on the ground. "Say something, damn it! You're willing to tear this whole thing apart for what? To prove a point?"

I found my voice. "I love you. But you're not the boss of me. Is this how controlling you're going to be? Is this what it's going to be like to be married to you? We're out seeing the world, and I can't talk to one person? You can't tell me what to do without constraining who I am. Without clipping my wings. You either trust me—and trust me in all that I do—or not."

Cap laughed derisively. "Legally, I am in charge of you. You signed on to *my* expedition, don't forget. I make the calls for our team."

"So what are you—my boss, or my future husband? There's a difference."

He picked his hat up, and dusted it off.

With his back to me, he added, "I don't know whether or not you still consider me your fiancé, but either way, I'm still your captain."

CHAPTER 48

WE WALKED BACK IN SILENCE to the hotel. As we walked, I averted my gaze from Cap. My tears had ceased, but my heart was heavy.

I didn't know where we stood anymore.

Cap flung open the doors ahead of me, and walked through the entrance without holding the door for me. He headed toward the large bar across the lobby without saying a word. As he rarely touched alcohol, I knew this didn't bode well.

I headed toward my room, my shoulders stiff with suppressed rage. Rounding the corner, I walked right into the Gallivanter and Chinook crews.

"Andi!" Paz yelled, his voice slightly slurred. "We finished dinner. We're headed to the beer hall!"

"Come join us," Willis said, grinning and slapping Rollie on the back. Rollie was beaming.

They'd clearly enjoyed themselves at dinner already, and they were going back out to drink more? *They'll regret this tomorrow,* I thought ruefully.

"Come on, Andi! It'll be fun!" Dessie said, giggling. Her bright red lipstick was perfectly fresh, even as she slurred her words, too.

I didn't feel like sitting in a bar all night, but more than that, I didn't want to be alone with my thoughts. I chose companionship.

"Fine," I smiled. Dessie grabbed my hand and linked arms with me, like we were schoolgirls out for a stroll.

"Whatever gets my mind off of Cap," I thought. A drink or two wouldn't hurt.

Our large group walked together through the lobby, laughing. Chito was crooning his Spanish song as Marceau tried to sing along.

"Cap!" Hudson called out across the lobby. "You devil, you're trying to drink without us?"

Cap's back was facing us, and an empty shot glass already sat on the bar. He had another in his hand.

"Come join us!" Hudson yelled, walking over toward him. "We're going down the street, to the beer hall. We're celebrating. Come on."

"I'm alright, thanks," Cap replied stonily, staring straight ahead.

Chito came up behind Cap and draped his big arms over his shoulders. "If I have to carry you out, I will," he laughed, pulling Cap off his seat.

"Get off," Cap said, pushing his hands away. "I'm staying here."

"I insist, Captain Gallivanter," Hudson said dramatically, bowing deeply. "From one captain to another, I must buy you a drink. Please. I can't rest until I do."

"You're outnumbered," Willis said, sidling up alongside Hudson and Chito. "We can easily drag you there."

"Fine," Cap groaned, standing up. He tailed along behind the rest of the group, Hudson chatting with him at the rear.

I could hear music and laughter from the beer hall as we walked down the street toward its warm glow. Outside the door, a dozen young men smoked cigarettes and watched as Dessie and I walked inside.

"Hey, sweetie," one of the men said to Dessie in German, cutting in front of her path. She deftly avoided walking into him, but winked and smiled as she passed him.

The hall was crowded and chaotic. Buxom young women carried heavy steins of sloshing beer over to tables of men, who laughed and smoked and clanked their drinks together loudly.

A man pounded away on the piano in the center of the room, and a few drunk men swayed together, arms around each other, singing a German folk song along to the music.

"Where do we go?" I said to Dessie, who stood next to me in the crowded room.

"We go have some fun," she replied, smiling at a man who held his beer up and whistled at her.

Cap and Hudson went up to the bar together, while Claude, Leonce, Paz and Chito crammed into one table together. "Over here, Dessie!" Paz called out, pointing to an open chair. She smiled and waved, and then turned to talk to a handsome man standing near the bar.

Marceau, Rollie, Patrick, Willis, and Bernard had grabbed another table. "Andi!" Rollie yelled, cupping his hands around his mouth. "We've got a seat for you! First round's on the Chinooks!"

Thanking my lucky stars that I wasn't alone with Rollie, I walked over. There weren't many other women in the hall, I noticed as I walked. The few that were there seemed to be flirtatious, hanging on the arms of men as they drank their beer and batted their eyes.

I was the only woman wearing pants, I realized. The rest, including Dessie, had on beautiful, form-fitting dresses. As usual, I was the odd man out.

I squeezed into the booth next to Bernard, who was on the end.

"Isn't this cozy?" I joked, as I squished in next to his shoulder.

"No," he grimaced. "How soon can we get out of here?"

"What are you having, Andi?" Rollie said eagerly, leaning across the table. "I'll go get you a drink."

"Um," I replied, looking around. "Do they have anything besides beer?"

Rollie chuckled. He was already quite tipsy. "I love your sense of humor," he laughed, dragging himself out of the booth. "I'll go get it for you."

Rollie and Patrick headed up to the bar, and ordered drinks for our tables. They carried them back carefully, Patrick pretending to trip Rollie.

"Here you go," Rollie said, bending his long legs down to slide the beers into our little booth.

I took a sip of my beer. It was tangy and foamy, a bit sour and smooth all at the same time. "Thanks," I smiled politely.

Unexpectedly, he reached across and used his two fingers to wipe my mouth. "You had a bit of foam there on your lip," he teased. "You don't want to wear that all night."

I felt my face go beet red, and I glanced to the bar, praying that Cap hadn't seen his action.

He had.

He stood across the room, glaring furiously, a beer in his right hand. Hudson leaned at the bar next to him, talking, oblivious to Cap's anger.

I stood up, abruptly. "I'm going to find the ladies' room," I said, setting my beer down. I made my way to Cap, weaving through the crowded room.

"Cap," I called, but he turned his back on me.

Hurt, I stopped. Wouldn't he let me explain? He had to see that Rollie was drunk. People did stupid things when they'd had too much to drink. But we'd had that terrible fight. I wasn't sure where we stood anymore. Would he question if I had led Rollie on again, tonight, after we'd just fought about it?

Impulsively, I wheeled around and looked for Dessie. Dessie would know what to do.

Shoot, I never thought I'd see the day when I went to Dessie for help, but here it was.

CHAPTER 49

I SPOTTED DESSIE QUICKLY by looking for the biggest cluster of men in the beer hall. Sure enough, she was in the center. I headed toward her.

"And there I was, gents, sittin' with my legs up on the dash and—Andi!" she squealed, pulling me toward her. "Boys, this here is Andi Gallivanter. She's a real star. You've seen her in the papers."

Drunk Dessie was complimentary, apparently. She'd never say such a nice thing about me sober.

"Fräulein," several of the men smiled, shaking hands with me eagerly.

"Dessie, can we talk?" I asked, speaking into her ear above the noise in the room. "I need advice."

She laughed. "You? You need advice from *me?*"

A tall blonde man grabbed me around the waist. "You're even prettier in real life than in your newspaper photos," he said in accented English, the sour smell of alcohol heavy on his breath as he leaned in close to my face. I wriggled away, shoving his hands off me.

"Dessie, come on," I wheedled. "Let's go sit down somewhere."

"What's the rush? Just enjoy yourself, for once," she said, smiling brightly at the young man who brought her another drink. She already had one in her hand, so she handed him the half-consumed one and traded.

I felt hot breath on my neck, and turned to see a young man about my age leaning in close to my neck.

"What are you doing?" I exclaimed, pushing him away. He laughed and stumbled, nearly dropping his drink. He sputtered nonsense at me as he giggled and his friends slapped him on the back.

"Please," I said, leaning in. "It's a serious situation. Have I ever come to you for advice before?"

"No," she replied thoughtfully, staring at me. She turned to the man who'd brought her the beer and smiled sweetly.

"Excuse me, darling," she drawled. "I just need to step away with my friend here for a minute or two, but don't you go wandering off. I'll be waiting for you when I get back. And you, and you too," she said, winking at two other hopefuls. They all grinned like idiots.

Dessie and I settled into a quieter corner, squeezing into a small table together. She leaned her head on her hands expectantly.

"This better be worth my time," she said. "He was a doctor. Or so he said."

"I don't know where to start," I said, suddenly feeling foolish. Could I actually confide in Dessie? I didn't know. But my heart felt shattered. I had to tell someone.

"Cap and I got engaged, several months ago," I blurted out, and Dessie choked on her beer.

"What? *You* and Cap?" She coughed hard, and wiped her mouth. "Is my lipstick smudged?"

"No," I said, looking at her mouth. It was perfect. She always looked perfect. It was a great mystery to me.

"We'd been falling for each other all along, on the first leg of our expedition. We went through Africa, while the Chinooks—before you were on the team, of course—went down through Scandinavia. Anyway, he proposed and I said yes. And we've been happy. So happy. Until—"

"Rollie," she interrupted, grinning.

"Why did everyone see it but not me?" I cried, exasperated.

She shrugged, and took another sip of beer. "He's cute," she said. "Puppy love. He talks about you all the time. It's not hard to see. You just didn't want to see it."

"So everything was fine, until we met up with your team and I started getting friendly with Rollie. And yeah, fine, he likes me. Chito and Cap both got on me about it, said he was falling in love with me—"

"He is," she interrupted again. "Duh."

"Anyway," I continued on, determined to get it all out. "Cap's upset. We had a huge fight tonight, after the press conference. He was furious that Rollie and I rode together, and especially that Rollie drove my car—a Gallivanter Ford—and I didn't think it was a big deal. And then what Rollie said on stage, in front of everyone? It just made Cap furious. We screamed at each other. I told him he's too controlling, that he can't control me and stop me from being friends with the people I want to be friends with. He blew up, and said that I don't understand men at all, and that he's in charge of the expedition so I need to do what he says."

She raised her eyebrow. "I mean, you clearly don't understand men. That much is definitely true."

"Tell me, then, Dessie. How do you do it?"

Dessie narrowed her eyes, her head tilted to the side. "Do you want the truth, or do you want what you want to hear?"

"That's a confusing question," I frowned. "I want the truth. Dessie, I don't know what's going on anymore. Things with Cap are bad."

I paused, blinking back tears that suddenly threatened. "He asked me tonight if I even loved him. If I wanted to be his fiancée. And we walked in silence the entire way back, and now he's ignoring me completely. What do I do? How do you manage men? You're so good at it."

Dessie played with her drink. "You want the truth? Here's the truth. I come across like I'm an open book, but I'm sealed up. I learned a long time ago that being a woman is dangerous."

"It's not dangerous," I replied, blinking to hold my tears in.

"It *is* dangerous, Andi," Dessie insisted. "Especially when you stand out. Whether it's you, who stands out because she's a woman parading as an equal in a man's world, or it's me, a beautiful goddess, we stand out. Like a target's been painted on our backs."

"Look around," she added, leaning in and staring at me. "Look at their eyes. All the men around us. Look at them."

I looked up and saw dozens of men staring at both of us.

"Look how many men are watching us right now," Dessie said in a low voice. "None of the men we know have ever been watched this way. They've never been studied, to this degree. No, we're like prey to some of these men. They want us. They want to control us. To make us cry out and hurt."

She paused and took a long, deep drink of beer. Her pulse was racing, I noticed, as she set the glass down.

"No, Cap and Hudson and Rollie and all the others have never had to walk into a room and pick out who has a dark soul," Dessie continued. "They've never walked down a street at night, by themselves, and been afraid just because they exist. *We* have. They can't ever understand what we face, every day, living in a world of men. They don't live in fear. We do."

Dessie's cheeks were flushed and her hands trembled slightly. *"There's an edge to her, a story she keeps to herself,"* I thought, watching her.

"My entire life, I've had guys coming after me," Dessie said, her voice low. "Even as a kid, I had to learn how to fend off their advances."

"As a kid?"

She paused and looked down at the table. "Yes."

"Oh, Dessie," I said, biting my lip. We sat in silence for a few moments, and she sipped her beer. Her hands still trembled.

I realized I had grossly misjudged Dessie, all this time. Sure, we were different, but life had been drastically different for us. She had suffered things I knew nothing about. I'd dismissed her, but it turned out she had her own type of strength, too.

"I wish I could be like you," I said finally, looking at her. "You know how to handle yourself with men. You know how to get them to do what you want, how to help you out."

"Believe me, you don't wish you were like me," Dessie replied, avoiding my eyes.

Just then, two tall men approached us. "Good evening, ladies," the dark-haired one spoke in English, "Please, we'd like to buy you a drink."

"No thank you," I started to say, and Dessie shushed me.

"Why, that'd be lovely," she said, smiling up at them. They grinned and elbowed each other, heading up to the bar.

"Lesson one," Dessie said as they got out of earshot. "Don't make instant enemies."

"We're here with a crew of eleven men, Dessie," I said, rolling my eyes. "We're safe. We're not going to get into trouble."

"Our men?" she said, craning her neck to look across the room. "They're clear on the other side of a crowded hall. Besides, they've been drinking for hours. Most of them were tanked before they even got here. The chef insisted on celebrating our press conference earlier, and gave us drink after drink with our food. No, we're on our own. They wouldn't be any help to us right now."

"Why do you do this, then?" I said, watching her smooth her hair. "You just string them along?"

"Some people get a thrill from seeing how close they can get to the edge of a cliff," she said quietly. "I like to see how close I can get to people, I guess, before I back off."

The men returned, and squeezed in next to us without asking. They pushed beers into our hands. Dessie lifted her eyebrows at me.

"So, how's your night?" I said awkwardly, trying to make conversation.

"It's pretty good," the dark-haired man said, smiling at me. "It just got a lot better, actually."

"Oh," I said, sipping my beer and searching for something to say. How on earth did Dessie do this so naturally?

The man casually reached across the back of the booth and rested his arm on my shoulders. "So what's it like to be famous?" he said.

"Um, it has perks and drawbacks. It's nice being able to travel, and see the world, and meet so many new people. I have a lot of little kids who come out to meet me, so it's fun seeing them and sharing our stories with them," I said, then stopped.

The stranger was trailing his finger down my arm, softly.

"What are you doing?" I said sharply.

"Just helping you relax a little," he grinned, pushing my beer toward me. "You're too uptight. Here. You haven't touched your drink at all."

"Don't touch me," I frowned, squirming away from him.

He laughed. "Andiamo Gallivanter, you're a feisty girl, aren't you?"

"Get out," I said, pushing his shoulder with my left hand. He stood up, his beer sloshing down onto the table and spattering us.

"Whoa," he said, then laughed again. His friend laughed with him and stood, hitting him playfully on the shoulder and mumbling in German. Dessie grabbed my hand.

"Don't," she said. "You're making things worse."

"How?" I asked, glaring as they wandered away.

"Some guys like a little fight in their women," she cautioned, looking at me. "You might be making yourself more of a challenge, if you're not careful."

I blanched. Dessie stared at me.

"Why do you think every girl on the planet wants to throw herself at Cap?" she pressed, studying me.

"I don't know. He's handsome. He's smart, and kind. And he's good and brave, and loyal."

"He's a good guy," she said. "It's simple. And so is Hudson. And pretty much every guy on both our teams. Why do you think I fought so hard to get a spot on the Chinooks? Because I saw immediately that they were good men. And it's worth it to end up with good men. Believe me, I speak from experience."

"Yeah," I said, thinking.

"You put up with their faults, because they're not perfect," Dessie said. "But then again, we aren't either."

"True," I replied.

None of us were saints. And even some of us who I'd always assumed were sinners had a bit more of a backstory than I'd ever realized.

CHAPTER 50

SUDDENLY, I HEARD A woman scream as a table crashed to the ground on the other side of the room. Men started yelling, and pushing toward movement in the corner, by the bar.

"What's going on?" Dessie cried, standing up as I jumped to my feet.

"It's a fight, I think," I said, craning my neck to see.

"Idiots," Dessie sniffed, sitting back down. "Some people just can't handle their liquor."

The crowds parted just enough for me to see what was going on. I froze, shocked.

Cap was on the ground, being pummeled by Hudson and Willis. Rollie was on his knees, cradling his head, and Chito was holding back Leonce and Patrick, who were shoving him.

"What—?" I shouted, sprinting across the room. I had to shove my way through the crowd to be able to see what was going on.

Paz was pushing Marceau back, shouting at him. "Stop! It's not your fight!" he hollered, as Claude tried to pull Hudson off Cap.

Cap still lay on the ground, wrestling furiously with Hudson and Willis and Rollie, who had joined into the fight.

The four men screamed and cursed at each other, violently throwing punches. The barman tossed a bucket of ice on them but they didn't even flinch as they rolled around in the slippery cubes that now skittered across the floor.

"That's it!" the barman shouted. "I'm calling the police!"

"Stop it!" I screamed, trying to pull Willis off of Cap. Rollie punched Cap in the gut, hard, and he doubled up in pain.

"Andi, get out of there!" Dessie screamed, grabbing me around the waist and pulling me out of the way just in time. The men rolled around, a tangled mess of swinging arms and legs, and knocked over a chair where I'd been standing.

The police must have been just outside, because the crowd swiftly melted as three beefy officers pushed their way into the melee.

"Hör auf damit!" I heard them yell. "Stop it! Lass das!"

The officers quickly dragged Willis, Rollie, and Hudson off of Cap.

I saw Cap's face and inhaled sharply. Both of his eyes were swelling already, and he had a gash in his cheek. Hudson had a black eye, too, and Rollie was holding his jaw with one hand.

"Meine Herren, Sie sind wegen dieses Straßenkämpf verhaftet," one of the officers said, pulling out handcuffs and locking them on Hudson.

The other officers slapped cuffs on Cap, Rollie, and Willis.

"You're under arrest?" I cried. "What on earth?"

The first officer pushed Hudson and Willis past me, through the crowd. Hudson's uniform was disheveled, the neat map he kept folded in his front pocket halfway out and crumpled.

Cap was behind him, his arms pinned behind him, hanging his head. He avoided looking at me as he passed.

"Cap," I sputtered, bewildered, as Chito and Bernard joined me, panting. What had happened?

Rollie was the last one, pushed forward roughly as the officers marched them toward the front exit. He looked at me as he passed.

"I didn't know!" Rollie yelled to me over the murmur of the excited crowd. "I swear! I didn't know that you and him..."

The officer pushed him forward and he stumbled, a painful bruise already blooming on his jaw, and kept him walking toward the door.

My knees felt suddenly weak. Dear Lord, please tell me this fight hadn't been about me? I clutched Chito's hands and squeezed. "What happened?" I yelled.

"There was a fight," Chito responded, shaking his head. "It was bad. I don't know what happened, but Cap and Hudson were up drinking at the bar for a while, and then Hudson started drinking with a pretty local girl. We tried to get Cap to come sit at our table, but he sat at the bar, alone, slamming them."

"He was mad when he got here," Bernard added. "Drinking made it worse."

"He's right," Chito said. "What happened earlier, with you two? Something must've set him off?"

"It's a long story," I said, my cheeks flamed with color. I couldn't believe this. "We got in a fight."

"Well, I assumed something like that had happened," Chito sighed. "He doesn't usually drink. And he can't handle his liquor, because he never drinks. Anyway, I don't know what started it, but Rollie went up to the bar to talk to Cap—he was drunk, too—and we saw him put his arm around Cap and say something. Cap yanked his arm off and cold cocked him, right in the face. Rollie went down, and Hudson turned around and jumped at Cap. Then Willis got into it, and the rest of us scrambled to hold the others back."

Dessie stood next to me, listening to everything. She caught my eye and shook her head.

"What are we going to do now?" I moaned, watching as the crowd drifted back into their seats. "They've all been arrested?"

"We'll have to bail them out," Chito rubbed his beard. "Good thing we've got a lot of money."

Patrick joined us. "We were just talking about that, too. Bailing them out. Gosh, I hope the Odysseus Society doesn't hear about this. We're already on thin ice."

"Let's go get them, then," I said, turning. Chito caught my arm.

"Hold on," he said, looking at Patrick. "I think they should stay in there overnight. Cool down. Sleep it off. Maybe talk it out, amongst themselves."

"I agree," Patrick nodded. "This has been simmering for a while. There's bad blood between your captain and some of the guys on our team. Paz, obviously. But with Rollie, too? He's not usually a fighter. He gets along with everyone."

Chito looked at me and I blushed again.

Dessie came to my rescue. "We need to talk about this somewhere else, boys. As a team. Or what's left of a team, anyway. Let's settle up our bills and head back to the hotel. We can talk it all out then and figure out our game plan."

We made our way back to the hotel. The lobby was empty at this late hour, so we grabbed several couches and chairs and pulled them close together, in a tight circle, in the farthest corner of the room. Leonce ordered us coffee, a few loaves of bread and thick butter, and wedges of cheese.

"We need to sober up, and fast," he said, pulling hunks off and handing them around the group.

"This is good cheese," Chito remarked, staring at the piece he'd just taken a bite out of. "What kind is it, again?"

Patrick grinned. "You can always spot the team cook."

"Are we going to spend all night talking about cheese, or talk about our friends in prison?" Bernard grumbled.

I smiled wanly, in spite of myself. "Bernard, you just called them friends. I thought you always said you didn't have any friends?"

Bernard shot me a withering look.

Patrick leaned forward, his coffee in his hand. "We need to clear the air here, Gallivanters. There's tension between some of our team members, and I suppose that's normal. You can't go from being rivals to friends overnight. But there's clearly some deeper resentment. The kind that makes people fight in public."

Dessie spoke up. "They're fighting over someone."

"Dessie!" I cried, exhaling.

"Come on, Andi," she said, staring at me. "Just tell them. They need to know now."

"Fine," I sighed. "We've kept it a secret so far. Just the Gallivanter team knows. But Cap and I are actually engaged to be married."

The others leaned back in surprise and made small exclamations. "Ah," Marceau said, exchanging a knowing glance with Claude and Leonce.

Paz crowed and slapped his knee. "I knew it! I told you, remember? You were too stubborn to admit it. But I saw it all along, when I was with you guys earlier. You and Cap couldn't keep your eyes off each other."

"We haven't told anyone," I continued, embarrassed. "I haven't even told my mother. We were afraid that it would look too hasty, because we hadn't known each other that long. And we were waiting, too, because Cap had a messy engagement a few years back and he was afraid she might come after him again and try to smear his name. Well, and she did. Or Dessie did."

Dessie ignored my hard look, shrugging. "I did what I had to do. I didn't lie, I just didn't bother to get Cap's side of it out."

"Yeah, it was really helpful for us," I said stiffly. I had a newfound respect for Dessie, but it didn't change my memory of the nasty actions she'd taken that had caused us so much trouble.

Patrick interrupted us, clutching his mug with both hands.

"Water under the bridge, ladies," he said, glancing at both of us. "We've come a long way since then, right? Let's focus on the future, not the past."

"Right," I said, "So we've tried to keep it a secret, especially from the press. We didn't want anyone picking up the story and blowing it up all over the world. We were getting so much attention. We decided to play it cool, and downplay our romance in front of everyone else. Including your team."

Marceau grinned. "Then there came Rollie."

I clenched my fists. "Seriously, did everyone see it but me?"

The Chinook men laughed, elbowing each other.

"Shoot, we told him we thought Cap seemed pretty fond of you, that maybe there was something there, but he disagreed," Leonce said, wrinkling his nose. "Rollie said he would've known, that you would've told him if there was something between you and Cap. But I guess you never did."

"We didn't tell anyone," I groaned. "Just Bernard and Chito."

Claude and Patrick grinned at me, shooting each other mischievous looks.

"What?" I said defensively.

"Oh, nothing," Claude said, biting his lip. His eyes betrayed him.

"Tell me," I demanded. They looked at each other again, and Claude burst out laughing.

"Who on earth ever would've thought that *Andi* would be the girl who caused something like this?"

All the men laughed hard, elbowing each other and slapping each other on the back. Dessie and I shrugged at each other. "It's not that funny," I said, confused. They merely laughed harder, in response.

Patrick made a concerted effort to reel himself back in, rubbing his face. "Alright, team. This all makes so much more sense now. Rollie must've said something to Cap up there at the bar, and Cap decked him. And Hudson and Willis jumped to defend Rollie. So it's all about Andi."

"Thanks a lot," I grumbled. I was mortified.

Chito caught my eye. "We're not saying it's your fault," he said gently. "The only thing that's your fault is that you were just too naive."

I rolled my eyes and crossed my arms. I felt like an idiot. But I suppose Dessie had been right. It was better to get all of this out there, to have our teams understand why there was tension, than to keep hiding it. Now we could move forward in the right direction.

Paz spoke up. "What's our plan, bailing them out of jail?"

Chito and Patrick looked at each other. "We think they should probably spend the night in there," Chito said. "They need to calm down and think. And they're still drunk. They'll sleep hard."

"So we'll go in tomorrow morning and post bail for all four of them?" Claude said.

"Yes," Patrick replied. "But I think we need to talk about what happens after that point. There's still going to be bad blood between Rollie and Cap. And maybe Hudson and Willis and Cap now, too. We made this expedition work with both teams for two months now, but a lot of that was because our captains had mutual respect for each other. Now? I don't know if that's still the case."

"So what are you saying?" Paz frowned. "It's going to be worse now?"

I thought about Cap. For as honorable and good a man as he was, he was also stubborn to a fault. He wasn't likely to get over this fight quickly.

"Yeah, probably," I sighed.

"So what do we do?" Dessie asked.

Chito spoke slowly. "What if we contact the Odysseus Society and ask if we can get out of our contract a month early?"

"Maybe," Patrick mused, tapping his coffee cup thoughtfully. "We've done two months on the road together, gotten them some great publicity the whole time. Our show tonight was the biggest yet."

"We'd have to bury this incident, though," Claude said. "Four of us just got in a huge public brawl and are sitting in jail. If the press finds out, we're toast."

"So maybe we tell them that?" Chito said, frowning. "We tell the Odysseus Society that we've done the best we can, but that old rivalries still exist and we can either implode and cause them massive public embarrassment, or go our own separate ways again, and resume the respectful attitude we used to have for each other, in the press."

"Will they let us out of our contract, though?" Paz asked. "Only Cap and Hudson know what it said. They signed for both our teams."

"So maybe Patrick and I call them up, and represent the teams," Chito said. "We tell them that both teams are in unanimous agreement, that we've served our time—learned our lesson, learned to respect each other—and need to split up now."

Patrick nodded.

"In order for that to work, though, both teams have to be in agreement," he said, looking around the room. "Does anyone have any objections?"

We stared at each other in silence. No one spoke.

"I respect you," Bernard said suddenly. His compliment, as ill-timed as it was, seemed sincere. The Chinooks grinned at each other.

"Same, buddy," Marceau said, with a smile.

"It's been frustrating, but still a good experience," Chito said. "I think we've reached a point now where we can go back to our own teams and not skewer each other in the press. We know now that this is a true competition between two worthy opponents. Even if we lost that million dollar prize in the end, I'd be content knowing that it went to good people."

"I feel the same way, Chito," Patrick said, patting his shoulder. "May the best team win. And we'll be cheering for you, along the way, even if you are our competition."

"When are you going to contact the Odysseus Society?" Dessie asked.

Patrick looked at his pocket watch. "It's almost morning. We could send a telegram now."

Chito stood up. "Patrick, let's go wire them right now. We'll go to bed and sleep for a few hours afterwards, and give them some time to meet and consider. Hopefully we'll have an answer by the time we wake up and go to bail them out."

CHAPTER 51

I HEADED DOWN TO THE lobby after a few hours of sleep to find Chito and Patrick already sitting there, empty coffee cups surrounding them, working on a letter.

"We got a telegram back right away," Patrick nodded at me as I sat down.

"What'd they say?"

"They're disappointed, but they're letting us split up since we're in unanimous agreement. As long as we agree to bury the story of the arrests. They said they realize the amount of publicity we've given them, and that these expeditions are invaluable to their society," Chito said. "Translation—we're their cash cow. They don't want to lose us."

"The winning argument was my last line, I'm pretty sure," Patrick smiled. "I told them that mankind is fueled by competition, that they were stifling the natural course of human progress if they continued to force us to be together."

"College boy, using his brain," I teased. "But shouldn't we run this by Cap and Hudson first, before we make a final decision?"

"We will," Patrick said. "But I don't anticipate that Hudson's going to want to stick around with you guys. No offense."

"I can't imagine Cap would, either," I admitted. "I suppose it's for the best that it's ending this way."

We waited for the rest of the team to join us for breakfast and filled them in as we ate. "Time to go free our jailbirds," Paz joked as we stood up from the table.

Claude, Marceau, and Bernard opted to stay at the hotel and spend the day tuning up the cars. The rest of us—Chito, Patrick,

Paz, Dessie, Leonce and I—made our way to the local police precinct.

———◉———

WE WALKED INTO THE busy lobby, officers and people crossing in front of our path. It was quiet, despite all the activity, and felt sterile. Patrick and Chito asked for Hudson, Rollie, Cap, and Willis by name and an officer took them to a side room to fill out paperwork.

"What are you going to say to him?" Dessie asked me, as we sat in the lobby and waited. She swung her leg in little circles, watching the handsome clerk behind the desk steal glances at her while we waited.

"I don't know," I replied. "What would you say to a man who just punched another guy over you?"

"I don't know," she grinned. "This is your problem, sweetie. Not mine."

After quite a long time, Chito and Patrick came back out to the lobby. Chito rubbed his face and spoke to the group.

"They were arrested for public disturbance, essentially," he said. "The police captain recognized them from the papers. They're cutting us a break and letting them bail out with a hefty fine, which is apparently unusual here in Germany. Normally these things go to trial, even if they're small offenses. We got a break—the bar owner agreed not to press charges after coming down to the station this morning and finding out who Cap and Hudson were. Apparently his daughter is a big fan. He didn't want to be the one responsible for tarnishing their image and breaking her heart."

"They got lucky," Paz shook his head.

"Yeah, they did," Patrick sighed. "We're going to make sure to mention that to them a few times, to really drive that point home."

We continued to wait in the lobby, taking turns pacing and wandering away. I bit my lip, embarrassed that I'd contributed to landing my own fiancé and people who had become friends in jail.

"Andi, I think you and Cap need to deal with your issues right away," Chito spoke to me quietly, leaning back in this seat and resting his head against the wall.

"I know," I sighed.

"I don't know where things with you two stand, but you need to work it out. He must have been pretty tangled up, mentally, to drink that much and fight Rollie. He's normally a pretty level-headed guy."

"I feel like all I'm ever doing is working things out with him."

Chito laughed. "Welcome to marriage."

I leaned my head against the wall with him and rolled my eyes. "I'm not married yet. Maybe we won't be. I don't know what he's thinking."

"What?" Chito frowned in concern. "Just how bad was your fight?"

"Bad," I replied. "The last thing he said to me was that he wasn't sure if I wanted to be his fiancée still or not."

"Oh dear," he uttered, shocked. "What did you say?"

"I didn't say anything," I admitted sheepishly. "We just walked back to the hotel in silence. We haven't had the chance to talk since then."

"Andi," Chito said reprovingly. "You're still so young and impulsive sometimes. Please let me give you some advice, from a man who's been married. You have to stop playing these games with his heart. I understand that you've never had many friends, so maybe you don't always know how to interact with people, but that means you need to listen to those people who love you when they try to give you advice. We're trying to help you."

I groaned. "I know. After you talked to me about Rollie, and I realized Cap had said the same thing about him liking me, I tried to pull back. But it was too late. He was already driving my car, and Cap was furious, and things just snowballed. We're both independent, stubborn people. When we clash, it's painful."

"And here we are now," Chito sighed.

We sat in silence for a few moments, as Dessie and Patrick and Paz chatted next to us. Finally, Chito turned to look at me.

"It's not over between you and Cap," he said in a quiet, comforting tone.

"How do you know?"

He smiled. "He loves you too much. I recognize it. It's the same way I felt about my wife, bless her soul. Cap will never be able to let you walk away. Not in a million years. Don't worry, this will work out. It might sting, for a while, and it'll require some humility and forgiveness, but it'll work out in the end."

CHAPTER 52

WE WAITED FOR NEARLY two hours in the lobby, before Willis finally came out. He carried his jacket and shoes as he shuffled out of the door and saw us.

"Thanks, guys," he said, shaking his head. "It smells terrible in that holding cell. Golly."

Leonce grabbed him around the neck and put him in a headlock. "Good to have you back, you hothead," he said, grinning. Patrick slapped him on the back, relieved.

"My first time in jail," Willis proclaimed, a small smile on his face. "I'm not sure it'll be the last."

"How was it back there?" Dessie asked.

Willis grimaced. "Let's just say they put all the drunks in the same few cells to sober up. You can imagine what that's like. All the bodily fluids it involves. It stinks to high heaven. I hope I don't smell bad."

Judging by Paz's expression, who stood near him, he did.

"We're still waiting on the others," Patrick frowned. "We've been here for hours. I thought it might take a while, but I didn't think it'd take this long."

"What's that they say?" Chito laughed. "The wheels of justice turn slowly?"

Leonce left to get sandwiches. The rest of us sat and waited.

Rollie came out next, his uniform neat and boots already on. He locked eyes with me as an officer held open the door for him, and I saw his lips purse quickly. His jaw had doubled in size with the painful swollen bruise left from Cap's fist.

"Oh Rollie," I thought desperately, feeling guilty. I should've just told him, privately, that Cap and I were engaged. This was my fault. Poor Rollie didn't know better.

Hudson was right behind him, still pulling on his jacket. His eye was swollen and bloodshot. An ugly purple bruise covered from mid-cheek up to his eyebrow.

"Team," he grinned dramatically, bowing as Patrick laughed. "I survived my first—and hopefully last—night in jail. I know, it's hard to believe this was my first foray into a jail cell, but it was."

"How's that eye?" Paz asked, staring at him and wincing. I doubted that Paz, the youngest son in a wealthy Spanish family, had ever even been in a real fight. He'd never even done his own laundry before coming along on our expedition.

"It hurts like hell," he replied, prodding it gently with his fingers. "I need a good steak to slap on it."

Rollie looked around, and spoke for the first time. "Where's Cap?"

It looked like it was painful for him to talk.

"He's not out yet," Chito replied, glancing at me.

"Well, we have some things to discuss when he does get out of there," Hudson said grimly, massaging the bruised skin under his eye.

"So do we," Patrick said. "We've been talking, too. There's a lot to tell you."

I felt uncomfortable and guilty, listening to their comments fly back and forth. It was my fault that these men were angry with each other. I decided to take the bull by the horns and pitch headlong into the tension.

I was the only one that could truly diffuse it now.

"Rollie, I need to talk to you," I said. Everyone turned to stare at me, and Rollie turned bright red.

"Um, no, it's fine," he said, looking guiltily at Chito, who stood next to me.

"No, it's not," I said firmly. "I want the whole team to hear this, too, because I've screwed everything up for everyone lately. Keeping secrets almost tore us all apart, and I can't do it anymore. I'm sorry. I know this is embarrassing for you, but everyone needs to hear it."

Rollie's face was a mask of shame, but I had to keep going.

"I'm sorry I didn't tell you this, but I'm engaged to Cap," I blurted out. "We got engaged months ago, in Africa, and we've been keeping it a secret. You know, Cap had a bit of a messy past and with all the bad news coming out in the newspapers about him, we just figured the world would rush to judgement against our relationship too quickly. We didn't want it to derail our team, or make people think we weren't professional. So we haven't told anyone at all, not even our own families. Chito and Bernard were the only ones who knew."

Rollie was stunned. Under his red cheeks, his skin swiftly turned pale with shock.

"I should've told you," I continued. "I don't know why I didn't. It was stupid. I enjoyed your company, and I liked having you as a friend, and I just didn't think to tell you. I haven't even told my mother yet. I don't know—it was just a part of my life that was mine. But I should've said something to you. As a friend."

"She told us the whole story last night," Patrick added. "She didn't realize you liked her, chap."

Rollie stared down at the ground, embarrassed.

"Damn, Andi," he said softly. "I didn't know. I swear, I wouldn't have pursued you if I knew that you and Cap were a thing."

"It's my fault," I replied. "You had no way to know."

"You hid it well," Rollie said, cheeks pink. "I mean, I thought—I don't know. You two were close, but I just didn't think…I'm sorry."

We jumped as the door opened and Cap strode out, carrying his jacket. He stopped short, looking at us all. Rollie blushed deep red again and looked away quickly.

"What's going on?" Cap asked.

"We're clearing the air," I said, looking at Cap's face. I felt guilty, like I'd helped put those dark bruises there, on both his eyes. His face was swollen in several spots, including the wound across his cheekbone.

"Oh?" Cap said, crossing his arms expectantly.

Rollie spoke quickly. "Captain Gallivanter, I'm sorry. Don't blame Andi. She's just a kid, she didn't know any better. It's my fault, I didn't know. I had no right."

Rollie *was* a good guy. And was trying to take the blame for something I'd screwed up.

"No," I interrupted, stepping toward Cap. "It's my fault. I'm not letting someone else take the blame for this. You tried to tell me, and so did Chito. I was stubborn and blind, and I caused a lot of pain and suffering on both teams. I was wrong. And I owe everyone an apology."

I reached up toward Cap's face tenderly, and touched the distended skin across his cheekbone. He winced, but reached up and held my hand.

"I love you, Cap," I said. "I'm sorry."

He held my hand and stared at me.

"I'll save the rest of my apology for later, when we're not standing around awkwardly with a bunch of other people who are listening to everything we're saying right now," I added, wrinkling my nose.

Behind me, the group laughed.

"Andi even steps up and apologizes like a man," Willis smiled, slapping me on the back. "Direct and to the point. Not wasting any words. You're a brave one, girlie."

"Now that we're all here, let's get something to eat and sit down for a little chat," Chito said, exchanging glances with Patrick. "We've been busy while you four have been sitting in lock up."

CHAPTER 53

I WOKE UP TO THE SOUND of a discreet knock at my door, two mornings later. Rubbing my eyes, I sat up and looked at the clock. It was later than I expected.

The knock sounded again, quietly. I smiled. I recognized Cap's tap.

I bounced out of bed, pulling the comforter with me and wrapping it around my body. My window was cracked open, and it was snowing again.

I swung open the door and threw myself into Cap's arms.

"Good morning to you, too," he said, kissing my head and laughing. He pushed the door closed with his foot, his arms still wrapped around me.

"It's freezing in here," Cap said, noticing my open window. I flopped down on the bed as he closed it, burrowing into my blanket.

Cap laid down on the bed next to me, and tucked my hair behind my ear. "So you still love me after all that, huh?"

"I do," I said, leaning in to kiss his face. "Even with that ugly bruised melon you have right now."

We'd had a long, heartfelt conversation after the men got out of jail, after Chito and Patrick filled Cap, Rollie, Willis, and Hudson in about our impending team separation. Things were good between us again. And the tensions between the men seemed to have lessened, too.

Chito had been right. It would be good for the Gallivanters and the Chinook Voyageurs to split and go our own ways again.

We'd spent the day in between restocking supplies and preparing our own itineraries, meeting in separate teams for the first time in weeks. The Chinooks had decided to head toward Milan, Italy, and were planning to cut through the western corner of Austria and into Switzerland. We decided to veer away from their route, and head east through Austria and up going through Czechoslovakia and Poland. It was like old times again, as both teams anticipated different routes.

Cap closed his eyes as I softly kissed his bruised right eye. It was still purple, but the exterior spots were starting to turn yellow.

"That helps," he said, his eyes closed, a content smile on his face.

"Oh, good," I said lightly. "I'd better kiss the other one, then."

He smiled again, his eyes still closed. Suddenly, we heard footsteps outside my door, then Bernard's voice. "Cap? Are you in there?"

Cap groaned as I playfully slapped my hand over his mouth.

"Stop!" I whispered, laughing.

"How does he know I'm in here?" Cap whispered back. "We have separate rooms."

"Cap?" Bernard asked again, through the door.

"If we're quiet, maybe he'll think we're both gone," I whispered furtively, grinning at Cap. We waited, holding our breath.

"Andi?" we heard Bernard say, frustration evident in his voice. "Where's Cap?"

Cap groaned again, and fell back onto the bed dramatically. I laughed and went to the door. Opening it, I saw Bernard standing there, hands in his pockets.

"Oh, good, you're both in there," he said, peeking around me to see Cap on the bed. "It's the Chinooks. They're ready to leave. They wanted to say goodbye."

"Yeah, let's definitely run down *right now* and say farewell," Cap grumbled behind me, just loud enough that I could hear it.

"Come on, you can put a smile on your face for a few minutes to send them off," I said, grabbing his hands and pulling him up off the bed. "We'll never see them again, after this."

"Good. I'm going to hold you to that," Cap said darkly, kissing me behind my ear as he left with Bernard. "I'll see you in a minute."

I closed the door, and changed out of my pajamas into fresh clothes. I brushed my hair quickly, and pulled it back with a ribbon. I pulled my boots on, and bounded down the stairs.

The Chinook Voyageurs were standing together in the lobby, their suitcases in hand and uniforms neatly pressed. Dessie's hair was perfectly curled and her lipstick was on, as usual.

"There she is!" Paz yelled, wrapping me in a big hug. He was shorter than me, and his head only came up above my shoulder.

"Good luck, Paz," I said, smiling. "Try not to get into too much trouble out there, you rascal."

He beamed. "Me? Nothing ever happens to me. You're the troublemaker. We both know it. Look what you did here."

I laughed, and traded hugs with the rest of the Chinook crew.

Willis nearly lifted me off my feet with his hearty hug. "You've got a new fan," he said, cuffing me playfully on the shoulder. "You'll go far, kiddo. I'll be following you in the papers."

"Yeah, Willis, like you can read," Patrick teased, wrapping me in a hug. "I'm proud of you, Andi. You're stronger than you even know. I'm glad that I can now call you a friend."

Hudson shook my hand with a smile. "It's been a pleasure, Miss Gallivanter," he said. "You're quite a girl. And you've got quite a man, there, in Captain Gallivanter. You make an impressive team together."

Impulsively, he pulled me in for a hug. "Don't you dare tell Cap I said this, but we'll take you on if you ever get sick of his tomfoolery and want to join a real expedition."

I laughed, and Hudson dropped his voice to a whisper. "And if you wake up and decide you want to marry a fun-loving man, you know where to find me."

He winked as I pulled away, smacking him.

Rollie was the last to say goodbye. Cap watched as he shyly approached me, offering his hand.

"Goodbye, Andi," he said. "I'm sorry for everything. But I did truly enjoy getting to know you."

"It's not your fault," I replied. "But let's not rehash this, not now. We'll part as friends. Tell those sisters of yours that I say hello."

He laughed, a wry smile on his face. "I still hope you get to meet them someday. But do me a favor? Don't ever mention any of this to them. They'll never give it a rest if they find out that I threw myself at Andi Gallivanter and she rejected me."

"There's an adventurous woman out there somewhere for you, Rollie," I smiled. "Best of luck to you, my friend."

I was glad we could attempt to joke about it now, even though it was still a touchy subject. I was thankful that Rollie hadn't tried to hug me, too.

We walked outside with the Chinooks and waved goodbye as they started up their six Fords and trundled away. I wasn't sure I could say we all parted as dear friends, at the end, but we at least had mutual respect for each other now.

Cap exhaled as he watched the last car, driven by Marceau, pull slowly down the street.

"I'm glad that part of our expedition is over," he said, running his hand through his hair. "I'm looking forward to just the four of us again."

"Me too," Bernard said.

"So when do you want us to head out, Cap?" Chito asked. "After breakfast?"

"You just want to eat here before we go," I teased. "You keep talking about their cheese, you know."

"I love a good cheese," Chito groaned. "I'd take an entire suitcase full with me, if we had the space."

"Sure," Cap smiled, putting his arm around me. "We'll eat breakfast before we head out. To celebrate surviving our time with the Chinook Voyageurs. Godspeed to them, and *good riddance.*"

CHAPTER 54

IT FELT STRANGE TO pack into our three automobiles an hour later.

I'd become used to hearing the noise and seeing the activity of a team of thirteen, and being back to just a small team of four again was jarring.

"It seems so quiet now, with just us," I told Chito as we enjoyed a short break, our Fords now resting in the outskirts of Munich. The countryside was fresh with a dusting of snow, and the air smelled crisp and new and cold.

"I wonder if they feel the same way," Chito mused. "Think they'll miss us?"

"I don't know," I said, thinking of the team. I had grown fond of Hudson and Rollie and Patrick and Marceau. Even Willis had his merits. And Paz, of course, though his obsession with Dessie irritated me. Leonce and Claude were quiet, but friendly enough. Even Dessie wasn't all that bad, once you got past her flirtatious attitude.

Chito sighed. "Sometimes I wonder if we could've made it work with them. They were fun to be around, for the most part."

"Yeah," I replied, watching as Chito reached into the small bag sitting in his passenger seat.

"Don't tell Cap," Chito replied, noticing my stare. "I did pack some of that cheese. Want some?"

The snow was blowing softly across the road, blurring the ground. It reminded me of the blowing sand we'd had as we drove through the Sahara earlier this year.

We drove leisurely through Germany into Austria, staring up at the mountains that soared around us. I wrapped my scarf tightly around my face, tucking it under my driving goggles, to keep the chill out. Even under the thick fabric, my nose was freezing. When we finally made it to Salzburg, we got out and stretched our legs, taking in the town.

"It's the birthplace of Mozart, of course," Cap said, rubbing his hands together in the cold air.

"Lovely," I winked at Chito. "What else can you tell us about it?"

"The name 'Salzburg' literally means 'salt castle,' from the barges that used to carry salt through here on the River Salzach," he said, sounding like a teacher. "They had to stop here to pay a toll. The name stuck, apparently. It's one of the best preserved old city centers in the area."

Bernard started to complain, but I swiftly elbowed him.

"Stop it!" he said sharply, rubbing his ribs.

"Let's go walk around," Chito said, linking his arm through mine. "The city's beautiful."

Salzburg was indeed charming. It looked like a storybook kingdom, with delicate spired and domed buildings peeking up over the baroque and medieval buildings in the center of town. A gentle river wove through its heart, flowing peacefully and drawing the eye up to the massive fortress perched on the cliff above the city.

Tourists and locals mingled together comfortably, the former admiring the buildings and beautiful gardens and the latter going about their daily routines, stopping to point out directions to the occasional confused individual.

"People seem so cheerful here," I said to Cap, as the four of us strolled down the wide streets. The sun was setting behind the mountains, and the temperature was dropping rapidly. Street vendors sold steaming mugs of mulled wine that we sipped. I cradled the tin in my hand, feeling the heat thaw my cold fingers.

"Hey," Bernard suddenly exclaimed. "I can feel the mug! My fingers!"

I grinned. "We told you the frostbite wouldn't be permanent. See? You'll be fine."

Chito grimaced. "Well, he can feel his fingers but I'm starting to lose feeling in mine. It's too cold here. Can we go in? We've been out all day."

"Let's get back to our hotel," Cap said, pulling his coat's collar up. "We can have dinner there. Stay in and relax."

"Let's get some photos here, too, with this light coming out above the mountains," I said, stopping to arrange us for a shot. Cap and I had fallen into an easy rhythm of noticing good spots to capture film and photographs, and he trusted my judgment to stop the group whenever I felt like it.

"Thank goodness we can start taking some photographs of our team again," Cap said, as I lined the boys up for the photo. "I didn't want to waste film on them."

I frowned. "Cap, they weren't that bad."

He made a face.

"Wipe that look off your face and smile for the camera!" I replied, taking their photo.

We dined at the hotel and slept well, cozied up under warm down blankets. After breakfast, we headed out toward east Austria.

"I think we can make it to Wels by the end of the day," Cap stared at the map. "There aren't a lot of big towns in between here and there, but it'll take us pretty close to the border of Czechoslovakia. We're making good time."

I drove the first leg by myself, whistling as I navigated my Ford. I never minded a bit of time to myself like this. It gave me time to think.

As I looked up at the mountains around me, I thought about how much my world had expanded in the last year. *"I've come so far,"* I thought to myself. *"For the first time in my life, I've been around people like me. I'm no longer the outsider I always thought I was."*

I'd found kindred spirits within the Gallivanter and even in the Chinook Voyageurs crew. They were fellow explorers and adventurers, like me. People who never wanted to settle into one place for long.

"People aren't as one dimensional as I've always thought. They're much more complex and nuanced," I pondered, thinking about Dessie.

Clearly, her life was not what I'd assumed. Neither was Bernard's life, who hid the tragic deaths of his brother, mother, and father behind his aloofness. Or Chito, who'd lost his wife and baby girl and had grieved them painfully. Or Cap, who'd pulled himself out of a terrible childhood, orphaned, and made something of himself even after being falsely imprisoned.

Our mutual losses and trials bonded us, and spurred us to live deeply in each moment. As we all keenly knew, the future was unpredictable. We enjoyed life now, unwilling to trade adventure for stability.

We all had our difficult pasts. Mistakes. Loneliness. Problems and challenges. But we were all here, together, pushing forward.

Had this all been worth it? Dropping out of boarding school to follow a bunch of strangers around the world in a car? Dealing with long days and dangerous situations and difficult people?

Absolutely.

"You've found yourself here, on this expedition," I thought. *"Not just because you met Cap, the man you're going to marry, but because your entire world has been opened up. You found your own strength, you discovered who you are, and you found real friendship in the people around you."*

On top of that, the joy of seeing the world and meeting new individuals was life-giving for me. I was especially struck when I met eager young fans. Somehow, my experience was opening new possibilities to an entire generation of new children who were growing up watching me and following my adventures.

The world had so many wonderful things—and people—and places to see.

And despite the moments of danger and plenty of discouragement I'd faced, I wouldn't trade any of it.

CHAPTER 55

WE PULLED OVER THAT afternoon for a late lunch, perching on nearby boulders to eat. I looked at the valley below us as I chewed my sandwich, marveling at how high up we already were.

"How much higher are we going, into these mountains?" I asked Cap, as he ate next to me.

"Pretty high up," he said, pointing. "We have to go up, and then make our way down. Let's hope it doesn't get too narrow."

"I hate mountain driving," I replied, my shoulders tense at the thought. It required absolute concentration, especially if we had to back our autos up the road, driving in reverse. The progress was maddeningly slow. One careless move could send any one of us sailing over the edge to our death.

"As long as the weather holds out, it shouldn't be too bad," Cap said, glancing at the sky.

"Smells like rain to me, though," Bernard remarked.

Sure enough, a light drizzle started a few minutes later, as we packed up our lunches and climbed back into the Fords.

"Be careful," Cap called, the drizzle dripping down his helmet and goggles. "This rain might make the roads a little slick. Go slowly."

I bit my lip. The last time we'd traveled through the mountains during rain, we'd been cautioned against it by a local. He'd warned us about mud and rockslides, and we ignored him, trying to stick to our schedule. As a result, Cap and Bernard's car had been hit by a violent collapse of a rock wall, and they both had nearly bled to death from their injuries.

"Stop it," I told myself, concentrating instead on watching Bernard driving in front of me. Cap and Bernard had made a full recovery. We were fine now. Nothing like that would happen again. Right?

It was slow going, climbing up the mountain and then back down. Several times, we reached a steep part and had to reverse up it, inching along the narrow path one after another. The rain stopped, but the road remained slick and soft.

"What a time to rain," I grumbled aloud, watching Bernard's tires sink into the ground. Now that his hand was regaining feeling, he insisted on rotating in to drive. I was sweating, even in the cold air. This thin lane of ground on this tiny mountain pass was made for a horse, not for an automobile. It was too narrow for me to feel comfortable driving on it.

Off to my right, the road dropped off alarmingly into nothingness. I knew from stopping earlier to assess that the drops were hundreds of feet here, in some spots.

"Why do people even travel these roads?" I thought, clutching my steering wheel tightly. *"If I lived here, I'd never go anywhere."*

My hands started to hurt from clenching the wheel so hard. I flexed my neck slowly, tilting it from one side to another. My shoulders ached.

I kept my car close to the rocky side of the mountain, and slowed down to a crawl as we went around sharp corners. I tried not to look down, but I couldn't help but see the ground so far below us on several occasions. I despised mountain driving.

Chito looked like he did, too, as I glanced up at him every so often up in Bernard's Ford. He was clutching the dash with his left hand, his right hand holding tightly to the passenger door. Poor Chito was closest to the edge of the cliff, and could probably see straight down it.

We drove this way for hours, unable to safely stop. A fine rain started again at one point, making the road even softer. My face was soon wet with sweat and rain. I wiped my driving goggles repeatedly with the back of my glove, but it simply left streaks across my lenses.

As I felt the strain starting to overcome me, we finally began to coast downhill. A stunning vista opened up before me, with a beautiful lush valley and large mountain stream curling through below, glimmering in the dense light.

"I just want to stop and stretch my legs," I thought. *"I need a break. This is miserable."*

Cap eased his car slowly over a rise, and I watched him with my heart in my throat. In my mind, I'd pictured his Ford slipping off the ledge and crashing right in front of my horrified eyes. Curse my vivid imagination. I'd die if something like that happened.

Bernard pulled forward behind him, the front of his car only a few inches away from Cap's rear bumper. He was a skilled driver, but I worried about him, too. If something happened to him, it'd be a double loss, with Chito as his passenger.

I imagined sending a telegram to Chito's sister and niece, telling them that he'd perished in the mountains in a terrible driving accident. Oh, little Molly would be devastated.

"Stop it," I said, biting my lip. *"We're fine. We're nearly out. Just concentrate on the road."*

We finally made it to the last drop where the worst of the pass ended and the road flattened again. The road rose up, then steeply declined down until it bottomed out on the banks of the large stream I'd spotted from several hundred feet up.

Cap raised his right hand in the air triumphantly from the front vehicle.

I grinned. We were finally out of danger. I could relax for the first time in hours.

Suddenly, Bernard's car started sliding. I watched in horror as the soft ground crumbled underneath the weight of his car, and it slid all the way forward and right off the road. I didn't even have time to scream as the Ford careened into the bubbling stream.

"Chito! Bernard!" I yelled, and honked my horn. "Cap! Stop!"

Cap slammed on his brakes, the sudden movement spraying wet dirt everywhere. I coasted down the hill and slammed on my brakes, too. I leapt out of the car, scrambling in front of it, as Cap sprinted to the banks of the river.

"We're fine, we're not hurt!" Chito yelled, climbing on top of his seat and dragging Bernard up with him.

The Ford was submerged in rushing water that was nearly at the top of the wheels. The stream bubbled around the car furiously.

"Damn it!" Bernard hollered angrily, his face red. "My car!"

"We've got to get in there," Cap said, looking at the hissing water. "It's not that deep, I think. Look at where it hits on the car."

"We should cross diagonally, just to be safe," I said. "The water still looks strong."

"Hold onto my shoulders," Cap said, tossing his helmet off on the sandy shore. "We'll go slow."

He waded in, and I followed him. The water was cold, even through my thick leather boots. As we crept in, my hands digging into his shoulders, the water pierced through my pants and gave me goosebumps. The wet fabric clung to my legs, making it hard to move easily.

"It's slippery," Cap yelled. "Careful!"

The stream was full of large, smooth stones on the bottom. We walked gingerly, the uneven and shifting ground making it difficult to stand against the weight of the rushing water.

We waded in until we were up to our knees. Chito and Bernard had already eased their door open and climbed out to join us.

"We need to get this car out of the water," Bernard squinted. "If it slips in any farther, we're going to have major issues."

"We'll have to push it out," Cap said, assessing the car with his hands on his hips. "We don't have a winch that'll reach, without risking another one of our cars getting pulled into the water. The ground's too soft."

"Hop in, Andi," Chito said, opening the door. "You're going to need to back it up, slowly, as we push from the front."

Bernard leaned over the side as I climbed into the driver's seat.

"You've got to do this carefully!" he yelled at me. "If you go too fast, we might sink it in farther. It wouldn't take much water to start pushing it downstream, either. We can't let that happen. Reverse her as slowly as you can."

I gritted my teeth as I settled into the seat. Reversing was a challenge on a good day. With my left foot, I had to depress the lowest pedal halfway down, releasing the transmission from high gear. I used my right foot to press down on the middle pedal to engage the reverse gear. At the same time, I'd have to control the throttle with my right hand and steer with my left. This would be tricky.

"Ready?" Cap yelled, as all three of the men leaned up against the front of their car, shoulder-to-shoulder, with their backs to me. "One, two, three!"

They pushed, and I concentrated on my movements. The car slid back with their effort, but I didn't reverse smoothly enough and the Ford whined as it revved up, then lurched back into the same spot.

"Again!" I yelled, and they pushed.

The car moved, but didn't get unstuck.

"I can't do this!" I hollered, standing up in my seat so I could yell over the glass windshield. "Bernard, you need to do it. You're better at reversing."

I shoved open the door and waded out into the water toward Chito and Cap. The water sucked at my ankles as I pushed forward.

Bernard passed me, slipping on the rocks, grunting as he climbed into the driver's seat. I took his place at the front of the car, bending my knees and leaning my back against the hot metal of the engine.

"Ready?" Cap said, looking over at me. I nodded.

"One, two, three!" he yelled, as we pushed with all our might. The car shifted a few inches.

"One more time!" Bernard yelled, and we squatted. "One, two, three!"

It slid back again, and then forward.

"Dear Lord," Chito said, wiping his sweaty brow. "I hate water."

"Come on, one more time," Cap urged. We lined up.

"One, two, three!"

With a mechanical whine, the car slowly eased out. We let out guttural yells of celebration.

Bernard skillfully backed the Ford all the way out of the water, up onto the bank. He turned it off, and hopped out to pop open the hood. We waded out slowly, shivering as the cold mountain air hit our drenched clothes.

"Let's change out of these wet clothes," Chito said, putting his arm around me and rubbing to warm me. "Andi, why don't you change first?"

I quickly retrieved a blanket from the back of my Ford and rummaged through my bag, grabbing clean clothes. I tossed the blanket to Cap, who held it up in front of me for some privacy as he looked away.

Shaking with cold, I stripped out of my clingy wet clothes as rapidly as I could, starting with kicking off my boots. I stood in the dirt in my bare feet, the ground freezing below me. My legs and arms had goosebumps on them as I peeled my wet pants and knickers off and left them in a heap on the ground, then pulled on my clean pants.

I next yanked my soaked shirt and camisole off over my head, then rapidly dressed in new ones. I was hopping from one foot to another as I buttoned up the shirt with chilly, stiff fingers.

"I'm done!" I yelled at Cap, who turned around. "Hold still a minute," I said, using his shoulder to balance on one foot as I pulled on a pair of dry socks.

"Wrap yourself in this and warm up," Cap draped the blanket around me, already unbuttoning his own shirt and dropping it on the ground.

His muscles flexing, he stripped down quickly out of his pants and jogged over to his car in his underwear, before disappearing from sight around the other side as he threw on pants and a new shirt.

Chito was already doing the same, his big barrel chest visible above the car as he put a new shirt on.

"Oh, to be a man," I thought to myself. *"They have no concern out here, stripping down to nothing in front of each other. It's the ladies that have all these layers and delicacy to worry about."*

Despite their acceptance of me as one of the crew, situations like this reminded me that I was still a woman living in a man's world. They didn't always see it, but I certainly did.

I sat in my car, bundled up but still shivering, watching as Cap and Chito joined Bernard, who was still in his wet clothes. I pushed my door open with my stocking feet and padded over through the dirt to join them.

"Your car must've been heavier than ours, with the two of you in it," Cap said, staring at the Ford. Mud caked the wooden spokes, and water dripped from them. "The ground gave way under the weight of the car. This was just sheer bad luck."

"She's going to be alright, I think," Bernard frowned as he tinkered in the engine. "She just needs to dry off a bit and we can hit the road again."

"Nice," Chito winked at Cap. "That was some expert-level driving there, Bernard."

"Thanks," he said shortly. Popping up the engine, he poked around. A few minutes later, he dropped to his knees and laid down flat on his back, shimmying under the Ford to inspect underneath.

After a few minutes, he yelled, "We should be good!"

He emerged, flecks of mud and oil on his face. Grunting, he pulled himself up and closed the engine.

"I need to say something," he said gruffly, looking at me. "I'll admit, Andi, when you first came on, I didn't think a girl could do this job."

"Oh," I said, taken aback. I'd always thought Bernard was fond of me. I didn't realize he had doubts about my capabilities.

"I liked you well enough, kid," he continued. "But this is a man's work, here. Dealing with cars."

Cap started to speak up, but Bernard shushed him harshly. "I'm not done. Let me finish."

He stared at me, and shook his head. "I was wrong. You've proved me wrong."

I smiled at him. We waited, in silence, for him to finish. He looked back at me, blankly. Chito broke the silence.

"Are you done now?" he said, catching my eye with an amused grin.

"Yes," Bernard replied. "We're ready to go."

Without another word, he pulled off his wet boots and reached for his bag. Behind his back, Cap and Chito doubled over with silent laughter.

I stifled my laugh, too, and smiled widely. If I could change Bernard's mind about something, that was nothing short of a miracle.

CHAPTER 56

AT OUR HOTEL THAT NIGHT, after dinner, Cap flopped down on the bed in my room.

"I just want to lay down and relax after this afternoon," he groaned. "What is it with this team and mountains?"

"Everyone knows they're dangerous," I teased. "You're the idiot that keeps taking us through them."

"Hey, the world is full of them. It's the only road through, in a lot of places."

"I'm kidding. Just lay back and relax. You're right. It's been a rough day for all of us."

I rubbed his shoulders for him, kneading his tense muscles. He stretched and groaned, and rolled over on his side.

"That feels good, Andi, but I want to talk to you. I've been thinking about something," he confessed, reaching out and toying with a strand of my hair.

"What?"

"Now that things have settled down with the Chinooks and we're not fighting each other in the newspapers anymore, is it finally time to tell the world about us?"

"You mean tell the public that we're engaged?"

"Yes," Cap said, grinning back at me. "You haven't changed your mind about it, right?"

I laughed. "No, have you?"

"No. I'd marry you tomorrow, if I could. Or tonight. Think we can find a preacher real quick?"

"Stop," I laughed, pushing him playfully. He rolled onto his back and put his hands behind his head comfortably.

"So? When do you want to announce it?"

"I hate to say this, but I should probably write to my mother first," I admitted, wrinkling my nose. "And to my sister, too. They need to hear it from me before they read about it in the paper. They'd never forgive me if that's how they found out. Besides, I might need to do some damage control. I don't know if they've seen the newspaper articles about you."

Cap looked at me. "You haven't said anything to your mother about me all along, right? Nothing about having feelings for me?"

"No. I didn't want her to be angry. We've only known each other a year now. We got engaged after only knowing each other a few months. She'll think I rushed into it. I figured it was better to keep it to myself, and let her think things progressed at a reasonable rate between us."

He sighed. "When are you going to write to her?"

"I don't know."

"Can you guess when you might know?"

I raised my eyebrows. "Are you in a hurry?"

"I'm just being practical," Cap replied. "It'll take a few weeks for a letter to reach America. And then if you want to wait for a response back from her, we're looking at a few more weeks after that. Then we'll have to arrange a press conference. So...yeah. We probably need to get the wheels in motion, if we're really going to make it public."

"I could try to write some thoughts out tonight, I guess. At least get the letter started."

"I'll just stay right here and supervise," he said, closing his eyes and nestling into my bed.

"I don't think so," I grinned, pushing him off the mattress. "I need to think. It's not going to be easy. I have a hard time putting my private thoughts into words."

"I hadn't ever noticed that about you," Cap laughed, kissing me on the forehead as he rolled off the bed. "I'll be in my room, then. I have work to do, anyway. Good luck, Miss Gallivanter."

He closed the door behind him. I sat down at the small desk in my room, slowly pulling out a piece of paper. The blank whiteness of the sheet stared up at me.

How could I possibly explain everything that had happened in the last year to my mother?

I'd been living away from home since I was eleven years old, and I'd never been good at sending letters home. All of my classmates had been well-behaved, conscientious daughters, making it a priority to spend their afternoons and evenings writing letters to their parents with regularity.

I'd been too busy tearing around the woods on my horse, with my friend Arnau, to sit down and spend an hour writing.

Since I'd joined the Gallivanter team in France last December, I'd dashed off a few letters here and there, sometimes with a few newspaper clippings inside. Because of the unique situation I was in, traveling from city to city, I hardly ever received letters back.

I sometimes worried that my sister or mother might fall terribly sick or die with me all the way on the other side of the world, living in blissful ignorance. But years of independent living and the thought that my mother would surely send a telegram if something serious was going on dulled that nagging worry.

As such a poor correspondent to my family, I now fretted over how to tell my mother about the whirlwind adventure and romance that led to me being engaged to Cap in just a few months.

Suddenly, her approval seemed so important. Why?

"Because he's the man you want to spend the rest of your life with, that's why," I told myself. *"You want your mother to love him like you do."*

I jotted the easy words down on the paper.

"Dear Mama, I miss you and Evelyn and hope you are doing well. I know it's been quite a while since you've heard from me. We're now staying in Austria and enjoying the cities here. We've been driving through the country here for a few days now, and we're heading to do some big presentations in a few days. The crowds love us, as they always do. I sign so many autographs."

Did that make me sound conceited? I frowned, and added, *"I can't believe so many people want to meet me."*

There. That was true. It still boggled my mind. But how to broach the subject of Cap?

"I've been so very busy, Mama, and there's always so much to tell you that I don't know where to start," I scribbled.

CHAPTER 57

"OH, DEAR," I said to myself, staring at the letter in front of me. *"I can't just launch into this. But what do I say?"*

For the last twenty minutes, I couldn't figure out what to write next. I was frozen in indecision.

My mother had no idea at all that I was interested in Cap. I'd never written about him to her, other than the quick mentions of him in my own stories. I'd been too concerned that she'd read into it and see my growing love for him, even when we first started traveling together.

As far as my mother knew, Cap was my boss—the leader in charge of our expedition—and the man who she had entrusted my safety to, as we traveled around the world. Would she be angry that he had fallen in love with me? Would she think I was too young, not understanding that my experiences with this expedition had made me far older than my years?

What would she think of him? Cap was a few years older than me, and had been engaged before. Not to mention the six months he'd spent in prison. Would she judge him?

I'd better build him up to her, first. She had no idea who he truly was.

"I realize how little I've told you about the men who mean so much to me," I wrote. *"The men who have been at my side as we've traveled the world have been the biggest blessing to me. They've been the best part of this entire experience."*

I watched the ink dry, little spots of wet slowly fading to matte on the paper.

How could I articulate the way I felt to someone else? Sometimes my mother felt like a stranger. A distant, foggy memory from my childhood. I knew she loved me and supported me, but it'd been so long since I'd seen her.

"These men I've traveled with—Cap, Chito, and Bernard—have been so kind and cheered me on. They've always included me as one of their own, and treated me fairly. They've encouraged me to be myself, without having to change a thing. You know how much that means to me," I slowed down now, thinking.

How could I tell her why I'd fallen for Cap?

"Captain Gallivanter especially has been—"

What was he, to me?

How could I put this into words?

"Captain Gallivanter especially has been an anchor for me," I wrote, resolving to throw caution to the wind. I scribbled the words quickly, from my heart.

"Mama, I'm in love with him. I've known it from the beginning. He's not the reason why I joined the team, but he's the reason the team exists in the first place and I can't help but love him for that, too. He's brave, and strong, and cares so much about everyone else. The only thing more incredible than his integrity and character is his soul. He's deep, and complex, and there's so much more to him than anyone else knows. I want to spend the rest of my life understanding what's in his soul.

We had a terrible accident a few months ago, in Africa. You probably remember it from the papers, it was when we first became very famous all over the world. We had traveled through a narrow pass after a rainstorm, and the ground was wet. Some large boulders gave way above us, and came tumbling down onto Cap and Bernard's car. Their car flipped over, pinning Cap and Bernard inside. They were badly hurt, gushing blood. My team and I got them both out, and I rushed them to the hospital all by myself.

It was then, Mama, when I saw Cap's lifeless face, that I knew for certain. I loved him.

I held Cap's wound in his leg, trying to stem the bleeding as I raced him to the nearest hospital. Every moment of that awful race against the clock, I prayed like I've never prayed before.

I would've traded my life for his right then and there, no question. And I'd do it again, if it meant I could save him. He's the most important person in my life.

I would give up everything for him. Everything. Without any regret.

I know this must come as a shock to you. I don't know why I didn't tell you about him sooner. I think perhaps I was embarrassed by how quickly I fell in love. I've always valued my independence, and worried I'd be on my own forever, that no man would ever want me. But Captain Gallivanter does. He loves my spirit, my fire, even my desire for independence. He encourages me to be just who I am.

I've never met someone who loved me for me like he does."

I paused, thinking deeply. A smile lit my face at the thought of Cap.

"It sounds silly to say this, but it's true: I think I love him more each day than I have the day before. It's the greatest joy in my life to know that he loves me just as much, too," I wrote.

"We saved each other's lives. Twice. That doesn't happen every day. It's a sign, right? We are meant for each other, like no one else.

I've never told you this, Mama, because I knew it would scare you, but I nearly drowned early on, in our travels in Spain. We attempted to cross a flooded river, and our publicist egged me on to go out into the rapids so he could film me and show the world how brave I was. I'll admit, I wanted to show off, so I did it—even though Cap and the others told me it was too dangerous. Well, they were right. I fell in and swallowed a lot of water. They managed to drag me back, and Cap saved me by forcing air into my lungs.

I realize now that I knew in that moment, staring up into Cap's eyes as I regained consciousness, just how much he loved me. His expression was naked terror at the thought of losing me. I denied it for a long time, but I see it plainly now. He loved me."

I laid the pen down and put my head in my hands, overcome at the memory. Even now, when I saw a gurgling, gushing stream, I'd flash back to the moment I'd been sucked into the dirty black water and swallowed so much of it so quickly. In a matter of just a few moments, I'd lost consciousness and drowned. My team had dragged my limp body to shore by the rope wrapped around my waist, and Cap had waded into the water to pull me out.

Closing my eyes, I could still feel Cap's lips on mine, frantically blowing his own breath into my lungs.

I felt his hot, eager lips on mine as he kissed me, hard, when I started breathing on my own again. I'd known then that he loved me. The thought kept me tossing and turning every night for months.

I bit my lip, thinking how he must have felt. Like no one else, I could imagine the exact feelings that had raced through his brain. I'd felt them as I stared at his white face, covered in blood, after pulling him out of the wreckage of his Ford after the rock slide.

It was the undeniable realization that he had to live—that if he didn't, it would kill a part of me, too.

I wasn't good with words. How could I ever explain all this to my mother?

"He's the love of my life. Cap has made me happier than I ever imagined I could be. He hasn't made me better, but rather, he's inspired me to be a better person. Wherever it is that life may take me, I know that if he's by my side, that's exactly where I'm meant to be.

I can't believe I get to be by his side every day. To share with him in the grand adventures we have as we see the world. To laugh and tease and cry and care and worry together.

And Mom, I want to live right there by his side, forever. We're engaged to be married."

I set my pen down again, staring at the words. It was impulsive and direct, there was no doubt. It would come as a shock. I didn't know how to ease her into the big news.

But then again, that's who I was. Impulsive and direct.

I'd learned so much about myself in the last year, as we traveled the world on our expedition. Sometimes it seemed like an entire lifetime had passed in just a few months. I'd found my own voice, and been forced to stand on my own two feet.

I knew my own strength now. And in large part, that was due to Cap.

Cap had seen my character before I even knew it fully myself, and given me the chance over and over again to test my own limits, without rushing to interfere or solve things for me. He'd treated me like everyone else, expecting the same commitment and service out of me as Chito and Bernard.

Where other men might have spared me from the disgusting chores of changing the oil and the gasoline, or digging the Fords out of the mud, or even carrying the bags and boxes to and from our hotels, Cap had wisely known the value in having me do it all, just like the men.

Because of that, they fully respected me.

He never talked down to me or coddled me, either. Like no one else in the world, Cap saw me as an equal. And he treated me as such. Under that strategy, I had blossomed into a strong, capable, fearless woman.

And because he hadn't interfered, I could proudly say that I'd done it on my own. That this was *truly* who I was.

I smiled, and picked up my pen again.

"I know this will come as a shock. I know you'll worry that I haven't known him long enough, or that he's not the right person for

me. But I know in my heart, with absolute certainty, that he is. I've never been more sure of anything."

But when should I tell her we were going to get married? We hadn't really talked about setting a date.

Frankly, it didn't matter all that much to us—we were mid-expedition, and already living together. Along with Bernard and Chito, of course.

Maybe I should have a little chat with Cap and make sure we were on the same page, before I wrote any specifics about a wedding day to my mother. She was sure to ask about it, if I didn't mention it first.

I tucked the unfinished letter under the inkwell and trotted down the hall in my bare feet.

CHAPTER 58

I REACHED CAP'S ROOM and knocked lightly.

"It's open, come in," he said absently, from inside.

I pushed open the door, and smiled when I saw him. Cap was sitting crosslegged in the middle of the floor, his bed pushed back to accommodate the dozens of piles of papers neatly stacked all around him.

"What's this?" I asked, looking around. There was barely room for me to tiptoe through, so I stepped carefully around the stacks and laid down on his bed, propping my head up on my arms.

"Work," he said, glancing up from a sheaf of papers labeled *"AUSTRIA"* at the top. "Upcoming stops."

"I see," I replied, sitting on the edge of his bed. He glanced down again, consumed by his task.

Staring at his tanned face, I could scarcely believe that a young man of only twenty-six could handle so much work and still have the energy to lead our crew and host such dynamic press conferences in every country we visited.

He had his faults, of course—punching innocent men in bars came to mind, as chief among them—but his leadership skills were unparalleled.

He pursed his lips, lost in thought.

"Cap?" I said lightly.

"Hm?" he replied, his eyes glancing over at a map. I could tell he was thinking about the trip.

"Can we talk a minute?"

"Sure."

I waited, but he didn't look up. I exhaled, and he caught my eye, guilty. He set the papers down in his lap.

"What?" he asked, searching my face. "Is something wrong?"

"Don't laugh at me for this. I want to talk about our wedding."

"Oh, look at you. I tell you to write one letter, and suddenly you lose your mind in wedding planning and romance and lace and satin? You're starting to sound like a real girl, for once."

"Very funny. But no, it's not the actual planning part. It's the date."

"The date?"

"Yes," I answered. "I'm writing to my mother about you, and I don't know what date to tell her we plan to get married. Shouldn't we discuss some possibilities?"

"Oh," he said, looking at me. "You're doing it? You're actually writing?"

"I'm trying to."

"I didn't think you'd already be working on a letter. You said it'd be hard to write it all out."

"It is. It's...awkward. I don't know how to let other people in to how my heart feels. But I know I need to tell her, somehow."

Cap laughed, setting the map to the side and getting up. "Hold on, maybe this will help."

He stood up, stretching his legs, and walked over to his bag. He rummaged around for a few moments, then pulled out something. He smiled as he looked at it, then turned to me. "Close your eyes."

"Why?"

"Just do it," he ordered. I closed them, and heard a rustling.

"Can I open them yet?" I asked, smiling.

"Yes," he said. I opened them.

Cap was kneeling on the ground in front of me, holding a small red velvet box.

"What are you doing?" I exclaimed. Had he bought me a ring? When had he possibly had time to do that?

"Just take the box," he grinned at me.

"Please tell me you didn't buy me something gaudy," I teased, remembering what he gravitated toward at the jewelry shop in Paris.

"What kind of woman mocks her beloved's gift when he's kneeling in front of her, patiently waiting for her to take the thing he's been waiting for weeks to give her?" Cap groaned in mock outrage, his eyes twinkling.

"Your kind of woman," I laughed, grabbing his shoulders. "I told you, I don't need a ring. It's not practical."

"Open the damn box, Andi!" he ordered sternly, as a smile tugged at the corners of his mouth. "I've been holding onto this for ages, waiting for the right time to do this."

I opened the box, inhaling at what I found. Inside, a small gold compass floated on a gold chain. The backing was dark, but tiny symbols marking north, south, east, and west gleamed in bright gold. A tiny needle spun around as I lifted it up out of the box. In the center of the needle, a large diamond sparkled.

"What is this?" I exclaimed. "A necklace?"

"It's your engagement ring," Cap replied, his eyes bright. "Well, it's what you're getting now, anyway, until we get you a proper ring. I sensed that you didn't really care so much about the ring. You kept saying you're practical and that you didn't need one yet. So, I designed something that I thought you'd like to wear now. This—a compass—it's *very* practical."

"Cap, I love it," I said, examining it closely. "It's incredible!"

He came up next to me, and studied it in my hand.

"You're getting a ring, too, whether you want one or not," he added, kissing my hair. "But at least you can wear this now, even before people know we're engaged."

"How big is this diamond?"

"Two carats," Cap grinned. "You told me you were modest."

"Modest, right," I swatted him. "Two carats is a bit extravagant, don't you think?"

"Have I told you lately, darling, how very rich we are?" Cap joked. "I used my own stockpile of money, by the way. Not our trip funds. Anyway, look at the back. That's my favorite part."

I flipped it over. In tiny cursive letters on the back, it said, *"Andiamo: Beauty, Brains, and Boots."*

"Oh Cap!" I cried, looking up at him. "From the newspaper advertisement you put out, trying to hire me?"

"Yep," Cap said, his eyes sparkling. "*That* fits you, doesn't it?"

Gently, he took it out of my hands and fastened it around my neck, as I lifted my hair up. "There," he said, stepping back to examine it.

I felt guilty, realizing he'd had this necklace the entire time he was watching Rollie throw himself at me. Poor Cap. He'd had more restraint than I'd given him credit for. No wonder he'd been so angry. I threw my arms around him.

"Thank you. It's perfect. Where did you get it?"

"Remember that jeweler in Paris, where we stopped and tried on engagement rings?" Cap replied. "I saved his information. And sketched out a design for this. He did the custom work. I designed it myself, just for you."

"I love it."

Cap grinned at me. "You're a survivor. An explorer. And every real adventurer needs a compass. So now you have your own."

He kissed my neck and added, "But your compass has a big old diamond. So don't go loaning it out to strangers."

"It'll stay safely on my neck," I smiled.

"Oh, you missed the best part," Cap said, picking up the box from the floor where I'd set it. "I have to read this to you."

From inside the box, underneath the velvet cushion, he pulled a small slip of paper and read it aloud.

"Congratulations! Best of luck to Bernard and his lovely bride. May you enjoy a joyous future together."

CHAPTER 59

WE SLEPT IN LATE THE next morning, happy to relax on a rare slow day.

The four of us met for a lazy breakfast in the small hotel restaurant. I smiled as I tucked my new necklace under my shirt, feeling the weight of the compass against my throat.

"The coffee's not bad here," Chito said, sipping it. "Remember how good it was in Morocco, though? I'd go all the way back there just for those beans."

"Do you ever think practically, or is it always with your stomach?" Cap joked, his maps sitting untouched in front of him. It was nice to see him relaxed, for once. So often, he was bent over his work, distracted from what the rest of our team was doing.

"Life's miserable if you don't think a little bit about your stomach," Chito protested, reaching for the cream. "Admit it, you know I'm right."

We laughed, but I noticed the hotel clerk pick up the ringing telephone at the front desk in the nearby lobby and frown, listening. I watched him, and wrinkled my forehead as he unexpectedly looked at me. Why was he staring at me like that?

"One moment, please," I heard him say, still staring at me. A jolt of fear raced through my brain.

"Miss Gallivanter," the hotel clerk called, jogging over to me at the breakfast table. "Miss, there's a telephone call for you!"

"A call?" I repeated, rising to my feet.

Cap frowned, setting his napkin on the table. "Who'd be making a telephone call to you? And this early? Would it be your mother?"

My heart was in my throat. I'd just been writing to my mother the night before. Had something happened? Would she never know the love I felt or the man I was planning to spend my life with? Was I too late in telling her about Cap? I rushed over to the telephone in the corner, behind the reception desk.

"Hello?" I breathed.

"Andi?" I heard a woman's voice say on the other end.

I realized in that instant that I hadn't heard my own mother's voice in so long that I couldn't be sure if it was her or not. Was my mother dying? Was it Evelyn, my little sister? What was going on?

"Andi!" I heard the voice say again. "It's Dessie!"

"Dessie?" I repeated incredulously. This couldn't be right. Why would Dessie call me?

"My—oh—Andi," Dessie yelled brokenly. Her voice sounded husky, like she'd been crying. "Something terrible's happened!"

"What?"

"We got attacked. We were robbed, all of us. They destroyed our cars, and—and—they tortured us, Andi."

I froze. Cap had followed me and stood watching me, perplexed.

"What?" he mouthed, clearly worried. I stared back at him, my eyes wide with horror. They'd been attacked? The Chinooks? How?

"Andi?" Dessie said again, panic making her voice crack.

"I'm here," I said, trying to collect my racing thoughts. "What happened? Are you alright?"

I heard Dessie breathing hard on the other end. "No," she choked out, after a moment. "I'm sorry, Andi, I didn't know who else to call."

"What?" I said, fear worming into my soul. They'd been tortured? How badly? "Tell me what happened, Dessie."

"They kidnapped Paz," she sobbed. "They wanted him all along. You know his family's rich. They dragged him away, and they have him. He's gone. We had to walk to a house on foot, to try to find help."

I could hear her bawling on the other end. Dessie was always so cavalier, and the sound of her brokenness petrified me.

"Where is he? What?" I asked wildly, knowing I wasn't asking clear questions. I just needed to keep Dessie talking.

"I don't know where they took him," Dessie cried. "A bunch of the men are hurt really badly. Patrick and Willis and Rollie. They're in the hospital. And Hudson, too. It's bad. It's going to be days, maybe weeks, before they can travel again. I don't even know if Rollie will make it. I don't think he will."

"Oh, dear Lord," I groaned, biting my lip.

Cap gestured wildly at me, frantic. "What?"

I covered the receiver. "The Chinooks were robbed! Paz was kidnapped, and the crew was tortured!"

Cap's face went white. "What?"

"It's Dessie," I said, holding up the phone. Swiftly, Cap grabbed it.

"Dessie, it's Cap," he said, his tone commanding. "Tell me what happened."

He listened for a moment, and then spoke more softly. "I'm sorry, but you need to calm down. Focus on my voice, and just answer my questions. You can do this, Dessie. But I can't understand you right now. You need to take a deep breath and calm down. His life depends on it."

The muscles in his jaw were clenched, and his skin was still white. But Cap spoke quickly, without hesitation, as he fired off questions to Dessie on the other end of the telephone. "How many of them were there? Where did they attack you?"

He listened, nodding. "What did they do to you?"

I noticed his fist ball up, as he listened this time. He winced involuntarily.

Chito wandered into the lobby and frowned, looking at us standing at the telephone. "What's going on?" he asked quietly, coming up next to me.

"The Chinooks got waylaid by robbers and Paz got kidnapped," I whispered, watching Cap.

"*What?* Is Paz hurt? What happened? Where is he? How did this happen?"

"I don't know yet!" I whispered. "Dessie's still on the phone, she's telling Cap now."

"Dessie called?" Chito said, reeling back. "Why not Hudson? Or Rollie or Willis?"

"They're hurt, she said," I replied. "She said they were tortured first."

"Tortured?" Chito groaned. "I can't imagine how badly they're hurt, if it's Dessie calling us."

He was right. They'd never given Dessie any real responsibility before. It must be dire. How bad was it if Hudson couldn't even make a phone call?

"And where are you now?" Cap said into the receiver. He listened, gesturing for a piece of paper.

I grabbed blindly for paper and a pen at the reception desk, handing it to Cap. He held the paper against his thigh, scribbling as he listened.

"We'll be there as soon as we can," Cap said. "Finish talking to the police, first, but we'll get there as quickly as possible. Go take care of them."

"Cap!" I whispered, clutching his arm.

"What?" he said, staring at me.

"Let me talk to her," I said, pulling the phone out of his hand.

"Dessie?" I said, holding the telephone to my ear.

"Andi?"

"Listen to me, Dessie," I said, willing myself to calm down. My heart was racing. "You're strong. I know that. *You* know that."

She sobbed in response, her words incoherent.

"Dessie, they need you right now," I urged. "You need to pull yourself together. You need to act like Hudson right now. Take charge. You can't fall apart."

"But Paz!" she gasped, her voice raw. "They have Paz!"

"We'll get him back," I promised. "But right now, you need to pull yourself together. For Paz. And for Hudson and Rollie and Willis and Patrick. For the whole team, Dessie. They need you."

She cried brokenly on the other end of the line.

"Damn it, Dessie," I yelled, trying to shock her. "Stop being an idiot for once in your life and be strong! I know you're capable! You told me, remember? Your childhood? Channel that strength now. It's there. It's inside of you."

I heard a hiccup, and then another sob. "I'll try," she whimpered through her tears.

"Don't try," I said. "You need to do it. They're depending on you, Dessie. Don't let them down. Don't let *me* down."

"Alright," she replied in a small voice.

"We're coming," I said. "Hold on. We'll be there as soon as we can."

I hung up and faced Cap and Chito.

"We have to go," Cap said, before I could say a word. "Chito, go tell Bernard to get his stuff ready. How fast can we leave?"

"Hold on now, we're not walking into a trap of some kind, are we?" Chito asked. "How'd they get robbed?"

"I don't know," Cap frowned. "I didn't even think of that. Did she tell you?"

"No," I said. "What, you think someone would be looking for the chance to rob us, too?"

The three of us stared at each other uneasily. "I hadn't considered it but it makes sense," Cap said quietly. "We have a ton of money. Expensive supplies. Cameras. Nice automobiles."

"But Dessie said they destroyed their cars," I replied. "Was Paz the target all along?"

"If Paz was a target, wouldn't we be an even bigger target?" Chito asked. "I know his family is rich, but so are we. And think about it—we've been sharing our itinerary with the entire world. People have been following us for a year, tracing our journey. If they know the area, or at least look at a map, they can figure out exactly what roads we'll be on, and when. The publicity we rely on can work just as well against us, to help criminals track us down."

Unexpectedly, a chill ran down my spine.

I suddenly remembered Bernard's comment weeks ago that we were dealing with a new wild now. He'd been right. Beauty and cruelty lay in the hearts of men, just as it existed in the wilderness. Ironically, humanity was even more vicious than nature. We could be hunted down ruthlessly by criminals as easily as we'd been hunted by a leopard in the jungle of Africa.

Cap groaned. "Yes. That's all true. But we've got to get to them. They need our help."

"Where are they, anyway?" I asked. "Dessie didn't tell me."

"Zermatt. It's in Switzerland, near the border of northern Italy," Cap replied. "I need to look at my maps and figure out how long it's going to take us to get there. I'll look now, while you three start packing."

He started to walk back to the breakfast table and stopped. "Chito, how much reserve gasoline do we have?"

"A fair amount, why?"

Cap thought for a moment. "Let's double it. And double the food and water supplies, too. Let's see if we can sleep along the road, in small shifts, and not stop at a hotel overnight. We don't have time to waste."

Bernard was walking toward us. "What's going on?"

Chito and I quickly filled him in. He reeled back in surprise. "How bad are they hurt?"

"I'm not sure," I said. "Dessie said they were tortured. I didn't ask specifics. She was pretty rattled. But she did say that a bunch of them can't be moved for a while. Rollie and Hudson and Willis and Patrick are hurt badly, she said."

Cap bit his lip. "It must be bad if Dessie telephoned us, not Hudson or Patrick or one of the others."

"That's what I said, too," Chito frowned.

"So we're going to help them?" Bernard asked, his head tilted. "You just got out of jail for punching them in that bar. I thought you hated them?"

"It's not about who they are, it's about who *we* are. We're helping," Cap said, shaking his head. "A stupid competition doesn't matter anymore. We know they're good people. And we don't have time to waste discussing it. Chito, supplies. Bernard and Andi, start packing and prep the cars. I'll plot our route and we'll meet at the Fords to depart as soon as possible."

The hotel clerk had been watching everything and tugged at Chito's arm. "We'll pack up some food for you," he said. "Anything that might help, so you don't have to stop for supplies."

"Thank you," Chito said gratefully. "But don't breathe a word of this to anyone, you understand me? Our friend's life depends on it. Word cannot get out."

"Of course," the clerk said. "I am so sorry to hear about this. But I'm glad the Gallivanters are headed to the rescue. If anyone can help, it's you."

CHAPTER 60

BERNARD AND I RACED to our rooms, while Chito rushed out to the Fords. I knew he'd be taking one of them to fill up more canisters of gasoline.

Cap was already back at the table, a map spread across it.

I quickly threw all of my belongings into my bag and brought it downstairs, dropping it next to Cap.

Wordlessly, without lifting his eyes from the map, he reached into his pocket and handed me his room key. I took it, and headed up to his room. I packed his bag just as quickly, and brought it down.

Bernard was loading, and I jogged out to help him. Months of the same routine had made us efficient, and we worked rapidly, without words.

A few moments later, Cap joined us outside, carrying his map. The hotel clerk followed him, his arms full of wrapped parcels.

"We're checked out," Cap said, nodding as I grabbed the food from the clerk and thanked him, putting it in my Ford.

We heard Chito's vehicle coming down the street, and he swiftly pulled in. He'd gotten several extra gasoline containers, and Bernard reached in to shift some of the food supplies from his vehicle into our other two Fords.

"Are we already ready?" Cap asked in surprise, checking his pocket watch. "Wow. We've set a new record for preparation."

I hopped into the driver's seat, and Bernard slid in next to me. Cap climbed into his car. As he did, Bernard and I pulled on our helmets and driving goggles and gloves.

"I never pictured us reuniting with those Chinooks," Bernard said, as Cap pulled out and started driving down the street.

"Me neither," I said, then bit my lip. It wouldn't be the same now, though, because Paz wasn't with them. And clearly Dessie wasn't her usual self. And how badly were Hudson and Rollie and the others injured?

I clenched my hands tighter as I held the steering wheel.

"There will be time to process this later," I told myself. *"Right now, you're driving. Just drive. Get there as fast as you can."*

We drove frantically, on the verge of pushing ourselves—and the Fords—too hard. We pulled over to refill the gasoline, and stretch. I was already sore, and sure that it was stress making my muscles hurt more than usual.

"Do you need me to drive?" Bernard offered.

"Yeah, maybe I'll drive the next leg with Cap," I said. He stood apart from us, furiously mapping out the next leg.

"Hey," I said, walking over to Cap and squeezing his shoulder. He glanced up briefly and nodded, before looking back down at the map.

"I think we can make it to Innsbruck by nightfall," he said, counting under his breath. "Just under three hundred kilometers. Then about four more hours to St. Moritz. But the driving conditions aren't ideal, and mountains...we'll have to sleep in our cars, maybe. Or could we sleep in shifts? No, there aren't enough of us to rotate, only one can sleep at a time," he said, talking to himself aloud.

I watched him in silence. He counted again, then one more time. He traced the routes on his map in pencil, doing complicated math calculations in the margins.

"If we pull off and sleep for just a few hours, that might be enough. We can make it through to Bellizona then, if we push ourselves, and pull over to sleep for another few hours. That means we'd be hitting Zermatt around tomorrow morning, or maybe afternoon, at the very latest."

"That's good," I leaned over his shoulder, looking at the map. "I can't believe we can make it there that fast."

He glanced at me. "Pray that we don't have some sort of mechanical issue. Or get a flat tire."

"They won't be the only prayers I'm saying."

Cap sighed. "Let's get going," he said tiredly. "We have a long day ahead of us."

We climbed in, and I rested gratefully against the passenger seat. Cap pulled his driving goggles down and glanced at me.

"Can you nap while I drive?"

"I can't possibly sleep," I said, as he pulled onto the road and increased speed. "I'm too worried. Do you think they're going to hurt Paz?"

"I don't know," he said, staring at the road.

"I know you regret it."

He looked at me. "What?"

"Being so distant with him these last few weeks."

"Of course I do," he confessed. "Paz might be injured, or maybe dying, and my last words to him were rude and dismissive. I should've been the bigger person. I shouldn't have given in to my resentment and let things fester."

"You didn't know. None of us knew this would happen."

"He was always running his mouth about being rich," Cap groaned. "How many times did he tell us? How many times did he mention one of his family's estates or properties, as we drove through Spain? He was always bragging about it. I'd be willing to bet he let it slip in front of the wrong person somewhere."

"Dessie didn't say who robbed them?"

"No. She was calling from a police station. She wasn't thinking clearly."

"How did she find us?" I wondered. "She knew which hotel we were at?"

"I don't know," Cap responded, thinking. "We'll have to ask her. It's a miracle that she managed to track us down."

The engine of our Ford shuddered and we both cringed.

"You can't push it this hard," I said. "We're going to burn the engine out at this rate."

Cap didn't respond.

I put my head in my chin and rested it on the door frame, staring out sightlessly at the passing scenery. The ground blurred together, an endless refrain of greens and browns and grays as we passed fields and barns and fences.

Paz. Where are you? What are they doing to you?

We stopped as infrequently as possible the rest of the day, mostly to refill the gasoline. We ate the sandwiches that the hotel staff had packed for us while we drove. Bernard's Ford overheated at one point, and we pulled over to allow the engine to cool down.

"We have to wait until the engine's completely cool, Cap," Bernard explained desperately, as we paced around his car. "It's just too hot right now to add any water and coolant to the radiator."

All three of us swore, kicking violently at the dirt. Our nerves were ragged and raw.

Time seemed to stand still as Bernard laid his hand on the engine every few moments, watching the temperature gauge. Finally, he gave us the thumbs up. "Let's go."

Sunset unfurled in front of us, the red glow painting our faces crimson. I drove now, while Cap rested in Chito's car.

Alone with my thoughts, my mind raced. How badly were the Chinook men hurt? Would they ever recover? What were they doing to Paz? How much pain could he tolerate? He'd grown up so pampered. He couldn't handle much hardship. And Rollie—would Rollie survive?

"Hang on, Rollie," I thought, praying silently for him. *"You're strong. Don't die. We're headed there to help you."*

How futile our competition now seemed in the face of this unexpected tragedy. It was clear to me now that we cared about each other, despite the bumpy road to this friendship between our teams. Why had we let such petty things divide us? What if we would've been there—would we have avoided this whole catastrophe?

Over and over, my mind circled around the biggest question of them all: how on earth would we possibly be able to track Paz down, now that he'd been kidnapped?

————◆————

WE PULLED OVER BRIEFLY, so we could refill the gasoline and Chito could dig out more sandwiches for us. It was dark now, and we had to use flashlights to see our canteens.

"How long are we going to drive tonight?" I asked Cap. "We need to take it slower, now that it's dark out."

He glanced at me in the glow of the flashlight. "How much farther do you think you can go? Honestly?"

I paused. Chito and Bernard looked up, and I met their eyes. They wore the same haunted look of desperation that I did. Despite what Paz had done, leaving our team, he was still a Gallivanter.

And one of the Gallivanters was in danger. We couldn't rest until we'd found him.

"We need to keep going," Bernard said, responding for me.

Chito chewed his sandwich, stretching his legs out slowly in front of him as he ate. "I've never been more tired, but more unwilling to rest. I just want to get there."

"I know," Cap said.

We ate quickly, in silence. We'd always been so jovial together. It was disconcerting to see the men I usually joked around with so profoundly affected. My heart felt heavy as I stood up, dusting the crumbs off my lap. It felt like I'd aged a thousand years since that morning, when I first got Dessie's telephone call.

The darkness swallowed us as we cut through it for hours, our small headlights carving a little hole a few feet in front of us as we drove through the night. My eyes started to burn, then blur, as I concentrated hard on Cap's bumper in front of me, following closely behind.

It was only when he veered in the road a few times that I blinked to attention. *We need to pull over and rest for a bit,* I thought, and honked at Cap. He braked, and pulled over to the side of the road.

"What's wrong?" he yelled tiredly from his Ford.

"We need to rest," I hollered. I was too exhausted to get out of the car and walk over to him.

"We can't," he yelled back. "We need to keep going! We're getting closer!"

"No, Cap," I groaned, wanting nothing more than to curl up and lay down in my car. "It'll do them no good if you get yourself killed. You're just about driving yourself off the road. We need you rested. Just a few hours. Please."

I heard nothing but silence. "Cap?"

Still, I heard nothing. Frowning, I pushed open my door and walked up to his car. He sat in the driver's seat, his eyes closed.

"Cap," I said, shaking him awake. He opened his eyes groggily.

"Sorry," he said. "I was just resting my eyes for a minute. I'm so tired."

"Go back to sleep," I said, pulling his hand off the steering wheel and reaching in to turn his ignition key off. "Lay down."

Without protest, he curled up on his seat. I trudged back to Chito and Bernard, tiredly.

"Cap's dead asleep already," I told them. "He needs to rest. His brain's been going a million miles an hour today. All of ours have."

"We all need sleep," Chito said, yawning. "We're lucky none of us went off the road already."

"Get some sleep then," I said. "Wake me up when you get up."

I climbed back into my car and closed the door. Before I knew it, I was fast asleep, too.

CHAPTER 61

I REGISTERED NOTHING until suddenly I realized that my face felt hot. Where was I, and why would my face be warm?

My eyes shot open, and I squinted against the rays of sun touching my face. It was dawn, and the morning sun spilled across the open fields where our Fords had pulled over haphazardly in the darkness, a few hours before.

I sat up on my knees, then stood up on the seat cushion of my car, straining to see into the other Fords. Cap, Chito, and Bernard were all still asleep in their vehicles.

Stretching my neck, which was uncomfortable from the painful position I'd been in all night, I climbed out of my car. I reached into the back of Chito's Ford and pulled out a tin of dried beef. This would do for breakfast. I needed to wake my brain up by chewing something.

I walked back to my car with the tin, looking for my canteen. My mouth was parched. I drank thirstily, staring across the fields.

Suddenly, I spotted a young boy in the distant fields. He appeared to be minding a field of sheep. I stood and waved my arms.

"Hello!" I yelled.

He waved back. I tossed my canteen onto the seat and jumped out of my car. I jogged through the fields, meeting him halfway. The sheep around him scattered as I ran up.

"We're looking for Zermatt," I said, breathing hard from my efforts. "Do you speak English?"

"Yes, I do, and it's not much farther," he said, wrinkling his brow. "Maybe forty kilometers from here? You'll recognize it. They have a big cathedral spire you can see from the road."

"Which direction?" I asked. He pointed with his hand.

"That way," he said, shading his eyes against the rising sun. "What are you doing out here so early, anyway? What's your uniform?"

"We're a traveling team, on a world tour," I replied, extending my hand. "I'm Andi."

"*Andiamo Gallivanter?*" he gasped, shaking my hand excitedly. "I've read about you in the newspapers! You're famous!"

I smiled. Even this young boy out here in the middle of nowhere knew me. As I smiled, too, I realized I hadn't smiled once since hearing about what had happened to the Chinooks.

"I'd love to stay and talk to you, but we have to get going," I said. "Thank you for guiding me." I turned and jogged back to the Fords.

Cap was sitting up, rubbing his eyes. "Who were you talking to out there?"

"A little shepherd. Good news, we're not too far away. He thinks about forty kilometers from Zermatt."

"Forty!" Cap exclaimed, grabbing for his map. "We went farther than I realized last night!"

"I don't even know what time we stopped driving," I admitted. "I don't think we've been asleep long, but I think we can make it forty kilometers now."

"Yeah, we can," Cap said, slapping his cheeks lightly. "Do me a favor and wake up the other two, and we'll get moving."

I grabbed the tin of beef from my car seat and jogged back to Chito and Bernard's car. Chito was sprawled across the front, with Bernard stretched out in the back seat.

"Rise and shine, gentlemen," I said, shaking Chito's shoulder and tapping Bernard's foot. They groaned.

"We're only forty kilometers away from Zermatt," I told them. "Let's go."

Bernard shook his head. "Already? That means we drove what, sixteen hours straight yesterday? Nineteen or twenty total, with stops to sleep? Our Fords aren't meant to be pushed that hard."

"Let's go," I said, tapping the side of the car. Chito yawned, and slid over as Bernard climbed into the driver's seat.

Cap was already pulling away, and I rushed to start my car and catch up with him. I heard Bernard grinding on the gravel behind me.

Again, we pushed the cars hard. After about an hour, the sun blazing overhead, I saw it. I honked at Cap and pointed as he glanced at me in his mirror.

"The cathedral!" I yelled, pointing up at a spire. "That's Zermatt!"

We rolled into town recklessly, not slowing down. I swiveled my head around like Cap did in front of me, looking desperately for the hotel Dessie had told us they were staying at. We cut in front of an old man who was crossing the street, and he shook his fist and cursed at us as we zipped by.

I spotted it the same instant Cap did, a tall gray building with a gilded lettering that spelled out the name "Atlantico Hotel."

He motioned, waving his arm, and we pulled over. The Chinook Voyageurs' Fords were conspicuously absent. *"Of course they weren't here,"* I thought a beat later. *"Dessie told me they destroyed the cars. How on earth did they make it to this hotel, then?"*

I had so many questions and so few answers to calm my racing mind.

CHAPTER 62

SLAMMING OUR DOORS, we rushed into the hotel. As soon as we entered, I heard a loud sob. I turned, and froze.

Dessie rushed toward us, crying, but it took me a moment to recognize her.

Her face was swollen and blackened with bruises. Her right eyebrow was split clean open. Her beautiful lips, normally perfectly lined with her red lipstick, were savagely split and dried blood pooled in the cracks. Even her throat was covered with ugly marks, as if she'd been strangled.

Cap pulled up short next to me.

"Dessie?" he gasped.

She threw herself into his arms, weeping. He stared at me over her head, his hands smoothing her hair, his eyes wide with shock.

Chito swiftly stepped next to Cap and peeled her off, leading her gently to a nearby chair.

"Sit down, sweetheart. Just relax, we're here now and it's going to be fine," he said softly, then turned to Bernard. "Can you get her a glass of bourbon, or whiskey or something?"

"Chito's compassion is a gift with power he doesn't even understand," I thought, watching him cradle her and smooth her hair, like a child who'd woken up crying from a bad dream. "We're here, sweetie, we're here," he whispered again, as she cried.

"I'm sorry," she choked out, staring up at us as tears cascaded down her cheeks. "Everything happened so fast, and I've been trying so hard to deal with it all and keep it all together and I just can't anymore."

She sobbed into her hands, hiding her face. "You're finally here. I need help. We need you."

"You have our help, I promise," Cap laid a hand on her knee. "You've been brave, Dessie. We're proud of you. You've done so well."

Even in this tender moment, my brain poked at me. *"No man's ever treated you this way,"* it whispered. *"You've always shouldered the burden of a man, and no one's ever come along and congratulated you for it."*

I pushed the thought aside. It was no time to be petty. The simple fact was that I *could* handle a stronger load, and maybe a lack of praise came with that ability.

"Where's the rest of the crew?" Cap asked, looking around.

"They're at the hospital," Dessie whimpered. "Willis and Hudson and Rollie and Patrick are all there, recovering. Leonce and Claude are here, at the hotel. They should be right here any moment, they only just left to get us something to eat. I don't even remember the last time any of us ate or drank anything. Marceau is at the hospital, keeping an eye on the others."

"We don't mean to stress you, Dessie," Chito said gently, stroking her hair. "But when you're ready, we need to know everything that happened."

Dessie's eyes filled with fresh tears, and her lower lip trembled. She nodded, but struggled to speak. I sat down on the other side of her.

"I know you're strong, Dessie," I said, leaning forward. "I remember what you told me in Germany, at the beer hall. Do you remember?"

She looked at me and nodded tearfully.

"You've always been strong, even as a kid," I reminded her, just loud enough that she could hear it. "Be strong again. Just a little longer. We're here with you. You're safe now."

She looked at me. I tried not to wince, looking into her bloodshot and darkly bruised eyes. She looked terrible.

"We stopped in Innsbruck, and were at a bar late after we did a presentation one night," Dessie started, breathing hard to control the tears that threatened to spill out.

"Paz was sitting next to me at the bar, boasting about how rich his family was," she said, shaking her head. "He was drunk. He was practically yelling. Everyone around him could hear him talking, bragging about his father's art collection and their horses and antiques and everything."

The color started to rise in Dessie's neck.

"There were a couple of rough men at the bar, listening in," she continued. "They started talking to him. Asking about our expedition. Asking where we were going next. How fast the cars go. Willis tried to wave him off and drag him away, but he just kept blabbing. You know how he gets."

"Yeah, we know," Bernard said. Cap shot him a warning look.

"They talked to him all night. The rest of us walked away and sat down without him. I don't know, he must've told them our next few stops. They were waiting for us out on a remote stretch of road, in between towns, two nights later. I assume they chose dusk intentionally, because we were tired from driving all day."

Her eyes welled up again, and she stopped. Chito put his arm around her.

"Take your time," he said, holding her tightly.

I watched as a range of emotions flickered across Dessie's face. She looked like she was about to fall apart completely, but then grimaced, as if she was choking her emotions down. Her expression went through a dozen tiny changes over the course of just a few seconds. *The spirit to fight is remarkable,* I thought, looking at her.

"They had a car of their own, across the road like it was stalled," she said. "There was only one of them there, standing outside the car. He waved us down. He limped, like he was injured somehow, and came toward us."

I inhaled sharply. I could picture the scene. The helpful nature of the Chinooks, a crew of good-natured childhood friends who saw the best in everyone, being used against them in such a brutal fashion.

"The rest of them were hiding in the woods, I guess," Dessie shook her head. "I don't know. It happened so fast. Hudson and Rollie and Willis were the first out of the cars, because they were all in the lead Fords. Hudson was checking with the man, to see if he was hurt, and..."

She paused again, biting her lip. She yelped, forgetting her lip was painfully split open. As she put her hand up to her mouth, wincing, I noticed that her fingers came away with fresh blood.

"Rollie and Willis were bent over the engine, trying to help out. One of the men clubbed them across the back of the head, hard. They went down right away. Hudson was held at gunpoint. The other two men had guns, too, and came at the rest of us, who were still in our cars."

She paused, her body shaking now as she relived it.

"I saw it all," she cried. "I watched it happen. I couldn't even scream. I was in the back car, with Paz. He shoved me down, trying to hide me. 'They'll hurt you, Dessie,' he said, peeling off his jacket and throwing it on top of me. He told me to fight for my life if they came after me."

"Oh, Dessie," Chito groaned, closing his eyes as he held her.

"Leonce and Claude were in the fourth car, and Patrick and Marceau were in the third car," she continued. "Patrick had come out charging right away. He knocked one of the gunman flat on his back, just barreled straight into him. He must've knocked the gun out of his hand, because I heard screaming and scrambling, and the gun went off. Then I heard another shot. The gunman shot Patrick, in the leg."

"Patrick was *shot*? Will he make it?" I gasped, dread flooding me. Not Patrick. He was so intelligent. Funny. And brave, apparently.

"I think so," she said. "The doctor said he was stable. We bound his leg right away. The bullet went straight through, which was good."

I clenched my fists. I couldn't stand to hear the rest. This was too painful to bear.

"They had a gun on Leonce and Marceau and Claude," Dessie said, her breath ragged. "Patrick was bleeding on the ground, and Rollie and Willis hadn't made a sound. They were passed out cold. The man who'd faked a limp had a gun to Hudson's head. Paz had climbed out of the car, I guess trying to distract them from me hiding in there. He gave them the money we had, in Hudson's bag. He tried to reason with them."

A shudder went through her body involuntarily.

"You're safe now," Cap said, watching her. His face was tight. "We're here."

"They remembered me, from the bar," Dessie said, tears falling down her face. "They yelled for me. 'Where's that blonde slut?' they yelled, searching for me. The Chinooks wouldn't say. None of them would say. I hid there, in the car, praying they wouldn't find me."

She closed her eyes, but the tears oozed out through her eyelids.

"I heard them ask each man," she said, her lips trembling. "When they didn't answer, I heard their fists. I heard them beating them. I heard the boys begging them not to, offering to give them money. I heard their cries as they hurt them."

I couldn't listen anymore. It was too savage—too unfair. I stood up, biting my fist to keep from crying out. Cap leaned forward out of his chair, his face white, as he watched Dessie.

"They grabbed Paz," she said, then cried out brokenly. "They recognized him. 'This is the rich boy, the one we want!' the one yelled, and took him. I could hear them pull him away. He fought like hell. But I heard him screaming, as they beat him. They beat him so much he stopped making any noise. I could just hear their fists hitting his body. Just—soft. The sound of blood, spattering. I thought they killed him."

Cap closed his eyes and bowed his head. For a long moment, none of us said anything. Chito wiped away the tears that dripped down his face, and rubbed his hand across his nose.

"What else, Dessie?" Cap said finally, lifting his head.

I knew he had to be thinking about what it would've meant if something like this had happened to us. How easy it would've been for this exact same thing to happen to the Gallivanter crew, as newspapers published our itinerary everywhere we went.

"I don't want to talk about it," she replied, the tears wetting her shirt now.

My fear, as a woman, was instinctive. Like a bad dream, I remembered what she'd said in the bar in Munich.

"We're like prey to some of these men. They want us. They want to control us. To make us cry out and hurt."

In my mind, I saw her pulse racing as she told me the men on our team couldn't understand what we faced in the world. "They don't live in fear," she'd told me. "*We* do."

"Dessie," I said, kneeling down in front of her. I took both her hands and held them. She bowed her head and stared at me.

"Forget them," I whispered. "Tell me. It's just me."

She stared into my eyes.

"They found me," she whispered back, her voice barely audible. "Two of them pulled me out, threw me on the ground. They knocked me around and laughed. One of them dragged me back up and—"

Dessie shuddered so violently that I could feel her whole body tremble as I held her hands.

"I head-butted him. That's when he did this," she said, pointing to her bruised neck.

"Good for you," I said, squeezing her hands. She stared at me. I understood now why her eyebrow was split open.

"He hit me," she replied quietly. "He swore at me as he did it. He was so angry. I don't even know what he was screaming at me, I couldn't understand him. And Marceau and Hudson and Patrick were screaming the whole time, threatening and bargaining and fighting. It was awful. It's all such a blur."

"Dessie?" I asked quietly, searching her eyes. She stared back, frightened. Seeing fear in her eyes unsettled me more than I wanted to admit.

"Their leader stopped them," she whispered. "He said they didn't have time for—for me. He yelled at them to leave me alone. They slammed me back against the side of the car and took off running."

"Oh, Dessie," I cried, holding her hands. They shook in mine.

I tried to still my heart, but it was racing as I listened. Dessie had been right. The world was still a dangerous place for women. I'd been living in denial, but I was shaken to the core now.

What if this had happened to our tiny crew of four? What if I'd been attacked by a couple of men, as Chito and Cap and Bernard watched on helplessly?

I bit back my fear. "Tell us what they did with Paz. What happened? Where'd they take him?"

She shook her head.

"They dragged him up off the ground. He was beaten badly, but alive. They tied him up and gagged him, and then shoved him into their trunk. I think they put something over him to conceal him. They tied everyone up. They got in their car and took off, after they slashed all our tires and smashed up our engines. It was dark, by the time they left. They drove down the road, but I don't know where. I was already trying to help the boys."

"What happened after that?" Cap asked.

"We made a sling and carried Patrick down the road, looking for a house," Dessie said. "Marceau and Leonce carried him, and I walked with them. We thought it'd be more likely that someone would open the door in the middle of the night to a woman, not just a bunch of men. And anyway, my face," she grimaced. "I couldn't fake that. It'd be obvious, looking at me, that something serious had happened."

She sighed, touching her split lip again. It looked like it hurt her to talk.

"Claude and Hudson stayed behind to watch over Rollie and Willis, who were still passed out. Patrick had the more serious injury, so we wanted to get him to a house and see if there was a nearby doctor."

"Good thinking," Cap said.

"I know," she replied. "Anyway, we walked in the dark, following the road, and we managed to find a little farmhouse. They heard us before we even knocked. Their dogs were barking at us. The farmer had experience with dressing wounds—my guess is from the Great War? He brought Patrick in and started working on him. His wife alerted the neighbors, who came out and brought the rest of us back in on their wagons. They drove half of us into town to the police station, and the other half to the hospital."

"I guess you knocked on the right door," Chito remarked.

"Yeah, we did," Dessie said. "Rollie and Willis both have concussions and some pretty serious swelling in their brains. They're in bad shape. Patrick is at the hospital, and he's healing well. He doesn't want to be in bed at all anymore, he just wants to go after Paz."

"I can relate to that feeling," Cap mumbled.

"Didn't you say Hudson's in the hospital, too?" I asked. "What happened to him?"

"He fractured some bones in his hand," Dessie responded. "He fought back, as they went after me. I could hear it. I guess the man ended up stomping on his hand."

"The human hand has twenty-seven bones in it," Cap answered automatically, then buttoned his lip.

"He's pretty banged up everywhere else, too," she said, regaining her strength. "Rollie's worse off. He's still in critical care. Willis is stable now. But Rollie—Rollie might not make it."

My stomach lurched. Oh, Rollie. How could something like this happen to him? Who could do this to *any* of them?

"Does his family know yet?" I blurted out, remembering how close Rollie was to his little sisters. What would this do to them, if they lost their beloved older brother in such a senseless crime?

"No one knows yet," Dessie responded. "The team didn't even know I called you. I called from the police station, as they took all our statements."

"They don't know we're here?" Cap frowned. "How can that be?"

"The three of us just got back from the police," Dessie said. "It's been absolute chaos. We've been up for almost two days now. I fell asleep in the police station and the hospital, waiting to talk to people. I stayed here while Leonce and Claude got food, because I wasn't sure how quickly you'd be able to make it. I didn't want to miss you."

"Hold on, how on earth did you know where we were?" Chito asked, frowning. "We haven't talked to you in weeks."

"It was sheer luck," Dessie admitted. "The detective had a newspaper sitting out, and it had a list of your upcoming travel destinations. I asked around to see if anyone in the police station had ever stayed in Wels, and what hotel they'd stay in. I imagined there weren't that many hotels to choose from, the town doesn't seem that big. I called a few places before I tracked you down. Luckily, I talked a police officer into letting me make several telephone calls."

The five of us fell silent.

"I guess we need to rethink sharing our itineraries with the public," Cap finally said. "This could've happened to us, too. I've never thought about people lying in wait to attack us."

I didn't want to think about the possibility of our team being attacked. Of what could have happened to the men I loved, sitting around me. Of what could have happened to me.

I pushed the thought from my mind, biting my lip. "What do we do now?"

CHAPTER 63

CAP STOOD UP, FACING the group.

"We need to go to the police ourselves, and get a plan in place," he replied. "We need to contact Paz's family in Spain, immediately, if they haven't already done so. They need to know what's going on. It's likely that they're holding him for ransom, and they might even go to his family's home and rob them."

Dessie paled.

"Paz loves his family," she said, holding her hand up to her mouth. "He's told me so much about them."

I swallowed hard. She was right. Paz often spoke about his family and his childhood. This would be so cruel for them to hear. What if Paz didn't survive this? What would that do to them?

"We'll go to the police first then head straight to the hospital," Cap said. "Dessie, you should stay here and get some rest. You've been through enough."

"No," she exclaimed wildly. "I don't want to be alone. Don't leave me alone!"

Bernard spoke up. "I'll stay with you. I don't talk much, Dessie, but I'm a good listener. Anything you want to say to me, I'll listen. And I won't judge. I'll just sit right next to you and be there."

The tears I'd been holding back threatened to burst out at Bernard's comments. He was odd and detached, at times, but he always came through when it mattered.

"We'll be back soon, Dessie," Cap promised, standing up and patting Bernard on the shoulder. "You've been very brave. Hang in there. Bernard, thank you."

Bernard nodded, and slid in next to Dessie, taking Chito's place on the couch.

Cap and Chito and I strode out of the lobby and climbed into the Fords. Looking at Dessie's battered face, I didn't want to see what the rest of the Chinooks looked like, but I knew we had to.

I bit my lip and exhaled slowly, trying to prepare myself for what we'd see at the hospital.

⸺ ◉ ⸺

WE DESCENDED FIRST on the police station in Zermatt, a small outpost. Cap's commanding presence stopped the hum of activity as we strode into the lobby.

"We need to see the chief immediately," he told the officer at the front desk. "I don't care what he's doing right now, but we need to talk to him."

Before we knew it, we were being ushered back into a small office in the back of the station.

"We know who you are," the chief said as he brought us into his office and shut the door. "You're that Gallivanter crew, the other ones traveling around the world."

He frowned as he sat behind his desk, the seat creaking as he lowered himself down. "How did you end up here, at the same place at the Chinooks? Don't you go different places?"

"They called us, from this station," Cap explained. "We're their friends. We came immediately, to help them."

Chito and I glanced at each other behind Cap's back. That was the first time Cap had ever referred to the Chinook Voyageurs as anything other than our competition. Usually, he called them our enemies.

We talked with the police chief, and Cap left Paz's personal information with him.

"He used to be on my crew," Cap said, handing over a detailed file with Paz's full name, date of birth, home address, and family information. "I keep all the details for my people, in case something happens and I need to contact their families."

I watched as the chief took the paper and read over it. I never realized Cap had information like that for each of us.

"The burden of responsibility is so heavy for him," I thought, unconsciously playing with the compass necklace he'd gotten me. *"He handles a thousand little details like this, all the time, and no one has any clue."*

"This is very helpful, Captain Gallivanter," the chief said, glancing up. "The Chinooks are lucky you had this. I'll call Paz's family right away and fill them in on what's going on, and what they can expect if the kidnappers demand a ransom."

"Thank you, sir," Cap said, as we shook hands and left.

I stared at him as we walked back to the cars. "What?" he asked, noticing my glance.

I just shook my head. There'd be time later to tell him that I was proud of him. That he was a rare leader among men. For now, we had to get to the hospital.

"I'll drive, if you want to navigate," I said instead.

"Yes," he said, handing me the keys.

CHAPTER 64

THE HOSPITAL WAS A few blocks away. We climbed out and quickly found the reception desk.

"We're here to see a few people," Cap said to the white-haired woman sitting behind the desk, knitting. She peered up at us through her glasses.

"Yes, what—oh my!" She dropped her knitting needles and struggled to her feet. "You're those travelers! The Gallivanters!"

"Yes ma'am," I replied. *"Please don't ask for an autograph,"* I added in my head.

"Oh, I just love you!" she squealed. "I've followed your stories since the beginning. When you went through Morocco, and then the rest of Africa...well, I haven't followed you too lately, though. My daughter just had a baby a few months back, so we've had our hands full with that. It's her fourth child, you know how it goes, the house is just busy *all* the time. Insanity, really. But I was reading all the stories about you earlier this year! Oh, you're so brave. I'm such a fan, you have no idea! What an honor to have you here, at our hospital! I can't believe this. I was just telling my husband this morning, nothing exciting ever happens here and—"

"Thank you," Cap interrupted her. "We wish we were here under better circumstances, but we need to see a few people. It's urgent."

"Certainly, of course, Captain Gallivanter. Who is it that you want to see?"

"Captain Hudson Landry and his crew, ma'am. Patrick, Rollie, and Willis."

She shuffled through the papers on her desk, shaking her head. "It's a terrible thing that happened to them, just awful. I heard about it from one of the nurses. Captain Landry is so good-looking, too. And the young one, with the sweet face—oh, that poor young man. I hope he makes it."

I grimaced. She must be talking about Rollie.

She rattled off their room numbers. Cap turned to leave as soon as she told us. "Thank you," he said over his shoulder, already striding away.

"You're so welcome!" she cooed, then frowned. "Wait, aren't there five of you? I only count three. Where's that handsome dark-haired one? The Spanish one?"

We pretended not to hear her, but her blunder stung us. Where *was* Paz? We were desperate to know.

We hurried down the busy hall, doctors and nurses and strangers weaving in and out across the hallways in front of us. We veered to the right, into a hallway that stretched down out of the lobby.

"I think this is where Rollie is," Cap said, reading signs as we walked. "He's in critical care, right?"

"That's what Dessie told us," I replied. I hated hospitals. We'd spent too much time in them ourselves, as a crew. Being back in one now made me anxious.

"We're looking for Roland, one of the Chinook Voyageurs?" Chito asked a nurse who came walking toward us.

"Yes, he's here," she replied, leading us briskly down the hallway. "But I'll warn you, he's in poor condition. He suffered a crushing blow to the back of the head. He has a concussion, of course, but his brain appears to be swelling. It's very serious."

She led us to a door and turned to look at us.

"Don't touch him," she cautioned. "Be very careful around him. Move slowly. Brain swelling is one of the most dangerous things for us to deal with, in his condition. The next day or two are the most worrisome."

"Yes, ma'am," we replied in unison.

We ducked into his room quietly. My heart sank at the sight of him.

If she hadn't led us here and told us this was Rollie, I wouldn't have been able to recognize him. His entire face was grossly swollen, the skin stretched tight.

"Good God, Rollie," Chito groaned quietly.

Cap frowned, studying his face. "He must've taken the harder hit," he whispered. "Didn't Dessie say they hit him first, and then Willis? It looks like he landed face first on the ground."

I nodded, trying desperately not to cry. Rollie's swollen brain looked to be pushing against the eye sockets. Everything bulged out grotesquely.

We stood watching him for a few moments. His breathing was even, but I couldn't tear my eyes away from his face. This couldn't be Rollie. Rollie was so happy—so full of life. He wasn't this empty shell, laying still in a hospital bed.

"Well, let's go find Hudson, I guess," Cap finally said. "We can't do much here."

I bit my lip and followed Cap out to the hallway. He stopped outside the door, and pulled me to his chest. He grabbed for Chito and pulled him in, too, unexpectedly.

I could feel his heart beating wildly. I knew he had the same thought as me. *"This could have been us,"* was all I could think.

It so easily could have been us who'd been attacked. We were the far easier target, too, with a smaller crew.

We stood there, the three of us clutching each other, for a long moment. I could feel Chito and Cap's bodies warm against mine. Finally, Chito pulled away.

"I know, but it wasn't," he said, answering the unspoken question that hung heavy in the air. "We're fine. And they need us right now. We need to keep it together. We have to talk to the others."

CHAPTER 65

FRANTICALLY, WE LOOKED around the hospital hallways for signs. Cap pointed to our right, his face pinched.

"Hudson's room should be close," he said. "I think down the next hall."

We walked as fast as we could. After a few turns, we came to it.

"Here, this is it," Cap said, pointing to an open door. He knocked. "Hudson?"

"Cap?" came Hudson's incredulous voice.

We stepped in, crowding around the foot of his hospital bed. Hudson lay on the bed, his long frame nearly hanging off it. His boots and jacket were sitting in the corner on a chair.

I tried hard not to react to his injuries, but I couldn't help it.

Hudson's face was distended and bruised, one eye completely swollen shut. Several of the dark bruises had gashes through them. His hand was bandaged, in a sling around his neck.

"What are you doing here?" Hudson stared at us in confusion.

"Dessie called us from the police station," Cap said. "She told us what happened. And about Paz. We're here to help."

"But...you weren't even traveling around here, were you? How did you get here?"

"We left as soon as she called, yesterday morning. We drove straight through the night to get here. We came as soon as we could."

Hudson still stared. "I don't understand," he said, shaking his head. "I'm sorry. I'm a little muddled. It's the medicine they gave me, I think. To help with the pain."

Cap pulled a chair up to Hudson's side and sat down, leaning close to him. "We're here to help, Hudson. You need us."

Hudson sighed. "Paz."

"Tell us what happened. Who were these men? Did you know them?"

"They were the same men we met in a bar a few nights before. Dark-haired fellows. Ruffians. Big and mean-looking. Paz was an idiot, blathering on about his rich family and his servants. He was trying to impress Dessie, you know. He has a thing for her."

"I know."

"There were four of them out there on the road. I should've recognized the one. He pretended to have a broken down Ford. It was across the road, and he was limping, like he was hurt. I should've recognized him, damn it."

"What about the other men? Did they have any distinguishing traits?"

Hudson shook his head. "They had dark eyes and dark hair. Vicious. I'd bet this wasn't the first time they pulled this ruse. It all happened so fast. It's a blur now."

"Think, Hudson. Did you notice anything that could help us figure out who they were? An accent? The name of a town? Anything?"

Hudson pursed his lips. "They spoke English in front of us, mostly. They said a few phrases in another language, but it was so quick. They had an accent, but I don't know what kind. One of the romance languages, maybe? It sounded musical. It wasn't French, but it sounded kind of similar."

Cap turned to me. "Can you say something in Spanish?"

"I'm not very good at Spanish, but I'll try," I said, then stumbled through. "¿Qué hay de esto? ¿Las palabras sonaron así?"

"No, I don't think so," he said, screwing up his face.

"I can speak some Italian," I said, thinking rapidly. It was hard to switch between languages so quickly. I'd always had a knack for it, even when I was young, but now the pressure of finding Paz was making my carefree hobby a matter of the utmost importance.

"Just calm down, Andi," I told myself, breathing through my nose. *"Italian. You can do it."*

"Forse le loro parole suonavano così?" I said, and Hudson's eyes lit up. "Maybe their words sound like that?"

"Maybe," he exclaimed, tilting his head to the side.

"Say something else," Cap urged.

I responded in Italian. "Hanno parlato così? In italiano? Vengono dall'italia? Questo è come suonerebbero."

"I think that's it," Hudson said, listening.

"So they're Italian," Chito said, crossing his arms in front of him. "A bunch of Italian thugs kidnapped him. How are we ever going to track him down? He could be anywhere."

"We will," Cap said firmly, looking at Hudson. "Captain Landry, we're officially rejoining your crew. I know we've had our differences, but I hope you'll agree that it's time to put those behind us now. Your team needs us, sir, and quite frankly, there's nothing more important to us than rescuing Paz. He's part Gallivanter too, you know."

Hudson blinked hard. Was he fighting back tears?

"Thank you, Captain Gallivanter," he said gruffly, his voice full of emotion. "I can't think of anyone else I'd rather have here to help us. We're grateful."

"You lay back and rest," Cap said, standing up. "We're handling everything now. The police are contacting Paz's family in Spain. We'll make arrangements to get some additional vehicles to replace yours, and we'll start working on tracking these kidnappers down."

"I don't think we should tell the press yet," Chito spoke up. "We don't want to tip the criminals off, right?"

We thought for a moment.

"You're right," Cap mused. "We want the element of surprise on our side. We don't want these men to know we're hunting them down, or that we joined forces to search together. But we're a part of the public eye—people know us everywhere we go. How are we possibly going to move around? We're all famous now. Everyone knows our faces."

"How on earth can we hide our travels? The world expects us to continue our expeditions," Chito responded. "It'll make headline news if suddenly we both drop out and stop traveling."

"Unless we give them a reason to think we've stopped," I said, an idea popping into my mind. "We tell the world that we're taking a break for a while. To celebrate."

Cap looked at me, realization dawning.

I nodded. "We tell the world that we're taking a break to celebrate a wedding. That Cap and I are in love, we're engaged, and can't wait another second to get married. We distract everyone with stories of our romance, our wedding planning."

The men looked at me.

"We take a break, tell the press that we're scouting the perfect location for our wedding," I continued. "The public will be so excited about the two of us getting married, they'll forget all about our expedition. *Both* of our expeditions. They won't even pay attention to what we're doing."

"And all that time, we're secretly looking for Paz," Cap finished. "We keep the element of surprise. We track down the kidnappers ourselves."

Hudson stared at me. "Genius."

"It's perfect," I continued. "We tell the world that we don't want to be bothered—that we're suspending all our scheduled press conferences and shows and presentations. We pretend like Dessie is my best friend, now that we traveled together, and that she's helping me with wedding planning. That the Chinook Voyageurs and the Gallivanters are all involved, planning our perfect day. I don't know, make all of your crew our groomsmen or something."

Chito grinned at me. "And this is why we have Andi on our team, boys."

I turned to Cap and smiled wanly. "Time to get me that flashy engagement ring after all."

"What do you say, Hudson?" Cap asked, turning to look at him. "Want to be best man in my wedding?"

Hudson laughed. "I'd be honored, sir."

Cap grinned. "It means you have to travel with me, my friend. Our crew is going to be scouting out locations for our wedding. You know, my fiancée has always dreamed of having the perfect wedding. Ever since she was a little girl. This matters to her, more than anything. And we just can't do it without your help."

I blanched, and Chito elbowed me.

"You have to sell it, Andi. You're the excited bride-to-be now."

"I will," I promised. "In front of the cameras and the public, though. We know the truth. We're the only ones who *can* know the truth."

Hudson looked at me. "Thank you, Andi."

"We're here to help," I responded. "Whatever it takes."

"Poor Rollie," Hudson said suddenly, biting back a smile. "He's going to be living a nightmare, when he wakes up. The girl he's embarrassed himself in front of is now back on his crew, and he's in her wedding."

We went quiet, exchanging looks with each other. Did he not know about Rollie? About how serious his injuries were? Privately, I thought it'd be a miracle if Rollie made it through the night.

After a long pause, Cap sighed, rubbing his neck.

"Hudson, we saw Rollie before we came in here," he said quietly. "He's not doing too well. He has swelling in his brain. They don't know if he's going to make it."

Hudson dropped his smile. Instantly, his face clouded. "Damn," he choked up. "Rollie's one of my best friends. I've known him my whole life. I barely have a memory without him in it."

We bowed our heads for a few moments, thinking.

"Paz, we're coming to find you," I thought. *"Please don't be hurt. Please be strong. And Rollie and Willis and Patrick, hang in there. We need you. We're stronger together, all of us."*

Cap broke the silence.

"We're going to get through this," he stated, looking at Hudson. "We've faced trouble before. We're not afraid of it."

He crossed the room and put his arm around me. "We're the Gallivanters. And now we're not on a mission of world peace, we're on a rescue mission for Paz. And we won't stop until we find him. I swear it."

Hudson smiled weakly. "Thank you."

"Get some rest," Cap said, laying his hand on his shoulder lightly. "We'll be back later."

We walked out of the room and crowded into the hall. Nurses veered around us.

"Ready for a whole new kind of challenge?" Cap asked us, looking at Chito and me.

We nodded.

"Alright then," Cap said, tugging at his jacket and lifting his chin. "We're going after him. Let's go find Paz."

AUTHOR'S NOTE

A CONTINUATION OF THE first book in *The Gallivanter Saga* series, I completed this novel as soon as I finished writing the first book. I didn't even take a day off, in between working on the manuscripts. I pounded this story out in three weeks flat, writing each morning and evening before and after working my full-time job.

Andiamo Gallivanter is a young woman who discovers herself, overcoming her own doubts and struggling to survive in the wilderness. But this book explores something even more real to most of us: how one survives in the wilds of society.

During the writing of this book, I encountered blatant sexism in my professional career. I found myself echoing many of the sentiments Andi did, in her moments of frustration. Our gender should never limit our capability or contributions to the world—yet a hundred years after women like Andiamo faced backlash, I found myself facing the exact same comments.

I've been told to have babies, not opinions. That I don't belong up on a stage, keynoting events. That I'd sell more books if I was a man. That men shouldn't bother to read my books. That I have no business teaching men, because they can't learn anything from women. That I should know my place. That my place isn't in the boardroom.

Even against all of those negative comments, I forged ahead anyway—because it's *my* life. *My* adventure to live.

Sometimes the battle isn't with the elements but with your soul. It's the battle to keep loving people—to keep believing that humanity is worth the effort—when it feels like the world lets you down. But, like Andi, we know that the people we surround ourselves with do matter greatly in our lives. It's worth the fight to keep loving people and looking for good in the world, even when we're stung. The world's a beautiful place, if you ignore the small-minded critics.

I was inspired to write this series after reading about a real-life adventurer, Aloha Wanderwell Baker. Her story is worth exploring, but my story and every character within it is entirely fictional. I peppered a few real-life details about Aloha into my manuscript, in tribute to a woman I admire, but this story is my own.

In my efforts to remain as historically accurate to the period as possible, I became an expert on a lot of topics that no one cares about. However, I wrote in a progressive manner regarding the way that women and various races and ethnicities were actually treated and talked about at the time, in many of these places.

Thank you to many people who helped me with this book.

To Tyler, my husband—your love was on full display as I worked feverishly on this novel. I can't count the number of times you made dinner and quietly put a plate in front of me, letting me throw myself into this. Your support, encouragement, loyalty, and deep understanding of my soul is the greatest gift I've ever received.

To my family and in-laws and dear friends, thank you for the excitement and support you've had for me all along. I am blessed.

My nephews and godchildren inspire me to keep writing about people who have the courage to embrace their own adventures. Beckham, Bentley, Arya, Kensley, Ingrid, and Henry, I'm behind you all the way—but it's up to you to convince your parents to pony up the money for a trip around the world together.

To my dear former students Robby, Brendan, and Logan, thank you for being my muse for the wild students at the Irish school. I wish I was making up some of that stuff, but I know from firsthand experience as your teacher that you actually acted like that, as middle schoolers. I did warn you that I would immortalize you in fiction, if you didn't behave better. You dear boys have grown up to be so wonderful—but we both know that your rebellious little hearts are still in there, somewhere.

Thanks to Emma, Marenda, and Jaden for giving me excellent and thoughtful feedback on the plot points. You three are a blessing beyond words.

To my wonderful friends—thank you for loving me and loving this story.

Ken, Chloe, Harry, Alisson, Pierre, Rena, Jessica, and Luca, thanks for checking the German, Spanish, French, and Italian in this manuscript. Your fluency in multiple languages astounds me.

Our world is perhaps more polarized than ever, yet we still universally rally around heroes. The qualities of integrity, courage, and unflagging tenacity inspire us all, whether we're young or old. No matter what you've been through, how checkered your past is, or how uncertain your future may be, those qualities can be yours. They make all the difference in your life. Fight to make your story a good one, my friends.

Soli Deo gloria.

OTHER BOOKS IN *THE GALLIVANTER SAGA*

*The thrilling adventures of a ragtag team of world travelers,
navigating danger and discovery in the Roaring Twenties.*

Saving Andiamo
Book One, *The Gallivanter Saga*

A New Wild
Book Two, *The Gallivanter Saga*

Savage World
Book Three, *The Gallivanter Saga*

Uncharted Within
Book Four, *The Gallivanter Saga*

Audacia Always
Book Five, *The Gallivanter Saga*

A Dream Uninvited
Book Six, *The Gallivanter Saga*

About the Author

Cassie A. H. Moore is an author, speaker, educator, and consultant with over 15 years of experience working with young people.

She earned her master's degree in organizational leadership from the Townsend Institute at Concordia University in Irvine, California, has published non-fiction books, curriculum, and articles, and has taught and spoken to thousands of students and leaders all over North America.

As a lifelong student of culture, Moore weaves her interests in humanity, history, travel, and new experiences into her writing and speaking.

A travel enthusiast, Moore has enjoyed her own adventures traveling to 50 states, 21 countries, 10 islands, 6 Canadian provinces, and one erupting volcano. She and her husband live in Hood River, Oregon, with their two dogs, where they hike or kayak every chance they can get.

Learn more at cassieahmoore.com.